The Last

The Story of Mary Allerton Cushman

The Last Pilgrim

The Story of Mary Allerton Cushman

Noelle A. Granger

ISBN-13: 978-1-944662-45-5

Library of Congress Control Number: 2020903835

The Last Pilgrim by Noelle A. Granger published by Realization Press, Willow Spring, North Carolina.

Cover by Mary Louise Smith and Michael Scott

Dedication

I dedicate this book in awe, respect and love to the brave and selfless Pilgrim women who came to New England on the Mayflower. The survival of the Plymouth Colony is their lasting legacy. Their lives have been largely forgotten, but from their bones was this country created.

Table of Contents

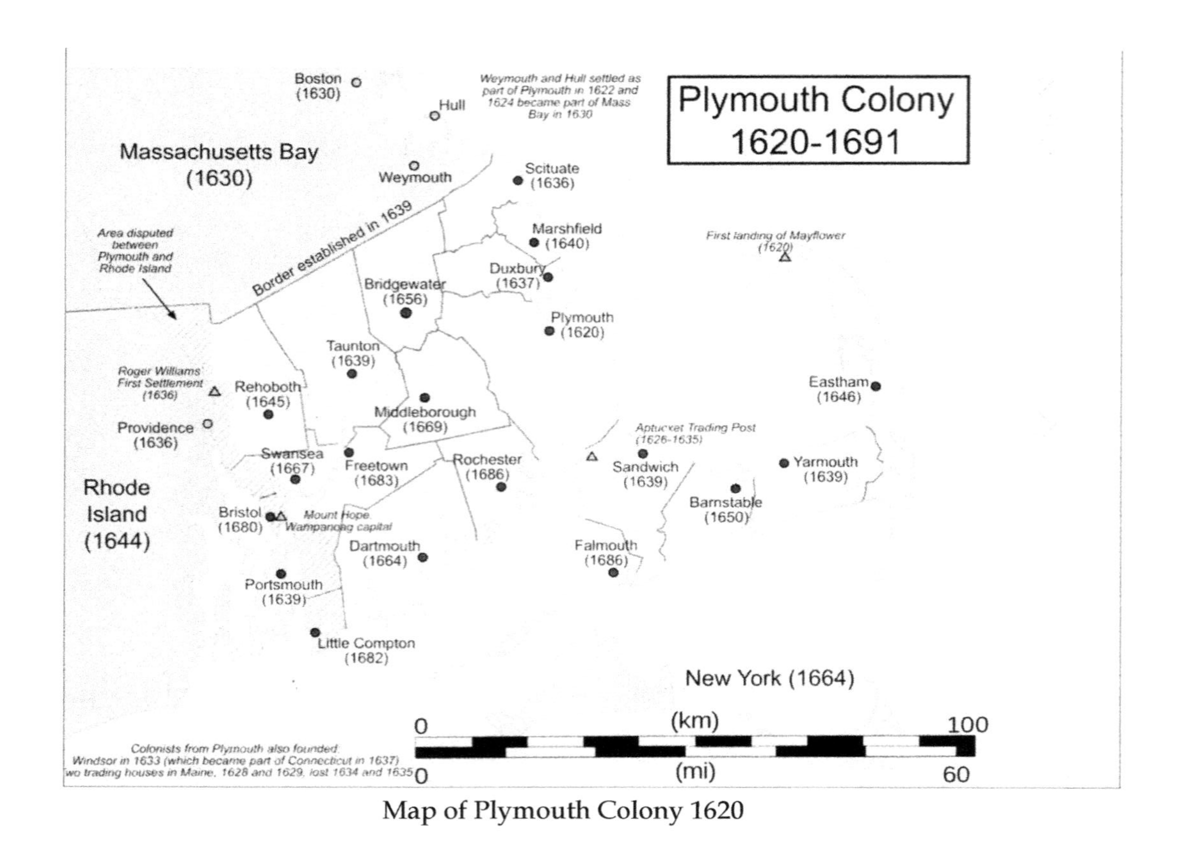

Map of Plymouth Colony 1620

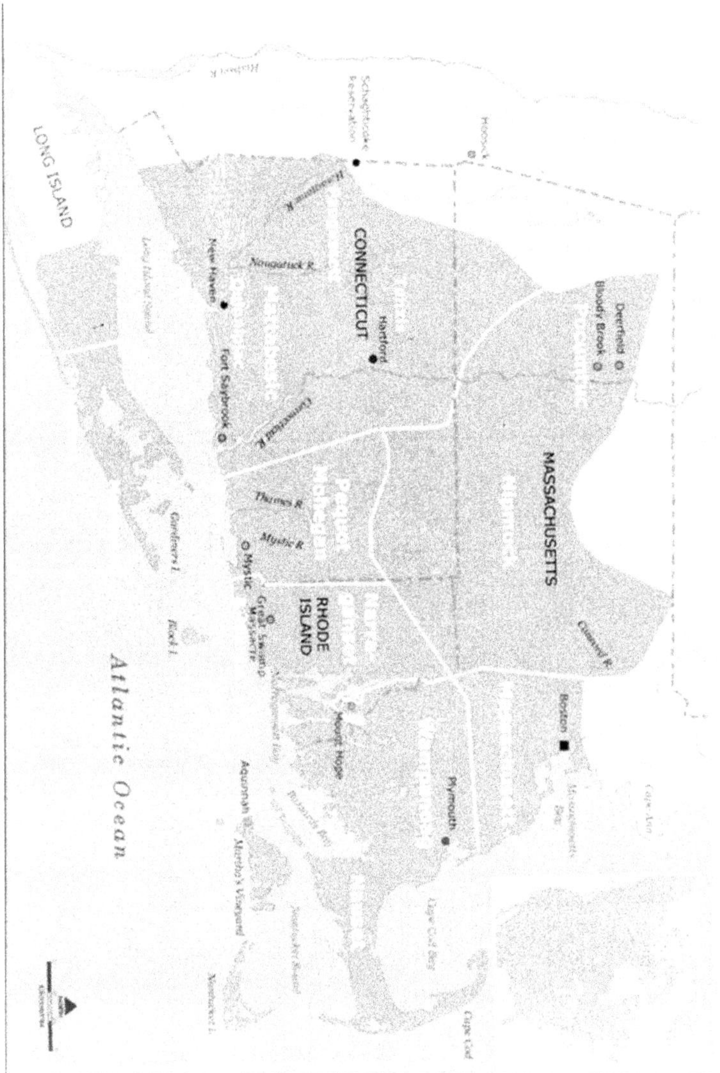

Map of Indian Tribes

THE LAST PILGRIM

The Story of Mary Allerton Cushman

Mary Allerton Cushman, Plymouth, Massachusetts Colony, September 1699

Using my gnarled cane, the one carved from the root of a sumac tree by my grandson Thomas, I step gingerly down the two stones that make my back stoop.

"Mother, be careful where you step!" my youngest daughter Lydia calls from inside the house. She knows my vision started to blur some years ago. I live with her and her husband William Harlow and their children in the house that had been my husband's in Rocky Nook.

I can still tell my garden thrives, just by its colors. The orange of the pumpkins, the green of the beans and the yellow of the corn, the burnish of the squash. *Almost time to harvest.* I slowly and carefully make my way to the bench under the beech tree at the edge of the garden and sit down heavily, feeling aches in every bone. *I wonder if this will be my last autumn.*

Tucking a stray wisp of white hair into my cap—my hair has ever been unruly—I lift my face to the warmth and the glow of the sun, filtered by the golden leaves. Closing my eyes I contemplate, as happens so often these days, how I came to be here. Who would have thought I would outlive everyone who came on the *Mayflower*? *Except Peregrine White, of course. But he came in his mother's belly... does that count?* I smile to myself.

Sometimes, that voyage seems like a blink of time away, although with the passing of years, I often cannot tell my own memories from what my father told me. After decades, I can still hear him, measured, reasoned, and, yes, loving. So many times he told me the story of it… and now I do the telling of those early days in his voice.

Chapter 1

Embarkation

Isaac Allerton, Plymouth, England, September 1620

"Mary Norris, are we ready to embark?"

"Yes, husband. The children are in hand."

I had worried that my youngest, little Mary, might have wandered off.

The frustration I was feeling must have shown on my face, because my wife, Mary Norris, placed her hand on my arm and asked, "You're as worried as I am about this voyage, husband, and it shows. We mustn't let our children feel our fear."

She was right, of course. After sailing from Leiden to England on the *Speedwell,* we had taken on more passengers before continuing on our voyage to the New World. Sailing together with the *Mayflower*, the *Speedwell* had unfortunately twice sprung leaks, the second time three hundred miles into our journey. Both ships had returned to port, where boatwrights had finally concluded they couldn't make the *Speedwell* seaworthy.

"I believe you made a true decision, Isaac, in moving our family to the *Mayflower*, even though she will make the journey alone."

"I pray that I did…but what we all face, only God knows."

On that early September day, I stood on the docks in Plymouth, England, with my family—my wife, two daughters and a son—waiting patiently for the signal to board the *Mayflower* for our third voyage to reach the land we had been granted. Next to me stood John Carver, a prominent member of our church in Leiden, and his wife, Katherine. I spoke with him about the trip. "Did you hear Thomas Weston expounding at our meeting yesterday?"

"Yes," Carver replied, "he was loud enough to be heard in the street. I know as one of our Merchant Adventurers, his goal is profit, but first we must get there. These delays have sorely vexed many of us, but having him speak on and on about the problems with the *Speedwell* and the lateness of our voyage has only added to people's fears."

"I agree. I'm sure his pronouncements are the reason some have become discouraged enough to leave us. Do you think the investors will pull out?"

Carver frowned. "I don't think so, but I anticipate trouble from those Adventurers who travel with us."

"Then we must pray our departure this day will be successful. I don't know where we will spend the winter if we have to turn back again and then have to wait until spring to leave." One of my wife's fears about any further delay was that our food would run out. We had used what little money we had to purchase our own supplies for the voyage and our first year in the new land, and some of the food had already been consumed during our two previous sailings.

Carver turned to answer a question from his wife, and I noted the gray clouds overhead and felt the chill wind lift our cloaks. I, too, was distressed by the lateness of the season, knowing autumnal storms would make our journey even more perilous.

That day, my wife and I thought we knew what faced us, although the truth of it would be far worse than our imagining. But even not knowing what was to come, the challenge of this voyage deeply troubled us, and we prayed daily we would reach the New World alive. We had made an irrevocable decision, possibly a mortal one for all of us.

So preoccupied was I with these thoughts that only the squall of diving seagulls and the snapping of ships' lines in the wind brought me back to the moment. My family drew my attention then-four-year-old Mary being held tightly by her mother's hand, all the children dressed in the clothes Mary Norris had made them for the voyage. Not moments before, my youngest daughter had splashed through some dirty puddles and her mother had admonished her, "Don't get your clothes dirty, Mary. You will be wearing them for a long while." Remember, two years older than Mary, was clearly bored by the long wait, while Bartholomew, at eight, was fascinated by the work on the docks.

I chuckled when I saw Bartholomew wrinkle his nose. "What bothers your nose, son?"

"The awful smell from the water, Father."

In truth, a rancid, fishy smell came from the greasy water that slapped on the dock's pylons. A dead fish floated belly up not far from where we stood.

Little Mary looked up at me, shielding her eyes from the sun, and I wondered what she thought of all this. An inquisitive child, she soaked up anything we told her. Her dark curls escaped from her biggen yet again, and Mary pulled away when Remember took it upon herself to tuck them in.

Finally, the word reached us that it was time to board, and I led my family down the dock to join the others boarding the *Mayflower*. The ship loomed above us as we neared, our home for the long trip. For perhaps the first time, Mary actually recognized it, because she cried, "Look, Father! See the castles at each end?"

"Silence, daughter. Your behavior is unseemly." In a quieter voice, I asked her, "Do you remember I told you they aren't castles?"

"Yes," she replied, now subdued. "They are where the men who sail the ship live, and they are shelters from storms. We'll live between decks." She frowned, apparently remembering our previous two sailings. "It's dark down there."

Later, as the ship's sails unfurled and the *Mayflower* lumbered out of the harbor, many of us remained on the deck. Captain Jones had ordered us to stand on the hatch covers and stay out of the way of the crew, and there we stood, silently watching the coast retreat to the horizon, deep in our own thoughts. Before going below, we lifted our voices in a final prayer for a safe voyage to our new home. I knew the others, like me, would be thinking of the dangers, devils, and hardships the future would bring, but it was risk we had to take to be free to practice our faith and live in the righteousness of God.

Chapter 2

The Hardships of Life Below Deck

Isaac Allerton, aboard the Mayflower, autumn 1620

"Mary! Mary Allerton! Leave poor Mister Hook alone."

"But Mother, he tells such wonderful stories. There's nothing to do this morning."

"Mind your tongue, daughter. Your father brought Mister Hook to work as his apprentice, not to amuse you. Come help me with the bedding." Keeping Mary occupied and out of trouble was a major chore for my good wife, especially within the dim, cramped confines of our living quarters.

While I tutored my son, Bartholomew, in his letters, and Mary Norris taught Remember how to sew and knit, little Mary would frequently wander off, visiting our fellow passengers and asking endless questions. While the older members of our congregation complained constantly that living between the decks was nearly unbearable—monotonous, endless, with the hardship of being confined with one hundred others, rocking endlessly on rough seas—Mary found everything and everyone around us interesting.

Bartholomew, to his dislike, was tasked with finding her in the warren of meager spaces, some with fabric walls, all packed with bedding and containers of food. My wife and I could only hope she didn't annoy all and sundry. We soon discovered she had a polite charm, and people would delight in conversing with her and answering her questions, with so little else to occupy their time.

Moving around between decks was difficult. Adults had to stoop to walk below the low ceiling and frequently staggered with the pitching and yawing of the ship, tripping over or bumping into the many people crowded in such a small space. Mary found the stooping humorous, since she could walk upright, and I watched in dismay when she began imitating the adults, walking bent over.

"Daughter! What are you doing?"

"This is the way everyone walks, Father. I should walk that way, too."

"You're disrespecting your elders, Mary, mocking them."

Mary looked at me with big eyes, the smile disappearing from her little face.

"You must always respect your elders, as you respect your father and mother. I think some extra prayers before you sleep tonight will help you remember this."

I couldn't help but pity her for her mistake—tears slid down her cheeks in response to my lecture—but we curbed her of this disrespect.

Mary had only a few friends close to her age, among them Mary More, Wrestling Brewster and Resolved White. When our Mary was particularly restless, which was much of the time, her mother and I allowed her to go with them to explore our very small, cramped world together. Early in the voyage, we often found them on a partially disassembled boat called the shallop. This had been stored forward between decks, to be assembled and used in locating a suitable living site once we reached Virginia. The children often climbed on it and pretended they were the captain and crew. Unfortunately, in this place some of us lived and slept, and the children had to be shooed away. After making apologies several times, I finally ordered the children never to play there again.

Sometimes her mother gave her a small job to do to make her stay put, but Mary, at four years, was as yet of little help with the daily chores. She did show interest in learning her letters and numbers. Although not a common practice, I wanted all my children to be able to read and write. At first, we taught Mary her letters to occupy her time, but soon she began to recognize words in our Bible.

The fractiousness of our daughters, being kept in such close quarters, complicated our lives on the ship. Remember was two years older than Mary, and she could be harsh with her sister, talking sharply when Mary failed to do task given her or did it poorly.

One morning, Mary decided she would carry the bucket we used as a chamber pot to the gun port where we emptied it. I saw her dragging the bucket, its contents slopping out.

"Mary!" Remember rushed over to where her sister stood, in a puddle of noxious liquid, some of it smeared on her dress. "What have you done? Mother, look what Mary has done." She grabbed the bucket handle from Mary and went to the gun port with an indignant expression. Mary, looking down at herself, started to cry.

My wife went to her with some rags and wiped down her skirt, then mopped the floor. Mary's cry became a wail.

"You cannot do anything correctly," said Remember as she came back, giving her sister a hard tap on her back.

"I try to help," said Mary.

"Remember, silence!" Mary Norris had little patience that day. "Mary, stop crying. You aren't hurt."

Mary gulped down her tears, looking miserable. My poor daughter. Her skirt reeked until my wife washed it out in salt water, but we hardly noticed this additional odor in the air of our living quarters. Certainly the people around us made no comments.

I worried that Mary would not have a cordial relationship with her sister when they were grown. Remember received a beating for her behavior, which only served to make her resentful. Extra prayers and reminders for them to love each other didn't seem to have much effect.

ꕤ ꕤ

We found we could endure the endless days below deck with a schedule of prayer, meals, schooling and work. Thus my family awakened early every day, prompted by the bells marking the beginning and end of the sailors' watch, rolled up our bedding, and followed me in morning prayer before we ate. Mary always fidgeted, and I couldn't scold her overmuch since an energetic four-year-old would naturally be distracted by so much going on around us. Her mother tapped her on the head again and again to get her to pay attention, and I wondered if that spot were sore from the constant tapping. With our prayers concluded, we ate a small breakfast.

Every other day it seemed my wife would complain, "How I wish we could have hot food, husband. Or at least cheese without mold. The children won't eat it. And they struggle to eat the hard biscuits, even soaked in beer or water."

Captain Jones had decreed there could never be a fire on the deck where we lived because with the constant movement of the ship, even a small flame would court disaster. Thus we ate cheese and dried fruits, pickled beet roots or onion root for many meals, along with the hard biscuits, called hard tack—tasteless squares made of flour and water with a small amount of salt, which Mary Norris had baked months before we sailed.

One day I noticed Mary playing with her biscuit. "Your food is meant to me eaten, Mary."

"But Father, look at these little wiggly things—what are they?" She proceeded to dig some out and poke them.

"Ugh!" Remember had some in her biscuit, too.

"They're weevils, children," replied Mary Norris. "Do not eat them."

"But how do we get them out of the biscuits?" Bartholomew asked.

We soon learned from the crew members to break the biscuits into smaller pieces and submerge them in beer or water. When the weevils rose to the top, we picked them off, rendering the beer and biscuits fit to eat. Later we had only beer for the children because the water had become fouled.

Despite my wife's best efforts, our children were always hungry, and we despaired of their growth on this terrible diet.

After breakfast, I would read to the children from the Bible, and then there were chores: washing of hands and faces with salt water, emptying the chamber pot, scrubbing the deck and hanging our bedding and clothes to air or dry. This had to be done because our bedding was infested with bed bugs and lice, leaving us all scratching their bites. Mary Norris applied vinegar for the bites, adding to the odor-laden air below deck. Heavy weather frequently flooded our living space, soaking anything left on the deck, another reason to hang our bedding.

To pass time, we quietly sang psalms and told stories, hard to hear above the noise level of our living quarters, and the girls played with their poppets. We all played cat's cradle or noughts and crosses, but later we increasingly needed to tend to the passengers who were sick.

There were more hard biscuits, pickled vegetables and perhaps some soaked peas or beans with dried meat or fish for our mid-day meal. My brother-in-law, Degory Priest, joined us then. Degory had married my sister Sarah but had sailed alone on the Mayflower, his wife worried about the hazards of the journey. He told us constantly how he missed his wife and their two girls and vowed again and again to send for them as soon as he established a home. Despite this monotony, everyone, especially Mary, liked him because of his lightness of heart – he often had us laughing over some small matter. He clearly missed his children, always taking time to tell stories or play cat's cradle with ours.

And, of course, we all prayed for God's blessing and a safe journey, with thanks for our food both before and after our repast.

༄ ༄

I spent part of each day with the other men on this journey, Separatists and Adventurers alike. Our discussions were filled with complaints about the weather, daily vexations arising from the closeness of the company, and the slow progress of the journey, dictated by increasingly foul weather. This last often led to heated interactions with the crew, if we were on deck and got in the way and even when we didn't get in the way.

Elder Brewster was our only conduit to Captain Jones, and while they had a grudging admiration for each other based on mutual interests, the Captain largely dismissed our complaints. During one of these discussions, William Bradford brought up the subject of the crew yet again with Elder Brewster. "You need to speak to Captain Jones again about his crew, Master Brewster. These men are low and vile, and they engage in crude behavior in the presence of our women. Some of them have taken to lowering their drawers in front of our wives when they ventured on deck!"

"You must remember the crew considers us religious radicals, Master Bradford, which dictates much of their interaction with us. This, however, is beyond tolerable, and I'll speak with the captain."

Elder Brewster climbed to the main deck and soon returned with word from the Captain. "I regret to tell you that while Captain Jones sympathized, he felt maintaining the spirit and good will of the crew was more important."

There was a lot of dark muttering to these words, but Elder Brewster had a fair response. "I propose that hereafter, any women seeking to take air on the deck will be accompanied by a small contingent of men. They can stand as a bulwark between them and the crew. What think you of that?"

We all gave our assent, and men were assigned each day to go with any women wishing to take the air on the deck, providing the weather were fair.

As a distraction to the men, our military captain, Myles Standish, encouraged us to tend to our weapons to prevent our muskets from rusting and to make sure our powder remained dry. He also attempted to drill us, insomuch as we could in our small space.

ꕥ ꕥ

At the end of each day, following our evening meal, I read from the Bible. Then we prayed, unrolled our bedding and settled in to sleep. At first, the pitching and yawing of the ship made sleep very difficult, along with the creaks and groans of its timbers, the sloshing of the water against the hull, and the coughing of the sick. We rolled from side to side or slid on the floor, but after several weeks, the sounds and movement lulled us to sleep.

When we concluded our evening prayers, our children were free to ask Mary Norris and me questions about our faith and what our future might be when we reached Virginia. Mary, perhaps the most inquisitive, couldn't imagine a future beyond our tiny world below deck and thus always asked to tell her about Holland, which seemed more real to her.

"Can you describe Leiden, Father?"

"Well, Leiden is a big city with many, many houses and streets. It has two castles..." —castles being one of Mary's favorite words —"... and lots and lots of people."

"How many?"

"Many thousands, child. Too many for you to count."

"Did we always live there?"

"No, we went there from England before you were born because we wanted to worship God in our own way. We couldn't do that in England."

"Why not?"

"Because the king didn't like it."

"The king must be a very big man. Did you like living in Leiden?"

"You're full of questions tonight, daughter. You know the story already, so permit me to finish."

Mary smiled and leaned in against me. Bartholomew and Remember were bored with this same story and rolled away in their blankets.

"Leiden was a very busy city, with lots of ships coming and going because the people who lived there made cloth and cheese and books to sell in distant lands. My father, being a man who sewed clothes, taught me that trade. Many of us worked at making cloth from wool, but others, like my father and I, made rich suits or shoes and gloves. Some of us built houses and made furniture. We worked very hard, six days a week from sun up to sun down." I closed my eyes, envisioning where our house had stood. "Almost all of us lived near a church, so big that it filled the eye up close. It is called Pieterskerk. I met and married your mother in Leiden, and all of you children were born there."

"Why did we leave?" Mary's eyes grew heavy.

"In order to remain ourselves and keep our faith, child. The children were pressed to work and some of our young people left us, preferring the easier life of a Dutch citizen. I didn't want my family to become Dutch…"

Mary had fallen asleep. Her mother shook her head at me and lifted her to her blankets, covering her tightly, as the nights had grown cold. "I'm worried about the food, Isaac. Even though Degory contributes his share, I fear we will not have enough. And the children need more…"

I had heard this complaint many times but replied with forbearance, "I know my decision to make this voyage has much affected them. This troubles me—all of us—and I pray daily it was not wrong. We mustn't speak of this when the children can hear us. They are not yet afraid, and I don't want them to be. God's hand is in this decision, and He will watch over us. Now let us pray together on this before we sleep."

Chapter 3

Increasing Misery

Isaac Allerton, aboard the Mayflower, autumn 1620

Life aboard the Mayflower worsened as the weather grew colder and with no heat below the main deck, we were chilled all the time, despite the warmth generated by the more than one hundred people living there. By then, everyone wore several layers of clothes, if they had them. Others remained wrapped in their blankets, day and night.

"Remember, please tie Mary's wool cape and put on her wool cap. And Mary, you must keep that on your head." Mary Norris was often cross with little Mary about this. Our youngest tolerated her linen cap, but the placement of a wool cap on top of it meant she might pull the wool one off at anytime, anywhere in our crowded living quarters. Bartholomew was often sent in search of it.

"We must thank God we have such warm garments," my wife reminded our children. "There are some who have only what they wore when they came aboard."

Storms came ever more frequently as we sailed into autumn weather, violently rocking the ship one way and another.

Walking and even standing in our living quarters became impossible as we were tossed and thrown about, water from above dripping on everything. Everyone had been seasick at the beginning of the voyage, but even those with hardy stomachs now became nauseated from the violent motion. I'd adjusted fairly quickly to the pitching and yawing but now had moments of queasiness. Mary Norris, Bartholomew and Remember, who had taken longer to toughen to the constant movement, were frequently nauseated and would not eat. Only little Mary seemed relatively unaffected.

The response of the ship to the large waves assaulting it made the voyage particularly difficult for my wife. We had left England knowing we would have another child, but its growing took a toll on her and even after the worst of the seasickness had passed, she still vomited and often had to rest.

Worst of all was the air between decks, a noxious mix of vapors worthy of hell. We couldn't escape the smell of vomit, feces, moldering food and sweat. The fetid odor compounded our misery from the flea bites, and our heads itched with lice. My poor wife spent hours picking and combing lice from our scalps.

The days of fine weather weren't many, but when they came, a few of us would climb the ladder to the main deck in defiance of the captain—Captain Jones didn't like having passengers about on deck, interfering with the crew's work. If little Mary went at all, her brother had to mind her, to prevent her from wandering and to protect her from the crew. These were rough men, unaccustomed to children, and they treated ours as meanly as they did the adults.

When I went with her, I could see her joy at being outside, which was always accompanied by a litany of questions.

"Can you smell the salt in the air, Father? Why do the sails flap? What makes the waves? Why is the water different colors of blue?"

In addition to trying to answer her questions, I also told her to ask God for the gift of obedience, particularly when I or her brother told her she had to return below.

A strange thing happened as the voyage lengthened and the challenges of dealing with the storms and the hardships increased:

the first officers came to respect us for our courage and our determination. This extended to the children, so when the officers' breeches were tugged by a young one begging for a story or an explanation, they bent down and indulged the interruption. Soon enough, these officers became part of our extended family.

Best of all, one of the passengers, John Goodman, had brought his dogs —a mastiff named Ruff and a springer spaniel called Agon. The dogs were often on deck, and Mary loved to pet them and Bartholomew played tug-of-war with Ruff, using a scrap of old rope. There were cats, too, who slunk around below deck and in the crew's quarters. One of the officers told Mary there were always cats on sailing ships, to kill the mice and rats the children occasionally saw lurking in the darkness. At night, the cats slept with anyone who would have them and their fleas.

Despite the daily challenges and aggravations, we never wavered in our belief that God had been good to us in many ways, although he continued to test us mightily with our hardships. Long days into the voyage, a huge wave hit the *Mayflower* during a bad storm, and we all heard a loud noise overhead. Nearly everyone pitched to the other side of the living quarters. Even my good wife, who, with practice, could now keep her balance in the rocking, was thrown and fell, trying to protect her stomach. Water poured in and soaked everything on the floor, and our living quarters filled with cries of fright in the dim light. "What is happening? Where is my child? Help!"

The captain and the ship's carpenter, Francis Eaton, descended the ladder and went aft to inspect the ship's structure. Some of us followed them and saw that one of the cross beams had bowed almost to the point of cracking. It was clear to everyone that the *Mayflower* in its present condition couldn't withstand the beating of the wind and waves any longer.

The idea of being marooned in the middle of the ocean spread quickly, gripping us all in dread. If the ship didn't break apart, would we die lingering deaths from starvation and thirst, buffeted by weather that would drive the *Mayflower* eastward before it?

There seemed little we could do, and I heard fervent prayers to God begging for salvation.

Captain Jones, after inspecting the beam from all sides, asked his carpenter, "Is there any solution to this problem, Master Eaton?"

Francis Eaton was a carpenter hired by the Merchant Adventurers who financed our voyage. Among our number was also John Alden, who had been hired in Southampton to make repairs to the *Mayflower* while it was in dock. A cooper by trade, Alden had stayed on in our company, making barrels during the voyage to replace those that became damaged or rotted. Alden and Eaton conferred, then approached the captain with their answer.

"There is a jackscrew in the hold," Eaton replied, "brought by our passengers to set the beams in the building of their houses. It might work to lift the bent beam back into position, until a footing can be constructed to support it. Master Alden and I can bring it up from the hold if we have help from some strong crewmen."

Little Mary left her mother and went over to peer down into the hold, where the two men struggled to position the heavy wooden jackscrew for the crew to lift. When I found her, she was standing near the edge between the legs of two of the crewmen. "Mary! You're in the way." I took her by the hand to pull her back, but she came reluctantly, eager to follow the efforts to lift the jackscrew, then carry it to a place beneath the beam.

God was with us that day, as the jackscrew lifted the beam and held it firmly in place, where it would remain until the building of a footing. Eaton pronounced the arrangement would suffice and Captain Jones called it staunch enough, but he reduced the number of sails so as not to overtax the ship's hull. Much to the relief of everyone, the *Mayflower* sailed on, more slowly but heading west.

Yet another delay to our voyage!

That night Mary Norris and I listened to a litany of whines from our children.

"The bedding is very wet, Mother. How can I sleep in these blankets?"

"There is salt water in the food."

"My clothes are wet."

Mary Norris stopped them. "Silence! We must thank God for saving our ship and for the wisdom of the men who repaired her. Our difficulties are small compared to what might have been." We then spent a long time in prayers of thanksgiving, but for once, I couldn't be harsh with the children because I had the same, but unspoken, complaints. But God had indeed been good to us that night.

ᘓ ᘐ

Not long after, we experienced another miracle. "Have any of you met a man named John Howland?" I asked the children following our evening meal.

The children shook their heads.

"He's an apprentice, like our own Mr. Hook. Today, he climbed up to the main deck to get some fresh air. As he stood there, a large wave struck."

"What happened?" asked Bartholomew. The children's eyes were large and for once, I had their attention.

"The deck pitched and he slid to the rail and fell overboard." I heard a long intake of breath from everyone. "But God saved him."

"How?" they all asked at once.

"A rope dangled over the side and trailed behind the ship—one of the long ones used to raise and lower the upper sail. Master Howland managed to grab it, even though he sank below the waves. Some of the crew members pulled him back to the boat and used a hook to drag him up to the deck. He was quite shaken by his adventure."

"Thank heaven," said Mary Norris. "His salvation is a sign from God. Despite our travails, God has blessed us again."

As the heaving ship tossed us about that night, Mary cried out in her sleep with a bad dream. When her mother roused her, Mary said she had dreamed of huge waves and plunging beneath the surface of the sea. Nightmares now plagued my youngest.

ꟗ ꟗ

As the days and nights of our misery dragged on, Mary Norris and I tried to remain constant in our trust that almighty God would sustain us. Being too young to fully comprehend God's will, the children despaired that our wretchedness would ever end, no matter how many stories we wove about our new home and the goodness of Our Savior. In truth, there were times when my own faith came close to failing, but I couldn't let my wife or children see this.

Our diet was now mainly the rock-hard biscuits, plus dried fruit and salted meat or fish. My wife and I and even the older children drank beer. Mary had first been drinking water, but when the water fouled, she had to drink beer with us. She hardly wanted to, claiming it tasted nasty and bitter, but there was nothing else.

About that time our mouths began to bleed, our gums swelled, and our breath stank like rotten meat. We were more tired than ever, especially Mary Norris, and all of us had pain in our joints.

One day, as Mary Norris wiped the blood from around Bartholomew's mouth, he wiggled one of his teeth with his tongue, then spat something out.

"Look, Mother, I've lost a tooth!"

"I lost one yesterday," added Remember.

Soon after, I lost a tooth myself, with some bleeding, as did my good wife. Little Mary had to be constantly reminded not to wiggle her loose teeth. The first officers told us we had scurvy, but they had no knowledge of a cure. We assumed our poor diet caused it and prayed that once we reached land, proper food would cure us of this affliction.

But life went on, even in the face of the added woes. One day we were all distracted by groans coming from the rear of our claustrophobic living quarters.

"Is someone being hurt, Mother?" Mary asked, moving close to my wife's side. The sound frightened her.

"No, child, Mary Hopkins is having a baby. I will, too, soon enough." Her mother cradled her swelling belly, and then frowned, before wrapping Mary in a hug. In the quiet of the time before sleep that night, Mary Norris whispered to me, "Isaac, I fear the stress of this journey and the lack of good food will affect this babe. Will it even be born alive?"

"Do you feel it move?"

"Yes, stronger each day."

"Then it's safe within you, and prayer will see the babe to its delivery. You must find strength in our Savior, whose suffering was worse than ours."

The next day Mary Norris took Remember and little Mary to see the baby boy the Hopkins had welcomed into our small, dark world. My wife told me on her return their son had been born healthy. They named him Oceanus for the ocean, and his thin wails could often be heard over the babble below deck.

The worst day for everyone was our first death, that of William Button, servant of Samuel Fuller, our physick. We knew death traveled with us, but its first claim reinforced our fear that it might take more of us before once again we stood on dry land.

Button's interment was at sea, on a bitterly cold, gray day with enough waves to make it hard for any of us to keep our balance. We held our children's hands tightly and stood with our congregation on the main deck of the *Mayflower*, surrounding the body. The goodwives had stripped it to just a shift and wrapped it in a sheet, and it lay on a plank. The men had placed lead shot within the shroud to help the body sink below the waves.

Mary, ever inquisitive, asked, "Mother, what are the bumps in the sheet?"

Mary Norris looked to me for assistance. In truth, I didn't want to answer, so I said, "This isn't something of which I'll speak. Bide your tongue, daughter."

As Separatists have no sacrament for a funeral, the crew slipped the body over the side to an audible sigh from the assembled crowd.

Later that day, Elder Brewster led us in common prayer in his sonorous voice, beginning with some readings from our Bible. He then told us God had predestined the fate of Mister Button, he had received God's grace, and as a boy, and thus sinless, he would be saved. During all this, Mary fidgeted, twisting around to see things behind her, but her mother held her hand fast, not letting her go. Finally, everyone sang a psalm, and we returned to our spaces, feeling no better for our Elder's words.

That night, Mary woke the entire family with screams. She had had that same nightmare again, and although her mother did her best to calm her, the bad dreams continued.

ꟸ ꟸ

In early November, Elder Brewster descended from the main deck with news from Captain Jones. "One of the crewmen has seen a seagull, and now there are more of them about the ship. We should see land soon," he told a gathering of our men.

These words brought tears to some, to think this long voyage would soon be over, and the news spread quickly through our living quarters, generating cries of happiness. When we heard the cry from above, "Land ho!" many of us climbed to the main deck. For once, Captain Jones didn't seem to mind. It was a bitterly cold, clear day but the seas had calmed, so I lifted Mary to my shoulders so she could see that the water had become green. Gradually, land emerged on the horizon—high cliffs and behind the cliffs, tree-covered hills. Everyone began to talk, excited voices filling the air. I put Mary down and she tugged on my hand, beginning to ask yet another of her thousand questions.

Before I had a chance to answer, the voice of Elder Brewster, asked us to kneel in prayer. "To almighty God, we give thanks for delivering us safely over the vast ocean, and from our misery and perils, to this new land. May His goodness and righteousness continue to bless us in our endeavors."

Chapter 4

The Search for a New Home

Isaac Allerton, aboard the Mayflower, November 1620

With land in sight, Elder Brewster immediately went to speak with Captain Jones. Several of us followed. "Do you know where we are?" he asked Jones.

"I do. As you and I have often discussed, the course forced upon us by the easterly winds has driven us north from our original destination. Based on our compass and astrolabe readings, the land we see is Cape Cod."

We all knew of Cape Cod, which had been named by an early English explorer and later mapped by John Smith.

"Given the northerly winds, we have only to turn in a southerly direction to reach the land you were legally granted. If this wind holds, I anticipate we should have an easy two to three day run."

Two to three days! We felt our excitement at seeing land for the first time return tenfold. Invigorated by the news, we went below to tell the others. Several hours later, we were still huddled together, praying in thanks and discussing our plans, which now seemed so close to fruition. Then we felt the ship change course. The noise of conversation increased, as many among us realized what was happening.

I returned to the main deck, where some of our group had gathered around Captain Jones once again. It seemed to me the wind now came from the south, rather than the north, and the Mayflower headed to open ocean. *Why are we turning back?*

"I regret to tell you we couldn't continue on the course I'd plotted," Jones told us somberly. "Not only has the wind suddenly swung to the south, but we've come to an unmapped area of shoals and sand bars. The tide is turning and soon we'd be sailing into a cauldron of waves and rip tides. With one of the ship's beams already compromised, I fear should we persist in this direction, the ship will founder. I've made the decision to turn north."

I could hear unbidden groans and whispered words rising like a black cloud. We have come so far and are so close to our goal!

Jones then said, "I'll repeat what all of you already know: this has been a long voyage, our food supplies are dangerously low, and a good number of passengers are sick. We need to find a place to land to replenish our water supplies, find game for food, and build shelter against the cold. Do you not agree?'

Although disappointed and frustrated with this turn of events, all of us saw he spoke the truth and nodded.

"We'll anchor off Cape Cod tonight," he continued, "and in the morning, make landfall north of the Cape."

Knowing there was nothing for it, and to the sound of waves breaking on the shallow shoals, we descended into our living quarters, which were as cold and dark as our mood.

When we'd planned this voyage, our group had thought to hire John Smith as our military advisor. He had sailed these waters six years before and knew the land north of Cape Cod. However, we feared his ego would dominate our wishes and we had instead chosen Myles Standish. It occurred to me that with this turn of events, our decision not to hire John Smith had been unwise.

Some of us—Adventurers, Separatists and other passengers alike—continued to express confusion and anger at the Captain's decision, and several returned to the deck to argue with him, trying to persuade him to continue south. They returned chastised. Jones, whose strong personality had impressed us, convinced even the most obdurate of us that his decision was the right one. So in the end, they agreed. Our water had long been fouled, the number of sick indeed increased daily, and the cold had become bone-chilling. The thought of our doughty ship foundering after so long a journey sealed his argument. Nevertheless, we had no patent for any land north of Cape Cod and knew nothing of what to expect.

Just as agreement with Jones' decision had settled in, another argument broke out, one which had occupied us since the beginning of our voyage and one in which I'd become deeply involved. With a landing soon, we needed to make a final decision on the type of governance the new colony should have. There were conflicting interests between the Separatists like myself, who fled England to avoid religious persecution, and the Merchant Adventurers, such as Thomas Weston, who had come with us. We had signed a contract with those paying the expenses for the voyage, promising them profits from whatever goods we sent back to England. Thus these Adventurers were focused on a governance to guarantee those profits. Even the non-Separatists and non-Adventurers amongst us were concerned about the government we would choose —some, like John Billington, almost to the point of belligerency.

I found myself in a confrontation with Billington, a cantankerous man, who together with his unruly sons had not endeared himself to those sharing our crowded living space. Mary had told me she disliked him, and while I tried to be accepting of his nature, she said Billington frightened her when she'd first encountered him. When he demanded, "Come here, girl," she'd run back to her mother.

We had gathered at one end of our living space, and Billington's voice was more than loud enough to be heard by everyone over the general din. "Since we will not be landing in the place of our contracted settlement, we are free to do what we want once we are ashore," he declared, not for the first time. "No one has power to command us, and I'll not be subject to the rules of religious radicals!"

"Mister Billington, yours is an unjust comment. We haven't pressed you to become one of us while on this journey, nor will we, when we have created our settlement." I replied.

"What guarantee do we have of that?" he said, still shouting.

The Merchant Adventurers had named Christopher Martin the governor of the passengers. Although he had claimed to be a Separatist himself, I had doubts he still believed as we did. His voice could now be heard by everyone. "In order to maintain peace and order, I propose we govern the colony without religious influence."

"You must not forget you owe a debt to the Merchant Adventurers, of which I'm one," added Thomas Weston. "If each of you goes his own way, how do we manage repayment of this debt?"

The argument dragged on, with John Carver supporting Weston. Carver, a well-regarded, wealthy man, had married into our church in Leiden and had donated much of his own money in support of our congregation. He was also one of the men who had negotiated with officials of the Virginia Company in London for land in the colony of Virginia. "I must remind you," he said, "that under the terms of our signed agreement, we must be self-governing, with the directive to repay our investors." His words carried great weight.

The vigorous discussion continued unabated, because now, without a patent for the land north of Cape Cod, we sorely needed at least a temporary solution for governing the colony. Men drifted in and out of the discussion, some wanting to be on deck, others tired of the monotony of the argument and of the intransigence of some. I saw Mary sneak away and climb up the ladder to the main deck, accompanied by her brother, as usual. My wife, now over-tired in body and mind, didn't tell her to come back. The baby would come soon, and she needed rest. I myself left to follow my children. The strong wind and the movement of the deck caused us to stagger, but both Bartholomew and I held fast to Mary's hands.

"All sails be lofted," Captain Jones ordered his crew, and soon the *Mayflower* had new-found speed. I wondered if the damaged beam would hold. When we were chilled to the bone, I brought the children back down, where unsurprisingly, many of our number were still in discussion.

William Bradford, who had been raised in Elder Brewster's family, now brought a reasoned view to the emotional debate. "If we mix temporal and spiritual authority, it will be no different than in England. King James is the head of the Church of England. Is that how we want it here? What we decide here will determine how we manage our new lives, both in the days ahead and possibly for years to come. We left England because of the king's will to determine how we worshiped. I strongly urge the establishment of a civil covenant as the basis of government for our colony."

I had long held to this idea, and agreement to his position gradually increased. And yet, the talking continued, even as some men—myself amongst them—left for the evening meal. Mary Norris was curious about the reason for the raised voices. "Why are the men so angry, husband?"

"We must decide on the form of our civil government. It's taken some time for the discussion to become less emotional and more reasoned."

"Is this important?"

"I wouldn't worry yourself with these thoughts. The men of our company will determine the outcome."

Remember had taken over the job of preparing food while her mother rested and demanded that little Mary and Bartholomew put away the remains of our poor meal. Both grumbled until I reminded them sternly to consider Remember's directives the same as their mother's. By evening, Bartholomew reported we were just off the tip of Cape Cod. I returned to the deck with him just as the crew set anchor and hove our ship to for the night, and as we watched the dark outlines of the crewmen furling the main topsail against the waning light, I prayed we were home at last.

We all arose early the next morning, and some were on deck as our ship glided into Cape Cod bay at sunrise. In the golden reflection of the sun on the water, we saw a vast expanse, protected on three sides by land, according to Captain Jones, and our hope rose that this might be our home. A few children ran around on deck, interfering with the surly crew and resisting efforts by their parents to control them.

After we had prayed and broken our fast, I went with the men to the cabin at the stern of the main deck, the captain's quarters, to make final what we had ultimately agreed would be our governance—a civil covenant apart from our religion. After hours of discussion, William Bradford had written it down and we would all sign the document as an indication of our acceptance. I thought Bradford a perfect choice to create this, well-regarded by everyone as intelligent, learned and thoughtful.

Mary and Bartholomew followed me above, eager to walk on the deck. Failing to get the children to return to their mother, for which they would be punished later, I told them, "Children, you must stay outside. This is no place for you." Once inside, I could see their faces peeking in the doorway, but they would not see much with the bodies of all the men blocking their view.

Sunshine from two windows at the stern lit the room unevenly, as we each stepped up to sign the document. In years to come, we would know it as the Mayflower Compact. This compact declared our group a 'body politic,' with a civil government, and we agreed to submit to all governing laws and ordinances drawn up by our elected officials. When I leaned over the desk to add my signature to those of the other signees, I had no idea this document would keep our colony in relative peace for many years.

With our compact in place, it remained to choose our governor. We considered several of us before deciding on John Carver, who had been the first to sign our agreement. Master Carver had brought with him the largest group of people, all servants, and a boy named Jasper More, who was a friend to Mary. She told us that Jasper was always sad, having been given by his parents to the Carvers as a servant.

After we had concluded our business together, a group of men planned to go ashore to scout the land and perhaps find water and food. I was amongst them and when I told Mary Norris, our youngest daughter overheard and jumped with excitement, tugging on her brother's hand, thinking everyone would get to go ashore.

"I'm going with you, Father. I can play by the water. I'll not be a problem."

"Mary, you cannot come with me. No woman or child will be on this first foray. We need to know if this landing is a safe place—there could be Indians around. Then we must find a source of fresh water and hopefully find some game for food. There is no place for a child."

"But I want to go!"

"Mary, you're being disrespectful to your father," said her mother. "Stop your whining right now! You heard him—no children are going. If you don't obey me, you will not be allowed to go ashore when the time comes."

Mary hopped about in frustration and finally sat down on the floor with a thump, her face screwed into a frown and her arms crossed on her chest. For this disobedience, she received a thrashing, and her sobs followed me as the other men and I armed ourselves.

Sixteen of us climbed to the deck and lowered ourselves into the ship's boat. Our number sank the ship so low that water slopped over the gunnels with each wave. We had a long row to land, because the shallow depth of the bay meant the captain had had to anchor the *Mayflower* far from shore. Like my daughter, I was excited at the prospect of being on land after so long a time but also feared what we might encounter. From the faces of the other men, alternating between frowns and smiles, I could see my feelings were shared.

Our heavily laden boat ran aground well before the beach, so we had to clamber out, encumbered as we were with armor and arms, and wade in the icy water, pulling the boat behind us to beach it. Reaching dry sand and with rivulets of water running from our breeches and boots, we together fell to our knees and gave a prayer of thanks to the God of Heaven, who had delivered us safely here. I couldn't help but remember young Button, who had not reached the end of our journey. With our prayer over, we wandered amongst the hills of sand to see what we could find.

ഇ ഉ

That night I told my family what I'd seen. "We first explored the area behind the beach. I noticed that after so long a time on this ship, some of us, myself included, had trouble walking straight. This made it difficult to climb over the dunes, but once there, we discovered low bushes and small trees of birch, ash, and walnut, plus the cedar for a cooking fire."

"And fresh water? Did you find some?" Mary Norris asked.

"We did find a fresh water pond," and here I smiled at my wife, "from which we've brought water. It's in a barrel on the deck. I'm certain some washing can be done in the pond."

She clapped her hands together at the prospect. Looking at our filthy clothes and bodies, she replied with a smile, "We indeed have a great need for cleaning." Without thinking, she rubbed her stomach. "But I am grateful for the squirrel and rabbit meat you brought us."

We had managed to kill a number of both, which we'd cooked over a fire on shore and brought back to be shared amongst all the passengers. "We saw deer, and we will hunt them next time. I hope we'll be successful, since it was apparent to me that we are long out of practice and some of us have never hunted."

"Will we build here, Father?" Bartholomew asked.

I shook my head. "The land isn't suitable for building homes— it's too low and the sandy soil won't support crops."

Everyone then started talking at once, making plans for the next trip ashore. Another question from Bartholomew broke into our conversations. "Did you see anyone else? Perhaps the natives we've heard of?"

"No, son, we saw no one. That doesn't mean they aren't there, so we'll need to stand guard over any groups going ashore."

"Can I go?" asked Mary. Clearly, her eagerness hadn't been inhibited by the thrashing.

"I think we will take at least some of the women and children on the next trip, so possibly."

We prayed fervently that night, thanking God for the abundance we had found, and for once, Mary had no nightmares.

The next day being Sunday, our day of worship and rest from work, we stayed aboard the *Mayflower.* Although an undercurrent of grumbling, especially from those not of our faith, spread below deck, everyone finally agreed to stay aboard, with Elder Brewster leading our congregation in Sunday services. Predictably, Mary couldn't understand why. "Why do we have to worship today, Father? God won't care if we don't pray this once."

"Hush, child," replied Mary Norris. "No, He does care, and your constant whining will bring down His wrath and also punishment from me if you don't guard your tongue."

With both a morning and an afternoon meeting, my frustrated wife had to scold little Mary on several occasions, with more punishment. She had her hands full keeping our children in check and advising Remember in the preparation of the midday and evening meals. I could understand everyone's impatience since I myself felt it.

Excited voices rang below deck, as we ate our evening meal. After so long a time in our low, cramped living space, the prospect of walking upright on dry land, breathing fresh air, and having clean clothes was invigorating. However, a few were now too sick to leave the ship, and some of the goodwives would have to stay aboard to tend them, creating resentment only somewhat repressed.

Monday finally came, a cloudy cold day with no sun, and Mary preceded me up to the main deck so she might watch as men loaded the pieces of the shallop into the ship's boat, then rowed them to shore for assembly. Once there, Francis Eaton, John Alden and a couple of assistants began the work of reassembling it, and the sounds of hammers and saws reached us across the water of the bay. When the boat returned, more men went ashore and finally some women and children, taking large iron kettles with them. Mary Norris, the children and I counted among the healthy and were amongst those on the fourth trip, bringing with us soap and dirty clothes that smelled as bad as our quarters. "I may just wash you first, Mary," I heard her mother comment as they waded through the water to the beach. "I can hardly see your face beneath the grime."

Mary Norris and the children long recalled this first wash day as the best of those that followed. Despite the bitter cold, Mary and the other children had taken off their shoes and stockings before wading ashore, squealing in delight, and they then galloped along the beach, our calls to be careful echoing after them. After so long aboard the ship, everyone was unsteady walking on the sand and had to adapt a rolling gait. Now I knew why sailors walked the way they did.

Some of the women told the children to collect wood, while the men filled the iron kettles with water from the pond and returned them to the beach. Other men drove forked stakes into the hard sand and hung long poles between them, from which we suspended the heavy kettles.

Using wood the children had gathered, we built a large fire beneath the kettles to heat the water. The children ran back and forth, bringing branches to keep the crackling fires going, then reluctantly followed their mothers to the pond. There, everyone washed in the icy water, as much as they could with dignity and without exposing themselves to the bitter air. After Mary Norris had scrubbed her youngest daughter as clean as possible, little Mary returned to the fire to warm herself and put on her shoes and stockings. Her little feet were blue from the cold. When she dawdled with doing this, I scolded her. "Mary Allerton, put on your shoes and stockings right now or you'll come down with the sickness from the cold." She was a light in our lives but could be irritatingly unruly.

While little Mary and the others warmed themselves around the fires, Mary Norris dumped our clothes into a kettle, adding lye soap. The women took turns stirring their brews with sticks, then carried the clothes to the pond for scrubbing and rinsing. Remember stayed with her mother, who because of her awkward size, couldn't bend and needed help with the washing. Finally, the clothes were wrung out and spread on top of bushes to dry.

In between gathering wood, the smaller children hunted for nuts and when John Alden, our cooper, found a hickory tree, he called, "Children, come pick up these nuts!" Under a blanket of leaves, he had found a great number of nuts, the frost having opened their coats to reveal the white interior. Mary gathered some into the skirt of her dress and brought them to a growing pile on the beach. With the washing finished, the nuts were put in the empty kettles to be brought back to the ship, along with kegs filled with fresh water.

Not all the clothes dried that day, but by nightfall, everyone was wearing something clean, and the smell below decks was almost tolerable for the first time in months, especially since nearly everyone had at least washed their faces, necks and arms. That night, because the protected bay was calm, Captain Jones allowed us to make a fire on the main deck in a brazier, using the cedar wood gathered on shore, adding its pleasant odor to the air. For the first time in months, we could warm ourselves. Nevertheless, it remained cold below deck and my wife shivered as she prepared the evening meal. She was clearly exhausted by the work of the day and had been chilled to the bone on the beach. Remember and Mary rubbed their mother's arms and legs to warm her. Even so, Mary Norris shivered through the night and began to cough, the sound joining the snorting and hacking of so many others.

Sickness was spreading.

Chapter 5

Fruitless Exploration

Isaac Allerton, aboard the Mayflower, late November 1620

Despite our carpenters' abilities, they took a long time to reconstruct the thirty-foot long shallop with its single mast. So much time that when our next exploration for a home site took place, we again had to use the much smaller ship's boat to reach shore, loaded as before to the gunwales. I was once more amongst the party, but before I could leave, Mary had to show me how well she had learned her numbers by counting the men assembled to make the trip.

"Sixteen, I think, Father," she said, after using all her fingers several times. "Will the boat not sink, with all of you in armor and carrying swords and muskets?"

I chuckled. "It almost did the last time, daughter, but we are one fewer."

"I remember the water is cold. You will have to wade in. Will your feet turn blue?"

Her concerned little face looked so pitiful that I almost laughed. "Don't worry, daughter. We will get wet but will soon dry as we walk."

Amongst us in the party were William Bradford and Stephen Hopkins and also another passenger of whom Mary was very afraid,

Myles Standish. He was not that much taller than Bartholomew, with reddish hair, a robust physique, and an aggressive manner. We had become used to it during our training with him on board.

Held up by Bartholomew, Mary's little head was just visible above the Mayflower's side as we rowed away.

This time the boat grounded even further from the shore. Dragging the boat behind us in order to beach it above the tide line, we waded in icy water soaking us almost to our waists. Once on land, Standish quickly organized us into a line. "We head to what from our map might be the mouth of a river," he ordered. "It lies northwest some miles away. Step lively. Forward, march!"

I was hoping, as were the others, that the land near the river would be suitable for building. Winter had set in and there was a growing sense of desperation to find a site for our colony and to get everyone off the ship.

ꙮ ꙮ

We had planned to return on the second day, and when we were delayed, we lit a fire on the beach. This was a signal we had decided on beforehand for just this situation, to let those on the *Mayflower* know we were well. When we finally returned on the third day, we were met with great rejoicing and prayers of thanks to God, together with amazement at what we had brought with us—dried corn, still on the cob, which we could use as seed. I knew it as maize, as it had first been called when it was brought to England from Virginia. But many had not seen it before and viewed it with some skepticism because of the color of its kernels—yellow, red and blue.

That night, my family and Mister Hook gathered to hear my story of our exploration. "We'd marched for several miles down the beach, led by Captain Standish, of course, when we saw five or six people and a dog walking toward us. At first, we thought it was Captain Jones and John Goodman with his dogs, but when they saw us, they ran away into the woods. Standish decided to chase them…"

"What did they look like, Father? Were they armed?" Bartholomew asked.

"We weren't close enough to see that, son."

"Don't interrupt your father, Bartholomew," said Mary Norris, coughing as she spoke.

"We couldn't follow them very quickly because of the weight of our armor and guns and our lack of strength after these long months at sea. Standish tracked their footprints, and we marched for perhaps ten miles before stopping for the night. The traverse of the rocky shore was difficult, and he pushed us to exhaustion."

"What did you have to eat, Father?" asked Mary.

"Nothing, daughter. We'd brought only some strong spirits, hard biscuits, and moldy cheese, and by morning we were all hungry and thirsty." At this point, I held up my hand for silence, because the children were jiggling up and down with their questions. "We resumed our march, still following the natives' tracks and finally, we came to some open land where we found an upwelling of fresh water. We drank long and deeply before marching to the shore and building the signal fire for the *Mayflower*."

"I saw it, I saw it," crowed little Mary.

"But where did the corn come from?" Even Mary Norris couldn't help but interrupt me in an unseemly way, but I indulged her curiosity.

"We found it the next morning. First, we encountered fields where the corn had grown, then burial mounds. As we marched on, we discovered an old, rusted, ship's iron kettle near the remains of a fort. Standish told us about a man named Martin Pring, who in 1603 commanded a voyage to these regions. Standish reasoned that we'd found the site of the stockade Pring and his men had built to house the crew while they harvested sassafras trees."

"Then we aren't the first from England to come here, are we, father?" Bartholomew asked.

"No, but unlike us, those who came before didn't stay. Exactly where we'll build is still uncertain though. The land near the river proved unsuitable."

"Oh, dear." Mary Norris dropped her head in disappointment.

"But where did you find the corn?" little Mary repeated her mother's question.

"We climbed a hill overlooking Cape Cod bay and found a mounded place where something clearly had been buried. By whom, we didn't know. When we dug down, we discovered it was not a grave but a storage place for corn, and after much discussion, we decided to take as much as we could carry in the kettle we'd found."

"You just took it?" The words slipped from Mary Norris' mouth.

"We did, and for that I'm heartily sorry. We argued about that because we took something of value from the native people. Some of us—Standish in particular—clearly had no qualms. In the end, his argument overcame our doubts. If we are to survive, we must have seed to plant in the spring."

"But we have wheat, barley and peas," replied my wife.

"What if they don't grow here? What will we live on?" I replied.

No one answered. Our theft of the corn indeed proved a troublesome act to some.

༺ ༻

Three days after our return, the people below decks once again heard groans and screams. This time, little Mary knew what it was. Mary Norris seemed irritated as she related to me what happened when she and Mary went to visit Mistress White and her new babe, Peregrine.

Observing the red, crying infant wrapped tightly in a blanket, Mary had asked Susanna White, "Peregrine is a strange name. Why did you name him that?"

"Because it means 'traveler,' child," she had answered. "He has come a great way to be born, don't you think?"

Mary had been so impertinent that I had to intervene, saying "Pray pardon my daughter, Mistress White. She speaks out of turn and isn't appropriate for a girl her age. Hush now, child. Your questions are disrespectful."

Mary Norris told me Mary had persisted with several more questions as they returned to our living space. When Mary Norris had refused to answer her, she had finally stopped, but her behavior would once again deserve punishment.

"It's the truth, Isaac," my wife said to me when she finished recounting this, "Mary is inquisitive to the point of disrespect, and you encourage her by telling her about everything that's happening."

"I'm sorry, dear wife. Perhaps I do encourage her, but she's clearly an intelligent child. I want all my children to take an interest in what we're doing, to understand the importance of our decision to leave England, as well as the perils we face. We cannot pretend we'll have an easy life."

"Perhaps you should spend more time with Bartholomew. After all, Mary is only a girl and very young at that. You shouldn't be filling her head with useless information."

I had to agree with my wife, but of my three children, only Mary showed the nature of a scholar.

ꙮ ꙮ

Ten days later, another group struck out from the *Mayflower* in search of building site. This time they left in the shallop, which Francis Eaton and his assistants had finally finished assembling. Much larger than the ship's boat, it had a mast and sail, but even so, the large contingent of men overloaded it, more men than Mary could count as they boarded. She held my hand tightly as we all watched, standing on the deck wrapped in layers of clothing to fend off the cold breeze.

"Father, I'm glad you're not going," Mary whispered.

Although my wife was close to giving birth and also ill, the other goodwives would care for her. I could have gone, but in truth, my spirit didn't seek further adventure. On this occasion, Standish didn't lead the group, but rather Captain Jones. He insisted that as the master of the *Mayflower*, he should lead, although some of us had our doubts because of his age. True, Jones seemed spry enough on the ship, despite his fifty years. However, he returned early after only two days, which confirmed our suspicions.

The remaining men returned a day later, and we gathered around William Bradford, pale with exhaustion, as he told us of their exploration.

"We numbered thirty-four at the beginning, and an unkind wind blew us to the other side of this bay. We overnighted there in the cold, our shoes and stockings freezing after wading ashore. It snowed that night, and the next morning we marched north through it for many hours before Captain Jones decided to make camp. However, we could at least eat a little, having shot six ducks and three geese.

"The next day, not having found any suitable site for a settlement, we returned to the mound where the corn had been found and retrieved what we had left the previous time and discovered many bushels more. As you know, Captain Jones, who had been taxed mightily during our march, returned in the shallop with two crewmen, bringing the corn. We all agreed that Standish would now take the lead.

"Later that day, we dug up another burial mound in search of more corn, but all we found were the remains of a man with fine yellow hair, a sailor's canvas bag, and the skull and bones of an infant. We thought him a seaman from Pring's command who had stayed behind, possibly with an Indian family. We reburied him."

My youngest stood quietly in the shadows, listening. How much she understood, I didn't know. But many shuddered at that news. *Is this to be our fate as well? To die and be buried in some forgotten place?*

Bradford continued, "Then we found a deserted Indian village. We concluded the inhabitants had left in haste because we discovered pots, bowls, reed baskets and an iron bucket."

"Did houses remain?" asked Francis Eaton. "How were they constructed?"

"Yes, there were houses of a sort and they were well made," Bradford replied. "They were constructed from young saplings, bent so that both ends stuck in the ground, creating a round structure. Woven mats covered the bent saplings down to the ground. Although we couldn't stand upright within them, the houses had mats on the floor, with a wide-open hole at the top for the release of smoke. All in all, these houses appeared quite comfortable, large enough for a few people to live in." He paused before saying, "We took things we thought we could use."

A silence fell on those listening to Bradford, because the men had stolen from those who had lived in that village. *Our Bible says thou shalt not steal… and if the natives discovered we had taken their possessions, could we ever form a peaceful bond with them?*

That night, we prayed as a family for God's blessing. Mary Norris, my ever sensitive and pious wife, asked His forgiveness of our theft of the natives' belongings and His strength that we might survive in this challenging land. Once in our blankets, Mary Norris clung to me tightly, not only for warmth but also clearly needing comfort from her fear for herself and her unborn child.

The following day, everyone heard what sounded like an explosion, followed by a great commotion in our living quarters. I went to investigate along with virtually every other man, and when I returned, I said to Mary Norris, "We have a family of troublemakers amongst us!"

My wife shook her head in warning, nodding at the children. Despite the noise of voices telling the tale around us, I said no more until that night, when I whispered to her what had happened.

"It was Billington's sons, John and Francis. With their father elsewhere, they decided to shoot off his fowling piece in their living area, producing a great many sparks. The shot buried itself in wooden ceiling, but its discharge created great danger, since there was a barrel of gunpowder nearby, along with their bedding. Their neighbors soon extinguished the sparks, and God be praised, no harm resulted."

"God be praised, indeed. The ship might have burned. What will happen to the boys?"

"I can only imagine. Their father isn't kind of heart."

The next morning, we saw John and Francis on deck. Neither Billington boy would look at anyone in the eye, and both walked very slowly. I doubted their belligerent father had spared the rod.

We then saw off yet another expedition. Perhaps this time they would find a place to build our settlement—an open area with good soil for crops and a solid anchorage nearby, so the unloading of the ship would be less arduous.

The death of one of Mary's friends dampened her usual excitement at such a departure. Seven-year-old Jasper More, the indentured servant of Master Carver, had succumbed to an illness. As men loaded his little body into the ship's boat for burial on shore, I wondered how his death would affect Mary's generally sunny disposition. Already Remember and Bartholomew had become somber beyond their years, though they rarely expressed their thoughts to either me or my wife. *This journey has changed us all and not for the better.*

I remained behind again, because by this time, nearly everyone between decks was wheezing or coughing uncontrollably, bleeding from their mouths, some shivering with fever and unable to rise from their beds. Although weak with lung congestion herself, my wife still cared for them, and I thought to relieve her of this burden.

I could only hope that where we all lived, below the main deck, would not become a place to die.

Chapter 6

A Home at Last

Isaac Allerton, aboard the Mayflower, December 1620

Little Mary, Bartholomew and I peered through the gun ports to watch the shallop leave. Mary could count the men going to shore, as there were less than half the usual number this time—the cold and the spreading sickness below deck had sapped the strength of many who might go. I myself had been suffering with gout for some years, and Mary Norris did her best to ease my pain with such herbs as she had brought. Without a cooking fire, she couldn't boil these herbs in water so she chose to grind them in beer—the seed of wild celery, sassafras root, willow bark, rosemary and sage —for me to drink. I found the taste most unpleasant and gagged trying to swallow it.

The day after our latest expedition left, all of us were shaken by news that William Bradford's wife Dorothy had fallen over the side of the *Mayflower* and drowned. The crew recovered her body and we buried her onshore. Mary, as usual, had questions about what had happened and pestered both her mother and me.

"How could she fall overboard, Mother? The sides of the ship are high."

"We don't know, Mary, but it was a certainly cruel accident," I replied for my wife.

Mary Norris took little Mary by the shoulders. "None of us has the right to question an act of God, daughter. Get on your knees and pray for the poor woman and for her son, left behind in England. He will never again know his mother. And pray for Master Bradford, too, who will be hit sorely by this news when he returns." To my surprise, she did as I asked.

Another death from the spreading sickness—that of James Chilton, one of our congregation—occurred the following day. The dark mood enveloping us deepened.

When the exploratory party finally returned after six days, the news they brought only partially lightened our growing sense of hopelessness about our future.

Every man not sick enough to be in bed gathered in the fore of our deck to hear what Bradford had to say about their adventure. My wife, now heavy with child and coughing, made the children sit with her where she could watch them, instead of letting them slip away to listen in. She thought what they might hear would frighten them, and she asked me to omit anything fearsome when I retold what I'd heard.

When I returned, they harassed me with questions, until Mary Norris threatened them with hours-long prayer, instead of the news. After giving God long and heartfelt thanks for the safe return of the expedition, we gobbled our scant evening meal of cold porridge. As Remember and Mary cleaned away our dishes, Mary Norris whispered, "Husband, how fares Master Bradford with the sad news of his wife?"

"I understand he was at first overcome with grief, but he told us he believed God had taken his dearest wife for a reason. His strength in the face of this adversity is much to be admired."

"Truthfully, I cannot see how he's accepted this," replied Mary Norris.

Then I asked the children, who now all sat around me, "Do you want to know what happened on the expedition?" The children's eyes lit up and they nodded in unison, wiggling in place with excitement. "Then you must allow me to tell you without interruption." I glared at little Mary and she giggled.

I did tell them most of Master Bradford's report, leaving out only the most frightening parts. "As they sailed along the coast, the men in the shallop first saw a whale stranded on the tidal flat."

"What's a whale?" asked little Mary.

"Did I not tell you to…it's an enormous fish, as big as the *Mayflower*."

Mary's eyes grew large at the thought.

"Indians had gathered around it, cutting strips of its blubber for food, but they ran, carrying the blubber, when they saw our boat. On shore that night, the men built a barricade of tree trunks and branches to protect themselves from possible attack. They warmed themselves by a fire within it, because they had nearly frozen in salt spray as they sailed. The next morning, the party split up. Some walked along the shore, where they found abandoned Indian dwellings but still no safe anchorage for the *Mayflower.* The rest of the men sailed along the coast in the shallop and both groups met up at a creek, where they built another barricade. Before sunrise the next morning, they were attacked with what Bradford called a rain of arrows.

"How many Indians were there, Father?" Bartholomew interrupted me.

At that point, I conceded to their interruptions. "Captain Standish estimated thirty. Perhaps because of the darkness and the stoutness of the barricade, there were no injuries."

"Did the men fire their guns? Did the Indians run away?" asked Mary.

"Captain Standish identified their leader and told the men to fire at him, Mary. When their leader realized he was the target, he and the others ran back into the woods. Standish and his men followed them for a while and shot off their muskets to show they weren't afraid."

I could see the children imagining the encounter, and they snuggled close to me and my wife. It seemed even my simple words worried them, despite the good outcome.

"What then, Father?" Remember finally asked.

"Reuniting at the shallop, all the men sailed north and slightly west, but ran into bad weather. They lost the shallop's rudder and couldn't keep true to their course..." and here I left out the details of the terrible storm—the high seas, the shallop swamping, the mast shattering and how close to death our men had come. "But using the oars, they rowed and eventually found a shallow cove at the end of a sandy spit of land. There they disembarked and built a huge fire to warm themselves. The next morning, they repaired the mast, which had been damaged."

"Where were they?" asked Bartholomew.

"On a wooded offshore island, at the outer edge of a large sheltered bay. When they explored the bay, they found most of it wasn't deep enough for the *Mayflower.* But they found almost everything else we seek. On the shore of the bay was a brook with clean water, as well as already cleared land, both situated at the foot of a high hill. Captain Standish thinks the top of the hill would be suitable for a defensive position, and a large rock marks a landing site."

"Did our men see any Indians about, Father?"

"No, but fallow fields lay close to the shore, so Indians had clearly lived there, Bartholomew."

"So this is where our new home will be?" asked little Mary, sleepily.

"It may, daughter. We shall see."

Her eyes closed, and as I looked at her pale face and stick-like arms and legs, I questioned yet again my decision to take my family to this land. Perhaps with this discovery we could at last leave the ship and begin to build our homes. Little Mary had a seemingly bottomless resilience, but I still feared for her life, for all our lives.

ꙮ ꙮ

When the *Mayflower* finally left for the new anchorage three days later, excitement stirred in our living quarters, tempered by the sickness afflicting so many of us. The ship finally anchored the following day, about a mile from the brook Master Bradford had described. During the next three days, little Mary tried our patience sorely, and her excitement only increased as she watched some of us leave each day to explore the shore. I went on two of those trips, during which we found other suitable sites.

After the third excursion, all the men gathered to consider which we might choose. "We must first consider the island in the bay where our last expedition sheltered," said Governor Carver. "We would have ample notice of attacks by the natives if we dwelt there."

"But it's heavily wooded," replied John Howland, "and clearing the land for planting would be laborious and would take time we don't have."

"And there is no source of fresh water—it would have to be hauled from the mainland," Edward Winslow said, ever thoughtful.

"All of this is true and makes this site less attractive," said Carver. "What of the land near the river that enters the bay from the north?"

"Here again, the land is thick with trees and would need to be cleared—we now have few able-bodied men to build shelters," William Bradford said with a frown. "And we could easily be attacked by Indians, coming upon us from the woods."

Everyone who had been on shore dreaded an Indian attack.

"There remains the original site we explored." Carver spoke these words with some conviction. "The fresh water is an advantage, and the land has been cleared and appears to have been planted with some crop a few years ago. We'll have to walk a good distance to find wood for building, but the harbor is full of fish."

At that point, Captain Standish could be heard over the underlying conversations. "Don't forget the hill at the top of that land, which affords us a command of everything around. We can place our ordinance there for protection."

After some discussion, most in attendance agreed that the site where we first landed would be where we would build our homes.

That night, after the children were abed and asleep, Mary Norris asked, "So will we build near that rock and the brook?"

"Yes, most of us agreed."

"Is it not a miracle we found land already cleared? But what of the natives who lived there?"

As she settled beside me in the bedding, I again dropped my voice, in case one of the children were still awake. "We found many skulls and bones just lying on the ground. I believe disease visited these people and killed many—so many that there were too few left to bury their dead. They must have fled."

"Let us pray for our survival, then, in case these people return," said Mary Norris, shuddering. Perhaps she had the same thought I had, thinking about building a house on top of those bones. I held her close for warmth while she drifted off to sleep.

The next morning, when we had finished our morning prayers, Bartholomew asked, "So it's settled then, Father? We will build our homes near the big rock on the shore?"

"Yes, and you can eventually help us with that."

"I want to help, too," said Mary. "May I go with you, Father, please?"

Mary Norris and I both said, "No!" at the same time, and Mary was so startled, she didn't say another word. Later that morning I could see her face at a gun port, when I and a score of men went ashore to start felling trees for our first house. We had no time to lose, as winter was upon us. Even as we began, a furious storm arose and lasted two days.

ꟻ ꟻ

When Mary Norris began to experience the pains of birth, the goodwives who attended her told me to take Bartholomew and little Mary and find another place to be, away from the birthing. Remember was old enough to stay with her mother and the other women. I sent Bartholomew up to the main deck with a request to Captain Jones that he be allowed to stay there until my wife had given birth. Then I tried to find some place between decks where the groans of my wife were faint. Mary hid her face in my chest for comfort, tensing with every moan she heard. She asked me many times, "Will Mother die?" to which I could only lie.

After many hours, we heard a final scream and then silence. I could hear voices.

"The baby isn't breathing. It's blue."

"This must be God's will. Mistress Allerton is too weak to care for a baby now anyway."

"It's only by God's grace she still lives."

In this way, we came to understand the baby had been born dead. The women came to tell me we had had a boy, as Mary Norris had predicted, and some of our congregation took his tiny body away for burial onshore. When Mary, Bartholomew and I returned to my wife's side, I knelt and held her hand, praying beside her, in joy and thanks that she had lived through her labor. Mary and Remember knelt beside Mary Norris, little Mary crying in relief to see her mother alive. My wife hugged both her daughters tightly and grasped her son's hand. "God giveth and He taketh away. We must accept this. Come pray with me for your little brother."

In truth, I believe that exhaustion, illness, and the difficulties of the voyage led to my wife's acceptance of our baby's death. Her stoicism and belief in God's will provided me with the strength to face the sorrow myself. As we prayed that night, I hoped my children would also come to accept what had happened. My good wife slept peacefully after our words beseeching our Lord and Savior for His comfort.

In the days that followed, Mary Norris didn't recover as she did with her first three children, needing to rest often and having no appetite. Remember, with some help from Mary, took over more chores, trying to get her mother to eat some meat and pickled vegetables to regain her strength.

Adding to our distress, my servant, Mister Hook, had also fallen ill. He lay close to us, now too weak to work ashore, and tended to by my exhausted wife, who rose from her bed to wash his bedding and clothes and to feed him. Little Mary emptied our foul bucket each day without complaint.

By December twenty-fourth, we had still not begun the construction of the first house. That morning, before I left for the day, Bartholomew and Remember began to tell their little sister what they remembered of Christmas celebrations in Leiden. Their mother stopped them immediately. "We don't celebrate Christmas, children. Does the scripture name any day as holy except the Sabbath? No, it doesn't. Christmas is a pagan festival, and we aren't pagans." My two oldest looked properly ashamed, as they should have been because this was one of our strongest beliefs.

On our first day of actual construction, I paused to take in the immense silence of the land, compared to the constant babble and creaking of our living quarters, and how once begun, the noise of axes and saws and our calls to each other punctuated the stillness of the cold air. As we worked, our breaths created isolated clouds of condensation, growing larger as together we dragged logs to the chosen site for our first house. This lay near the brook, at the base of the smaller of two hills marking the site. We had begun to erect its framework when, toward sunset, we heard whoops erupting from the forest near us. Dreading an attack, we returned to the ship. Mary, who had heard the whoops, clung to me all evening, thinking something was out there in the dark, waiting to hurt us. Mary Norris had to rock her to sleep, my daughter clinging tightly to her poppet.

Our building of that first house was my youngest daughter's entertainment for a full two weeks, because bouts of icy rain interrupted it completion. Each night I would bring the family news of our progress, which I delivered as we sat together on the floor following our evening meal and prayers.

"What will it look like, Isaac? Anything like our houses in England?" asked Mary Norris from where she lay wrapped in her blankets.

"No, this first one will be crude, a common house, just enough to provide shelter and some warmth. We are making the walls of tree trunks and we'll interweave branches between them. We found a place along the marsh with some reasonable clay, with which we can use to fill in between the branches."

"But what will you do for a roof?" Remember asked.

"There are cattails and reeds in the salt marsh. Bartholomew will go with some others to gather them."

Bartholomew beamed with pride at his inclusion.

"I want to see it!" Mary said loudly.

"None of you will, at least for a while. The decision has been made to transfer some of our sickest men there, where they can be cared for separately from those who are still healthy."

Conditions on the ship had long ago become nearly unbearable, and although I doubted it could become worse, it had. More and more of the women suffered with fevers, racking coughs, and flux of the bowels, so there were fewer available to care for the sick. With little heat, the cold penetrated even the warmest clothes, and our only hot food was cooked on shore or if permitted, in the ship's galley. It was hardly warm by the time it reached us, and we still had to eat the odious hard biscuits. The men who were still healthy could at least spend part of everyday away from this fetid place of sickness.

After a few more pleas from my youngest child to go ashore, my wife threatened her with still more prayers that night. Mary crossed her arms with a dark look on her face. Before Mary Norris could scold her again, I said, "Daughter, if you will but obey your mother, you may watch us this coming week, when we climb the hill from the common house. Captain Standish plans to build a platform at the top of that hill, on which we will place our cannon. With the view from there, we can make a plot for our village, and in a few days, I can tell you where our house will be."

Mary Norris leaned back in her bed, coughed, and took in my news with a wan smile. "That will be nice, Isaac, especially for the children." She looked around our tiny, dismal living quarters. "Do you realize that Mary doesn't know what it's like to live in a real house? All she can remember is living here."

Chapter 7

Construction Begins

Isaac Allerton, Plymouth Colony, January-February 1621

My dear brother-in-law, Degory Priest, who had been so kind and loving to my children, died January first. He had tried to work ashore with the other men, but toward the end of December, feverish and racked with coughing, he took to his bed aboard the *Mayflower*. Mary Norris tended to his needs, placing a cloth soaked in cold salt water on his head to cool him, and little Mary sat by his side, hoping when he recovered from a coughing fit he might tell her a story. She took it upon herself to feed him broth made from deer meat. Despite these ministrations, he eventually raved with fever and then fell into a fitful sleep from which he never roused.

When he took his last rasping breath, the world shifted. We had lost a member of our own family, and our grief was deep and abiding. I went ashore with his body for burial and returned to continuing tears and sobs. That night, we prayed for his soul and that he had found peace in the loving arms of his Savior.

My family's depression only lifted with the completion of the common house. Crudely made of logs with clay daubing between them and a thatch roof, it nevertheless gave us the belief we could build a settlement and soon be in our own homes. The construction had proved difficult, as winter storms had halted our work for days at a time and washed away the daubing.

One evening, after a bitterly cold day of felling trees and gathering rushes, Bartholomew and I climbed down to our living quarters aboard the *Mayflower*, swinging our arms and stamping on the deck in attempt to warm ourselves. Remember fussed with our evening meal—cold food, as usual, but at least we had some meat. "Is the common house yet finished?" Mary Norris asked, coughing between her words.

"Yes, and tomorrow we'll bring the sickest of our men there, where they can be isolated and kept in fresh air. Did you know William Bradford is now sick as well?"

"Yes, I saw him today. Who will care for them?"

"Some of the healthier men, I imagine."

There were only a few healthy men remaining to assume this task, amongst them Elder Brewster, Myles Standish, Samuel Fuller, and myself. We fetched wood for the fire, fed the sick if they were too weak to feed themselves, undressed and dressed them, and washed their clothes when they became vile. Our cheerfulness as we worked convinced me that God's love was why we cared so well for our friends and brethren.

But the work of the devil interrupted us. A spark from the chimney of our common house caught in the thatch. We dragged the sick outside and retrieved the muskets and the powder stored in the house, but we had no water to douse the flames. Calls to those chopping down trees some distance away went unheard. When someone finally noticed the smoke, they ran back to help. It was too late, and we watched our first house burn.

"Was the powder removed from the house, Governor Carver?" Master Winslow asked. He'd been the first to run back.

"Yes, by the grace of God."

"We'll just have to rebuild." I spoke the obvious, with a deep sigh. "But God blessed us, in that no one was hurt."

We stood there until the house became just a glowing pile of logs, then began the rebuilding, disheartened.

༺ ༻

Little Mary bounced on her toes with questions for me when I returned for the night. She had seen the huge fire on shore.

"What happened, Father? Was it Indians?"

"No, the common house burned when a spark from the chimney caught on the thatch. No one died, but we have to rebuild. No one was injured, though."

Mary Norris shook her head. "So much work wasted, but thanks be to God, husband, everyone survived." She sighed deeply, discouraged at yet another setback to leaving the hell that our quarters on the ship had become. Now so weakened by her illness she couldn't rise from her bed to tend the others who were sick, she clung to the hope of living in fresh air and enjoying the warmth of a fire.

"Perhaps this will bring you some cheer, everyone. We've discussed a plan for our settlement and have decided where our houses will be sited. A street will lead to the top of the large hill, where we have begun building the platform, and our homes will line the street on both sides."

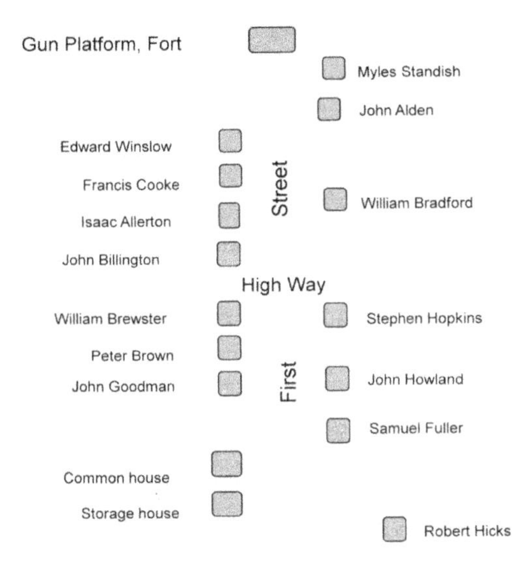

Plots of Houses along First Street

Everyone's eyes lit up with that news. "Soon we'll have a real home," Remember said. "Just think, a home of our own!"

I had hoped this news would encourage my good wife, but she knew as well as I did there was no way of knowing how long this would take.

Since each family would build their own house, and since construction skills varied from man to man, the erection of houses could take a long time. Further, Captain Standish was determined to build the gun platform, and at the end of December, some of us had been assigned to work on that, rather than on our houses. The bad weather continued as well.

"Do you know where our house will sit, Isaac?" Mary Norris asked.

"Yes, about halfway up the hill. We chose by lots, so no one had the advantage. Governor Carver's home will be across the street from us." I could see the family's eyes sparkling in the dim light, thinking about our home and seeing our settlement. "We are also planning for a cross street."

Mary Norris paused for a moment and then asked, "How big a plot do we have for the house?"

"Each family will have a plot eight feet wide and roughly fifty feet long, multiplied by the number of its members. Bartholomew, can you calculate how wide and how deep our plot will be?"

Bartholomew scrunched his forehead as he did the mental calculation. After a moment he replied, "With five of us, that would be forty feet wide and about two hundred feet deep, I think."

"That's rather small," said Mary Norris, "but we will make do."

"We'll have a still larger lot because each of the unmarried men has been assigned to an existing household."

Why?"

"Because with our numbers so depleted by sickness, we haven't the men to build the number of houses originally planned. Our plot will be somewhat larger when we include Mister Hook." I looked at the boy, wrapped in blankets and lying against the hull of the ship, but listening intently to the conversation. *I doubt he will survive but I must give him hope.*

Only thirteen years of age, young John had grown dear to us during our long voyage. He had been more of a playmate and companion to our children, there not yet being much for him to do in assisting me. While he lay ill, Mary often sat by his side, telling him fanciful tales to make him smile.

My wife shook her head slightly, so slightly that only I could see it. "He is as sick as the others here," she whispered with tears in her eyes.

Over the next few days, my wife, when she had the strength, and Remember worked to keep Mister Hook alive—wrapping him in our blankets, feeding him broth, and making him drink a decoction of herbs to help with his coughing. Sadly, nothing proved effective.

Like my brother-in-law, he grew hot and bright-eyed with fever and talked loudly in his sleep. I believe it was God's blessing when he died in the middle of January, after suffering for so long. My family shed tears, watching as some of our men took his body ashore for burial that evening. The children were especially distraught, his death coming on the heels of their uncle's, and they refused to eat that night, going to bed silently after our evening prayers. I could hear muffled sobs from Remember and Mary until they fell asleep.

Watching bodies being rowed to shore had become commonplace, and I was surprised that with all this misery, we still had tears to shed. Despite the constant specter of death, our faith still sustained us—but for how long?

༺ ༻

Bartholomew and I grew sinewy from our exertions on shore, even with little to eat. The clean, cold air filled our lungs, and the sound of chopping and the voices of the men working were unexpectedly soothing.

We had to travel some distance to find the best wood, but since the Indians had burned much of the underbrush, they'd made it easy to walk amongst the trees. We had our choice of tall white pine and black and red oak. Later we would make use of the chestnut, hickory, birch alders and maple trees. Once the trees were felled, we used our axes to shape them from round to square for the framing. We welcomed the exertion on sunny days, despite the cold, but even rain and snow didn't often impede us. We frequently saw Indians and thus had to be constantly on our guard. Having women and children on shore would be dangerous, so they remained on the *Mayflower*. Nevertheless, I prayed for the day when Mary Norris and my daughters could come ashore with me.

One day, the younger of John Billington's two unruly sons, Francis, climbed to the top of a tall tree and from there spotted what he called a great sea. He and some others went to find it, discovering two great lakes, full of fish and with many water fowl, along with abandoned Indian dwellings. This was a rich land.

Another day, when I returned to where I had felled a large pine, I found my axe missing. I called to Stephen Hopkins, "Is my axe there where you are cutting?"

"No," he replied. "And another axe went missing two days ago."

In this way, we discovered that while the Indians never came near us and we never saw them, tools disappeared if left unguarded—a great loss since they were irreplaceable. We had neither the time nor the strength to pursue the thieves, so we then kept our tools always in our sight.

ꟿ ꟿ

Work on the houses proceeded apace in January, and our leaders decided a few women and some of the older children could come ashore. Remember was chosen one day, much to little Mary's frustration and anger. The women gathered such greens as they could find and looked for clams at the ebbing of the tide. Unfortunately, our first meal of clams sickened us, so it was some time before we tried eating them again.

Master Jones sent the shallop out into the bay to locate where fish might be caught. The men returned with three seals and an excellent cod, but we found that most of the fish hooks we had brought with us were too large to catch the fish. We remained hungry since the men were busy with construction and few would hunt.

Also that month, Peter Brown and John Goodman, the latter our member with the two dogs, disappeared while cutting thatch. We prayed John's mastiff would protect them from wild animals and Indians, but their long absence became increasingly concerning. When they finally returned and told us what had happened, I had a fine story to tell Marry Norris and the children.

"Well, I thank God they returned safely," Marry Norris said first, with her usual piety.

"Where were they?" asked little Mary.

"It seems the dogs were to blame. They spotted a deer and took off in pursuit. When Mister Brown and Mister Goodman finally caught up to the dogs, they had lost their bearing and were unable to orient themselves to our harbor. They spent a cold, snowy night walking to keep warm and became further afraid with the wailing of two lions. The next day, they finally found a hill high enough to give themselves a view of the harbor. When they reached us, they were close to fainting from exhaustion and want of food and warmth."

"Lions!" exclaimed Mary. "Is the devil out there, too, Father?'

"Hush, child," said my wife. "Your imagination is worse than reality." Still, she looked worried. We all believed the forest to be the devil's last preserve.

With tensions running high from seeing fires in the distance and the disappearance of tools, Captain Standish attempted to create a militia with some of our members. Standish took to this task with energy but with so much officiousness that he engendered considerable contempt. Standish's boldness particularly irritated John Billington, who berated the captain in an insolent voice. "You have no right to order me about. We didn't come this long, perilous way for conscription into an army! We know how to shoot, and we've repelled the Indians during our expeditions on shore. Our time would be better spent building our own houses or preparing fields for planting."

After several long-winded, seditious speeches by Billington, Governor Carver thought to punish him by tying his hands and feet together and making him sit in a public place, but the pleas of his family earned him a reprieve. "Billington has become a thorn in the side of our community," I told Mary Norris. "I wonder what he'll do next."

At the end of January, we finally took some of our stores ashore, placing them in a shed built after we'd completed the common house. Some of us would be set to building other sheds to hold the rest of our goods, since Captain Jones wished to unload and set sail back to England as soon as fair weather returned.

With the gun platform completed at the end of February, Jones, with many of his sailors, helped us drag our cannons up the hill—one great and one smaller—to set them on bases we had constructed.

Because of all the communal construction, Bartholomew and I had made slow progress on our house, having only dug the post holes and set the posts. Nevertheless, to raise the spirits of Mary Norris and the children, we would relate even the smallest of progress each day when we returned to the ship.

Mary Norris grasped her son's hand like a lifeline one night while he described what we had done that day. "The frame is finally up—it's a small house, Mother, with only one room, but it will be fine and cozy for all of us. We are now splitting the logs to make clapboards for the siding. Once that's done, we can make the inside walls. I think little Mary and Remember might help us collect the sticks to make the wattle. Then I can show them how to use clay, straw, and sand to mix into daub. Mary should enjoy that, don't you think?

My wife smiled at the thought of Mary playing in mud. She cradled his faced with one hand and said, "Look at you, my son. You have grown so much in the last several months. And now so strong." The love in her eyes encompassed us all.

Chapter 8

Death Comes to Call

Mary Allerton Cushman, Plymouth, September 1699

On the bench in my garden I shudder, despite the warmth of the sun on my shoulders, thinking of the time of the great sickness. I do have some memory of our first winter in Plymouth, although my recollections are indistinct, as if I'm seeing them through a shifting veil of gray and black.

Mary Allerton Cushman, Plymouth, October - November 1620

The place where we lived was dark and smelly and all I could hear were groans and coughing. Every day men came to lift another body and take it away. I can remember sneaking up on deck during those times, despite the admonishments of my mother, just to feel the sun and breathe fresh air. I longed to go ashore with my father. During this time of blackness, my Uncle Degory died, succumbing quickly to a congestion in the lungs. Father tried to remain strong for us all, but the absence of Uncle Degory created a sadness in him that even Mother couldn't touch. We had shared so much during our journey here, and we children missed his smiles, stories and kindly ways.

Mother was tired all the time and racked with coughs, yet she tried to tend the other sick, even when doing so left her too exhausted to continue without a day of rest. Remember told me Mother had little strength left to keep me from wandering and that I mustn't tax what strength she had. Both Remember and Mother were cross with me most of the time. My sister, being two years older, had to stay by Mother's side. She gave me nasty looks when I returned from wherever I'd roved, and those looks continued for many years. I knew she blamed me for making my mother's life more difficult. Bartholomew, when he was on board, had the task of finding me. I remember his kindness as we'd always play some game together and he'd make me laugh before he brought me back.

One day I told my mother, "I'm bleeding from my mouth again."

"Hush, daughter, we all are." She coughed. "It's because of our poor food. No! Don't wiggle that tooth!"

My stomach always hurt from hunger. The hard biscuits now tasted strongly of mold, and what little food we had crawled with maggots. The best times were when some of the men killed a deer or rabbits and we ate roasted meat.

My mother often had me or Remember sit by her side, reminding us in a rasping voice, with gasps to take in a breath, how to behave, what was expected of us, and to take care of Father. At the time, I didn't understand why she did so.

Then Mother died.

Isaac Allerton, Plymouth Colony, February 1621

My dear wife and mother to our three children joined her Savior at the end of February, despite the ministrations of our physick, Samuel Fuller. The long, brutal days of living below decks, the lack of food, the piercing cold, the stress of a stillbirth, and her determination to care for others finally overwhelmed what strength she had. I held her hot, fevered hand through that last day, as her breathing became more and more labored, while Remember laid cool cloths on her forehead. Silently I urged her to fight, but I knew she had no strength left in her. She lay, wrapped in soiled blankets, struggling to breath, too tired to cough to clear the phlegm that choked her. For the children, I prayed aloud for her soul, to prepare them for what would come.

I couldn't imagine life without her. As I watched her care-worn face and noticed the streaks of silver in her dark hair, the guilt of having brought her on this perilous journey weighed heavily upon me. *What have I done? What will happen to my children?*

The children surrounded her, little Mary grasping her mother's hand to her face and urging her to get well. Finally, after many hours, my wife's breathing slowed and then stopped. Her struggle to live was over. I stroked her face for the last time.

Little Mary wailed, "Don't leave me, Mother. I'll be a good girl. I'll do whatever you say." She clasped her mother's still body and cried. Bartholomew hid his face to cover his tears, but his shoulders shook. Remember wrapped her arms around her sister, adding her own sobs.

"Children, your mother has gone to be with God. Her labors in this life are over. We must pray for her soul." I bent my head to hide my own tears. It took some moments to gather myself, but I knew I had to be strong. "Come, on your knees, and join me in prayer for your mother's soul. She was a righteous and kind woman and the best mother to you all." At this, Mary's voice grew loud in her grief and Remember collapsed, kneeling on the floor.

By now, others who were still able to walk gathered around us, and together we offered a prayer of gratitude for my wife's life and of hope she rested with her God. Finally, several goodwives shushed the children away and dressed Mary Norris in clean shift and wrapped her in a shroud made from a blanket. Some of the men took her body up to the main deck. The children and I followed and continued to pray until the ship's boat arrived from shore to take the body for burial. The children remained behind, and I went with my wife on her last journey.

In the days that followed, Remember took over the household chores, and Mary now stayed by her side and did what small tasks she could, always clutching the now bedraggled poppet her mother had made. Their eyes were empty, and after our evening meal, Mary stopped asking for stories and went to bed without a word.

Despite the best efforts of our physick, forty-nine of us died by the time spring finally came in April, including all but five of the adult women and three entire families. Master Fuller often recalled this time with profound sadness because there had been little he could do to ease the suffering of the sick. We buried our dead, including Mary Norris, at night, on the smaller of the two hills overlooking the harbor. We didn't wish the Indians to know how depleted our numbers had become and we leveled the soil and sowed grasses over the graves to disguise them.

Chapter 9

A Treaty with the Indians

Isaac Allerton, Plymouth Colony, Spring 1621

By the middle of March, most of us could spend our days ashore building, and as a result there seemed to be less illness. A few houses stood complete with others nearly so, and the absence of the bitter winter winds lifted our spirits and our energy. With the great guns installed at the top of the hill, we felt for the first time a modicum of safety—we could now defend our little community. Furthermore, due to the depletion of his crew with sickness, Master Jones had postponed leaving for England and, with his healthy crew members, hunted for food so everyone's diet was enriched with fish, meat and fowl.

Despite the need to finish binding bundles of reeds and rushes for the roof of our own house, yet another call from Captain Standish for further discussion of military matters interrupted our work. We slowly came together at the bottom of what now looked like a street leading up the hill, the passage of many feet having pounded the dirt and sand flat. Just as Standish began his usual long-winded pontification, a solitary Indian appeared at the top of the hill on the other side of the brook.

As the Indian walked down the hill towards our settlement, one of us hit an iron pot with a sword, the signal for the women and children to go to the common house. After crossing the brook, he headed directly to our gathering. We stood rooted to the ground in surprise when he stopped, raised his hand with an open palm, and said, "Welcome, Englishmen!"

After we'd recovered our wits, Governor Carver replied, "Welcome to our settlement."

Mary had not gone with the women but instead came and stood behind me, peeking around my legs. She tugged on my sleeve, saying, "A real Indian, Father! Why isn't he wearing any clothes?"

"Silence, child." He was indeed naked, except for a fringed leather strap around his waist—a tall man with black hair, cut long in back and short in front. Mary continued to hold tightly to my breeches and viewed the Indian with total fascination, shaking off her sister's attempt to drag her to the common house. I could see the women and children looking out from the door, equally interested.

"You must suffer from the chill air, sir," Carver said with concern. Someone thought to hand the governor a long coat, which he draped over the Indian's shoulders—not only to offer him something warm to wear but also to hide his nakedness. "How are you called?" he asked.

"I am Samoset," he replied. "Have beer?"

We didn't have beer, but Bradford offered him some aqua vitae we'd brought, and soon Samoset sat on the ground surrounded by our company of men, eating hard biscuits, cheese from our stores, and a slice of roasted duck. The expression on his face indicated he had eaten this food before and enjoyed it.

He spoke to us in broken English, telling us he came from an island off the coast of Maine. He had learned our language from the English fisherman who frequented that area. "This," he said, gesturing at the harbor and adjacent land, "Patuxet. Many people live here, now all dead. Big sickness."

Although we had occasional difficulty understanding him, we learned the Indian leader of this area was named Massasoit, who lived some forty miles to the south at a place called Pokanoket.

"Man there speak good English," Samoset told us. "Name Tisquantum. I bring him."

Samoset told us the Indians of the Cape area where we first landed—and from whom we had stolen corn—where called Nausets. He said they were not kindly disposed toward us, since an Englishman named Hunt had abducted twenty or so of their men eight years earlier. Samoset's promise to bring another Indian elicited some whispering amongst our group about a possible attack. Nevertheless, establishing trade with the natives, especially for furs to be sent back to England, would enable us to pay some of our debt. In the end, we reached consensus that this proposed meeting with Tisquantum was worth the risk.

As dusk fell, Samoset pointed to the *Mayflower* and said, "I stay there." He rose from the ground and headed to where we had beached the shallop, climbing into the boat. After we persuaded him of the difficulty of rowing to the ship against the tide and wind, Governor Carver invited him to stay the night in Stephen Hopkins' house. Nervous comments from some of us led Carver to mount a watch outside the house. Bartholomew and I slept with other men in the common house, while Mary and Remember slept in another completed house, along with some of the women.

In the morning, Samoset received food along with gifts of a knife, a bracelet and a ring. He promised us to return in a few days, bringing some Nausets with him.

True to his word, Samoset returned that Sunday with four other Indians, the man named Tisquantum among them. They were clothed in leather pants, with all but one wearing a deer skin, and their faces were painted in black, red, yellow or white. Their leader bore a wildcat's skin, his face was painted a dark red, and his long black hair glistened with grease. Not surprisingly, their appearance impressed some, especially Edward Winslow, who had a deep interest in the natives and their culture. The Indians frightened the women, who provided food but would not serve them. After they had eaten, they sang and danced, to the rapt attention of Master Winslow.

Mary, curious as ever, once again snuck away from her sister and sat cross-legged on the ground with some of the boys, observing the activity intently.

Tisquantum explained how he'd learned English. "My name is Tisquantum or Squanto, which is my shorter name. I am Patuxet and, along with some Nausets and some men of my tribe, was taken captive by Thomas Hunt when he came here to trade for furs. He was a very evil man. He kept us below in his ship, took us across the water to a strange land, and sold some of us. Some holy men took those remaining to save us. I," he said, pointing to his chest, "only I, have returned to my home."

"What happened to the others?" Master Winslow asked.

"I do not know. The holy men tried to make us Christians, but I escaped on a boat that took me to the place called England. I lived there with a man who wanted to trade with Indians, and from him, I learned your language. I returned across the great sea in one of his boats to a place called the Newfoundland Colony, then left and came back here. A great sickness occurred during my absence, and now all my people are dead. I am the last." The sadness in his face told me how much he mourned their loss. "Now I live with the Wampanoags."

A few days later, Squanto returned, this time with the chief of the Wampanoags, Massasoit, along with many of his men. The appearance of so many had us picking up our muskets, but the Indians stopped on the hill across the creek. Squanto brought us a request from Massasoit that we send someone to speak with him. Edward Winslow, clad in armor and with a sword at his side, stepped forward, agreeing to go—a good choice to represent us.

Noticing that Mary once again stood by herself at a distance from this scene, absorbed in its drama, I left our gathered men and walked to where she stood. "Daughter, this isn't a safe place for you. Go back to the women." The women were currently standing outside but close to the common house, should they need protection.

"But I want to stay here!" Mary said, frowning in determination.

"Then you will not be spared the rod tonight for your disobedience," I replied. At that, she walked slowly back to the women, dragging her feet.

By the time I returned to the group of our men, Master Winslow had reached the contingent of Indians, having walked steadily toward them with no obvious fear. He brought Massasoit gifts: two knives, copper kettles, some alcohol and biscuits.

Winslow later told us he had made a speech, which Squanto had translated. "Massasoit asked me for my armor," Winslow told us, "which I had to decline as politely as I could. He then said I would be their hostage while he went to meet with the rest of you."

I was amongst the men who went with Governor Carver and Captain Standish to greet Massasoit and his men. They left their bows behind which reassured us they wouldn't attack, and we welcomed them warmly after they'd crossed the creek. Massasoit appeared the same as his tribesmen, except for a great chain of white bones around his neck. Like his warriors, he wore red face paint, and he was oiled, both skin and hair.

The two parties then walked to William Bradford's house, where a chair of Bradford's and a rug had been arranged on the dirt floor. I heard faint whispers coming from the small window on one side of the house's single room and knew at once that some of the children had slunk away from the women. I also knew without doubt that Mary and Bartholomew were amongst them. *What am I going to do with these willful children?*

I watched while Governor Carver kissed Massasoit's hand and had him sit in the chair as a place of honor. After some food and drink, Squanto translated a speech by Carver to the effect that King James sent Massasoit words of love and peace, accepted him as his friend and ally, and wished to trade with him. Carver proved an admirable diplomat.

However, as the speech progressed, I noticed that Massasoit broke into a sweat. He visibly trembled as he and Carver, with input from both our group and the other Indians, negotiated a peace agreement, a formal treaty between our two peoples.

࿇ ࿇

After our meal that night, I had much to tell my family. "First, I'm disappointed in the behavior of my children today," I said, looking sternly at Mary and Bartholomew. "This was an important event, and I could hear you whispering outside the house. What if this had distracted the meeting? You would have interfered with everything Governor Carver worked to achieve. You've been disobedient and disrespectful and for that, you'll be thrashed. Then you will spend some time tonight on your knees, praying for God to forgive your sins."

The children hung their heads, but I sensed they weren't truly repentant. Remember looked smug, since she was not the object of my anger. Mary glanced at me sideways with her impish face and asked, "What did you think of the Indians, Father? They looked very fierce, but this time they were wearing clothes."

"And I didn't understand them when they spoke," said Bartholomew.

"Children, they have a language of their own, much as we do. Squanto, the one who speaks English, told them what we were saying and told us what they were saying."

"What did they say, Father?" asked my son.

"They were interested in a treaty of peace with us, and one was made—a great accomplishment for our governor."

"Does that mean they won't attack us?" asked Remember.

"Yes, I think we'll be friends."

Sitting with us for our meal that night had been John Alden, the cooper hired for the *Mayflower*. He had decided to remain with us and because of the deaths of my wife, my brother-in-law, Degory Priest, and our servant, John Hooke, Governor Carver had assigned Alden to live with us. He hadn't been amongst those meeting with the Indians, so he asked, "What type of agreement did we forge, Master Allerton?"

We had yet no furniture, so I sat on a stump, placed so I could lean back against the wall of our house. "Massasoit agreed that none of his people will injure any of us and if that happens, the offender will be sent to us for punishment. We will do the same if any of us do harm to them. He agreed if any of our tools are taken by a member of his tribe, he'll have them restored."

"That sounds fair and reasonable," Alden said.

"There was more—we agreed to help him if any tribe wages war against him, and he agreed to do likewise should any war against us."

"Is there a reason he wanted this particular agreement?"

"He's in a position of great weakness. The Wampanoags have been much reduced in number by sickness, and he fears attacks not only from the Narragansetts to the south but the Massachusetts to the north, as well as from other tribes in the Wampanoag confederacy. Massasoit will let our agreement be known to the neighboring tribes, as a means of showing his strength. We can only hope that the other Wampanoag tribes will abide by what Massasoit pledged."

Bartholomew had been sitting quietly, listening, while Mary, sitting next to him, rubbed her eyes with sleep and hugged her poppet. "Father," he asked, "did you notice Massasoit perspired?"

"I did, son, and he seemed nervous to me. I heard later that Squanto told him we had plague stored in barrels beneath one of our storehouses."

"But that's a lie, isn't it? Why would he say that?"

"Yes, it was a lie, but Squanto explained he said it to persuade Massasoit to reach an agreement. I'm not sure I agree with that strategy, but perhaps when Massasoit saw our sheds were guarded, he was inclined to believe Squanto."

"Are the Indians still here in the village?" Alden asked, frowning slightly.

"No, they left a short time ago, except for Squanto. He will stay here as a gesture of friendship. There is much we can learn from him, Master Alden. Massasoit and some of his people have pledged to return with corn seed to help us plant our fields, which is a gracious and welcome gesture.

"I hope the Indian corn will sustain us during the coming year. With only barley and peas to plant, and without either cows or pigs, what did the Merchant-Adventurers think we would eat? And we gave Massasoit a kettle of dried peas, further reducing our stores." This added to my frustration with the poor foresight of the men who had financially backed our voyage.

The next morning, Squanto went to fish for eels. Bartholomew was eager to go with him, along with some of the other children, much to their parents' concern. My son had often been near the tidal creek, gathering reeds and rushes for our roof and more recently, for mud to make the daub to fill in between the boards of our house. I never saw him as happy as when he was mucking in the creek.

That night, after we had all feasted on the fat and sweet eels Squanto had caught, Bartholomew told us how he had learned to catch them. "Squanto waded out into the creek and used his feet to squish them out, Father. You should have seen how many he found! Now that I have seen him do it, I can do it, too. We will have eels to eat now...but that water is very cold."

ꙮ ꙮ

In early April, we gathered on the shore of the harbor. An old friend was leaving. With the weather now fair, Captain Jones had decided to take the *Mayflower* home to England, her empty hold ballasted with stones. He left with only half his original crew—the rest had died along with half of our own number during that long, miserable winter. Before Jones left, I gave him a letter for my sister, telling her with great sorrow of the death of her husband.

Sadness and anxiety showed on our faces as we watched the *Mayflower* unfurl her sails and sail east out of the harbor into the rising sun. Aboard were many men who had become our friends, and now, without the ship, many of us felt for the first time truly alone and isolated in this vast and unforgiving land. Our last link from whence we'd come had disappeared, and whatever our future, we faced it here, alone but together. We stood on the shore and watched until the ship disappeared over the horizon.

ꙮ ꙮ

As spring progressed, Squanto proved to be a true friend. He showed our men and boys how to hunt and trap and thereafter, we had abundant game to eat. One day, Alden and I went with Squanto, some Wampanoags, and all the members of our settlement, including the women and older children, to the land cleared south of the brook. There he showed us how to plant the strange, multi-colored corn kernels that would be our staple until other seed arrived from England.

We returned to the house for a midday meal, which Remember prepared with the other women, who had to cook together for all of us because they were so few. Little Mary dragged behind, tired and quite dirty, clutching her equally filthy poppet. We washed our hands and faces in water in a bucket outside the door before entering the house, but Remember had to remind Mary to wash and ordered her to leave the poppet outside when she saw its condition. I must tell my Remember to clean it. It's little Mary's one reminder of her mother.

We no longer had to stand or sit on the floor to eat, as we now had stools to sit on, and Mister Alden had made us a table from boards he'd split from oak logs. Bartholomew came in last, drinking from a dipper of water from another bucket near the door. He sat on a stool, removing his felt hat and wiping the sweat from his forehead with his sleeve.

I looked at him with some sympathy. "I know planting is women's work, son, but we must all share in the work so we can plant enough corn to sustain us though the next winter. Once the corn starts to grow, you and I and the other men will work the fields together."

The planting had proven very interesting. Squanto had shown us how to gather mounds of earth and then put inside each mound some of the corn seed and several fish.

"Why do you think Squanto put fish in with the corn?" Bartholomew asked.

"To feed the corn when it sprouts," Alden replied. "I think the Indians know the soil isn't rich enough."

"He brought so many baskets of fish. Where do you think Squanto got them?" My son had many questions that day.

I knew exactly where. Soon after the Mayflower left, the waters of our brook roiled with fish—alewives and bluebacks, a type of herring, working their way up the brook to spawn. "From the brook. You should go there to see it—there are so many fish there, you can catch them in your hands. If you do, we can have fish cooked on the fire for our meal tonight."

That morning, we had used hoes we'd brought with us on the Mayflower, but I'd noticed Squanto worked with a crude tool that looked just like our hoes. It had a stone head and a wooden handle, and he called it a mattock. I wondered if we could make such a tool for those of us without hoes, and I mentioned this to John Alden.

"Let me look at this mattock more closely," he replied, "and I'll ask Squanto about its construction.

Thus we began to fashion our own tools.

ꙮ ꙮ

After the harsh winter, April was unseasonably warm, and nearly all the men now labored in the fields of planted corn. Some of the corn had sprouted, and Squanto directed us to add beans and squash, both native plants, to the mounds. As I understood his explanation, the creeping vines of these plants would grow up the cornstalks, shading the roots of the corn from the hot sun and providing us with more food. I shook my head, looking at the areas where we had planted barley and peas. They grew, but poorly. We would need to ask Squanto about how we might improve the growth of these crops as well.

April also brought great despair and sorrow because we lost our governor. John Carver had been working in the fields beside us, red-faced and sweating copiously. After a while, he began to complain of a throbbing pain in his head and dizziness. We half-carried him back to his house, where we lay him, burning with heat, on his bed. His wife tended to him, along with Samuel Fuller, our physick, but after a short while he became unresponsive and remained that way for several days, until dying.

We gathered outside his house on the evening of his death, and led by Elder Brewster, gave thanks to God for his life and prayed for his soul. We buried him where all our burials had been, on the small hill at the bottom of the street we now called First Street, and we marked the significance of his passing by firing our muskets. There he joined my wife Mary Norris, my brother-in-law Degory Priest, my apprentice John Hooke, Captain Standish's wife Rose, Edward Winslow's wife Elizabeth, and so many others from that first winter.

Carver's death shook the members of our settlement. After the horrors and deaths of the long winter, we'd now lost a man on whose good judgement, courage, and advice we'd come to depend. Some days later, John Alden and I spoke quietly together, as the fire in the hearth burnt down and crackled as logs fell into the ashes. The children had fallen asleep on their mattresses in a corner of our house, and a sense of peace filled the room, at least until we considered that the loss of Carver was not our only problem.

"We need a strong leader now, Master Alden. Consider the troubles we face. For one, the *Mayflower* returned to England without goods. How will the Merchant Adventurers respond when they find an empty hold? Will they withdraw their financial support? Will they send no more people and no further supplies?"

"Agreed, Master Allerton. And there is rancor even amongst us. That man Billington continues to rail against Standish and there are petty arguments by the day. We need strong and steady leadership. Who do you think can take Carver's place?"

"I think the logical choice is Bradford."

Alden looked thoughtful, then added, "But he's young, though, only about thirty, and he's been sorely ill for the last months. Will he accept? And if he does, when will he be well enough to take over Carver's duties?"

Soon thereafter, the men put it to a vote and chose Bradford. Although still not recovered, he accepted, but only if I served as his assistant. So I became one of our colony's leaders, and together with Elder Brewster, Edward Winslow and Miles Standish, assisted the new governor in making decisions for our future.

Chapter 10

Health, Hope, and Turmoil

Isaac Allerton, Plymouth Colony, Spring and Summer 1621

In May of 1621, we celebrated our first marriage in the colony—that of Edward Winslow and Susanna White. Both had lost their spouses during the terrible winter. Susanna White's husband William had succumbed in February, leaving her with two young sons—Resolved, six, and Peregrine, born aboard the Mayflower. Edward's wife Elizabeth, whom he had married in Leiden, had died in March after a long illness.

"Do they love each other, Father?" asked Remember. "Mistress White's husband only just died."

"I'm not in a position to answer that question, my daughter, but I'm sure they'll come to comfort and support each other."

"Then Resolved will have a father," said Mary, matter-of-factly, referring to the boy she had occasionally played with on the *Mayflower*.

"Yes, he and Peregrine will have a fine, honest, educated father," I added.

"Didn't Master White have servants, like our John Hooke? What will happen to them?" Bartholomew had the most practical outlook of all my children.

"Yes, he did, and they will become part of their household and a great help to Master Winslow, since he and I have had to assume some of the duties of Governor Bradford."

"Will there be singing and other things?" Mary's eyes lit up with excitement.

"No, child, it's to be a short ceremony, consistent with our faith. Governor Bradford will officiate."

"Oh-fish-ate?" asked Mary.

We all chuckled. "He will say the words to make them married, Mary."

Remember frowned. "Will you marry again, Father?"

"Possibly. We'll see. You children clearly need a firm hand and a mother to teach you."

We all attended the union, although the winter deaths dampened its joy. As was our custom, no rings were exchanged, but the brief ceremony marked a milestone in our colony's survival.

ℰ ℰ

With the corn growing high, a few houses built, and gardens planted, we thought to send some representatives to meet with Massasoit, the sachem of the Wampanoags. Governor Bradford and his advisors decided to give him gifts to secure our treaty. We were also curious about how he and his tribe lived, and we needed to determine the numbers of his warriors.

On July 2, Edward Winslow and Stephen Hopkins, with Squanto as their guide, set off on what proved to be a forty-mile journey of several days. They brought with them a red cotton horseman's coat and some copper chain as gifts for Massasoit, plus necklaces, beads and some other small trade goods to exchange for furs and corn. An intellectually curious man, Master Winslow would note everything on the trip.

When they returned the following week, footsore and hungry, with a guide named Hobomok instead of Squanto, they had quite a lot to tell us. After they'd eaten, since it seemed they'd had little food during the trip, they met with the governor and his advisors in Bradford's house. To my relief, this time the children didn't hover outside.

Winslow began. "Soon after we left, we encountered a dozen natives along a well-worn, hard-packed trail—men, women and children returning to their home, Nemasket. They had been gathering lobsters at one end of our harbor. This seems to be a seasonal activity for them. Most interesting, we encountered a series of circular holes in the ground along our way. These holes were well-maintained."

"Are they holes for standing beams?" asked Bradford.

"No," replied Hopkins. "The natives told us they were dug to mark places where something significant had happened to their tribe. In addition to maintaining the holes, it's each Indian's responsibility to inform his or her fellow travelers about what had happened there."

"In this way," Winslow added, "the tribe is taught its history and its connection to their distant past. The importance of these memory holes became even more apparent because we encountered no other natives. The land is empty and desolate, despite the fact thousands of them lived here until just a few years ago. With the sickness taking so many, these holes are slender threads to their past."

"When we reached the Nemasket village, the women fed us," said Hopkins. "A fairly decent meal, if I do say so—corn bread, herring roe and boiled acorns—but we didn't tarry since Squanto said if we pushed on for a few miles, we could reach Pokanoket the next day.

"We slept that night in the open, at a site where some Indians had built a weir to catch fish and were harvesting striped bass. Six of them decided to travel onward with us the next day, wanting to visit relatives in Massasoit's village."

Winslow then took up their story. "We reached Massasoit's village before nightfall —a well-situated, fertile piece of land with two rivers running through it. Massasoit greeted us warmly and invited us to his longhouse, what they call a nush wetu, where we gave him his gifts. He seemed very proud of himself in the red coat, standing tall with the copper chain around his neck."

"We were mightily hungry by then, I tell you," said Hopkins, unconsciously patting his stomach. "We'd had nothing to eat since the day before, but it soon became clear the village had no food. Massasoit and his people had only just returned there, and they don't keep stores of food. They seem to follow the food during the seasons—game and wild fruits and vegetables. Before asking us to sleep with him and his wife on their sleeping platform, Massasoit launched into a very long and tedious speech about each of the villages that paid him tribute, I believe in an effort to impress and convince us he was King James' man. Finally, we lay down for the night with the sachem and his wife, along with fleas and two more of his warriors who decided to join us. Did you know they sing themselves to sleep?"

A deep chuckle went through the room.

"When did you finally eat?" I asked.

"Not until the next afternoon," replied Winslow. "Several other leaders of Wampanoag tribes came to see us, and while they played what looked like games of chance with painted stones and reeds, Massasoit went fishing and brought back two large striped bass. Unfortunately, there were by then nearly forty mouths, so the fish didn't go far. We spent another sleepless night sharing Massasoit's bed and decided to leave the next day."

"Why didn't Squanto return with you?" asked Bradford.

"We decided together he should remain at Pokanoket with our trading goods and travel from village to village to establish trade relations for us," replied Winslow. "Massasoit designated Hobomok to be our new guide. He is a pniese, or, as I understand it, an elite warrior with special abilities and stamina, and he's recognized for his valor. He was with the warriors who accompanied Massasoit on his first visit to our settlement."

Hobomok looked familiar to me, strong and lithe in his appearance. He stayed, living amongst us and giving us assistance and advice in adapting to the challenges of this new land, and he became a greatly trusted friend of Captain Standish.

ᘓ ᘓ

It seemed the Billingtons couldn't exist without causing difficulties for our small settlement. Toward the end of July, their son John, a young man of eighteen years, disappeared. His parents told us they had last seen him in the woods south of our settlement.

Goodwife Billington appeared at my door very early on the third day after he went missing.

"Good morrow, Goodwife, how fare you?"

"Good morrow, Master Allerton. I came to learn if there are plans to find my son."

Elinor Billington had impressed me as a woman of strong opinions and a sharp tongue. She was not uncomely and dressed as neatly as possible at that time, but this morning her hair escaped from her coif in a wild array. All of us wore clothes many times patched and mended—but hers were nearly rags. Knowing our conversation would likely be unpleasant, I didn't welcome her into my house but remained at the door. "Have you spoken with Governor Bradford?"

"He did not ease my mind."

"What did he tell you?"

"That he would send a messenger to Massasoit in a day or two, if John fails to appear."

"Then that is what we will do. Good morrow to you."

She spun on her heel and tromped next door to her house. Seeing her, rather than her husband, at my door didn't surprise me. John Billington showed little concern for his sons, other than what work they could shoulder for him.

When a few more days passed with no news and his mother's increasing agitation, Bradford did indeed send word to Massasoit, asking if he could find the Billington's son. We finally heard the

Nausets held him, the same tribe which had attacked us the previous November and whose graves we had disturbed and corn stores we had stolen. It seemed they wanted revenge. At least the boy was still alive.

Bradford sent ten of us, more than half our grown men, to see if we could rescue him from the Nausets. Squanto, recently returned, went with us as our guide, along with Hobomok. As we sailed to the Nauset's encampment on Cape Cod, we were beset by tremendous thunderstorms that forced us ashore onto some tidal flats. There we spent a foul and wet night in the shallop because we didn't know what might await us onshore. At dawn, we saw several Indians gathering lobsters. Through Squanto and Hobomok, we were introduced to their sachem, who offered to guide us in the shallop to the Nauset village some twenty miles away.

When we finally reached the Nauset settlement, a large number of Indians appeared, and, unlike the apparent emptiness of the land we'd encountered when we first came ashore, there were many natives about. One of the first to speak with Squanto and Hobomok was the one whose corn we'd stolen.

When Squanto related this information to us, I told him, "It's important to make peace with these people if we are to reclaim John Billington. Promise him we'll reimburse him with corn from our harvest."

This seemed to appease him, and we sat in the shallop, arms at the ready, to wait for their sachem, named Aspinet. He finally arrived at sunset that day, with more than a hundred of his warriors. One of them carried John Billington, who looked unharmed and healthy and wore a necklace of shells. Some of us waded to shore, where we had an unexpectedly cordial interaction with Aspinet, more so after we gave him a knife. After some discussion between Aspinet and Squanto, Squanto gave us some disturbing news.

"Narragansetts, their land lies east of your settlement, took Massasoit. Killed several of his men." Squanto's expression hardened.

Edward Winslow immediately saw the consequence to us. "If the Narragansetts have taken Massasoit and killed some of his tribe, then we are at war with them. Our treaty with Massasoit guarantees him our help. What if the Narragansetts decide to attack our settlement? There are so few men there to defend it."

We pulled on our oars mightily to get the shallop on its way and then prayed for a good wind to speed us home. But still it took us three days.

ജ ഇ

The colony's relief at the return of John Billington was short-lived. Bradford called us to his home soon after to give us more serious news. Smoky air from the hearth filled the one room, redolent with the aroma of the meat and porridge provided to him by one of our goodwives. He had been quite ill during the previous months, without a wife to care for him since Mistress Bradford's drowning the previous winter. He looked pale and gaunt as he leaned back in his chair.

"We have good news," he told us. "The Narragansetts only kept Massasoit temporarily, and there'll be no war between them and the Wampanoags. However, I've learned there is a sachem of a minor Wampanoag tribe who is trying to turn some of the other tribes against Massasoit. His name is Corbitant and he's vehemently opposed to our treaty with the Wampanoags. Squanto tells me Corbitant is now in Nemasket, trying to win over those who live there to his side. I've prayed on this but am unsure what to do. Have you any ideas on how to proceed?"

Standish stood up, his normal ruddy color becoming more reddish. "We should uphold our treaty with Massasoit and immediately march as many men as we can spare to Nemasket to confront him. I'm certain he'll back down in the face of our armor and muskets."

"But what if he has an overwhelming number with him? What if the Nemasket turn against us as well?" asked John Alden, a man of great practicality.

Bradford's longish face drooped. "I'm unwilling to put our few men at risk, given this possibility."

"Why don't we sent Squanto and Hobomok to discover what Corbitant is doing?" asked Stephen Hopkins.

A murmur of assent arose from our small group, and Bradford agreed to this suggestion.

The next day, I worked in the fields with Bartholomew. Little Mary trailed along with us, since Remember tended our garden and prepared our midday meal under the direction of the women. I paused for a moment from weeding and stood straight up, to release my back from the bending and to admire the field. Just then I saw Hobomok run past the field toward the village. Suspecting some urgency, I ran after him, children on my heels. More followed us to where he stood, covered with sweat, bent over and gasping.

"What's wrong?" I asked. 'What's happened?"

Governor Bradford was one of the last to arrive, wheezing and short of breath from his recent illness.

Hobomok panted out between breaths, "Squanto, possible he dead…Corbitant warrior held a knife to his chest. Corbitant blames Squanto for treaty…he say if Squanto gone, you lose your voice."

"This cannot be tolerated if our treaty with Massasoit is to hold," said Bradford. "Corbitant must suffer the fate of a traitor, as is our custom. Captain Standish, you will take ten men, capture this man and cut off his head. Bring it back to our settlement for display."

His order startled me, but this was the English way of dealing with traitors. Since Hobomok and Standish had become good friends, bonding as warriors, they soon developed a plan to capture Corbitant.

I found myself marching with them in the rain the next day to a location some distance from Nemasket, where I and other men waited until it grew dark, becoming soaked and chilled. With a quiet hand signal, Hobomok led us into the village and to Corbitant's long house, larger than any of the Indian dwellings I'd previously seen. I imagined a good number of people slept inside, including women and children. Standish placed us in positions around this dwelling, with orders to shoot anyone trying to escape. Not being a military man, I had deep qualms at the thought of shooting anyone. Indeed, I'd never even shot at a person before.

Standish then burst into the longhouse, shouting Corbitant's name loudly. The alarm thus sounded, the people within tried to escape by pushing through the mats that made the walls or by rushing around Standish, who stood stooped in the doorway. Total chaos followed in the darkness, the only light coming from dying campfires. I maintained my position but was unwilling to fire my musket, although some around me fired their guns in nervousness. Women and children screamed in fear, and I could see the natives running here and there as shadows against the campfires, adding to the noise and confusion.

Hobomok helped to restore order by pulling himself through the smoke hole at the top of the long house and calling out to the villagers. Morning revealed that Corbitant had fled with his men, but Squanto was still alive. Although we failed to capture Corbitant, our attack proved useful, since it sent a strong message to him and any allied with him: if anyone should try to overthrow Massasoit, we would have our revenge.

Our attack had left two Indians wounded—a man and a woman. Along with Squanto, we brought them back to our settlement, where our physick, Samuel Fuller, tended to them. They left for Nemasket some days later, when they were healed.

Because of our show of force, sachems of various tribes sent gifts to our governor. On September 13, nine sachems, including Corbitant himself, came to our settlement to sign a treaty to signify their loyalty to King James. Naturally my children couldn't keep to their chores with so large a group of Indians in our midst, all of them having painted their faces in wild colors and wearing little but skins. Even the women came out of our houses to watch the event.

At least for the time being, this treaty assured us of peaceful relations with the natives who lived around us. Only the Massachusetts tribe, which lived to the north and which had threatened the Wampanoag confederacy in the past, didn't take part. At Squanto's urging, Bradford's advisors, including myself, decided to pay them a visit.

Chapter 11

A Good Harvest and More Separatists Arrive

Isaac Allerton, Plymouth Colony, Fall 1621

We sailed north in the shallop in hopes of making a treaty with the Massachusetts tribe, ultimately entering an island-filled bay where they were known to live. We marveled at our surroundings, the immensity of the bay producing expressions of awe. I couldn't help but think we should have settled here, an idea discussed by some of the others over the next few hours. Here was a harbor deep enough to accommodate the draft of any ship, with moorings possible close to the shore. Had we but travelled a little further north in our explorations, we would have found it.

"Do you think we should relocate here?" asked Edward Winslow.

My heart sank at the thought of moving to a different site and beginning again.

"I'm content with our present home," Standish replied. "We've already suffered much to find and make a home in what is a protectable site, and moreover, this time of year isn't good for such a move."

John Alden broke the silence that followed, pointing as we approached what appeared to be the confluence of several rivers.

"Over there…there's high ground where the rivers meet. We could live there, and it's easily defensible."

Winslow took the middle ground in the discussion. "We should describe this place to our governor and ask him what he thinks when we return."

Squanto directed us to a place where we could beach the shallop on the south side of the bay. After wading ashore in our armor, hot and heavy in the sun, we followed him to meet the northernmost sachem who recognized Massasoit as his leader. Following a back and forth conversation between Squanto and this sachem, we learned the leader of the Massachusetts tribe had been killed during a recent incursion of Micmacs from the north. The sachem agreed to guide us to the widow of this leader, a woman called Squa Sachem, who wielded considerable power and with whom we could perhaps make a treaty. On the following day we sailed to the north side of one of the rivers entering the bay, where we were led to the grave of the former sachem of the Massachusetts people—an elaborate affair within a dwelling and protected by a palisade.

We were disappointed when Squa Sachem couldn't be found, but we met some women of the tribe, who fed us boiled cod. When their menfolk were persuaded to appear, one agreed to give us the animal pelts they had accumulated, for which we traded. The warriors trembled and shook throughout the transaction. I wondered if they had heard of our attack on Corbitant's village and were afraid of us, since they'd been greatly reduced in numbers by the same sickness that had decimated the Wampanoags. The women gave us the skins off their backs, leaving them naked but for the leafy branches of trees they tied around themselves.

In this strange way did we establish relations with the Massachusetts people.

Our governor didn't look favorably on the idea of moving to that region, having no plans at the time for a much larger settlement. He was content to remain in our snug village by the brook, and in the end, so were we.

ꕤ ꕤ

By late September, we had harvested our crops of corn, squash, beans, barley and peas, and we rejoiced in having enough to last over the coming winter. Bartholomew came running into our home one day, shouting, "Come see the harbor! There are thousands of fowl there!" While some of us worked on catching a supply of cod, bass and other fish—the appropriately sized hooks now having been made—others took their muskets and returned with ducks, turkey and geese. Our governor sent four men hunting for deer and other game, resulting in a true abundance of meat to smoke and dry and adding to what we already had for our tables.

In celebration of the harvest and of our good fortune by the grace of God, we entertained and feasted with our Indian friends for three days in early October. Massasoit came to our settlement with ninety of his men, some of whom went out to hunt and brought back five additional deer. There was much eating, drinking and playing of games, but we also devoted time on our knees in thanks to God.

Such seats and tables as we had were brought out into the sunshine, but many of us, including most of the natives, squatted or sat on the ground or on tree stumps, clustered around outdoor fires. There the venison and fowl were cooked on wooden spits and served with onions and nuts. We had a dwindling supply of some spices—salt, cinnamon, ginger, pepper, and nutmeg—but we added them to our food to mark the celebration. The women created salads of greens found growing wild and many pottages. These simmering stews, filled with different meats and vegetables, filled the air in our village with enticing aromas. The goodwives also boiled some of our corn and pounded it into a mush, then sweetened it with wild fruit they had gathered. The Wampanoags made something they called nasaump, made from dried corn, berries and nuts boiled in water over a fire to a thickness like porridge. Both the Indian children and our own loved the corn mush and the nasaump.

After the previous winter and the backbreaking labor of the spring and summer, it felt like heaven to have full stomachs and days of little to do in the fields. John Alden and I sat outside our house on stools he had crafted, relaxing in the sun and feeling confident that our stores of food would sustain us through the hard winter months.

The children were free to roam or to play games of their own. Suddenly, some of the children thundered by, playing lummelen. It seemed Bartholomew had been chosen to capture as many children as he could. Most of the girls didn't join in, since it was inappropriate for them to do so, but Resolved White, Samuel Fuller, Giles Hopkins and Joseph Mullins ran away from my son, whooping and hollering. As usual, little Mary tagged after them, calling for them to wait for her. She was impossible to restrain.

Earlier I had seen Love and Wrestling Brewster teaching some of the Wampanoag youth how to play noughts and crosses, using a stick in the dirt to make the board. In the field, a target had been erected of logs, and the Indian boys were having shooting contests with bows and arrows made of reeds. They had been instructing some of our boys in the art of bow and arrow hunting, when they were not having running races. The happy voices of the children at play was a near forgotten pleasure, after all that we had endured.

I breathed a sigh of contentment. As we looked up and down First Street, as it had come to be named, people were everywhere, Separatists and Indians, enjoying the warm sunshine and bright skies. "We are indeed blessed," I said in a lazy tone.

"I haven't eaten so well in many days," replied Alden, "although our diet did improve this past summer. I'm surprised the children—in fact everyone—are in such good health, considering we've only water to drink. I'd always thought water most unhealthy."

"I think the reason is that the water here is pure and clean. I hope we'll get a supply of hops if another ship arrives, so we can make beer again. I have such a mind for it that I'm going to try to brew some using corn."

"I have never seen such colors in the trees as we have here," my friend said, looking at the forest surrounding us.

Indeed, the muted fall tones of England were translated into bright yellows, oranges and reds in this new world, wrapping the land in a bold quilt. "Our new land is indeed remarkable," I replied. "But these colors are a warning of harsh weather to come, a season we know well. We'll need to hunt and fish as often as we can before the first snows. There's time now that the harvest is in."

"And we need to fell more trees for wood." Alden gave a small groan at the thought of the endless chopping.

"I'm grateful to the goodwives for teaching Remember how to preserve our meat and fish. I only hope she'll soon be as skilled as her mother in cooking."

Alden smiled. "We've had some interesting meals in past months."

I smiled too, thinking of what Remember put on the table. "Mayhap you won't have to suffer those meals much longer."

He blushed. We both knew he had more than a passing acquaintance with Mistress Mullins.

We both sat quietly for a few minutes, during which I reflected on all that had happened to us over the past seasons. Finally I said, "I do think in many ways we've become like our Indian neighbors."

"How so?"

"Have you noticed that like us, they share their food? The sachems support widows and they care for their sick and elderly as a community. While we do fence our yards for growing vegetables, we hunt and fish together and share in the corn and other crops we've grown."

"I agree. Our life here is so much different than in England. There each fended for his own."

That night, as he had on every night of our celebration, Elder Brewster offered up our thanksgiving in a lengthy sermon and prayers. We did indeed have much to be thankful for.

ꕥ ꕥ

In early November, our governor received a message from the Nausets that a ship had made landfall in Cape Cod bay. When the ship didn't appear in our harbor for more than a week, I gathered with Bradford, Winslow, Brewster, Standish and a few others to discuss what might have happened to it.

"It's too early for a supply ship from England," said Bradford. "Do you think it's a French expeditionary vessel?"

"If so, we must make sure there's a lookout on the top of our hill ready to signal us if it enters the harbor," replied Standish. "We are a rival settlement to those in Canada, and I doubt the French would come here to trade."

We all knew of the established French settlements of Port Royal and Quebec City in the eastern reaches of Canada, and the English and French had been at war with each other for centuries. If the French sought to claim the land in this region for themselves, with our own hold here still tenuous, a French attack was a possibility.

"Then we must prepare for the worst," Bradford said. "Captain Standish, ensure the readiness of your men. They must be able to repel an attack, if it should come. The rest of you, tell the women and children they are to go to the common house if they hear the drum."

"We should also include any of the boys who can handle a musket," added Winslow.

We worked in a heightened sense of anxiety every day until the end of the month, when our lookout finally sighted a sail heading for our harbor. Many of us were out in the countryside, fishing, hunting, or gathering nuts and other food, when we heard the horn calling us back to our settlement. Voices rang out as we came from all directions, bringing our guns, pikes and halberds, to assemble into a fighting contingent under the direction of Captain Standish. The women and children were already gathered at the common house by the time we proceeded to the harbor.

"It's English," shouted Wrestling Brewster when the ship had come within good sight. "It's English!" More huzzahs arose when we discovered it was the small ship *Fortune* with thirty-five settlers on board, some Separatists and some Adventurers. As the passengers came ashore, there were warm welcomes, hugs and shakings of hands as we recognized familiar faces, such as the eldest Brewster son, Jonathan, and the brother of our newly remarried Edward Winslow.

Chief amongst our new arrivals was Robert Cushman, who came with his fourteen-year-old son, Thomas. He had been a wool comber when we were in Leiden and had known losses like ours—his wife and two of his children had died before we left Holland for England. Cushman and John Carver had been the ones to secure the patent from the group of Merchant Adventurers and the financing for the establishment of our colony.

Our governor now faced the problem of dividing thirty-five new settlers amongst our various homes. As a result of his decision, our little house became, if only temporarily, even more crowded. Most of the new arrivals were young men in good health, who would help us greatly in farming and building, but, as we soon discovered, they brought with them no supplies.

Bradford assigned to our home William Hilton, a married man who came singly on the *Fortune*, along with the unmarried Thomas Prence. Prence told us that he was an armiger, entitled to bear arms by right of birth, and he felt he could work with Captain Standish. Both men would be busy building a home for Hilton's family that winter, along with learning about our way of life. Nevertheless, I worried what effect their presence would have on my children, especially little Mary. I knew Remember would be most unhappy at having to tend to the needs of two more men.

That evening, our governing group crowded into Bradford's home, and we were formally introduced to Robert Cushman, who, together with his son, now housed with our governor. Bradfords' dour look conveyed his unhappiness with the new arrivals. "We have found not so much as a biscuit-cake or any other food, nor any bedding, pots or pans on the *Fortune* to sustain these people, and, indeed, they have hardly any clothes for the coming winter. Since we now must house, feed and clothe our new arrivals, I am sorry to say we may once again face privation."

Winslow added, "We also have to consider that while many of the men are married, only one woman came on the ship. This will only increase the burden on our goodwives, who already struggle to support us."

"I, for one, see one good grace with the arrival of the *Fortune*." Captain Standish gave us a rare smile. "I'm pleased to have more strong men to join our militia, although I doubt many have any experience with arms."

Bradford then reminded us of his plan for housing the arrivals. "I have assigned some of them to our common house. I trust the rest have been fairly divided amongst our families. In advance of the bad weather soon upon us, we must put them to work on building more houses and teaching those unskilled how to hunt. Who will offer to oversee them and help with the building?"

Once that was decided, Bradford said, "Master Cushman has brought news from Thomas Weston, and I'll let him convey that." He sat down wearily, a look of anger clouding his face, and Robert Cushman stood to address us.

Cushman had fallen out with both John Carver and Bradford before the *Mayflower* and the *Speedwell* had set sail from England. Although not privy to all the details, I knew both men felt Cushman had too readily accepted harsh terms from the Merchant Adventurers, mainly one named Thomas Weston, in order to gain the money we needed for supplies. The contract stated we would work seven days a week for the investors and shareholders in the company and that our houses, land and goods would be treated as company assets and divided at the end of seven years.

Clearly this would not be workable, and although we'd rejected these stipulations at the time we sailed from England, Cushman had agreed to Weston's demands anyway. He'd been aboard the *Speedwell*, and when she returned to England for the second time, he'd decided to remain behind. Now he had arrived to take stock of our colony and report back to Weston.

Cushman was not a tall man, but his stern visage and piercing brown eyes captured our attention. "As you know, I've had many interactions, not all of them cordial, with the Company of Adventurers, specifically one Thomas Weston. What I have brought you is a new patent, specifically for this colony, in the name of John Pierce of London, who is one of the merchants supporting this endeavor. Thus, the legality of having settled in this place, instead of Virginia, is established. My duty now is to convince you to accept the terms of the contract imposed by Weston and the other London investors."

"Are these the same terms we rejected before we left England?" asked Edward Winslow, his round, kindly face now mirroring the sternness of Cushman's.

"Yes, they are. But I'm sure after a year's work to establish this settlement, you can understand why supplies must keep coming from England and therefore you must agree to the terms. There is more—I have a letter from Thomas Weston, addressed to Governor Carver. Your current governor," and here he tilted his head in Bradford's direction, "felt you should know its contents. I'll not read it to you, but instead present Weston's opinions in my own words, to abate the anger this letter will undoubtedly cause."

Silence filled the room. We could only imagine what Weston had written, and it proved worse than we'd anticipated.

"Weston feels that your weakness is the reason the *Mayflower* returned to England empty

of goods, a weakness in your judgement rather than of your hands. He believes you wasted time in discourse and argument."

At that, voices rose in reply. "How dare he?"

"Bring him here to live as we do!"

"Make him hunt and fish for food and work in the fields in the hot sun."

"His demands caused the death of our good Governor Carver!"

"He is eager to reap quick profits from us!"

Containing his emotions, Cushman stood unwavering while he waited for our company to calm.

At that point, Bradford said to him, "The loss of John Carver, and so many others of us, cannot be valued at any price. You need to make him see this."

Cushman cleared his throat, then said, "I truly believe Weston is one of the few men who will stay the course with us. Despite his harsh words, I beg you to sign this agreement. I'll do my best when I return to London to make the investors see the error of this contract."

Several minutes of general muttering followed his statement, but, in the end, we looked to William Bradford for his decision. When he nodded, we all signed. We had now agreed to the original conditions put forth by the London merchants, knowing full well these terms could not and would not be met. *How do we improve our families' lots if we work only for the merchants? And we'll have to give our homes to them for their profit. Then we are no more than slaves!* The signing of this agreement was a farce.

Toward the end of the meeting, Edward Winslow told us he and Bradford planned to send a lengthy letter on the *Fortune* when it left to return to England, addressed to George Mount, an old and loving friend. There followed a discussion of what might be included in that letter. We decided to tell him about our presently good relations with the Indians, the weather, the abundance of game, fish, fowl and wild fruit. To that we added a list of those things direly needed: cows, pigs and sheep, paper and linseed oil for windows, candles, soap, clothes and bedding. Thus our meeting ended on a more productive note.

ꙮ ꙮ

The *Fortune* departed less than two weeks after she had arrived, but with a hold full of beaver skins, sassafras, and split oak clapboards for barrel staves, which we had amassed over the previous months—a valuable cargo we hoped would appease the Merchant Adventurers.

Robert Cushman returned to England on the *Fortune.* He left his son Thomas in the care of Governor Bradford, with the intent to rejoin us the following year. Our missive to George Mount went with Master Cushman, along with other letters to kin and members of our congregation who were still in England or Holland.

Over the next year, we saw the wisdom of the governor's plan to employ our new arrivals in the growth of our settlement to twenty houses, stretching up on either side of First Street and onto Fort Hill and in either direction along the path of the future highway that would bisect the village.

Mary Allerton, Plymouth Colony, late fall, 1621

My poppet! I remember the day I lost my poppet, Charity. She had given me comfort during our voyage, because other than the constant reminders to be respectful, behave, sit still, not speak out of turn and do chores willingly, no one paid much attention to me or even played with me. Charity was my sole and constant companion. I talked to her every day and took her with me everywhere. She became bedraggled, stained, and ripped, hardly looking like her original self, but she comforted me at night and I couldn't be without her.

Mary's Poppet, Charity

One evening, as I helped Remember prepare the evening meal by adding wood to the fire, I suddenly realized Charity wasn't there. I dropped the kindling and ran towards the door, but my father blocked the way.

"Where are you going, Mary? It's time for our meal and evening prayers. You may not go out now—it's getting dark." He kindly but forcefully moved me back to the hearth.

I looked up at him, tears welling. "But Father, my poppet is gone. I must find her. I need her."

"Don't be silly, daughter. You're too old for a doll. You can look for her in the morning."

"Look at Mary," Remember said, "crying over an old, dirty rag. Put that kindling on the fire and stir the pottage or you won't eat tonight."

I looked at Father, who frowned at her words. "Remember, don't be cruel to your younger sister. And Mary, you must listen to her."

When the older people were seated at the table and I stood with my brother and sister at our places, Father began what turned into a long and hearty prayer about love for family, understanding, and forgiveness. Remember's cheeks flamed, but my mind raced frantically, trying to recall where I might have left Charity.

That night, I tossed and turned, unable to get to sleep without the comfort of my cloth companion. Remember, sleeping beside me, grumbled for me to lie still. Finally, when everyone was asleep, based on the snoring, I tiptoed to the door in my bare feet, unlatched it and went out—making sure to close the latch with as little sound as possible. In the darkness, only the glow of the banked hearths through the windows of nearby houses lit my way, as I ran here and there, retracing my steps of the day, hoping to trip over what I had lost. In the bitter cold of the night I could see the white tendrils of my breath against the dim light. Without shoes, my feet felt like blocks of ice and I shivered without a cloak.

Suddenly a hand clamped on my shoulder. *Oh no! The men on guard have seen me!* I spun around and opened my mouth to scream, but no sound came out.

"Mary, what are you doing out here with no cloak and no shoes? What possesses you, child?"

It was John Alden. "I saw you creep out. Your father will not spare the rod if you don't return to bed."

"It's my poppet. I cannot find her," I sobbed.

"Hush, child." He stopped and picked me up, wrapping me in his cloak. "I know she means a great deal to you, but she cannot be found in the dark. Will you go back to bed, if I promise to look with you first thing in the morning?'

I gulped back my tears. "Yes, and thank you, Master Alden."

We both managed to return to the house and bed without disturbing anyone, although I swore I saw my father's eyes gleaming in the low light of the coals on the hearth. Remember grumbled that I made her cold as I slipped beneath my blanket and skins. I slept as soon as my eyes closed, overwhelmed by exhaustion and worry.

I awoke to sound of water being poured from the bucket into our iron kettle and the lick of flames as the fire built up. I rolled over to get off my mattress, and there was my poppet, lying beside me. *But how?*

When I had gotten up and rolled my mattress, I saw Master Alden sitting at the table along with my father, eating corn bread. Instead of the scolding or, worse, the beating I expected for being so late arising, Master Alden gave me a wink. My father gave me a small smile and said only, "Go help your sister, Mary."

But I still had no friends, and Charity would remain my companion for a long time to come.

Chapter 12

A Year of Discontent and Challenges

Isaac Allerton, Plymouth Colony, 1621-1622

With November came threats from the Narragansetts, with whom William Bradford believed we were on good terms. A messenger from their sachem, Canonicus, arrived, bearing a bundle of arrows wrapped in the skin of a rattlesnake. It was intended for Squanto, but Squanto was away from the colony. When he returned, Squanto met with Bradford and his advisors to explain this odd gift.

"Not a threat. Only a challenge to me," he told us.

"Then I'll answer it in your stead," replied Bradford. With that, he removed the arrows and poured gunpowder and musket balls into the snakeskin. "Take this back to Canonicus."

Although Squanto insisted this gift didn't constitute a true threat, many of us were troubled, Captain Standish foremost. "I have often said that we're wide open to attack. Look at you—hardly a man amongst you can manage your muskets. I could track and kill a rabbit in the time you take to reload." As he said this, he drew himself as tall as he might for his short stature, trying to look intimidating.

"But what of our cannons on the platform?" I asked.

"Hmmph. Do you think you could repel many Indians at night with those? In the dark?"

He humbled me with his common sense.

"I think now is the time to build a palisade around our town," he said.

We had long discussed the idea of enclosing our settlement, but other more pressing needs had pushed it aside. Now, in the face of this perceived threat, Bradford said, "I agree. But this will take a mighty effort from everyone. I anticipate it will consume much of our time, and all of us, without exception, need to share in its construction."

After some consideration, we together decided to build an eight-foot high wall, enclosing the gun platform and all the houses lining First Street and its crossing. It would be more than half a mile in length and would require the felling of hundreds of trees, to be chopped or sawn square and then set tightly side by side into the ground.

As the plan for the palisade developed, Standish added more details. "We'll also need at least two flankers, to allow people to enter and leave."

Despite my reluctance to again show my ignorance of military matters, I asked, "What's a flanker?"

Standish glared at me, shaking his head in disgust. "It's a projection from a fortification which can enclose a gate. It can also serve as a shooting platform."

With the plan for the palisade complete, our work began and proceeded more quickly than anticipated because of the contributions of the newly arrived men. But building our palisade cost us dearly in hunger and exhaustion—we were working on half rations to accommodate our increased population and the men with big appetites. I was deeply affected by seeing my children go hungry again, and Bartholomew, John and I fished and hunted whenever possible to feed us all.

ꝏ ꝏ

Tensions between Separatists and newcomers grew as winter arrived with snow and bitterly cold winds. Our sense of community, already strained by the sharing of our limited food supplies, was further stressed by the crowding of our houses with people not of our faith. My house alone now sheltered four adults, all male, with my three children. Luckily, Master Alden had helped me build a sleeping loft, where the children could be separated from the adults. At night the men slept side by side on the floor, rolled in whatever bedding they had and filling our one room with their snores.

At our table one evening, we shared a meager common meal of smoked fish, bread made from corn, and a pottage of the vegetables we had stored. The room was cold and dim, lit with only oiled paper candles, and my two daughters, after placing the food in a trencher on the table for me to apportion, stood to eat. Mary spoke out of turn. "This is like living on the *Mayflower*, Father. We were always hungry then, too. So many people in a small, dark place. Will we get sick again?"

"Silence, daughter! It is not your place to speak at meals. Expect punishment tonight for your disrespect."

Mary knew this meant a thrashing and she said no more, but Master Pence, who had paused after spearing a piece of smoked fish on his knife, said, "It's not my place to comment on the behavior of your children, Master Allerton, but I can see your daughter only speaks from her hunger. I understand the children suffered greatly during their time on the *Mayflower* and what she said is only what many of us think. I pray you don't punish her, but reassure her that our lives here will improve." Turning to Mary, he said, "They will, child. Be of good faith."

In this way, a man without children taught me to calm and reassure my own, and although his comments pricked, they also humbled me, and I prayed that night for better understanding.

ꟷ ꟷ

In coming to the New World, we sought to live a pious life according to the principles laid down in our Bible, but the newly arrived men challenged this every day with their unwillingness to work and complaints about the lack of food and crowded living conditions. Things came to a head when many of them expressed a desire to celebrate Christmas, which we did not, resulting in several heated discussions with our governor. In the end, Bradford decided they would not have to work on Christmas Day, in order to ease the tensions.

This turned out to be a bad decision because the newcomers took advantage of Bradford's fair and good nature. On December 25th, when some of us returned from working on our palisade and others from hunting or fishing, we found our two streets filled with revelers playing a game called stool ball, which uses a ball and paddles. I had seen this only once, when I was very young. One man would throw a ball at a tall square piece of wood or a stool, while a member of the opposing team would attempt to protect the stool by hitting the ball with a wooden bat. In this case, the men had erected two posts, and the batter ran between the posts when he hit the ball. The shouts of encouragement and derision from the two teams created a great disturbance. The children, of course, were mesmerized, and our few women were calling to them in harsh voices to stay away and tend to their chores.

Our group stopped at the edge of the street and just stared, until feeling our distaste, the men paused in their game.

"What are you doing?" said Bradford loudly, so all could hear. "When I gave you permission to celebrate Christmas, I expected you to spend the day in quiet prayer and convocation, not boisterous revelry. Captain Standish, please collect the pieces of this game. This must cease immediately!"

As Standish carried out his orders, we could hear loud grumbling from the players. They retreated with sullen and grim faces, casting challenging looks at our governor, but we couldn't tolerate this activity in our midst. Everyone who lived here had to abide by the governing rules of our colony, and these men had taken advantage of Bradford's forbearance.

As they left the area, Bradford announced to everyone, "It's illegal here in our settlement to follow the customs of the Church of England and celebrate its holidays!"

ജ ഇ

While we were building our palisade, Standish drilled us mercilessly in the use of arms and the firing of our cannon, as well as military maneuvers, and this caused more grumbling amongst the newcomers. He assigned groups of men to duties such as standing guard, handling any fires that might break out, either by accident or caused by Indians, and he made contingency plans for when he might be absent.

When we finished the entire palisade by March, we felt a sense of safety in that we now had a defined, stable and permanent settlement. Furthermore, our governor's wisdom in returning the snakeskin from Canonicus filled with shot and gun powder had become evident. Word came that when Canonicus received the snakeskin and saw its contents, he expressed great fear at our intentions. Thereafter, Bradford's gift passed from sachem to sachem within the Narragansett tribe, as if it were poisonous.

ജ ഇ

By early spring, our food supplies became so limited that the governor's council decided to send some of us north by boat to the Massachusetts tribal area, seeking to trade for corn. Ever mindful of our duty to the Merchant Adventurers, we hoped to purchase furs as well.

Before we could set sail, there came troubling news. Hobomok, on whom we had come to rely and who had been living with us during the winter, had just met with Standish and Bradford, after which Bradford called in his closest advisors.

With Hobomok standing by his side, Bradford told us, "It seems our presence has created some unbalance between our native neighbors. Hobomok has brought word that the Massachusetts, together with some Narragansetts, plan to attack our trading party. They plan to kill Captain Standish during the fight, so they can then attack our settlement without its military leader."

"Then we shouldn't go," Edward Winslow replied.

"But we cannot confine ourselves within our palisade. We need food, and we must trade for goods to return on the next ship that comes here from England," Bradford replied. "And there is even more unsettling news. Hobomok tells me that Squanto involved himself in this plot during those times he was away from here."

That revelation struck a profound blow based on the looks of surprise and then frowns of anger on everyone's faces. Squanto had long been our friend, and we trusted him with our lives. We couldn't imagine this treachery. Bradford motioned Hobomok to leave us, wishing a private conversation.

"I don't know if this is true," he told us. "It's hard to imagine. Perhaps there is some rivalry between Squanto and Hobomok. Do any of you have thoughts on what we should do?"

Elder Brewster stepped forward. "Although this troubles our hearts, we must believe God will protect us, especially after all we have endured. We must be steadfast and resolute, as we have been in the past."

Standish replied with his customary bravado, "I agree. I don't fear this journey. Hobomok and I have developed strong ties, and I trust and support him."

"While I myself have had a long and productive relationship with Squanto," said Bradford. "So perhaps we can use our relationships to balance one against the other. What say you? Should we proceed with the plan to sail north to find food?"

With a chorus of "Ayes," we together decided that both Hobomok and Squanto would accompany Standish and the ten other men selected for the party. Edward Winslow would go in the hopes he might be a mitigating influence in any confrontation.

On the day of the departure in the shallop, myself amongst the travelers, we set out with a light following wind and fair weather. As we reached the point of land called the Gurnet, which marked the northern end of our bay, the wind died and we prepared to row. Just then, we heard cannon fire. Fearing an attack on the colony, we came about and rowed back in a great hurry, fueled by fear.

Bradford met us on the beach. With him was a member of Squanto's family, who had arrived after we had left and who claimed he'd been beaten and chased from Nemasket. According to him, some Narragansetts had joined with Pokonokets, one of Massasoit's Wampanoag tribes, to make an assault on our settlement.

Bradford took his group of advisors aside, ignoring Hobomok. "The arrival of this man after you left, Captain Standish, seems suspicious. Without you here to organize a defense, we would be in a poor position. What think you?"

Standish stood, hands clasped behind his back, frowning. "I cannot see why Massasoit would want to attack us. Are we not in good accord with him? Have we not been willing to defend him and his people? I suspect something strange is behind this."

Hobomok rejoined us at that point, anger suffusing his face. Pointing at the Indian who had supposedly come from Nemasket, he said, "Lies. This man tell lies. I am Wampanoag warrior. Massasoit would tell me about any attack." He spat on the ground. "Squanto behind this. He makes trouble. Send my wife to Pokanokets. She will find truth."

Upon her return, we met with our governor and learned that as Hobomok had predicted, the Pokanokets were peaceful. No

Narragansett attack occurred, and Massasoit was infuriated, believing Squanto had planned to turn us against him. "We have received reassurance from Massasoit that his promise to us remains," Bradford told us. "He will warn us of any threats and come to our assistance, if need be. It seems we have become pawns in a battle between Squanto and Massasoit for leadership of the Wampanoags."

Some weeks later, we learned that Squanto, in his travels during the winter, had been telling various native villages we had the plague and planned to release it on them. If they paid Squanto tribute, he would prevent that from happening. Bradford told us if Squanto had managed to bring a significant number to his side with this lie, he would try to take Massasoit's place as the preeminent sachem in the area. Most of us now viewed Squanto as supremely deceitful, although Edward Winslow insisted Squanto only wanted to revive the fortunes of his family, which had been wiped out by disease, and to reestablish his family's honor.

Through it all, Bradford remained loyal to Squanto, insisting that his position as interpreter was vital to the survival of our settlement. Massasoit felt this traitor deserved death. While his murderous rage eventually abated, many of us didn't regard Squanto with the same respect ever again. I myself felt torn. Squanto had been a good friend to my children, teaching Bartholomew how to hunt and catch eels and making a corn husk poppet for Mary. I couldn't understand how such a kind person could plot against us.

Our planting that spring had gone poorly, due to the multiple distractions with our relationships with the natives. When we finally sailed north in search of corn, we were unable to obtain any from the Massachusetts, who regarded our request with humor. In addition, Thomas Weston had in May sent three ships to Plymouth—the *Sparrow*, the *Charity*, the *Swan*—carrying a total of sixty-seven more men, whom we were now obliged to support. Our anger at Weston's latest affront didn't lessen in subsequent months. Although Weston intended for them to create a settlement to the north, and we had to house and feed them until the site for their settlement could be determined.

Despite the warmer spring weather, we were starving. We had proved to be but poor fishermen, despite the plenitude of fish in our waters, and we spent much time hunting for shellfish. Worst of all, Weston's men took our immature cornstalks for food, ruining our crop.

A letter from Robert Cushman sent our spirits even lower. The *Fortune*, with its cargo for the London merchants, had been captured by the French and had returned to England with an empty hold. He also wrote something Elder Brewster emphasized in his sermon on Sunday. "I pray you not to be discouraged, but live through these difficulties cheerfully and with courage until your days improve." While meant with all good will, his admonition was a bitter drink to swallow.

At one of our now regular meetings, Bradford, with Stephen Hopkins serving as his aide and secretary, had some hopeful news. "We have received a communication from the north that the cod fishing season is active, with hundreds of vessels from England and elsewhere catching fish to bring back to London. One of Weston's ships is among them. I propose we send Master Winslow north in the shallop to secure us some fish."

There were no objections to that plan, but the next news was a blow to our sense of security. "This same ship's master also informed me of a massacre at Jamestown. Indians attacked thirty towns along the James River, burning homes and killing livestock. Over three hundred souls were lost."

It was if all the air had left the small room in which we gathered. *A massacre!*

"Our heretofore good relations with our Indian neighbors have been sorely tested by Squanto's deviousness," said Bradford. "I confess my own reluctance refused to allow Massasoit to take Squanto's life in retribution. With this news from Virginia, there is real urgency to increase measures of protection in case of an attack from the combined forces of the Narragansetts and the Massachusetts. I'm grateful Captain Standish convinced us of our need for the fort."

ꕥ ꕥ

In the early summer of 1622, Captain Standish had strongly inveighed to our governor and his advisors to build a fort on the hill where our cannon stood, a secure place where our community might gather if attacked. Given our uncertain situation with our neighbors, Bradford had agreed, saying, "I believe we will need the work of all the men to accomplish this, if what remains of our poor crop is to be harvested."

"How can we persuade the new men to help us?" Master Winslow had then asked. "We certainly cannot offer them more food."

"Perhaps the fear of an Indian attack could motivate them?" Standish's face took on such a fierce look, I believed he could frighten them on the spot.

"Given the undetermined nature of these attacks, our lack of food, and the time this building is going to take, you must be very persuasive," Bradford had replied.

And so Standish proved to be. In a short time, the hard labor of more men built the fort at the top of Fort Hill, as it came to be called. Made with good timber, it stood two stories tall, with a flat roof and battlements, on which we mounted our ordinance. Some of our cannons were fixed on their mounts, while others, lighter and moveable, could be sighted in any direction through various gun ports. Standish had once again made a wise suggestion, since the fort also served for many years as our meeting house for larger discussions, as well as Sunday services.

Fort on Burial Hill

After the completion of the fort, Winslow said to me, "I'm amazed at how men can be made to reason when it comes to their own safety."

ꟾ ꟾ

Until they left at the end of July, the tensions between us and these Strangers, as we called them, emerged daily in ugly confrontations and arguments. We also had to keep close watch on the women, girls and children. Weston had written these men were 'lusty,' to confirm to us they were strong and vigorous, but he had no knowledge of their personal backgrounds or temperaments. Thus we felt it better not to trust them.

I had returned from the fields for our mid-day meal one day in the summer and found one of our guests standing at the hearth, close to my daughter Remember, speaking to her in a low voice. She turned away to ignore him, but he grabbed her arm to turn her back. Mary watched wide-eyed from where she sat at the table.

"What do you do, sir, with my daughter?" I asked.

He turned, startled, and stammered, "I did but ask her when we should eat."

"That isn't what I observed. You laid a hand on her, and for that I'll report you to our governor. Leave this house and find accommodations elsewhere."

The man left, after angrily grabbing up his poor possessions.

"What did he say to you, daughter?"

Remember reddened from her neck to her forehead and shook her head, unwilling to answer.

"Did you encourage him in this?"

"No, Father."

Mary spoke up. "He has often been around my sister when you aren't here, Father. He talked to her in a strange voice. She tried to walk away but he wouldn't leave her be. Remember is afraid of him but was more afraid to tell you."

"Why, daughter?"

"Because you might not find me blameless," replied Remember.

Thereafter, I made sure a goodwife was present with Remember whenever I or Master Prence were absent from our home and when these newly arrived men were not in the fields or otherwise engaged. Governor Bradford sent the offender to live in a common house with a stern warning that he would be expelled from the colony if his actions continued.

When they learned of this, our goodwives allotted the man less food and would not mend or wash his clothes.

Tensions eased when Weston's men left for the site of their new settlement at the place named Wessagusset. Everyone in the village felt relief when they were gone.

ꟃ ꟃ

John Alden, who had lived with us for more than a year, had now married and lived with his wife Priscilla some doors way. Some evenings, Alden came to discuss the business of the colony. We would sit by the hearth, the children asleep in the loft above, the only light and warmth that from the fire.

"What do you think of this new colony at Wessagusset?" I asked.

"I think it a fool's venture," he replied. "They are without help for their everyday needs. They need to build their houses, but I'm not sure they can do even that."

I frowned. "I agree. I fear they'll return and burden us further for food and lodging. Standish told me the men are spending their energy on building a fort for protection. No one hunts or fishes. They'll have to trade with the Massachusetts for corn, and I fear the natives will be unwilling."

John's face looked thoughtful in the flickering light from our fire. "I think their problem is that they have no goodwives." Then we both smiled. "And we haven't enough." Our smiles faded.

Chapter 13

Village Life

Mary Allerton Cushman, Plymouth, September 1699

I still have some recollections of my days as a young child in Plymouth, during our first years there—of the constant hunger, a house crowded with strangers, the frequent absence of my father, the calming presence of John Alden, and Remember's attempts to make us a home—all these I can still see and feel.

There were but five goodwives in our settlement at that time. With six older girls, they took on the tasks of cooking, cleaning, and washing laundry for all of us, fifty or more in number. They also cared for their own families, of course, as well as nursing any of us who fell sick. Looking back, I cannot imagine how these women sustained us. But they did.

The women pressed me into duty, although I was only four, but more often than I can freely admit, I escaped to play—only to be reprimanded by the sharp tongues of the goodwives when I reappeared. Of these, Goodwife Billington's was most harsh.

I can still hear her voice. "Mary Allerton, where have you been? You were to weed our gardens this morning. Look at you! Your skirt has a new rent."

Of the older girls, Priscilla Mullins was my sole friend. Being courted by John Alden, who lived with us, she visited our home frequently. Her kindness was evident in her patient explanations of each task assigned me, such as planting seeds and leaving room for their growth, and she often stood between me and the barbed comments. It was Mistress Mullin who combed the tangles and lice from my hair and turned up the bottoms of the clothes given me from others, so I would not trip on them.

The boys, even those near to me in age like Resolved White and Richard Moore, with whom I'd played on the *Mayflower*, now worked by their fathers' sides in the fields or joined in hunting. There were no girls near my age, my sister being closest, at six. But she usually stayed with the goodwives and young women, being schooled in the preparation of our food, washing clothes, the uses of plants for medicine, all tasks for the keeper of a home. I think secretly she liked that, working with the older girls, rather than minding me, the baby. I tended to be ignored and would wander here and there in the village when nothing but make-work existed for me.

I remember that fences were everywhere. Made with split wood rails, they enclosed many of our small plots of land and the houses within. They bordered our main street, the one leading up the hill from the harbor to our cannon. Another street crossed the main street part the way up, running to the north and south gates in our palisade. Our governor's house stood at the intersection.

I was often tasked with weeding the gardens the women had planted, behind or beside each of the houses. Remember, with the help of the goodwives, had subdivided ours into small beds, with paths between them just wide enough for us to weed the plants. I disliked all the weeding.

At first, I weeded under the careful direction of Mistress Mullins, who gently admonished me when I pulled up something not a weed. I quickly learned edible from intruder and then moved on to the other gardens. To kill what she called cutworms, Mistress Mullins threw cinders from the hearth on the plants and she also dumped water from the washing of dishes on them to keep the ground moist. She told me this kept down other vermin.

Plymouth Village Scene

At first, the women mainly grew squash and pumpkins, along with onions, garlic and herbs. They'd learned to grow the squash and pumpkin from the Indians. Mistress Mullins helped me plant beds of parsley, lettuce, spinach, white things called carrots, cabbage and turnips, along with some herbs, all grown with seeds the goodwives had brought. Later, with the arrival of more seed, we grew beans and a large, long, green vegetable called a cowcumber. These beds provided food for our families and were added to that doled out from common stores.

I liked to chase the chickens. There were but a few chickens at first, wandering freely in the village, and the women fed them worms, so they often asked me to dig for worms. This was something I liked to do, and it was one of the few tasks Resolved and Richard would do with me.

Remember soon had me helping to wash our clothes and then hang them over fencing and bushes to dry. She hated this chore, mainly because she had to bring large amounts of water from the creek to heat in a kettle, and she burned her hands with the harshness of the lye soap. Bartholomew and I walked several times to the brook each day to fill our buckets with water for drinking and washing. We always took our shoes off to wiggle our toes in the brook, until some goodwife in a shrewish temper caught us and told us to stop dawdling.

I loved those splashes in the brook because work in the gardens during the summer had everyone running with sweat in their heavy clothes. All the women wore a shift and over it a skirt of wool or linen, a waistcoat and an apron, and they told me frequently that first year it was never so hot in England. I wore Remember's outgrown clothes and each day I suffered as she tied the strings of my biggen tightly under my chin. It didn't matter how snugly she fitted it, my curls escaped from the cap and eventually the biggen would slip from my head and dangle down my back. Richard and Resolved had been breeched the past winter and now, instead of a shift, wore shirt, breeches and a jacket. They could take off the jacket while working, and I often thought how much cooler it would be to dress like them.

Usually I didn't dare to venture into the woods, although sometimes a frog or a butterfly would lead me there. After the palisade went up, my father made me stay inside it, unless he was going out to work in the fields. Each day groups of people would head for the fields—mostly men and boys, but during planting women and girls also worked. I went out with them one day to pull weeds from around the corn but soon became hot, tired and bored. The shady woods surrounding our fields beckoned me. Looking around, I could see everyone was either chatting with their neighbor or intent on their work, so I walked into the woods.

The shade of the trees surrounding the fields offered respite from the heat, and there I found a brooklet, which I followed to find its source. It was a long walk, and I drank thirstily from a little pool deep in the woods from which the brooklet meandered. Then I cooled my feet. I never wore shoes in the summer and my feet were used to hard ground, but the woods had things that spiked my feet, so after a while they hurt. I built a house of twigs and mud on the side of the pool and imagined it to be my house.

There were bugs in the pool, so I poked them for a while for fun. It was so lovely and shady there, with dapples of sunlight shifting with the leaves in the trees. I could hear birds and lay down by the pool to listen to them. I fell asleep, only waking up when the sun had gone down, and insects had formed noisy clouds. I decided to follow the brook back, but it went another way and I couldn't see the field. I remember becoming more and more fearful and finally stopped moving because I had often been told by Father and Mother that devils lived in the deep woods. I sat down and waited, wrapping my arms around my legs, shaking at the thought of a devil getting me. *Surely Father will find me.*

After a long while, sitting quietly, I heard movement in some nearby bushes and made myself as small as possible, holding my breath but unable to stop shaking. *Mayhap it's a devil? Or a wild animal?* We'd all heard the cry of the lions before. *Would I be eaten?* I shook as I heard skittering amongst the leaves and tried hard not to cry out in panic.

"I see you, Mary." The deep and resonant voice startled me.

I had heard that voice before—Squanto!

"How fare you?"

I took a deep breath of relief and wiped away tears that came unbidden. "Well, I think, thank you, but I seem to have lost my way. Did Father send you?"

I heard a deep chuckle. "You are a big trouble. Everyone looks for you. Come with me."

"How did you find me?"

"Not difficult. Follow your trail."

He took my hand since I was having difficulty following him in the dark, and with that simple gesture came a sensation of complete safety. It had been this kindly and caring Indian who had brought me a new poppet made from corn husks when my Charity had finally fallen apart. I thought of him as almost a father.

A horn sounded my return, and all those who had gone looking for me came back to the settlement. I heard a lot of muttering as Father first offered thanks to Squanto for finding me and then turned to me with a hard face. "Don't give me any meal-mouthed excuses, daughter. You have caused grief to many of us. All children are born wicked, but I thought you had changed. Your good mother and I tried mightily to bring you up in the ways of God, but I can see you persist in a stubbornness and contrariness of mind. This must be corrected."

I received a sound beating with a rod that night and was made to pray endlessly on my knees, petitioning God to forgive my transgressions. The strangers in our house grumbled loudly as they tried to sleep. I didn't sit well for almost a week, and thereafter, I was less attracted by adventures. Resolved and Richard were angry, since their fathers were more strict with their freedom as a result, and they mocked me, pretending to swat each other's buttocks. My father also worked me like a turnspit for months, but Remember didn't escape punishment either, since she had been charged with minding me in the fields. That made me feel better.

ᘓ ᘐ

Everyone had worked on the building of our home. Father and Uncle Degory, before he'd died, had dug the post holes and built the framework, then Master Alden helped nail clapboards over the frame to enclose the house. Bartholomew had gathered grasses and reeds from the nearby marsh and bundled them, so they could be fastened to the rafters as a roof. A stray spark could set the roof on fire as the reeds and grasses dried out, so we kept a bucket of water handy, alongside a wooden ladder. There were constant leaks in our roof, particularly at the top, and rain dripped down on us or ran down the walls. Repairs to the roof were constant.

Master Alden and Father had built the chimney, lining the firebox with rocks they had gathered, and they filled the spaces between the stones with clay. It seemed to me they called often upon the Lord when these rocks would not stay in place. The chimney above was made of sticks, mud and clay, covered with clapboards on the outside.

Remember and I had created the inside walls, gathering small sticks to make a framework called wattle between the posts. Father showed us how to make daub out of clay, soil, grasses and water. I liked mixing the daub—it felt squishy and soft in my fingers—but Remember criticized me constantly for getting it all over my clothes, creating more washing for her. Then we pushed the daub in between the sticks and made a smooth surface with our hands or straight pieces of wood. Despite our best efforts, cold wind found passage into our house in winter, pushing its way around the door and stealing through the grasses of the roof.

Aside from that door, made of planks, we had but one source of outside light—a small window—so the inside of the house was quite dark. Father covered the window with parchment in the winter, which he soaked in linseed oil to keep out the cold. Our floor was just bare earth, dampened with water, then tamped and smoothed. Drying herbs, corn and onions hung from the rafters. We had two chairs and two stools, which John Alden had fashioned, along with a table made of boards. A small cupboard my parents had brought sat to one side of the room—this held our wooden plates, called trenchers, and four wooden spoons. Father had a knife, as did Mister Alden, who had carved the trenchers while teaching Bartholomew how to work with wood.

The room's sparse furnishings proved fortunate since with the arrival of more people needing to be housed, our one room became crowded. Father and Master Alden built a small area above, under the rafters and accessible by ladder, where Remember, Bartholomew and I slept. Food stores and Mother's trunk, containing what spare clothing we owned, were also kept there. We all slept on canvas sacks filled with corn husks and shared the blankets that had survived the voyage. Later we had deer skins for warmth. Father and Mister Alden slept in a small bed at one end of the room. When Weston's men arrived and were assigned to our house, they slept on the floor with whatever coverings they had brought with them.

Inside a Typical Early Separatist Home

Our home, being only one room, was crowded, dark and smoky most of the time, and although we Separatists washed hands and faces regularly and bathed twice a year, Weston's men avoided water and smelled horribly. Their rank odor filled our room, overpowering the smoke.

Once Father, on returning home for his mid-day meal, found one of these men, not one living with us, rummaging inside our cupboard. Father took him to the governor for judgment, and right after that, moved the cupboard and its contents to our loft. I worried about the weight placed on the floor planks each night, when my brother and sister climbed up there to sleep beside me. The flooring groaned with each toss and turn. We were all happy when Weston's men left our settlement and we could take the cupboard back down.

Set at one end of our room, our hearth was a place of warmth and the always enticing smell of food. In the fireplace were lug poles, pot hooks and kettles my parents had brought, with a fry pan and pots on the hearth. One of my tasks was to keep a close eye on the hearth because of the ever-present danger of fire. This was not a hard task, since it enabled me to snitch small bits of food when Remember's attention went elsewhere.

The strangers eating in our house ate from plain wooden planks rather than trenchers. When we finally had bread made from corn flour, we would put the food on rounds of stale or fried bread. We ate with just our fingers, using such knives and spoons as we had.

Eating a meal became fraught with tension with the accommodation of these strangers in our home. The increased number of mouths to feed led to smaller portions for everyone. Father would dole out the food, so we all received a fair portion. This did not prevent complaints and demands for more. One evening, Father and one of Weston's men nearly came to blows.

"Why does your youngest child get nearly as much pottage as me? I'm a grown man and need food to fuel my labors." I heard mutterings of agreement from the other man housed with us.

"Because she is still growing and needs the nourishment," my father replied. "My other daughter prepared the food for you and washes your clothes, and you sleep in our house. You have little to complain of."

"I shall speak with Bradford about this," he replied, his face growing red with anger. "You are free to discuss this with him, but remember that everyone in the colony goes hungry. I doubt he will offer you anything but words of comfort.

Until the time when the goodwives could make cornbread from ground corn, we ate mainly pottages or sops of vegetables, and dried or fresh fish, eels, some clams and mussels, or occasionally game if Father or Mister Alden were successful at hunting. During the warm months, we had salads of fresh greens. We were hungry, but for the most part, we were healthy.

ꕥ ꕥ

One thing I dreaded most in those early days were our services on Sunday. Although Sunday meant a rest from our labors, I experienced only the boredom of the unending prayers until I was old enough to appreciate the word of God. There were two services on Sunday, one in the morning and one in the afternoon. To my child's mind, they differed little in wearisome sameness.

Before the fort was built, a drum called us to our meeting in the common house. Inside it was dark and dank, with benches facing the pulpit in long rows. I had to sit on the left side with the women, servants, and all the children. Resolved and Richard were looking forward to becoming sixteen, when they could move to the other side of the room with the men, who wore their hats, carried their arms with them, and were allowed to speak during the meeting.

Everyone on our side of the meeting room was expected to keep quiet, except for singing psalms and saying "amen" at the end of a prayer. We all had to stand for the long prayers given by Elder Brewster. We stayed standing while he preached on this theme or that until, at last, we could say "Amen" again and collapse down on the benches. Our leaders would then expound on readings of the scripture, during which we could also sit, a blessing because they droned on and on. This was when eyes drooped.

Our goodwives did their best to control the children, but the youngest—Oceanus Hopkins and Peregrine White—would cry, and Samuel Eaton often tried to escape the hands holding him, wiggling and twisting until swatted hardily on his buttocks. Richard More and Resolved White squirmed constantly, as did I, as I recall. A thunderous "Quiet!" from Elder Brewster often shook the walls, which only caused the babies to startle and scream anew.

The only true joy for me was the singing of psalms, our only music, when we all joined in. These could be lively, and the children would sing at the top of their lungs. In the afternoon, something called 'prophesies' occurred. Elder Brewster would read from the Bible and one after another of the men would rise and speak for a long time, with questions coming from others. I amused myself by staring at each speaker to see how many times he would blink or by looking around to see who had fallen asleep. I confess I often did myself, until nudged awake by Remember's sharp elbow. After Elder Brewster gave the final blessing in the afternoon, the women and children could leave—with dire warnings not to run—while the men stayed behind. I didn't know at the time, but later learned, that the men discussed things large and small about our settlement and gossiped about various members of our community.

I'm thankful our services have changed over the years, as have I, and they are interesting and uplifting to me now.

Thinking about those first years of the Plymouth Colony, it seems like a far-away place where we lived most crudely. At that time, survival and the laws of God were all anyone thought about.

Chapter 14

Problems at Wessagusset and War with the Natives

Isaac Allerton, Plymouth Colony, Fall 1622- Spring 1623

My evening discussions with John Alden about the Wessagusset Colony proved prophetic. Despite all our prayers to the contrary, the colony, settled in August with around fifty men, was ill-prepared for life in this new world. The penurious and greedy Weston, who had financed its settlement and whom Bradford had come to despise, had supposedly provided the men with provisions to last them over the winter, but they proved woefully inadequate.

Bradford called his advisors to meet with him in his home to discuss the situation. We gathered in its one room, either squatting or standing, while he sat facing us, as usual, in his spindled chair. "I have had news from Wessagusset, and I fear it will have a profound impact on us."

What dreadful news will this be?

"As you already know, a native emissary came with a complaint that the colonists there were stealing their corn. I sent a letter to the leader of the Wessagusset settlers, Richard Greene, rebuking them for the thieving. Richard Greene is Thomas Weston's brother-in-law." His mouth twisted in disgust as he said this. "Now I've learned that rather than growing corn for the winter, these men have spent their energies on building fortifications.

"Master Winslow," whom he indicated with a nod of his head, "has secured more food for us, mainly fish, during his trip to the north. Nevertheless, it will be insufficient for the number we now have to feed, and especially so if we must feed those at Wessagusset. Since both colonies now face a similar shortage of food, I proposed a joint trading mission, to which Greene has agreed."

"Where do you propose to seek food?" I asked. I had always been interested in trade and hoped one day to set up a trading company of my own. This trip might prove useful.

"To the south of Cape Cod. We will sail on the *Swan*, the ship owned by the Wessagguset colony."

"Shall I lead this expedition, Governor?" asked Master Winslow.

"No, I think Captain Standish should assume leadership since we may encounter some hostility."

Standish, sitting to one side, nodded in agreement.

ꙮ ꙮ

Captain Standish unfortunately took ill just before we left, so Bradford went in his stead, along with Squanto as guide and interpreter. We had doubts about Squanto's motivation for making this journey with us, but he repeated several times that he once again had Massasoit's trust.

As we rounded Cape Cod sailing south, we faced the shoals we had encountered on the *Mayflower*. For one of the few times in my friendship with our governor, I saw fear and doubt in his face, and he told me privately he wondered if he'd made a good decision in sailing south.

When the *Swan's* master confirmed we had no hope of sailing through the breakers, Squanto used his knowledge of the area and guided our ship through a nearby narrow passage to a harbor where the *Swan* could anchor.

A tribe of the Nausets, the people we had first encountered when we landed on Cape Cod, lived in that area. After some persuasion, their sachem and some warriors met with Bradford and Squanto. This interaction gave us hope, as Bradford secured many hogsheads of corn and beans in exchange for the trade goods we'd brought. Buoyed by optimism, Bradford decided to make a second try at crossing the breakers.

However, before we set out, Squanto suddenly fell ill. We stayed at anchor during his illness, and when I visited with him, I found him weak and feverish from a disease no one recognized. Bradford never left his side, sitting in a chair beside Squanto where he lay in the ship's master's quarters. Bradford held his hand, frequently placing cold clothes on Squanto's fevered brow and urging him to take some broth. The air in the cabin became close and fetid, and Bradford sagged with exhaustion. But he still talked with his friend, recalling their times together and asking him for advice on working with this or that tribal leader.

When I told him I would stay with Squanto, he shook his head. "I cannot in conscience leave him. He's been my trusted advisor and companion and has in many ways ensured our survival. We owe him much."

On his last day, Squanto bled from his nose. Bradford tenderly wiped away the blood and many of us stayed with them, crowded into the small cabin. Squanto now observed the practice of our faith and had often told us of his belief in its strength. Taking Bradford's hand in both of his, Squanto said, "Pray for me so I go to your God in heaven. Give my things to my English friends and remember me with love."

Bradford nodded and prayed aloud for him until Squanto stopped breathing. Then he wept at his terrible loss. I could see that Bradford felt alone and bereft, despite our company. Without Squanto to guide us, Bradford's and our hopes rested on Hobomok to lead us in our dealing with Massasoit and his tribes and in handling the hostility of the Massachusetts and the Narragansetts.

After burying his friend, Bradford decided not to make a second attempt at crossing the shoals and we sailed for home with heavy hearts. Edward Winslow and I sat on the deck, regarding the lonely figure of Bradford at the rail.

"Squanto was indeed an intelligent, albeit, wily leader. He would have been a powerful sachem, if not for his attempt to overthrow Massasoit," said Winslow.

"I found him often talking with Bradford and their regard for each other was evident. We will all feel his absence."

Bradford joined us. "We were blessed to have his friendship. Without him, we would not have survived. I consider him a special instrument sent from God for good beyond our expectations, and I cannot see our way forward without him." He sighed deeply and fell back into silence.

ꙮ ꙮ

When we reached home, I had to tell Mary of Squanto's death. I waited until the beginning of our evening prayers. Her little face first registered disbelief, then screwed itself tight, as tears streaked her cheeks.

"But Squanto was my friend. He found me in the woods. He made me a new poppet. He taught Bartholomew how to fish for eels. Why did God take him from us? God is not kind!"

Her last comment shocked me, especially after everything we had survived. I supposed as a young child, Mary would take Squanto's death as a cruel and personal blow. I chastised her gently, but still I heard her crying in the loft that night.

ꙮ ꙮ

In November, our governor reported that Richard Greene had died, and John Sanders had become the new governor of

Wessagusset. Conditions there worsened over the winter, with some colonists entering a form of servitude with the natives, doing various tasks in exchange for food.

Some traded their clothes for food, and ten men died. The situation at Wessagusset had soured our own affiliations with both the Massachusetts and the Wampanoags, and these relationships continued to deteriorate during the winter months.

The news that Massasoit suffered from a grave illness only intensified our nervousness. Bradford sent Edward Winslow and Hobomok as his interpreter to Pokanoket to see Massasoit. When they returned, Bradford called his advisors together to hear their news. An overnight snow, still falling fitfully, had cloaked the ground outside in a heavy white mantle, and the cold day, overcast with gray clouds, suited our mood. We huddled close to Braford's hearth, our cloaks clutched tightly to us.

Winslow stood with Bradford sitting off to the side. "We had a long, difficult journey," he began, "and partway, we received word that Massasoit had died. This news struck us hard and affected Hobomok deeply. He grieved openly at the loss and wanted to return here, but if Massasoit had died, Corbitant—and I know he's a hollow-hearted friend to us—would be the new sachem. I felt it would be proper to stop at his village and pay him our respects.

"We found Corbitant had left for Pokanoket, so we sent a messenger there. The messenger returned with the news that Massasoit still lived. We traveled immediately to Pokanoket." He stopped and cleared his throat, in preparation for continuing. "When we arrived, we saw that people had jammed into Massasoit's longhouse and there were several groups of warriors arguing loudly in the village. We discovered Massasoit in extremis, unable to see. He could still hear, however, and I made him understand we had come with food and medicines to help him heal. I fed Massasoit some of the fruit preserves we had brought, his first food in two days, and scraped corruption from his mouth and tongue. After eating more of the preserves, his sight returned, and we prepared a broth of sassafras and strawberry leaves, which he readily drank. Thereafter, his recovery was rapid."

Winslow sat down before resuming the story, twisting his hands together as he did. "Before we left, Massasoit told Hobomok that the Plymouth colony is in great danger. He knew the Massachusetts who live around the Wessagusset colony were seeking help from other tribes to attack both Wessagusset and Plymouth at the same time and wipe out both settlements. With his words, we saw we were at the edge of a deep pit, of which we had been little aware. Massasoit told Hobomok we must act without delay to remove those who would lead this attack."

Those gathered sat in stunned silence, except for the snapping of the fire on the hearth. *Are we all to die after surviving so much?* I could see from the frowns on the faces of the others that they shared my th oughts.

Then Bradford stood. "I rejoice that our brother Massasoit lives and that by the grace of God, Master Winslow cured him," he began, always putting God first. "Yet news of this plan by the Massachusetts makes clear we're in mortal danger. I agree with the great sachem that we must strike first and kill the Massachusetts' leaders."

"And I also agree—we have no choice in this matter," said Standish, his faced flushed nearly as red as his hair. "There are many tribes who might be involved in this threat—not only the Massachusetts, but also the Nauset. I propose to lead a small force to Wessagusset to kill those who would lead the attack, in order to discourage others from joining."

Bradford concurred, and we assented to his plan as a group.

Before Standish and his men could leave, John Hampden, a gentleman from London who had come recently to the settlement, brought to us a Wessagusset settler named Phineas Pratt. He'd encountered Pratt while walking a well-worn trail north of Plymouth. Pratt had escaped from Wessagusset and from under the watchful eyes of the Massachusetts by pretending to search for groundnuts, which had become a staple in our food. After spending the night in the woods, alone and frightened, he was exhausted and sweating in fear. He thanked God for encountering Hampden. After spending a long time expressing his gratitude for being saved, he told us what he knew of the Massachusetts' plan: They would kill all Englishmen in a single day and only waited for the snow to melt so they couldn't be tracked.

The next day, as Standish and his party departed for Wessagusset, Standish proclaimed to those gathered to see him off, "We shall take them in such traps as they lay for others!"

Normally, Bradford would be a restraint to Standish's bellicose statements, but this time I heard him say to Standish, "You must make an example of the Massachusetts and their leader. Bring back the head of that leader as a warning to all who want to force us from this land."

I was not amongst the small force selected to march north. Instead Bradford gave me the responsibility of the defense of our settlement, using our remaining militia. Due to the existence of the fort, I felt relatively secure after Standish and his party left, but still I drilled the men relentlessly.

Standish returned in triumph. He marched in at the head of his men, resplendent in his armor and holding a pike with the head of an Indian at its end. The women and children, who had gathered in front of the governor's house, gasped and turned away, and I heard a scream which had to have come from my youngest child.

My men and I followed Standish and his group up the hill to the fort, where I gathered them in formation. From the corner of my eye, I noticed Mary running up the hill to me, sobbing. "Is that Squanto's head, Father?" she asked, hiding her face in my breeches.

Remember was fast behind her, panting as she reached the top of the hill, and pulled her from me. She dragged Mary back down the hill to her loud objections, but the damage had been done. There were whispers behind me, and I knew my fellow Separatists would once again criticize me for my wayward daughter and her lack of discipline.

I was grateful for the diversion of following Standish into the fort, where he gave his account of the military action. "We found the *Swan* deserted offshore and discovered some of the Wessagusset colonists living in the Massachusetts' longhouses. Hunger seemed to be their only complaint.

"I then marched our party to the fort at Wessagusset and spoke to their leader, John Sanders, as well as the men assembled there, telling them what we had heard of the plot and that we intended to kill as many Indians as possible. I told them that once our objective was accomplished, they could either return to Plymouth with us or sail the *Swan* north to the Maine territory. At that point, they left to tell the others in their settlement to come to the fort."

Here Standish cleared his throat. "Later that day the Massachusetts warrior Pecksuot, with whom I'm acquainted, came to the fort with their sachem and made a great show of insulting us."

I could only imagine what those insults might have been, because I heard whispers amongst some of Standish's men that Pecksuot was a tall man.

"I ignored the insults and instead invited both men to one of the few existing houses to share a meal of corn and pork with us. I know Indians like pork and they themselves were starving, so with some reluctance they came to eat, along with a few others. We attacked them as they sat down and killed them all with our swords. We then spread out through the surrounding settlement, killing whatever Indians we found and taking the native women prisoners."

I saw our stunned looks at the violence of Standish's words, uttered in such a calm and deliberate way, but later most of us expressed our their agreement with his actions.

"There was no resistance?" asked Bradford.

"Aye, some natives hid behind trees and fired arrows at us, but we chased them into a swamp, where they disappeared," Standish replied.

"What of the women and Wessagusset settlers?" asked Edward Winslow.

"We released the women, and most of the surviving Wessagusset colonists boarded the *Swan* and sailed north, hoping to find food and a safe place to settle."

When we finished asking questions, Standish placed the Indian head on the end of a pole on the fort's roof. The smell from the decaying flesh seemed to seep into the conscience of our settlement, and many avoided looking at it.

That evening, the questions from my children challenged me to answer in a manner they could understand.

"How many Indians did Captain Standish kill?" Bartholomew asked me.

"I don't know, son. A few. Many ran away."

"Why did he have to kill them?"

"Because we'd received word that they were going to attack us and the Wessagusset colony as well."

Remember shuddered and remained quiet, but Mary, of course, didn't. "Whose head was that on the stick Captain Standish brought in?"

I didn't answer but instead beckoned to her to come sit beside me. "Mary, you were most disrespectful and badly behaved today. You have brought shame on our family, as you often have with your thoughtless ways. Did you think it Squanto's head? That couldn't be! Squanto died some time ago."

Mary's eyes began to fill with tears. "It frightened me, Father. Then I thought of Squanto. I'm sorry."

I sighed deeply, for in truth I knew not how to change her. She received the rod regularly and it seemed to make little impression. Not for the first time did I long for Mary Norris' counsel and advice. Finally, I told her, "I cannot excuse your behavior. You're confined to the house for now, unless there is some task for which you're needed. And you will pray on your knees for an hour each morning and each night for God's guidance in following His righteous path."

Remember turned away from this interchange, but not before I saw the scowl on her face. She would be confined with her sister and would have to ensure she performed her punishment.

ꟾ ꟾ

The past two harvests had been poor, and as planting season approached, Bradford met with his advisors to consider how we might improve the situation.

"You must agree that our communal farming has, with the exception of our first year, been unsuccessful in providing sufficient food for our settlement. I know there are good reasons for this—our increasing population, the thieving and destruction of Weston's men, and the unwillingness of some to do their fair portion of work in the fields."

A noise of agreement came from those present—Edward Winslow, Thomas Prence, John Alden, Stephen Hopkins, John Howland and myself, now as Assistant Governor.

"What do you have in mind, Governor?" I asked, knowing full well what his answer would be, since we'd discussed this problem beforehand.

"I wish to allot each colonist at least one acre of land, where he can plant, grow and harvest his own crops for his own family. If there is surplus once his family is provided for, he may use it in trade."

"I think that's a sound idea," said Master Winslow, "but it may prove difficult for families such as Master Allerton's, with naught but small children."

I nodded at the thoughtfulness of his comment.

"Then perhaps two or more families could agree to farm their acres together, dividing their harvest proportionally as to the effort put in." Bradford not for the first time showed his forethought and wisdom, and I thought again how fortunate we were to have him as governor.

We then plotted out our individual acres, and arrangements were made between families to work the land. The Aldens shared their acreage with us. Even Mary contributed, and after the birth of their daughter, Mistress Alden worked beside us in our fields with her baby resting in a sling. Such was our enthusiasm to tend our own crops that Bradford's plan worked well, yielding a healthy harvest later in the year.

ℌ ℌ

One evening at dusk, I sat outside on a bench, enjoying a moment of respite from the labors of the day and looking around at our settlement. Much larger now, more than thirty houses, it stretched over the hill to the fort and crowded the palisade. The evening filled me with peace, the sounds of children and prayer drifting in the air. Swallows dashed here and there in the dwindling light, swooping to catch the last insects before the sun set.

Edward Winslow, on an evening stroll, stopped to talk.

Knowing he was most knowledgeable in the affairs of the natives, I asked, "What do you hear of our Indian neighbors to the north?" I beckoned him to join me on the bench.

"Little, but the news isn't good. The Massachusetts are much in fear of us now and have taken to living in the swamp. Many are dead of disease and those remaining have been loath to return to plant crops, so they starve. We haven't done well by them. None of the tribes will now trade their furs with us."

"Yes, I noticed Bradford has urged we fish for cod, not only to carry us over the cold months, but also to have food to offer them. I must admit," I said with a low chuckle, "I'm no fisherman. I went out with Bartholomew just a day ago and we came home with only a few fish and sick from the waves."

"Perhaps we could learn from the settlers and natives in Maine, who seem so skilled at catching fish? That's one reason I plan to journey there again soon."

"What do you think of our relationships with the other tribes? Do we have anything to fear from them?"

Winslow shook his head. "Many of the sachems we've known are dead. This has proved a benefit for Massasoit, who can now draw his various tribes together without opposition. In the meantime, alliances between the native nations seem to change constantly. I believe we now stand alone, except for the good will of Massasoit. How long that will last, I don't know."

This conversation troubled my mind, my anxiety only increasing with the contents of a letter Governor Bradford received from John Robinson, our Pastor in Leiden. In it, Robinson criticized the governor for his trust in Standish, writing that Standish lacked the tenderness toward life that a man should have. Bradford read to me from the letter, "...where blood is once shed, it's seldom staunched for a long time after." While he agreed the Massachusetts may have deserved their fate, Pastor Robinson questioned what role the Christians in Wessagusset had played. "...I'm indeed afraid lest, by your actions, others will be drawn to your aggressive course in the world."

I felt, deep in my soul, that even though he lived far from us, Robinson saw the future more clearly than we.

Chapter 15

A Tragic Fire and Mary Is Taken in Hand

Isaac Allerton, Plymouth Colony, Summer-Winter 1623

By the summer of 1623, I was increasingly anguished by my youngest daughter's willful and wayward spirit, and it seemed no amount of punishment or prayers would change her behavior. I welcomed some help with the arrival in July of the ship *Anne*, and a week or so later, a smaller companion ship, the *Little James*.

More than seventy people had sailed on the two ships, and many of its passengers were relatives of those already here. Elder Brewster and his wife Mary were most happy to see their daughters Fear and Patience again. Bridget, the wife of our physick, Samuel Fuller, came as well. Richard Warren, a strong survivor of that first winter, welcomed the largest contingent of the *Anne*—his wife Elizabeth, their five daughters, his wife's mother and her four sisters. I couldn't imagine how all these newcomers would manage in his one-room house, but we welcomed the increase of women in our colony. The inclusion of so many families and children reassured many of those who had preceded them that our settlement would continue, and I knew our heavily burdened goodwives would be overjoyed with the addition of hands for their work.

When these travelers came ashore, I saw dismay on the faces of more than a few, and I knew what we viewed with pride, they saw as poor conditions. I even overheard some say, "I would be back in England." True, our houses were roughly made and such roads as we had were rutted and pitted with stones, but we had created a thriving community and a place we called our home.

My sister, Sarah Godbertson, was amongst those who came ashore. She had remarried after hearing of the death of her husband Degory Priest. With her, apparently unafraid of the long journey and trials ahead, were her new husband Godbert, her two daughters by Degory, Mary and Sarah Priest, and a baby, Samuel Godbertson. These newly arrived members of my family were reticent at first, not knowing how they would be greeted, but Godbert proved a fair and godly man, and we soon struck upon a friendship. Our own house would now be overfull, but I welcomed the inclusion of a goodwife to my household, with the hope my sister would take Mary in hand.

Not surprisingly, there was soon friction in the house. Remember, after having charge of the home for some two years, prickled at the overbearing nature of my sister and her older daughters, as well as at the additional work entailed with so many now living there.

At the breaking of our fast the next morning, my sister looked around our table and said, "Remember, you will now clear the table, put away the food and rinse off the dishes. Bartholomew, bring in wood for the fire. Mary, fetch some fresh water. My daughters, you begin preparation of our mid-day meal while I inspect the garden. Are there clothes to mend?"

Remember stalked from the table with an angry look, since Sarah had given her only menial tasks. Later, she took me aside to complain. "Father, she thought my garden poor and didn't believe me when I explained the difficulty in growing some vegetables. And she gave me little Samuel to mind. He fusses constantly, and nothing I do soothes him."

"My daughter, they won't be with us for long. Construction on their own house will begin within a few days. Pray to God for patience and understanding."

Remember was not the only one having difficulty with my sister. Within a few days, Sarah approached me with a look of frustration, and I knew Mary's behavior caused it. I had anticipated such a conversation with dread, almost since Sarah had arrived.

"You daughter is unkempt, disrespectful with her words, and disobedient. How have you let her become such an unruly, impolite and undisciplined child? Today when I told her to weed the garden and bring water from the brook, she said she always did that anyway and that I didn't need to remind her! Then she spent the rest of the morning somewhere else in the village."

I did my best to explain how supervision of Mary had been nearly impossible because of the scarceness of women in the settlement, but she paid little mind to what I said.

"You must thrash her tonight for her disobedience, but I have serious doubts she can be brought to righteousness."

ജ ഇ

An idea came to me the next day. Mary was almost eight, an age when she could be put out. Perhaps I might find her a place her in another household where there would be learning to focus her interest and where she could be disciplined in a proper way, without the over-love—or over-harshness. Clearly my sister was not the instrument to do this. Mary needed a comforting touch as well as the rod.

With this in mind, I approached our governor the following evening. Despite the additional mouths to feed, his mood had been most pleasant since the arrival of the two ships. The widow Alice Southworth had come on the *Little James* with her brother-in-law, Thomas Southworth, and her sister and her husband, George Morton, and their two children. It was fairly common knowledge that after the death of Edward Southworth, Bradford had sent for Alice, whom he had known in England. A marriage was planned, and everyone could see the change in our governor, who had been lonely and dour since the death of his wife Dorothy on the *Mayflower*.

We sat outside, enjoying the last light of the day and the peace of the village. "What brings you here, Master Allerton?" the governor asked, looking at me with curiosity.

"This isn't an easy thing for me to tell you, Master Bradford, but you know my children have been without a mother for nearly three years. Although Remember and Bartholomew have dealt well with life here, my youngest daughter has grown independent and fractious. I feel she would benefit greatly from being placed with another family for instruction and discipline."

Hearing this, Bradford smiled. "You would like Mary to be schooled in my household, after my marriage?"

"Yes, begging your good will. I know these arrangements are common with our sons, but Mary knew little from her mother but love, and my sister will soon have a household of her own. Mary has already made a poor impression on her, and I confess I'm at wit's end as to how I might raise her in godly and submissive ways. The child wanders hither and yon, speaks during meals and only grudgingly does what she is told…well, you have seen her disobedience. She is more than old enough to begin learning her future role in our community, but it seems I am a poor teacher."

"I'll speak with Mistress Southworth about this, but I feel certain she will agree to take Mary into our household. There is room for her—only Thomas Cushman resides here permanently, and everyone now living here will soon move to their own homes." He paused for a moment, then said, "I think my new wife would welcome a girl child, and I know she can put her on the path to goodness and a disciplined life."

My relief must have been visible, because Bradford clasped my shoulder. "I realize how difficult it's been, raising the young children. You should consider yourself most fortunate that all three of yours survived. Be assured that when the time comes, your daughter will be welcome here."

The following day, I told Mary of this plan. As I had anticipated, she cried and begged me not to send her away, even though she would only be living on the other side of the street. When I pointed out how close she would still be, it made no difference. In the end, I made her pray with me, which seemed to calm her. Remember, for her part, looked relieved, but Bartholomew told me privately he would miss Mary's presence.

ꟼ ꟼ

The *Little James* proved to be a thorn in the side of our governor, because once again the Merchant Adventurers had been shortsighted and imprudent when they sent the ship. They not only didn't purchase sufficient food supplies for the crew, but they also failed to provide us with enough trade goods to exchange for furs. Further, the crew was unhappy with the arrangement for their wages—they were paid in company shares in place of any actual money. The *Little James* left soon after its arrival at the end of July, because its captain, one of our investors, decided to waste no time setting up trade relations for furs. After sailing to the south of Cape Cod, he and the crew soon discovered the Dutch had been there first with trade goods the Indians had wanted. The ship returned in the fall with nothing in its hold. To compound their misfortune, when a storm threatened to run the anchored ship aground in the bay, the crew had to chop through the mainmast and cut away the rigging to save it from sinking.

Bradford appeared on my doorstep early the day after the storm, and we sat outside discussing the future of the *Little James*. "The crew is in a bad temper, Master Allerton," he said. "Some of them believe they were fooled into making the voyage, and in truth, I must agree. The merchants have once again handed us a problem. And now the ship isn't fit to sail."

"Have we the men and means to refit the ship?"

"There's no question—we have to do it. But it's too late in the season for the ship to sail elsewhere, so they must spend the winter anchored here."

"Which means we will be dealing with an increasingly restive crew and even less food to go around."

"We must share what we can," Bradford said, shaking his head.

Would the problems created by those merchants never end?

ꟹ ꟹ

The arrival of family members on the *Anne* and *Little James* strengthened the roots of our colony, although this would not be apparent for some time. More than a few still viewed the settlement as miserable and were vocal in their resentment of the crowded housing arrangements. Our food supplies were so limited that we often had only lobsters, clams, eels and cornbread to eat. In the end, some decided to return to England. Our governor told me privately he thought these people unfit for the challenges of life in the colony.

Yet new houses were quickly being built and our settlement spread. Everyone still lived within walking distance of the fort, so they could attend Sunday services. Governor Bradford led us in a prayer of thanks to God each Sunday for the safe arrival of so many and for His goodness in providing for our wants. He also addressed God about our despair with the little rain that had fallen during the growing season. Soon thereafter, his prayer was heard, and we had soaking rains. Our crops flourished during the end of summer and beginning of fall, and the green and yellow of the fields surrounding the settlement gave it the aspect of an English village. This soothed the complaints of some of our newest comers.

In September, the *Anne* returned to England, taking with it the timber and furs we had amassed to pay our debts to the merchants. Edward Winslow sailed on the Anne as well. He was a skilled diplomat, and Bradford hoped he could inform our investors of the colony's situation and history and reassure them their investments would prove productive. At the time of Master Winslow's leaving, we had well over thirty houses in our settlement, with others under construction. There had also been births in the past two years, so our numbers grew to more than three hundred.

We had a reason to celebrate twice that fall, the first being the September marriage of our governor to Mistress Southworth.

Although only a civil ceremony, Massasoit attended with one of his five wives, along with other sachems and six score of men with their bows and arrows. The Indians brought four deer and a turkey, so there was plentiful food for all who attended: roast venison, venison pasties, pottages, plums, nuts, and grapes. The Indians also entertained us with their dancing and loud whooping. The marriage weighed on my mind, because it meant Mary's time to leave approached. I wavered between relief at having her finally in hand and sadness at her leaving.

With the harvest in, we celebrated again with a feast of thanksgiving, along with a long service of gratitude to our God, for His provision for our welfare. The harvest had proved more bountiful than the previous two, proving the wisdom of Bradfords decision to allow each man his own land.

ꕥ ꕥ

On a late November night, Mary awakened me by tugging on my night clothes. "Father, can you hear the screaming and smell the smoke?"

In truth, I hadn't because I was so deeply asleep.

I ran out of the house, children close behind, where the view of flames coming from the roofs of several houses stopped us where we stood. People were running to and fro, throwing buckets of water on the fire and helping the owners of those nearby or those with homes not completely aflame to remove their belongings. Bartholomew and I grabbed our buckets, and after I told Remember not to let Mary out of her sight, we ran to get water. The fire lasted only an hour, but that one hour was hard-fought. In the end, seven houses were reduced to piles of smoking ashes. So much hard work undone, so many families and their boarders without shelter, having lost their few possessions and now facing winter.

We were exhausted from our efforts and now sat mute and overwhelmed by the ruins. I sat on the ground with Governor Bradford, John Alden, and my son, all of us in such low spirits we couldn't even rise to go home. Looking around, I found myself smiling at the sight of our soot-smeared faces.

"How can you find humor in the face of this tragedy, Master Allerton?" asked Alden.

"Because we look like blackened scarecrows," replied Bartholomew for me.

Slowly the others smiled, then Bradford sighed, "I'll need to assign those without homes to other houses, and we'll need to begin rebuilding. With the harvest in, we can all contribute to the effort. Praise be to God no one died."

At that, we finally got up and went home to wash. Soon thereafter, the governor and his counselors decreed that roofs of new houses could no longer be of rushes or reeds but must be made of clapboards, if such were available.

so cs

As we had foreseen, with the freezing weather, short rations, and only water to drink, the crew of the *Little James* became sullen and mutinous. We all felt relief when the ship sailed for Maine in the early spring of the next year, and as she left our harbor, I could only hope we'd never see her again.

Chapter 16

A Trial, Banishment, and Mary Is Put Out

Isaac Allerton, Plymouth Colony, 1624

By the spring of 1624, our governor had grown tired of his responsibilities. He often spoke with me about the weight of his duties in the face of a new marriage and the work of his farm. He believed the colony now had a firm economic footing. Therefore it came as no surprise when, at a meeting of his usual advisors, he expressed his desire to be excused from the governorship.

"If there is any honor or benefit to this job, I welcome others to have it. But it has proven to be a burden," and here his shoulders slumped, "and I think it's only fair that I should share it." He gave me a half-smile. Since I was his assistant governor, he knew I understood his burdens very well.

Although I felt qualified by this time to become governor, I could see from the faces of the others that Bradford's announcement had created real anxiety.

John Howland stood to speak. "I cannot agree to another governor, Master Bradford. You have steered us safely through many perilous times, and I know there will be others. There's no one more qualified than you to lead us." Everyone nodded in agreement.

"Perhaps there is a way we can assist our governor," I said. "I'm currently his only assistant, and even with my help, he has too much to do. Just think on it: keeping track of our immediate and future needs, obtaining supplies, trading, overseeing rationing if necessary and finding housing for colonists who have none. He must keep accounts, although I do much of that, make treaties, greet visitors, assign tasks, inventory our goods, discharge our debts to the Merchant Adventurers, act as judge and jury—"

John Alden interrupted me, saying, "Clearly his tasks are overwhelming, Master Allerton. I suggest we give him more assistants, in addition to yourself."

After further discussion and with input from the governor, another four assistants were named to help him and were given the title of magistrates or Governor's Council. We were assigned as a group to vote on important matters of governance. With this guarantee, Bradford agreed to remain as governor. In his usual practical way, he asked each of us what tasks we would accept and, over the next months, parceled out his duties.

Soon after, Edward Winslow, named one of Bradford's assistants in absentia, returned from England on the ship *Charity*. He brought with him three heifers and a bull. The animals were regarded with joy by the population, but their arrival did prove, in Bradford's words, "a fatal thing to this plantation," because most gave up the idea of ever being fishermen as result. We were all farmers now. Oddly enough, amongst the things Robert Cushman sent us on the Charity were seines and hooks. Of more use were goods for trade with the Indians.

More colonists arrived with Winslow, two of whom Edward had specifically requested: a man knowledgeable in boat construction and a salt maker. After several months, Bradford's Council discussed the progress of these two.

"I'm pleased with our boat builder, Master Winslow," said Bradford. "He's an industrious man."

"He certainly is," Winslow replied. "He's already constructed two ketches with masts and a flat bottomed lighter for unloading goods from ships in our harbor. I see he's now working on some rigged boats the size of our shallop."

"These latter will be very useful for our trading ventures," I said.

"But will any of them be used for fishing?" asked Bradford, knowing full well the answer when no one replied. "And what of our salt maker?" he then asked.

"I find him ignorant, foolish and self-willed," Standish replied.

I smiled inwardly at the 'self-willed' criticism coming from Standish.

"I have watched his progress, or lack thereof, in making salt in the French way, and I doubt he'll succeed," said Winslow.

"Why is that?" asked Bradford.

"Because he digs shallow pools and lines them with clay for evaporation. He hasn't taken into account that our weather is ill-suited for this approach, there being more rain than he's used to."

"I still hope he makes enough salt to allow us to send salted fish to the English markets," Bradford said wistfully. "But since few want to fish and our salt maker seems destined to fail…" His voice trailed off. Then he added, "But we must allow him to continue, lest he tell our investors we didn't permit him to finish what he'd begun."

Tragedy struck when our ship builder died in the summer of that year, before he'd had time to train someone else in his craft. As for the salt maker, he returned to England and it would be another twelve years before we had a licensed and competent replacement. In the meantime, we obtained salt from England and what we could from salt water evaporation.

ꟻ ꟻ

I found myself strangely glad when my sister Sarah and her family finally moved to her new house, despite the fact we would again have to rely on Remember to prepare our meals. I hoped she'd learned from her aunt, so what she made would be more palatable.

Remember seemed quite content that the fretful Samuel was gone and that she was in charge of the household again.

Before she left, my sister's interactions to my youngest daughter had become only stern reminders to Mary of her chores in the morning and requests of me to thrash her at night. This I definitely would not miss.

As I'd anticipated, she left me with a parting word. "Mind that daughter of yours. She's going to be the bane of this community and will bring shame on us all."

I had not told her of my plan to have Mary live with the Bradfords, fearing she would think herself a failure in taking Mary in hand. Which, of course, she was.

I continued trying to persuade Mary of the advantages of being in the Bradford household, but my conversations with her were one-sided. We prayed together on it every evening, but all she would say is, "I don't want to leave you, Father," and cry herself to sleep.

ᘓ ᘔ

Contrary to our hopes, we had not heard the last of the *Little James*. Later that spring, its captain, a man named Altham, returned to Plymouth in a small sailboat and came directly to see the governor. I was with him that morning, going over accounts, when the captain arrived and walked in unannounced.

"Captain Altham, I'm surprised to see you. How fares the *Little James*?" asked Bradford, rising from his desk. On seeing the captain disheveled and in an agitated state, he said, "Please, sit and rest yourself. Can I offer you some water?"

The captain, a young man of English landed gentry, sat down wearily. "Yes, please. Water would be most welcome. I also beg of you some food. I haven't eaten since I left the coast of Maine some days ago."

Bradford poured water into a wooden cup on the table, then told his wife to bring corn bread and some meat. "Why have you returned? What's happened that you return here alone?"

Altham drank thirstily and Bradford refilled his cup. Mistress Bradford brought fried corn bread, samp, and smoked meat in a trencher, which she handed to Altham with a napkin, before giving her husband a questioning look. He shook his head and she moved away. We waited while Altham fairly inhaled his food.

When he'd finished, he wiped his hands and face on the napkin and sat back with a sigh of relief. "The news isn't good, Governor. When we reached Pemaquid, the crew mutinied and threatened to destroy the ship. They are keeping the ship's master hostage until I return with food." Clearly the master of the ship, an experienced sailor, had felt Altham would be the best person for this task, despite being completely unskilled at sailing.

Bradford's face didn't reveal his thoughts, but I knew his thinking. Being a man of laws and righteousness, he would naturally condemn the crew. Yet the words he spoke were fair. "I'll call Edward Winslow to provision you with bread and peas, so you can return as quickly as possible. I trust you can then restore order."

When Altham left, Bradford said, "This latest turn pushes me more to resigning as governor. I don't think I can handle any more of this stupidity, brought down on our heads by our investors."

"Why don't you leave this situation to Master Winslow and myself, Governor? Let us take this on."

He sighed with a half-smile. "No, I must deal with it—it comes with my office. But I thank you for the offer and I'll most certainly consult with both of you. Perhaps this is the last we will hear of that vessel."

Sadly, his words were proved wrong. After Altham returned north with food, a fierce storm drove the *Little James* onto the rocks in the harbor of Damariscove Island, killing the ship's master. After the disaster, the crew mutinied again. Bradford received word that the masters of several ships with homes on the island would salvage and rebuild the *Little James*, but only if our colony would pay their bill in beaver skins. Bradford agreed. Within six weeks, these men made the *Little James* ready for sea again, but her four small boats, important for coastal trading, had been lost. Because of this, Bradford sent an order to the ship's new master and its crew that they should return to England—another loss for our colony at the hands of the investor group, whom we privately came to call 'the Mis-Adventurers." Even more galling to Bradford was news that the leaders of the mutineers sued the investors and our colony for forty pounds, the wages the crew hadn't received.

ꟾ ꟾ

We had long hoped John Robinson, our pastor from our days in Leiden, would come to join us. He had sought funds from the merchants for his passage to Plymouth, but the Merchant Adventurers, being uneasy with our separation from the Church of England, had sent us an Anglican minister instead. John Lyford, along with his family, had arrived with Edward Winslow on the *Charity*.

Bradford read to his Council from a letter written by Robinson and carried on the *Charity*: "My hopes of coming to the Plymouth colony are now smaller and weaker than ever," Robinson wrote. "The Adventurers seem to have neither the money nor the will to send me."

Bradford's frustration and anger were evident to those who knew him, but despite this, our governor greeted Lyford with good grace, assigning him the best house in town and the largest food allowance. Lyford, for his part, impressed our congregation with his humility. At the same time, those living in our midst who were not of our faith were also pleased.

Lyford sat at our Council meetings alongside Elder Brewster and had a voice in matters of governance. He soon asked to be admitted to our church, an unheard of request. Bradford and his Council considered it and, given that we had no ordained minister for our church, acquiesced. Within a short while, Lyford shared the pulpit with Brewster and because Elder Brewster had not been ordained, Lyford baptized both Separatists and non-believers alike. This didn't sit well with the Council, but we reasoned that non-believers should be baptized too.

Soon some members of the Council noticed non-Separatist groups forming around Lyford and learned of meetings being held in his house, meetings of which we were not a part. Men who had complained most loudly and vilely of the colony were amongst those who attended those gatherings.

Bradford met with me soon after the *Charity* left to return to England, carrying our trade goods in her hold. He told me he'd been suspicious of Lyford's intent from the start. "So after the *Charity* sailed, I set out in the shallop to intercept it, knowing she had to be carrying letters from Lyford to the London merchants. The captain, knowing me well, hove to while I explained my unusual visit.

"He willingly gave the letters to me to read. Some I copied and some I kept, before leaving the ship to continue on its way. These letters are full of lies, slander and prejudice, aiming to ruin the colony!" He slammed his fist on the table in anger.

"What do you want to do about Lyford?" I asked him.

Bradford paused to regain control of his choler, then said, "Although Lyford is guilty of subversion, I plan to do nothing for now. I wish to gather more evidence, and I'm sure this traitor will find some way to show I'm persecuting him."

I didn't need more persuasion of Lyford's guilt but reluctantly agreed to the governor's plan.

Only a short time later Bradford discovered other letters written to the merchants by both Lyford and John Oldham. Oldham, a fiery and headstrong Anglican, had become a close friend of Lyford, along with the belligerent John Billington. This association was natural, since Billington railed continually about Bradford's management of the colony. The governor's Council soon came to the conclusion that the aim of Lyford and his followers was to establish an Anglican church here.

Oldham himself brought the situation to a head when he refused to take his watch standing guard, even after being ordered to do so by Captain Standish. As Standish told me later, Oldham quarreled with him and drew a knife. Despite his small stature, the captain was perhaps the last person in the colony I would confront, and he had Oldham arrested and imprisoned in the fort.

Bradford called the Council to meet with him at the fort early the next morning. As I walked up the hill, I marveled that such trouble roiled beneath the surface of such a sunny and peaceful spring day. The ocean breeze lifted the hair from my neck with a warm touch, the smell of baking bread filled the air, and the bird song of mating came from the eaves of some of our houses. People were about, calling to one another, and heading to their acres to prepare them for planting. Goodwives were outside to wash clothes, carry cornbread to bake in our communal ovens, or tend to their gardens. When I entered the fort, all such pleasant observations disappeared, and I took a deep breath, knowing Bradford, whose patience was formidable, had had enough.

When we were seated on benches, he stood and began. "We founded this colony so we might worship as we saw fit, without interference from the Crown. Now we have an Anglican priest amongst us, sent here by the merchants, fomenting discord, and supported by such men as Oldham and Billington. I have learned Lyford now plans to convene a religious service apart from ours on Sunday, and this cannot be tolerated." He turned to Standish. "Arrest Reverend Lyford and take him the jail. He and Oldham must be tried for plotting against us and disturbing our civil and religious peace. If any of you're in disagreement, say so now."

A profound silence followed.

"What about Billington?" Elder Brewster asked. He was the one person I had thought would not agree with our governor's decision, being a man of God's peace.

"John Billington must be watched, but he is bluff and bluster and not clever enough to be at the center of this plot," Bradford replied.

A day later, a public trial was held at the fort. When Mary heard there would be a big meeting, she asked to go. In addition to her request being forward and unseemly, she was too young to understand. I remonstrated her gently. "This is no business of yours, daughter, nor of any woman. This is the task of men, and the comprehension of it is beyond your ability. This is not a celebration."

For once, she did not pout, and when Remember asked her to feed our chickens, she went willingly. She loved chickens.

Bradford announced the charges of subversion and treason to all in attendance. Several of the non-believers were absent, not wanting to be identified as followers of Lyford. Both Oldham and Lyford stood, saying Bradford had no proof to support his charges.

Oldham raved like a furious beast, calling us traitors and rebels and using vile language. "Your governor is nothing but a wantwit. These charges are false. God's blood, he is but a bedswerver, stealing the colony's money to his benefit. May he be struck with palsy and all of you be cursed by the devil."

Bradford stood silently, waiting until Oldham was spent. Then he took Lyford's letters from his pocket and began to read from them, barely restraining his anger. "I advise you to send to the Plymouth colony as many as possible of those faithful to the Church of England, so their numbers will overwhelm the Separatists. It is especially important that the Leiden group, Pastor John Robinson and his congregation, be kept back or this plan will fail."

There was a collective gasp, followed by so profound a silence that I could hear the birds singing outside.

Lyford had grown red in the face and refused to look anywhere but at the floor, as Bradford continued to reveal his duplicity. He finished by asking Lyford, "What say you, Reverend? Why would you write this treason, if not to destroy our colony?"

Bradford sat down stiffly and Lyford stood, shaking and crying. "I admit have made a terrible error, for which I beg your forgiveness. I have been deceived and let myself be led astray by certain dissident opinions in the colony. I may have, in my own interest, encouraged them further. I'm but unsavory salt and have learned a great lesson."

With that, he raised his voice to God, asking for his forgiveness and charity.

Bradford would have none of it. "You and Goodman Oldham are indeed unsavory salt, and like such salt, you must be cast aside. You are permanently banished from this colony."

Both men left that day with several other families who were followers of Lyford. We heard later they had traveled north and founded a settlement called Nantasket, and their activities remained unknown to us for some time.

ꟸ ꟸ

I had chosen a day, with our governor's agreement, to bring Mary to his household, to be trained in religion, humility and such tasks as would eventually make her a good wife. I asked Remember to dress Mary in clean clothes and to pack her belongings in a bundle. Mary, in her stubbornness, refused to obey until I used the rod, spending some time telling her that she must behave in her new home. Sobbing, she finally did as told, took her little bundle, and followed me out the door and across the street to the Bradford's house.

As I approached their door, I prayed I had made the right decision. *She is so young. Still…I cannot raise her in the right way. This must be done.*

The door opened as we came in the front gate. There stood Mistress Bradford, offering us both a smile. Alice Bradford was a godly woman, generous of spirit, and already far gone with child. Mary could be a great help to her, if she would only accept the situation.

"Mary, dear child," Mistress Bradford said, "come in. I have some goat's milk on the table. Would you like some?' She took Mary's hand.

"Yes, mistress, I would, thank you."

I thanked God that Mary, for once, was suitably polite.

"Here, let me take your bundle," Mistress Bradford then said.

The relief on my face must have been obvious, because the governor's wife's smile widened, and she gave me a wave of the hand, which told me I could leave. The door shut behind them and I left, wondering what the future had in store for my independent, unruly daughter.

Chapter 17

Mary Settles in a New Home

Mary Allerton, Plymouth Colony, 1624

I remember the look on Mistress Bradford's face as I wiped my mouth on my sleeve after finishing the goat's milk. I couldn't decide if it was one of humor or horror.

"Well, well," she said. "I can see we first need to teach you manners. Do you see the cloth on the table in front of you?"

"Yes, mistress."

"It's called a napkin and you're to put it over your left shoulder and use it to wipe your hands and your mouth whilst you're eating and when you've finished." To emphasize that, she got up, placed the napkin on my shoulder, then had me remove it and wipe my mouth. "There, a first lesson." She sat down again. "Come here, girl, and let me take a closer look at you."

I did as she asked, standing nervously in front of her, shifting from one foot to the other.

She gave a soft cluck. "Tsk, tsk. Your clothes need some work."

Previously uncaring of my appearance, I immediately reddened as I looked down at my dress. I wore an old one of Remember's, made of rough brown wool, often mended, and also too short because I can recall seeing my feet sticking out from under it. My bidden already hung down my back from its tie around my neck, and my hair sprung out in tangled curls.

Mistress Bradford shook her head. "Let me see your hands."

I stuck out my hands and for the first time noticed how dirty they were, with soot under the nails and long scratches from the chickens.

Taking me by the hand, Mistress Bradford led me outside to a water bucket, which had a washing cloth hanging on it. There she proceeded to do a more thorough washing of me than had Remember, who had just wiped my face. While she did that, I took notice of her for the first time.

Although I was destined to know her for a long time, my first impression of the governor's wife was one of substance. She had a pleasant, round face with dark hair bound back and neatly tucked under her linen coif. Her dark eyes regarded everything around her seriously, but she smiled as she cleaned me, even to my legs and feet. Her clothes were somewhat better than those of some of the goodwives—a clean linen smock, which showed beneath her waistcoat of blue wool, and a skirt of brown, with a soiled linen apron that hung to the bottom of her skirt. A linen collar graced her neck. There were none of the mending marks most of our clothing bore, nor the wear at the cuffs and hem.

"There," she said when she'd finished. "We need to do something with your hair and you're more than ready for a proper coif." She led me back inside to a corner of the room where I noticed a bed, a chest, a bedside chair and some candlesticks that shone with polish. I thought at the time the Bradfords must be rich.

Mistress Bradford stood me in front of her, facing away, and energetically tackled my tangles. It proved to be a laborious task and eventually she took a knife to some of the most stubborn mats. Then she used a fine comb to remove the lice from my hair.

When she'd finished and sat back with a sigh of accomplishment, I felt my head and was surprised that my hair was smooth and tangle free. I hoped the constant itching from the lice would go away.

After binding up my hair, she covered it with a coif from the chest. "Finally. You look quite presentable, Mary. Now let's see if we can find you some proper clothes. I have only sons, both of whom are still in England, but mayhap something of mine can be reduced to fit, or we can make new." Lifting the lid of the chest, she pulled out clothes and laid them on the bed, amongst them a skirt in a dark green wool and a bodice in brown. "There," she said, choosing that skirt and bodice. "They will do but will require alteration."

I was awed by the thought she would give me clothes, especially of these colors.

"Have you a shift beneath your dress, Mary? I don't see one."

I shook my head no. "There were none to fit."

"That will never do. You cannot go without a proper undergarment. What do you sleep in?"

"My dress."

She shook her head again in amazement and took out of the chest a length of linen, which I'm sure she'd brought with her to make articles of clothing for herself and her husband. I suspected I would soon have a shift. Remember had one of our mother's and had hemmed up a great length of it and wore it with the sleeves hanging long.

ഇ ഇ

I recall my first night with the Bradfords very clearly. I had seen Nathaniel Morton and Thomas Cushman, the two boys who lived with the Bradfords, around our village but had never spoken to them. Nathaniel was my age. I learned his family had come on the *Anne*, and after his father died, the governor had taken him on as a son. A serious and sturdy boy with light hair that flopped in his face, he was tall enough at eight years old to help in the fields. I soon learned Nathaniel had a mischievous side and he often played pranks and jokes on his friends, encouraging my participation.

Thomas was the now seventeen-year-old son of Richard Cushman, who had come on the *Fortune*. He had remained in the care of our governor when his father left, since Master Cushman intended to return in a year or two.

The governor viewed both boys with affection, not only because they were the sons of close friends, but also because his own son John was still in England.

That night, Thomas appeared late for the meal, hurrying into the room and sitting down, the food already on the table and the Bradfords seated. Nathaniel stood beside me. Thomas looked at me with a squint, clearly wondering where I'd come from, then looked down in his lap, unwilling to meet the eyes of the governor.

"Thomas, why are you late?" asked Master Bradford.

"I, uh, I stopped to talk to some friends on my way in from the fields, sir." His voice broke and squeaked and his face immediately flushed.

"You have made us wait on you for prayers and the meal. That is disrespectful, so tomorrow, in addition to your regular work, you will milk the goat."

Thomas clearly didn't like that job because he grimaced, but he said, respectfully enough, "Yes, sir. I beg your forbearance and please accept my apology."

"Don't let it happen again. We will pray for you this night." And with that, Bradford launched into a long prayer of thanks and of how God might consider disrespect. When he had finished, he said, "Thomas, this is Mary Allerton. She has come to live with us and be a helpmeet for Mistress Bradford. Mary, this is Thomas Cushman, late of London, who is living with us for now."

I gave him a bold look, such as a child will do, noting as I did a gangly lad, with dark, shoulder length hair and the wisps of a hair on his chin, which was dotted with small pustules.

Under my gaze, he reddened again and turned to his food.

I saw little of him thereafter, except at meals, but observed him in the settlement, enjoying his little free time with his friends.

ꕤ ꕤ

Over the next several weeks, Mistress Bradford measured, cut and sewed until I had appropriate clothing. I sat with her outside the house while she sewed, and she showed me how to make different stiches on a small piece of cloth. My stitches were at first of different sizes and crooked, but her patience never faltered as she had me take them out and do them again. By the time my shift had been made and the bodice and skirt altered to my size, she had me make and hem an apron and pronounced my work acceptable. She introduced me to the stays I would eventually have to wear over my shift. I remembered my mother wearing them but never imagined I would have to.

'Why do women have to wear stays?" I asked Mistress Bradford. "They look binding and uncomfortable."

"It is, child, and to say truth, I don't often wear mine."

I examined what she laid before me and saw a rigid piece of clothing with rows of heavy stitching and no sleeves and with straps which fitted over the shoulders. "What does this do?"

"It supports and shapes your body, to help you fit your clothes. Sometimes there are reeds sewn into the cloth for stiffness and some have a flat piece of wood we call a busk in the center front. Most uncomfortable. We will eventually make you one and show you how to wear it."

When I received a gift of my own stays, I hated the confinement and, imitating Mistress Bradford, found any excuse not to wear them. There were still wool petticoats to add to my clothing, but for the first time in two years, I had stockings and leather shoes that fit. Mistress Bradford knit the stockings and taught me how to knit, and Governor Bradford somehow found me the shoes. In my new clothes I felt like a proper girl and took to my tasks with enthusiasm, if not joy.

I had much to learn in the Bradford house and my days were filled with so many chores I scarcely had time to play. Mistress

Bradford seemed to enjoy teaching me how to do my work properly, saying she'd never had a daughter. She didn't spare the rod when I transgressed, but she more often than not laughed at my missteps.

I saw my father from time to time, but he didn't stop to talk with me other than to remind me to be respectful and obedient. At first, I found his decision to put me with the Bradfords hurtful, but gradually, as I grew in skills and knowledge, I came to see the wisdom in his decision. Moreover, I was no longer lonely nor overlooked, since I was in the constant presence of Mistress Bradford.

ꟸ ꟸ

Mornings began when the sun rose and Mistress Bradford called to me where I slept on the floor. "Mary, time to get up and get dressed. Hurry child, and don't forget to tie your coif in the back, so the ties don't catch on fire like yesterday."

I struggled donning all my layers over my shift—how simple it was when I lived with Remember and Father and slept in my dress—and then shook my corn-husk filled bedding and rolled it into a corner. Despite my tired state each night, I couldn't help but notice my bedding often had a freshly washed cover with a new, sweet-smelling fill.

By the time I was dressed, Mistress Bradford was usually at the hearth, beginning to make the midday meal, usually samp or a pottage. Slices of corn bread were already in a frying pan on the coals of the fire banked the night before.

Samp was one of the first things I learned to make, from the corn leavings after grinding corn for flour. To the leavings I added water and then boiled the mixture down to a thick, pudding-like texture. If there were berries, we would use them to sweeten it, our supply of sugar being small.

"Tend the fire, Mary, while I put our meal on the table. Did you know I'm unaccustomed to cooking over an open fire?"

"You are? Why, mistress?"

"In England, we cooked over coals or perhaps peat. I'll admit to you privately that here I have scorched a goodly number of my husband's meals."

I felt proud that she would confide any of her shortcoming to me and went outside quickly to bring in kindling. Adding this to the banked coals, I roused the fire from its overnight slumber, then added split logs of oak, turning them with long iron tongs as they caught. While the samp slowly bubbled in an iron kettle over the fire, I put wooden platters, spoons and napkins on the table, along with the fried slices of cornbread and smoked meat left from the previous night's meal. We might have jam, if there were berries. Without cows, there was no butter, although goat's milk made a reasonable cheese. The food in the Bradford household differed little from that in all the other homes in the village.

Next, I took a bucket to get fresh water to drink, and the household had assembled for breakfast by the time I returned. The Bradfords sat at the table where they were joined by Nathaniel Morton and Thomas Cushman. After prayers, I distributed the fried corn bread, and everyone helped themselves to the meat and any preserves we had. Nathaniel and I stood during our meals, the custom for children, and one which I had rarely followed in my father's house.

After breakfast I helped to clear the table and wash the plates, then fed the chickens some corn and collected eggs from the hen house. The Bradfords kept their chickens in a pen in the yard, unlike the brood running freely in the village. I noticed more and more of the villagers shutting in their chickens. I missed digging for worms to feed the hens, but I was a proper girl now.

The governor had purchased a goat, which lived in a fenced area within the large yard behind the house. Mistress Bradford told me the fencing kept the goat from eating everything in her garden and warned me to always make sure the door to its pen was closed. Milking that goat became one of the first tasks I had to learn.

The governor's wife had a twinkle in her eye when she told me to follow her to the goat pen. She carried a bucket and asked me to bring the stool sitting beside the back door. Once inside the pen, she tied the goat to a post and gave it a handful of corn from her pocket to keep it occupied. Then she sat on the stool, placing the pail underneath the goat.

"Watch what I do, Mary," she said as she bent over. I noticed this was difficult for her because of her growing belly, and she frequently straightened up and rubbed her back.

Soapy water filled the bucket, and Mistress Bradford told me, "Before you can milk her, you need to wash her udder and her teats to get rid of the dirt. Here is her udder and these are her teats. The udder contains her milk. Wash your hands when you wash her. If you fail to do this, the udder and the teats will become hot and red and pus will flow out." She gave me a stern look. "Never forget to wash the goat and your hands."

Once I had done the washing, I took the bucket and emptied it in the garden and rinsed it with clean water before returning to the goat's pen. "Here," I said, handing her the bucket. "Is it clean enough?"

Mistress Bradford inspected it and gave me a nod, placing the bucket under the goat's udder again. "Watch carefully," she said, and she squeezed one of the teats. Milk came out in a steady stream. After a few minutes, she got up. "Now you try."

I did try, but it took some time before I could get the milk to flow, and then it went all over me and even on Mistress Bradford's feet. I expected a fast slap for that, but she only laughed.

On the way back to the house, she told me, "Soon you will need to be able to do this on your own. The goat must be milked morning and evening, and this baby grows big," she paused to pat her belly, "so soon I will be unable to do it. You came to us just in time, Mary, and you will be a good helpmeet for me."

I felt myself beaming. No one had ever called me helpful or made me feel of use before. When the goat got used to my touch and voice, she became a new friend and so much nicer than the chickens.

ꕤ ꕤ

During the next few weeks, I showed Mistress Bradford I knew how to weed and water the garden, which earned me a smile. But instead of using ashes from the hearth on the soil, she told me to muck the plants with goat manure to make the garden soil rich for planting and growth. That meant collecting the goat manure with a wooden spade and working it into the ground. I didn't enjoy that at first, and Mistress Bradford found me walking around and drawing with a stick on the ground instead of mucking.

"Why do you dawdle so, child?" she asked.

"Because I hate mucking," I said without thinking. For that, I got the rod plus a stern lecture and more prayers from the governor that night.

Of the many things I needed to learn, guarding my tongue was the hardest. I often thought Mistress Bradford would send me away for my speaking out of turn, but she just clucked, and I would be thrashed. I hated this more than when my father did it, because disappointing her was worse than the thrashing.

Cooking became one of the things I most liked learning. I had never been particularly interested in what I ate, only that when I was hungry, I needed food to quell the pangs in my empty stomach. I learned to make many foods with Mistress Bradford's instructions—samp of course, but also corn bread, various meat and fish pottages and stews, jams from fruit I gathered that summer, roast fowl, boiled fish, cooked pumpkin, mashed turnips, and an onion sop—onions boiled in chicken broth with garlic. She also began tutoring me in the use of herbs and spices.

In the evenings, Governor Bradford would read to us from the Bible and we would pray together. Afterward the governor would tutor Nathaniel, Thomas and me in numbers and reading. I took pride in being able to read a little and count to numbers higher than ten. Before long, I could read short passages from the Bible. The Bradfords owned chalk, and they taught me how to hold it and write my name. Mistress Bradford even taught me to do simple sums.

ꙮ ꙮ

My teeth had begun to fall out again when I still lived with my father, and when the first one had come out of my mouth, I had run crying to Priscilla Mullins, who was in the garden with Remember, teaching her about tending the vegetables. "Priscilla, I've lost a tooth. I must have the disease from the *Mayflower* when everyone's teeth got loose and came out. Soon I'll have no teeth!"

"Then you can be an old toothless hag, Mary," said Remember.

"Remember!" Priscilla turned on her. "That's a cruel thing to say. Mind your tongue or I'll tell your father."

I had to smile. Remember rarely got the rod.

"Mary, hush your crying. You're only losing your first teeth. All children get new teeth about your age. You're perfectly healthy."

"Really?"

"God's truth, child."

The last of my first teeth fell out during those early days with the Bradfords. When Mistress Bradford found I had lost the tooth, she told me, "You must clean the ones you have now, Mary, because you'll get no more."

"How do I do that?"

"I'll show you tonight," she said smiling.

That is how I learned to rub charcoal on my teeth, and then use the frayed end of a birch twig to scrub them, rinsing well with water so I didn't have a blackened mouth. She also showed me how to scrub my teeth with a wet cloth and salt. I retained many of my teeth for a long time, thanks to those instructions from Alice Bradford.

ꙮ ꙮ

Mistress Bradford had her baby in early June of 1624. When her labor began, I'd just returned from milking the goat and found her bent over and panting near the hearth, unfinished cornbread in a bowl on the table.

"Mary, it's time. Please run down the street and fetch Mistress Fuller," she said, between grimaces from the pain.

Bridget Fuller was the wife of our physick Samuel Fuller and, as Plymouth's first midwife, she gave a measure of relief to expecting women. I arrived back from her house in a matter of minutes, carrying an odd-looking stool with a seat like a horseshoe. "She will be here soon," I gasped out.

"Put that near the hearth, will you, Mary? And take the old linen sheet from my chest, double it over and put it on our mattress." By now, my mistress was walking slowly around the room, stopping whenever a pain hit her. I started crying in fear for her, and she said with great insight, "Mary, you mustn't cry. This is a natural thing, to give birth. I know your mother nearly died with the delivery of her last child, but I have done this twice before." She smiled. "I think I'm now an expert."

Nevertheless, I stood there, clutching my hands together and not knowing what to do until Mistress Fuller arrived. Bridget Fuller, a short, round, pink-faced woman, immediately rolled up the sleeves of her bodice and donned an old but clean apron. She carried a large bowl along with a burlap sack containing various things that bulged through its sides.

"There, there, mistress, this should be an easy birth. You've had two babes before without difficulty. Mary—Mary isn't it?—put some water in a pot on the coals to heat, then get me some clean rags."

I did as I was told.

"Now get me a bucket of clean water and some soap."

"Yes, ma'am." I ran to the brook for water and brought the bucket and soap back to the hearth. Mistress Fuller had laid out a small blanket on top of the chest and emptied the contents of her sack—some instruments, for what I didn't know.

"Thank you, child. You're old enough to learn the way of things, but for now, you can stand aside and wait until you're needed."

I stood there with my mouth hanging open. I knew nothing of birthing a child, except my memory of groaning and shrieks of pain.

"Has your water come yet, Alice?"

"Yes, early this morning."

Water? What water?

"Does the governor know you're laboring?"

"He does, and he, Nathaniel and Thomas will take their midday meal with Master Allerton."

"Mary," Mistress Bradford addressed me between her pains, "please fetch my gossip."

I knew that a gossip was the women, usually friends, who attended a childbirth. In this case, they were Mistress Warren and Mistress Alden. Elizabeth Warren had five daughters and would soon have another babe herself. Priscilla Alden had recently given birth.

I ran, glad to be away from the house, and breathlessly fetched both women. Once they had joined the midwife, they chatted amongst themselves about childbirth and accompanied Mistress Bradford as she walked around the yard and in and out of the house. From time to time, she lay down to rest. Mistress Fuller occasionally put her hands on my mistress's belly and twice made her sit on the stool while she examined her from beneath.

I finished the corn bread and placed it in the outside oven, swept the floor, went for more water, and began to make a stew of salted fish for the evening meal. Finally, after a particularly loud grown from Mistress Bradford, the midwife sat her again on the stool. At that point, I could see Mistress Bradford was in good hands and willingly focused my attention on the evening meal, bringing in the corn bread from the oven and cutting carrots and turnips from the garden to add to the stew.

Governor Bradford knocked on the door once during the early afternoon to inquire about his wife but didn't come in. Mistress Warren had a brief word with him and sent him away.

I spent the afternoon in and out of the house, doing the things I would ordinarily do: finishing the evening meal—although it seemed unlikely anyone would be there to eat it—milking the goat again, mending some clothes, then sitting outside while I made a new broom from twigs I had gathered. The moans and grunts coming from Mistress Bradford and the low and soothing words of the woman often distracted me from my work. Finally, in the early evening, I heard a loud shriek and Mistress Fuller say loudly, "It's a boy!" followed by the oohs and aahs of Mistresses Alden and Warren.

After a while, all was quiet, and Mistress Fuller came out and told me I could see the baby. My mistress was sitting up in the bed, cradling a small, red-faced mite of life in her arms. She smiled at me. "Mary, come see our son. His name is William."

As I approached, the governor ran into the room, stopping short at the bottom of the bed. "God's grace, Alice. Are you and the baby well?"

"Yes, William, and it's a boy, named for his father as we decided."

He fell to his knees in prayer and I joined him, happy at the day's outcome and considering for the first time that God may have had a hand in all of it.

Chapter 18

New Colonies and Their Relationships with Plymouth

Isaac Allerton, Plymouth Colony, 1625

I would be telling a falsehood if I didn't acknowledge I missed Mary after she moved to the Bradford home. Of my three children, she brought light to the darkness of those first years of our colony with her happy disposition. The only problem was her lack of self-discipline.

Mary had lived much in her imagination and, when not tasked with some chore, had wandered around quite freely, much as she had done below deck on the *Mayflower*. When I could, I'd continued talking with the children after our evening prayers, telling them of the happenings in the settlement. Remember had little interest, Bartholomew some, but Mary had always asked questions and interrupted when she didn't understand. I often regretted I spent so little time with my daughters, but then they were girls and didn't need to be schooled.

Remember, two years older than Mary, had become a solemn child of whom we asked much. Without her mother and only five adult women in the colony to teach her—before the arrival of the

Anne—the running of my household rested heavily on her shoulders. She'd had to learn a great deal with few to help her and few in whom to confide. I gave thanks to God for Priscilla Mullins' care of both my daughters.

Remember hadn't had a kindly relationship with her sister, viewing her as one more chore to be managed. I had many times admonished both to love one another as God would wish. Remember had become sullen and snappish when she discovered the new clothes Mary had received from Mistress Bradford, so I sent an order on the next ship returning to England for clothes for both her and Bartholomew, which Remember could alter to fit.

Bartholomew continued to spend his days with me, learning how to work the fields, to hunt, and to gather shellfish or eels. I spent what time I had instructing him in his expected role in our settlement, but I was often absent on some task or other for the governor. I hoped he would eventually become one of our colony's leaders, but Bartholomew had an abiding interest in England. Being my oldest, he had the most memories, and he asked many questions about where in England we had come from, the reasons for our division from the Church of England, and the manner of business in cities like Leiden and London. Although he seemed content with his lot, I wondered if he would remain with us here.

Mary, of course, now lived at the edge of my life. I saw her on those days when I had business with Governor Bradford, but her chores left her little more than a moment or two to talk with me. On one of those days, when Mistress Bradford welcomed me in to see her husband, I took the opportunity to ask her of Mary's comportment and progress.

"Oh, Master Allerton, she is such an intelligent child. She enjoys being taught, but she is stubborn and often not respectful." Because a smile played at the corners of her mouth, I thought this wasn't an issue that would lead to Mary's dismissal.

"I hope you haven't spared the rod."

"No, indeed, my husband and I have both used it from time to time. Without much effect." Another smile. "But she does make progress."

"Has she shown you she knows her letters and numbers?"

"She has, and we are impressed that she learns so quickly. We continue to teach her in the evenings, and she is now reading from the Bible. You would be proud of her accomplishment in this area."

"I must thank you for your generosity toward my daughter. I hope she will be of good help to you."

Alice Bradford placed her hand on her hips and replied, "She already is. I don't know how I could accomplish all that I must each day without her." With that, she motioned me to where the governor sat at the table and with a swish of her skirts, returned to the hearth.

Bradford wished to talk to me about our relations with the colony at Cape Ann. Edward Winslow already sat at the table, present that day to give us information based on a patent he had brought back from England. While there, he'd secured permission for a fishing center at Cape Ann from a member of the Council of New England. We had dearly hoped for this, since we wished to fish, hunt, and trade in that region.

"I fear Lord Sheffield has only the vaguest idea of the vastness of this land and doesn't understand that our colony encompasses so much land to the north," he told us. "Sheffield thinks this fishing center is nearby and easy for us to settle and oversee. I just returned from a journey to Cape Ann, Master Allerton, to see how we might establish a good site for fishing there. The drying racks we had built in anticipation of this patent were still there, but I was surprised to find a fishing center already in place."

"Who lives there? Who sent them?" I asked.

"A small group of fishermen, who identified themselves as the Dorchester Company, were sent by Reverend John White, a Puritan. These men had been fishing those waters for some years but without a base on land. I spoke with their overseer and told them of our legal patent, and, for the now, they're willing to share the site."

I then expressed hope that our relations with this group would continue to be peaceful, benefiting both of us, and that the fish we caught there could be sent to England to pay some of our debt. As the person who managed the financial records of our settlement, I knew that the Merchant Adventurers had initially invested somewhere between 1200 and 1600 pounds in the colony before the *Mayflower* sailed. We were obligated to repay this investment by 1627 with fish, fur, timber, and such food as we could spare. The Indians had taught some of us how to whale and rend the blubber for oil, which was much sought after. We hoped this could be another source of income, but we had made little progress in reducing what we owed, and Governor Bradford despaired of clearing our debt.

ꙮ ꙮ

Our sole pastor during our years in Leiden, John Robinson, had been the backbone of our church, and under his leadership, our congregation had grown steadily. Even though the Merchant Adventurers had refused to pay for him and the Separatists still living in Leiden to come here, Robinson continued to provide us with moral support and guidance through his frequent letters. Thus when Governor Bradford received a letter early in the spring of 1625 telling of Robinson's death, we all felt our loss profoundly, none more so than our governor.

Our community gathered in sorrow at the fort on the evening the news arrived. When all were settled and the children had calmed, Elder Brewster led us in prayer for the soul of our pastor. Then Bradford rose from his seat at the front, looking as if he bore a huge, unseen weight.

"I would like to read to you part of a letter sent to us several years ago from Pastor Robinson. This letter shows the depth of his love for God, for us, and his concern for our future. I think it's a fitting tribute.

"'Much beloved brethren, the distance between us cannot dissolve or weaken that bond of true Christian affection by which the Lord hath

tied us together. My continual prayers are to the Lord for you. I exhort you to obey those whom God has chosen to govern you, both in church and commonwealth. God forbid I should need to remind you to always follow peace, by which all good is tied together. May the God of peace and grace and all goodness be with you, now and forever.'"

With that, Bradford sat, and I could see tears coursing down the cheeks of many of our congregation, mine among them. I had a sense of emptiness when I thought of our congregation without his guidance, even from afar.

ꕤ ꕤ

Unfortunately, the peace exhorted by Pastor Robinson didn't endure in our relations with the Dorchester Company, largely due to the men who had joined that group. Amongst them was John Conant, a Puritan who had come to Plymouth on the *Anne*. He had left our settlement, along with Reverend John Lyford, and relocated to Cape Ann. We therefore anticipated trouble in our arrangement with the fishermen there. Myles Standish persuaded our governor to allow him to visit Cape Ann, to determine what had happened to our fishing stage, and to regain it, if it had been seized by the men of the Dorchester Company.

Standish's natural bellicosity and predilection for violence worried us all until he returned and gave his report to the Council.

"When we arrived there, we found that indeed the fishermen had taken over what we had built for drying and salting the fish. I demanded its return. Roger Conant, whom I'm sure you'll remember, appears to be the governor of this place. After I threatened violence if they did not return what was ours, Conant arranged for them to build us a new staging, stating that he had no wish for hostility, despite his religious differences. I'm sure he did this because there is already amongst them insubordination and anger over the lack of profits from their venture, and he didn't want more trouble."

All of us, but our governor in particular, worried that John Robinson's concerns after Standish's actions at Wessagusset, followed by the expulsion of Lyford and now the confrontation with the Dorchester Company, had given us the reputation of a colony of fanatics—soiling the image of peaceful comity Bradford tried so hard to create. As we had predicted, the Dorchester colony proved unable to sustain itself, and its men returned to England, leaving us the rebuilt fish staging. The restoration of our good reputation proved more difficult to repair.

ꙮ ꙮ

In 1625, another settlement began some distance to our north, named Mount Wollaston. Thomas Morton and a Captain Wollaston, along with a substantial number of indentured young men, had founded it as a Puritan colony. Unfortunately, we soon learned that Morton and Wollaston traded guns and liquor to the natives in exchange for furs and provisions, a practice which was not only illegal but which threatened the security of our own colony.

On the day the Council met to discuss this issue, Bradford banged his fist on the table to emphasize his anger. "Guns and liquor! This is completely illegal. I cannot tolerate it! What more can Morton and his men do to provide the Indians with a better means of attacking us?"

"You could send a small party to intercede with Morton and the natives," suggested Edward Winslow.

I heard several emphatic "no's" from those assembled. "Respectfully, Master Winslow," I replied, "Captain Standish's tendency for force has already damaged our reputation, and even if our delegation were non-military, I fear we would be met with discourtesy."

Bradford remained quiet for some moments, calming as he usually did after an outburst. "Perhaps it would be better if I wrote to Morton to indicate the danger in which he puts us all with his trading," he finally said. As usual, he sought the way of moderation.

He was sadly disappointed when Morton wrote back that he much preferred the civilized and humane culture of the Algonquians to the intolerance of his European neighbors. Bradford didn't accept this insult with good grace, and his contempt of Morton and the activities at Mount Wollaston grew. He often said it was only by God's grace that the Algonquians never attacked us.

꧁ ꧂

The Bradfords invited my family to share a mid-day meal with them not long after the letter arrived from Mount Wollaston. I believe Mistress Bradford wished Mary to have some time with her family to show how she had progressed in her comportment, respectfulness and piety.

We had all dressed in clean clothes, with Remember's new from London. Bartholomew bore a basket of wild blueberries he had gathered that day in the woods. When we arrived, Mary ushered us in, looking very much the proper nine-year-old in her skirt, bodice, jacket and coif.

"How good to see you, Father!" She smiled at me and then hugged Remember, who for once didn't pull away, and Bartholomew, who blushed. She led us to the table, where we greeted the governor and Mistress Bradford, who stood holding baby William in her arms. I already knew the two boys, Thomas Cushman and Nathaniel Morton. Remember blushed when Thomas greeted her. Nathaniel dug his elbow into Bartholomew's ribs in play, for they were often up to mischief together.

"Let us pray in thanks for this day and this food," said the governor, and, after his wife had placed the baby in his cradle, we all knelt in prayer. It proved long, and my aging knees protested before he finished, so it was with a sigh of relief that I rose after we said, "Amen."

"Please be seated," Mistress Bradford told us.

I saw there were chairs for the adults and a stool for Thomas, while Bartholomew, Remember, Nathaniel and Mary would stand.

"Mary, could you help me bring our meal to the table?" Mistress Bradford went to the hearth and returned with a bowl of what smelled like a vegetable pottage. Mary followed with a plate of cornbread, then a bowl of boiled onions and a green salad. When her mistress sat, Mary brought a platter of roast venison with drippings and then some preserves.

"My husband and the boys were fortunate to fell a deer yesterday, and Mary helped me roast a portion," Mistress Bradford said. "She's also learned how to make fruit preserves."

Mary looked very pleased with herself as she stood at her place. I couldn't believe this was the same belligerent and willful child I had left here just over a year before. After she served us and we ate, I noticed she used the napkin she had placed over her left shoulder and ate daintily with her fingers, a spoon, and a small knife to spear the meat.

When we had finished, Mary hastened to the hearth and returned with a true treat: fermenty. I was surprised to see this, since its basis was usually cracked wheat, of which we had none. I noticed Mistress Bradford smiling at my amazement.

"We altered the recipe, Master Allerton, to suit our circumstances," she said, rocking little William's cradle with her foot. "Instead of wheat we used cracked corn and for now, goat's milk, along with our abundance of eggs. Mary takes good care of our chickens."

Mary apportioned the fermenty to each of us, and I delighted in the flavor of cinnamon, such a precious commodity, and in the sweetness of the berries. Remember's and Bartholomew's faces lit up seeing the treat, and Nathanial jiggled in place with anticipation, until warned by the governor to stop. Needless to say, this treat did not last long.

Thomas remained silent for most of the meal, eating as if he had not had food in days, all the while stealing looks at each of us. He was a comely lad, and it did cross my mind that he might make a good husband for my oldest girl.

Just as we finished our meal, the baby started to fuss, and Mistress Bradford stood and asked forgiveness, so she could nurse him. She went to the bed in the corner, asking, "Mary, can you clean away everything?"

The children were permitted to go outside, and Mary joined them when she had finished her chores. Thomas, now a young man, left to join some friends. The governor and I remained sitting. "Would you care for some beer?" he asked. When my forehead rose in surprise, he chuckled. "Not the beer we have enjoyed in England or Leiden," he said, "although we'll have a good crop of hops before the end of the growing season. This is made with corn and sassafras. There's so much wild sassafras here that I've decided to export some to London. It's in such demand there that we may be able to reduce our debt with its sale."

He went outside to the back of the house and soon returned with two wooden cups containing a brown liquid. I sniffed it. "It has an interesting smell."

"My good wife made it with fermented corn and the roots of the sassafras tree, boiled together in a pot with water, to which she added a little cinnamon. It keeps well. What do you think?"

I cautiously took a sip and found the drink much to my liking. "I'll send Remember to your wife to learn how to make this. My friend, I'm pleased with Mary's progress and offer my deepest thanks to you and your wife for raising her in godly ways. I hope she's of help to you."

The governor leaned back and smiled. "It's God's blessing she came to us when she did. She had been a good helpmeet for my wife, and I hope we may have her with us for some time to come."

I nodded in agreement, because I knew Mary lived in the best of places for her future.

Chapter 19

The Colony's Debt Remains

Mary Allerton, Plymouth Colony, 1625

Thomas Cushman had been looking forward to his father's return to Plymouth, since Elder Cushman had written he would be a passenger on the next ship to the colony. While Thomas didn't speak much at our evening meals, when he did, he talked of seeing his father again, what he would show him, where they might live.

On an evening, soon after the news of Pastor Robinson's death, the governor and Thomas sat facing each other at the table, with the golden light of a summer's late afternoon coming from the door and window. I had poured them mugs of the corn beer, as they were relaxing after a day in the fields, then I'd withdrawn to the hearth.

After some silence, Bradford leaned forward and placed his hand on Thomas' arm. "Thomas, we've received some sad news. Your relatives have written me that your father has died. I know not the cause, but it happened during his visit to them before embarking on his voyage here. He is buried in St. George's Churchyard in Kent."

Since Mistress Bradford and I were both preparing the evening meal, we couldn't help but overhear. My mistress walked to Thomas' side and placed her hand on his shoulder, as he sat silently, his eyes glistening with unshed tears.

Bradford continued, "I know your grief is profound. Let us pray for your father's soul. Perhaps that will provide you some comfort." Thomas sat as stone for several minutes, then brushed his eyes with the sleeve of his shirt and stood. Grim-faced, he sank to his knees. Mistress Bradford and I joined them, as the governor prayed to the Almighty for Robert Cushman to find eternal rest in the arms of our Lord.

After we stood from our prayers, Thomas left the house. He returned long after dark, when Nathaniel and the Bradfords were already abed. Little William cooed contently in his cradle, his stomach full. I had begun to unroll my mattress when I heard the door open softly and close just as quietly. When I saw Thomas take a seat on a stool near the fire, I went to the hearth.

"There's food for you in the bowl here, if you're hungry," I whispered.

"Thank you." Thomas picked up the bowl.

I sat on another stool and regarded him carefully. His eyes were red, but he seemed composed. "I can stay here while you eat, if you wish. I hope the food is still warm."

He just nodded, making no objections to my presence as he ate.

"I'm sorry about your father. When I lost my mother, I felt such sorrow and emptiness. I don't know if it's the same or different for a father."

Thomas raised his eyes from the food and stared at me. "You're but a child. How would you know?"

With his words, the vision of my mother on her last day came to me, and my eyes filled with tears.

"I beg pardon, Mary. I can see my words were hurtful."

"No, not your words. The thought of my mother as she was dying."

"The governor told me about the sickness of the first winter and how many people died. Your mother was amongst them?"

"Yes, below deck on the *Mayflower*. A more foul and disease-ridden place you cannot imagine. Death lived there. So I think I know a little of the pain of losing a parent."

Thomas thought for a moment, then said, "Thank you for your sympathy, Mary. Forgive me for lashing out in my sorrow. Perhaps our pain is the same."

"Of course, you're forgiven," I said, standing and taking his now-empty bowl. "You're in anguish. I will bid you good night and leave you to your thoughts."

After that night, Thomas and I spoke more frequently, and I indeed now felt like his younger sister. He spent one evening showing me how to tie knots, something he had learned on his voyage from England, and he told me of his life there. I, in turn, showed him where to find sassafras trees and wild blueberries. If he was not working in the fields, he would help me milk the goat, whom we named Old Obstinate because of the difficulty in catching her and tying her up.

Isaac Allerton, Plymouth, Autumn 1625-1626

Without Robert Cushman to work on our behalf, Bradford had to name another as an agent to represent our interests with the Merchant Adventurers, a difficult task. He finally decided to send Captain Standish in the hopes his obstinate temperament might prove useful. As the governor often told me as we worked over the colony's finances, he was continually stressed by the burden of what we owed. He hoped and prayed Standish would be able to renegotiate the debt.

Standish returned in April and, to the governor's great frustration, told us he had not been able to accomplish a great deal. There had been a terrible outbreak of plague in London the previous summer, lasting into the fall, and little business had been done. The Merchants were of no mind to negotiate.

We reaped an abundant harvest the following autumn, so Edward Winslow traveled north to the Kennebec River with corn to trade, returning with a large number of beaver pelts. On the same trip, Winslow had also established a trading post with the Massachusetts Indians at Cape Ann, so our trading businesses expanded and with it our hopes of paying off the debt. Based on the abundance of our trade goods, the Council named a different representative to travel to London with the new shipment, to make another attempt at negotiations with the Merchants. This time the Council chose me.

Mary Allerton, Plymouth Colony, 1627

It seemed strange to me not to have my father close by. Remember would occasionally visit me on some pretext or another. She worked hard and I think she came by in order to rest from her chores for a while. Mistress Bradford didn't mind the time we spent together and often remarked how nice it would be if she had a sister.

At the end of a late spring day, when the world sprouted bright green with promise and the birds were noisily mating, Remember and I were outside, talking. We had both come from planting the fields and she had followed me back to the Bradfords, where we'd washed the soil from our hands and faces and had sat down for a rest on the edging of one of the herb beds. "How are you, sister?" I asked. "You appear more than usually tired." Indeed, she looked very thin and I noticed her rough and worn hands, with broken and dirty nails.

"I am, Mary." She took my hand. "I have no time to spend with friends because of my chores. And Father hasn't thought to provide help for me."

I took her hand, unhappy at her obvious distress. "Perhaps Mistress Bradford can spare me from time to time to help you. How is Bartholomew? Does he work well with Master Godbertson in Father's absence?"

"Yes, and I thank God each night there is no friction between them. But Bartholomew's mind often wanders to thoughts of England. He speaks of Father daily and wonders what news he will bring from London. His eyes shine when he talks of that city."

Mistress Bradford interrupted us when she came outside, carrying William. "Remember, let me give you some herbs to take home. I noticed your garden does not have as many as mine." She smiled at both of us, and I think she had a good idea of the difficulty of Remember's daily life. My sister left, promising to join the Bradfords soon for an evening meal and to bring Bartholomew. Mistress Bradford recognized Remember needed companionship, and my sister's eyes lit up at the thought of a meal she didn't have to prepare.

ꙮ ꙮ

Since the death of his father, Thomas had grown closer to the governor and frequently had long conversations with him in the evening. I could see sadness in the governor's face after these conversations, perhaps because Thomas stirred thoughts of his son John, who had been left behind in England.

The governor delighted in little William, who no longer needed the support of a walking chair, but staggered unsteadily here and there. He had to be watched constantly lest he fall into the fire, and his father took on the chore of minding his son in his little free time. Bradford would dandle him on his knees, listening to William giggle, and then his usual solemnity would fall away.

I loved being in the Bradford home. Although I toiled from sunup to sundown, I lived at the heart of the colony and was privy to many discussions of the colony's business. Bradford on occasion would talk with his wife about Council issues, although because she was a woman, I'm not sure he valued any of her opinions. Nevertheless, I believe she knew more of the colony's workings than did her husband.

Isaac Allerton, Plymouth Colony, 1627

I sailed for home early in 1627 with good news and feeling some satisfaction with my accomplishments. With input from four Separatists living in London, I had drawn up a new contract that the Merchants had accepted. These Separatists, together with Bradford and as many others of the Council who could be persuaded to participate, would assume the debt of the colony, a sum in the amount of 1800 pounds. In this way, we were finally free of the misguided oversight of the London merchants, as well as the high rate of interest on that initial loan. I also used the time in London to secure us further supplies. All this I told to the Council who gathered in our meeting house upon my return

Bradford spoke first. "You worked a good conclusion to our difficulties with the Merchants, Master Allerton. What are the details of our payment?

"The debt will be paid off in nine annual payments of 200 pounds. James Shirley, John Beachamp, Richard Andrews and Timothy Hatherley, all of London and with whom some of you are acquainted, have already agreed to assume some of this debt. I count myself with them. I'm hopeful more will join us, which will lessen what each man owes."

Bradford, Standish, Winslow, John Howland, and Thomas Prence stood forth, and with that agreement, the Council decided to send me back to England on the next ship, with power to conclude the contract. I brought with me beaver skins to pay part of our debt and to defray my costs. I also received authorization to procure a patent for a trading place on the Kennebec River.

One cool evening soon thereafter, with the town settled for the night and the soft smell of banked fires filling the air, I sat in front of Bradford's hearth after a meal with his family. Mary had clearly grown in both height and deportment while I had been gone. I thanked Mistress Bradford again for all her effort and goodwill.

"Oh, it's I who should thank you, Master Allerton. I could not manage without her now, and with another babe soon to join us, I'll need her even more."

I silently thanked God the Bradfords had allowed Mary to remain with them.

When the children and Mistress Bradford had retired for the evening, Bradford and I went outside and sat for a while, smoking our pipes with tobacco I had brought from London and speaking quietly together.

"While you were gone, Master Allerton, the Council and I authorized a second allotment of land. According to our decision, each man will retain the one acre originally given, but in this second division, each will receive twenty acres, five in breadth and four in length, with division by lot. These farms will spread north along the shore from Plymouth, and five acres of each allotment will front on water, so there is easy access to boats. I can take you tomorrow to see your land."

My surprise must have shown, because the governor smiled.

"This is a generous allotment, Governor, but with my travels, I'll have to pay men to work the land."

"I'm sure you will find some willing and able, perhaps together with your brother-in-law. I believe this decision will increase our harvest and bring in more corn and other produce to send to London, as well as to use in trade with the Indians."

"What about our jointly owned cows and goats?" I asked. "How will they be apportioned?"

"It's my plan to divide the cattle," Bradford replied. "When we have more than just the few, each man will have one cow and two goats, counting single men as part of a family. Pigs will be allotted according to the same rule. Eventually, with nature running its course, all families will have cows, swine and goats."

I felt Bradford's decision to be very fair. I was already considering how my return to London could earn me enough to pay workers for my fields and caretakers for my livestock, by selling my own trade goods separate from those of the colony.

"With that, I'll say good night," said the governor, standing, "but I implore you to relay to our friends in Leiden our desire they join us here. We would gratefully accept their partnership in this adventure. With the colony now stable, they shouldn't fear to come here, and they would certainly add to our able-bodied farmers."

As I walked across First Street to my home in the quiet darkness, I had much to think about. Another subject that had been on my mind recently was marriage. When I returned home from this next trip to England—how easily I now thought of our colony as home!—I would seek a wife. I had long missed Mary Norris and recognized my household needed the care of a goodwife. My sister

Sarah now had a home of her own, and Remember did her best to maintain mine, but she lacked daily supervision and help. There were several young women of marriageable age in the settlement, and I had already considered their suitability in terms of temperament and background. I finally decided on Fear Brewster, third daughter of Elder Brewster and now nineteen years of age. While in England, I would consider how to approach both her and her father.

Mary Allerton, Plymouth Colony 1627

With my father gone yet again to London, I found myself too busy to think much about his absence. For one thing, Mistress Bradford would soon give birth again, and helping with little William and the work of the household demanded all my time. My life with the Bradfords was easier but still not easy.

One day in May, I knew Mistress Bradford's labor had begun when she spent the afternoon walking around the garden, occasionally sitting or lying down. Without her asking, I took little William by the hand and walked down the hill to the Fuller home. Mistress Fuller returned with us immediately. I spent the long hours of Mistress Bradford's labor tending to little William. At two years of age, he had boundless energy and when I tired of running after him, I tied him to me or to some structure so I could work. If I didn't, his long shift would catch on everything, creating more holes and rents to mend, and he would run into things and cry loudly, disturbing his mother.

Mistress Bradford had a shorter labor this time, and before the middle of the night, she delivered a girl named Mercy. I could only hope Mercy would be less boisterous than little William.

Over the months, Nathanial Morton and I had become friends. When there was time, he would blow soap bubbles with me outside, using a hollow reed and soapy water, or toss small, round pebbles into a circle drawn in the dirt. Of Thomas Cushman, I saw little. With the division of land, he had received acreage in addition to the two acres he had first received, and he worked these along with the Bradford's land. Farming occupied all his time.

One evening, when the children were asleep—Mercy in her cradle and little William now in a trundle bed—Thomas returned late from the fields. When I heard him washing outside, I went to the hearth and placed what remained of our evening meal on a plate for him—grilled fish, corn bread, and a turnip mash.

The Bradfords sat at the table, Mistress Bradford mending and the governor writing yet another letter in his voluminous correspondence, their only light that of smoky tallow candles. Nathaniel sat beside the governor, his head drooping with tiredness. Thomas dropped onto a stool by the fire with a sigh. "I'm not sure I'm meant for this farming life," he whispered, as if conspiring with me.

"Why do you say that?" I handed him his food.

"I find the work unfulfilling. I don't mind that it's difficult, but it's endless and numbs the mind. I would like a job where I could use my learning. Thank you for the food," he added. After a brief inspection of what lay on the trencher, he ate hungrily.

I knew Thomas was intelligent. I had watched him at his frequent lessons with the Governor Bradford. He could read difficult texts and also write fluidly. I could also —Mistress Bradford, as one of the few women in the settlement who could read and write, had been teaching me for some time with the governor's permission.

"So what would you like to do?"

"I don't know," he replied between mouthfuls, "but I hope God will show me the way."

Thomas was very devout. He never missed an opportunity to pray with the Bradfords and frequently disclaimed against sin during our Sunday services. I often wondered if he might become an elder in the church. He never looked happier than when we heard the beat of the drum calling us to our meeting on Sunday.

Our congregation, drawn out of their homes by the sound, walked in a group to the door of Captain Standish, at the top of the street. From there, we marched three abreast to the fort, led by Elder Brewster on the right, the governor in the middle, and Standish with his side arm on the left. All the men carried their firearms.

I'll be honest in my recollections: although I'd been baptized, I felt little attraction for these church services, finding them long and boring. However, sitting next to the calm and devout Alice Bradford kept me from squirming most of the time. Holding little Mercy and trying to keep her quiet also helped. Mistress Bradford had a more difficult task, minding the wiggling William. Nathaniel usually sat on my other side, fidgeting. Mistress Bradford clucked softly at him from time to time. Occasionally I would look to the right at the men. It would be six years before Nathaniel could sit with them, but Thomas was already there and sometimes I caught his notice, eliciting a smile from his eyes.

My personal prayers were never uplifting. I only prayed that the service would end so I could begin my chores for the rest of the day. Work for girls and women didn't cease on Sunday.

ﻩ ﻩ

We were expecting the arrival from England of Mistress Bradford's two sons from her marriage to the late Edward Southworth. She had been disappointed when they were not on a previous ship, so when we saw a tall mast in the harbor, she didn't go down to the wharf lest she be discouraged again. Instead we were weeding in the garden, with young William alongside us, pulling up whatever his little hands could grasp. A noise at the gate made us rise.

I saw two gangly boys hesitantly open the gate and stop before entering. Mistress Bradford's face grew bright with joy. and she ran to the boys, saying, "My sons, my sons, how you have grown!"

Mistress Bradford's eyes glistened with tears when, after hugging the boys—to their apparent embarrassment—she turned to introduce us. "This is Constant Southworth, Mary. He is now twelve and will be of good help to my husband. And this is Thomas, two years younger. My sons, this is Mary Allerton, who lives with us as my helpmeet."

Constant was tall, thin and long-legged, with light, lanky hair and a long, narrow nose, down which he looked at me. Thomas was much shorter and wider than his brother but smiled when we were introduced. He had tied his long dark hair back from his face with string. Both boys shuffled their feet and said nothing, until my mistress asked them, "Where are your things?"

"Still at the dock," Thomas said in a high, piping voice, nudging his brother. "Constant thought we would have too far to walk with such heavy burdens."

"Well, you may now return and fetch them. Nathaniel!" she called to the house. "Come and meet my sons."

Nathaniel came to the doorway and slowly walked to the gate, where Mistress Bradford introduced them. I sensed some reluctance on his part with these new arrivals, but by the time the three boys had returned with Constant's and Thomas's bags, they were chattering away like the squirrels in the forest.

Nathaniel and Mistress Bradford's sons soon made a gang of three who were impish and fun-loving, which fretted both the Bradfords. For my part, I missed Nathaniel's company, as he now had boys of his own age in the household. Unfortunately, I became the frequent object of their pranks, such as hiding my shoes.

ഇ ഇ

At the end of the year, a group of visitors arrived in our settlement—three Nauset Indians along with two Englishmen. One of these men bore a letter for the governor. Mistress Bradford and I listened in fascination to the tale he told, sitting at our table while the Indians remained outside.

"I'm John Fells," one said, "and this is John Sibsey. Several months ago, we sailed on the ship *Sparrow Hawk* for Virginia, having a land grant to settle there. After a desperate crossing, our captain was laid low in his cabin with sickness and we lost our way. We were driven ashore some miles south of here. No one was injured and our goods are safe, albeit wet, but we didn't know where we were. We were approached by some Indians who spoke English, and they asked us if we were destined for the Plymouth colony, a name we recognized. They agreed to bring us here, along with a letter from the captain of the ship."

Bradford opened the letter and read its contents. He then told them he would need to call his Council to organize assistance. Soon after, the Council convened, crowding into the house. Bradford introduced the visitors and had them again recount their tale.

When they'd finished, the governor said, "Master Winslow, could you organize supplies for their crew and passengers and material needed to repair their ship? Are there any amongst you willing to go?"

Both John Alden and Captain Standish volunteered, and Master Alden proposed to find some other builders to join them. They set off in the shallop within a few hours, sailing south with some lumber, nails, oakum and corn. I overheard a little of the outcome when Master Alden returned with the others and reported to the governor that the *Sparrow Hawk* had been repaired and had set to sea with its cargo.

Unfortunately, our settlement's involvement with this ship didn't end there. Soon after the *Sparrow Hawk* sailed, a violent storm drove her onto the shore yet again, this time rendering her beyond repair. Both the crew, the passengers, and their Irish servants had to move to our settlement, and the governor agreed to feed and house them until such time as they could leave for Virginia. In return, they traded clothing, hosiery, shoes and cloth for their food, and come spring they were allotted some land to cultivate.

Among them were rowdy men, whose presence taxed our governor's patience with their drinking and revelry. But some proved competent at husbandry, and Bradford used some of the colony's trade goods to buy their crops before they were ready for harvest.

One day, when Mistress Bradford and I were sitting outside grinding corn, she told me John Fells had brought shame to the *Sparrow Hawk's* company.

"What did he do?" I asked, stopping for a moment.

"He got one of his maid servants with child and now has run away with her, I think looking to find passage to Virginia or elsewhere. I suspect he will return."

Indeed, a short time later both Fells and his servant returned. He slunk to our house and asked to meet with the governor. I was present when Fells abased himself and asked for forgiveness. Once he agreed to submit to Bradford's rule, he and the governor prayed. William Bradford never doubted God's forgiveness, and, in His name, he gave his as well.

Although ships sailing up and down the coast would often stop in Plymouth harbor, we waited some time for one that could take the *Sparrow Hawk's* passengers and crew to Virginia. Finally, at the end of summer and some nine months after the wreck of the *Sparrow Hawk*, two vessels heading down the coast took these people to their destination. We were all very glad to see them go, especially the governor, but we benefitted from the harvest of their fields.

Isaac Allerton, Plymouth Colony, 1627

When I returned from England, I was still firm in my decision to marry Mistress Brewster. I sought her out one Sunday after our services, finding her in the garden of her father's house.

When I approached, she asked, "Do you wish to see my father, Master Allerton?"

"No, it's you I've come to see."

She smiled, as if knowing my purpose.

We spoke for a few minutes before I returned home, and it became my habit to visit with her each Sunday. I found Fear comely, with light brown hair and sparkling eyes, very direct in her speech and solemn in her faith. My conversations with her only grew my attraction. Still, I was twenty years her senior and unsure my proposal would be accepted.

Finally, I felt it was time to ask. We sat together on a bench in her family's garden, and I was aware of her father tarrying nearby. After a moment of silence, I asked, "Mistress Brewster, I find your company most pleasant. As you're aware, I'm without a wife these many years and wish to remarry. Would you accept me as your husband?"

She didn't smile, but replied, "At last. It's taken considerable time for you to explain your interest in me, although I suspected from the first. My answer is yes."

She called to her father, who approached saying, "Master Allerton, if you wish to take my daughter as your wife, you have both God's blessing and mine. You're a pious and righteous man, and I couldn't wish for better."

In this way, our marriage was settled. I was not sure at first if my feelings for Fear were fully reciprocated, but she must have felt honored by my proposal.

She moved her belongings to my house on the day we spoke our marriage vows before Governor Bradford. I anticipated my family would need some time to adjust and felt relief that Mary had remained with the Bradfords. Fear would have enough with Remember to oversee and Bartholomew to care for, along with whatever children we might have together.

At our evening meal the first night, I sensed some displeasure from Remember. She was now thirteen and didn't seem particularly welcoming to yet another women who would run the household—this time, one who was my wife. She fidgeted in an unseemly manner during our evening prayers and responded slowly to Fear's directions to bring the food to the table. Accustomed to being by my side during the meal, she now sat, scowling, next to her brother on the other side of the table.

"Daughter, you will treat Mistress Allerton with respect. She is now in charge of the home in all respects and you *will* obey with grace when she gives you a chore."

Remember didn't reply, but Fear said to her, "We will be sisters, Remember. We aren't that far distant in age, and you'll need to help me find things here. We can work together."

I thought this was a kindly thing to say and gave Fear a nod and a smile. Remember didn't reply, but she stopped frowning, so perhaps my new wife's words had soothed her.

Bartholomew remained indifferent to my new wife, needing only someone to clean his clothes and put food on the table. Despite Fear's kindly overtures, Remember continued to show resentment from time to time. I hoped this would pass, as Fear was soon with child.

Chapter 20

Bradford's Hatred of Mount Wollaston Grows

Isaac Allerton, Plymouth Colony 1628

I returned in the spring of 1628 from another trip to England as the colony's agent. With a sense of pride, I reported that I had confirmed the new contract with the London merchants, freeing us from our perpetual debt and its usurious interest. With me came supplies for the colony: shoes, leather, cloth, stocking, rope and twine. I also brought tools: hoes, hatchets, scythes, shovels and spades, along with saws, files and nails for new building. For the goodwives, I had purchased iron pots, herbs and spices. We also now had a secure patent to establish a trading post on the Kennebec River far to the north, which the governor greeted as the best part of my report. Trade was something I had long planned for myself, one of the bases for my decision to leave England on the Mayflower. For now, however, this trading post would be just a colony venture. Discussing the situation with Bradford the evening after my arrival, he told me of a development that had occurred whilst I was in London.

"I'm uncertain whether fishing will ever be a source of income for us. Because so few want to engage in this task, I believe our future is in the fur trade. While you were gone, we established a trading post at Aptucxet on the Manamet River some miles south of here."

"Aptucxet? What word is that?"

Bradford chuckled. "It's Wampanoag for 'little trap in the river.' I believe they used to having fishing weirs there. We'll use it as a site for trading for corn and beans with the natives, and possibly for trade with the Dutch. A man named Isaac de Rasiers visited from New Amsterdam in your absence. He is the secretary of New Netherland, appointed by the Dutch West India Company, and came so he could report on our colony. I have it on good authority that his impression was reasonable—thus I think we'll be able to trade with the Dutch."

"What of the Kennebec patent?" I asked.

"We'll send some men as soon as possible to erect a post there. We can trade with both the natives and the fisherman, who live in great numbers in that area. Perhaps we can gather fish that way?" Bradford gave a rare smile and seemed well pleased with the financial footing of the colony, now certainly more solid than ever with the expansion of our trading posts.

ꙮ ꙮ

Before I had left on my latest voyage to England, I had contracted with a carpenter to build my family a new house. I decided to build in the colony's northern district, on my lands adjacent to the Jones River. When I returned, the house was nearly finished —a more spacious accommodation with two rooms, much to Fear's delight, and now needed, since in my absence she had given birth to a boy named Isaac. Remember's relationship with Fear didn't seem much improved, especially as my daughter now had the care of my son, who had lusty lungs and was subject to colic. Despite her earlier kindly approach, Fear had developed a sharp tongue in dealing with her, and Remember resented our moving, since she would be far from her friends in the settlement, and, of course, from her sister, Mary.

My son Bartholomew had always had a greater interest in England than in our colony, and after my return from this last trip, he told me he wanted to talk with me about his future. He was now a young man of sixteen, and I knew he'd been thinking about what he would do and where he would like to live. We sat outside of my old house, where he still resided, on an evening warm with the smell of newly turned soil and filled with the noisy screeching from nearby nests of baby birds wanting to be fed.

"I'm unhappy here, Father. I think you know that. This isn't the life I would choose to lead."

That day I saw my son as an adult, perhaps for the first time. His dark, shoulder length hair was the same color as his mother's, and he had her eyes. With his facial hair, neatly trimmed, and his deep voice, he could have been a year or two older.

"Have you not enjoyed working with your uncle? Is he a hard master?"

"No, Father, he is hard but fair. I have learned much from him."

"I recognize your life here hasn't been an easy one, but when we came, I made it clear that creating a home here would be difficult, with many challenges."

"But I didn't choose this life."

His words struck deep. I thought of the many nights aboard the Mayflower when Mary Norris and I prayed we had made the right decision, that we would survive and our children prosper. It was perhaps a selfish choice, since I had given little thought to whether my children would have chosen the same, had they been older. Now I reaped what I had sowed, and the truth of it hurt. "What do you consider your path?" I asked, almost in a whisper, as if not speaking about this aloud would make hearing what he had to say easier.

"I have thought about some business venture, apprenticing to a merchant."

"But I'll be going into a trading business soon. Does that not appeal?"

"No, Father. I wish to find my own way in England. This isn't home to me. It has never been."

"I'll think about what you've told me."

Bartholomew sat up straight and said, "I know I must honor and respect you, Father, but this decision is mine to make. I'm old enough to do this without your blessing, but I would prefer to leave with your good will."

"Will you not miss your sisters?"

"Yes, I'll miss them, but they have been but a small part of my life since we came here."

I sighed. "I understand, Bartholomew. I would ask that you think on this for some time more, while you either work my fields or help me set up my trading business. If you're still determined to leave us in, say, one year, very well. I have some relatives in Suffolk to whom I can recommend you for a place to stay when you arrive." I shook my head. "I have always prayed you would find a satisfactory life here, my son."

From the set of his chin, determined and proud, I doubted waiting the year would change his mind.

ꕥ ꕥ

The activities at the settlement of Mount Wollaston finally caused our governor to lose his patience. He called a meeting of the Council, telling us, "I have learned that Captain Wollaston wants even more profits than can be had by trading guns and liquor for furs. He plans to sell the indentured men who came with him to the Virginia tobacco plantations as slaves."

"I don't know what each of you think about this," said Elder Brewster, "but I find the enslavement of Englishmen to be immoral and abhorrent."

"We've had a few indentured servants here in the colony, as you know," replied Bradford, "but the years of their servitude are limited. We don't keep slaves."

"Is Captain Wollaston still there?" I asked.

"No, he decamped to Virginia with such men as he might sell."

"And how does Thomas Morton view the sale of those men?"

"To curtail the practice, he persuaded the remaining men to throw off their servitude and join the free members of the colony, to trade and live in harmony with the local tribes," Bradford replied.

"How does the settlement fare without Wollaston?" asked Edward Winslow.

At that point, Bradford's face flushed, and he banged his fist on his desk as he was wont to do when angered. "Morton mocks us as pious fundamentalists and has written off Standish as Captain Shrimp. He sells villainous commodities to the Indians, and now comes this latest news: Morton has renamed the settlement Merry Mount. He wants the name to reflect the freedom of the place.

"I call him the Lord of Misrule, as he governs over a dissolute life there. In this letter," here he waved a paper in his hand, "I'm told his latest feat is to erect a large Maypole, decorated with ribbons, garlands and flowers—meant to accompany revels and merriment in the old English custom, along with food and drink. This is a scandal, a beastly practice of mad Bacchanalians. It cannot be tolerated!"

His voice had risen to a pitch we'd not heard before from our otherwise level-headed and normally calm governor. We sat shocked at his outburst and didn't speak for some minutes, while Bradford gathered control of himself. "I'll first write that wantwit a letter," he then said, "asking him if what we've heard is true, and if it is, asking him as gently as possible to cease these practices. They are anathema to the Puritans as well as to us. If there is no reply, then we must decide on stronger measures."

The Council left the meeting shaken by Bradford's emotion and hoping for a resolution without confrontation. Morton did reply to Bradford's letter, scorning his advice, and so at Bradford's order, Captain Standish and a band of soldiers set out for Merry Mount in early June.

Mary Allerton, Plymouth, 1628

Sharing Mistress Bradford's running of the household filled each day, especially with looking after the impatient, active young William, whose interest jumped from one thing to another, never lasting more than a minute. Mistress Bradford had encouraged him to walk as early as possible by placing him in a walking stool, which supported him and in which he could move around. It had a small tray attached for his toys. I cannot count the number of times he ran that stool into my ankles and legs, which were constantly bruised. Once he had mastered walking on his own, he would run in his long gown, trip and fall, then cry. After being soothed, he would run again until he tired, then he would sit down and fall asleep. The only thing that saved his poor head from being broken was the pudding tied around it—a roll of soft cloth that cushioned it. That, and the strings attached to the shoulders of his gown. I could sometimes grab him by the strings before he fell. Outside, I tied him to my apron on a long rope.

Mercy usually was in a sling on Mistress Bradford's hip or in a highchair. She was a contented, smiling child, unlike her boisterous brother, and had her mother's dark hair and perceiving eyes. I thanked God in my prayers each night for her easy spirit.

In this now crowded and busy house, where nine of us now lived, we couldn't avoid hearing the governor complain about the colony at Merry Mount. "A fine name for a dissolute place," he would grumble. Mistress Bradford would offer soothing remarks, but nothing seemed to calm his thoughts on this subject.

On the day Standish returned from Merry Mount, I heard commotion in the street and ran outside, pulling William with me. There I saw Standish, marching up the hill to the meeting house, dragging a man in chains. His armed militia marched in formation behind, the sun glinting off their armor. Mistress Bradford sent someone to bring her husband from the fields, but I didn't know what had happened until later that evening, after the Council met in our house.

The two youngest children were in bed. I lay above in the loft newly added to the house, alongside the beds of Nathaniel and the Southworth boys, but we all could clearly hear what Standish had to say. These men never paid any mind to what women and children heard.

"We found Morton absent when we reached Merry Mount," he reported, "so we followed him to a nearby settlement, where we made his arrest. To my regret, he made an escape and returned to Merry Mount. There we arrested him again."

"We thank you for your efforts," said Bradford. "He will stand trial tomorrow."

Women were not allowed at the trial, but I did listen to Bradford the following night when he described what had transpired to Thomas Cushman, who'd been unable to attend. The conversation on this subject began as we sat at the table for our evening meal, with a question from Thomas. Naturally, the boys listened intently, as they were very interested in soldiers and warfare and would use sticks as swords in their play.

Before he could answer Thomas, Mistress Bradford, ever mindful of her husband's choler with regard to Morton, admonished him, "Good husband, please try to restrain your anger with this situation since children sit here with us. You could frighten William and little Mercy, not to mention inciting the imaginations of the boys." She glared at them and then at me as well.

Bradford gave her a stern look but replied to Thomas in a very calm tone. "We brought him to trial on charges of villainy. His trading of firearms with the natives is forbidden by royal proclamation. The licentiousness of his settlement has proved a magnet to evildoers, runaway servants, discontents and hoddypeaks."

"Did he not present his side?" asked Thomas.

"Aye, he did, claiming he only sought economic freedom and social equality under English customs and rule. He is a half-faced, mewling, gorbellied—"

"Husband!" Mistress Bradford got up and removed William in his chair away from the table and indicated to the boys that they should leave.

"Pray pardon me, my good wife. I'll mind my tongue better."

The boys stayed rooted where they sat, and I pressed my lips together to control my response. When I looked at Thomas, I could see he also tried hard not to smile.

"What was the judgment, sir?" he asked.

"We are sending him back to England on the first ship, as a prisoner. Until that time, he will stay under guard in the fort."

And so Morton remained, until he returned to England in chains on the second ship named *Mayflower*, which arrived in 1629.

Isaac Allerton, Plymouth, 1628

I had returned from England with the goods Governor Bradford had requested for the colony, but also with some I had purchased on my own. These I sold for furs and other items I could then use for trade in London. Those buying my goods seemed well-satisfied, and no one on the Council made any complaint, since I had been of good service to them in England. In this way, I benefited myself and made a better life for my family.

I'd brought with me this time a preacher by the name of Rogers. Although not recommended by the church in Leiden, he still seemed a fair choice to me, since he was both pious and well-spoken. Regretfully, it soon became clear this young man was crazed, based on his wandering, ungodly sermons and inappropriate social interactions. The Council had to decide what to do with him.

When we met in the meeting room in the fort, our governor stood and glared at me. "You made a poor selection of minister, Master Allerton. This man is clearly unbalanced, and we must send him back."

"I agree," said Edward Winslow, "but what did it cost to bring him here?"

"Not a small sum," I had to admit. "Three pounds, eleven shillings. I have it in the accounting, which details the cost of his provisions, clothes, and bedding."

"And this will become a larger sum if we send him back." Bradford looked most unhappy. "Master Allerton, you must pay some of these costs yourself."

I readily agreed. While this would lessen the profits from my trip, I feared more the distrust of the Council.

"This is the second preacher to come here who has sown discord rather than religion," said Bradford. "I hope the next will prove better."

I counted on the Council's trust to weather this situation, and in this, I was correct. The Council ascribed no blame to me, a great relief since I planned to expand my trade to other sites and needed their goodwill.

ꙮ ꙮ

Having been absent for some time, I saw our colony with fresh eyes and its growth amazed me. With the additional acreage granted to the various citizens, some were considering doing what I had already done—building new homes on their land, which meant leaving our settlement.

Bradford expressed his sadness about this one evening. He had come to my old home when I was in the settlement on business. We sat in chairs newly brought from England and smoked our pipes, since we now had a good supply of tobacco. I had sorely missed my pipe during our early years here.

"I'm pleased with that patent for the Kennebec site, Master Allerton. We're sending some men to begin building the trading post as soon as the weather improves."

I nodded at his compliment.

"However, I must admit I'm distressed to see that some, like you, leave our settlement to live nearer their farms, when we have struggled so long and hard to set down roots and establish our colony. Now that we are stable, people wish to move on."

"Your feelings are understandable, Governor. To you especially, with all you have given to ensure our survival, this must seem a cruel blow. On the other hand, you should feel a sense of accomplishment that the colony is expanding. Perhaps you could call a general meeting where we could discuss our future."

"I plan to do so, but in the meantime, the Council would like you to return to England again to purchase more goods and supplies."

I must have looked surprised. "I had not thought to return."

"We need an agent who understands our needs and can relate our situation to our London partners, and you have proved yourself more than capable."

In actuality, this served my purposes well, since I had decided it was time to open my own trading posts, and I needed to purchase goods to stock them. I agreed without objection.

Mary Allerton, Plymouth, 1628

So my father left yet again for London, this time sailing north to the newly established Massachusetts Bay colony and then taking a ship to England. After he'd left, I overheard that the governor had called for a meeting with the members of our congregation to discuss their thoughts on creating settlements elsewhere and establishing churches to serve them. On the night of the meeting, Governor Bradford offered long and dreary prayers before we ate, and he sat gloomy and withdrawn at the evening meal.

"Dear husband, please eat some food. Mary worked hard on both the bread and the stew. And look—we have butter for the first time, a gift from Mistress Warren."

"I have no mind for butter, wife. The colony must grow, but I hoped not to see the day when our congregation scattered and other churches formed."

Thomas looked thoughtful. "It's a natural consequence, sir, due to your long and challenging years of careful oversight and management. You should find comfort in that."

The governor looked unconvinced and left for the meeting before we finished eating. Thomas went with him, because he was also a landowner and wished to know what was said. The boys naturally wanted to go, too, and only Mistress Bradford's sternest warnings kept them at the table.

I knew nothing of the meeting until Thomas and I sat outside after our meal the next evening, enjoying the sunset and the tranquility enveloping the settlement at the end of the day. I minded William, who ran around in the yard, stopping only to inspect an insect or play in the dust. "What happened at the meeting, Thomas? Was anything decided?"

"You're but a girl, Mary. Why would you be interested?"

"I have interests in many things, Thomas. In that, I hope to be a calming voice to my husband, whenever I marry."

Thomas chuckled. "You're too young to be considering that. You're still a child."

"I'm not a child!" I could feel my face grow hot. "I'm twelve years old and can keep a house as well as any goodwife."

He smiled. "I can see you're as headstrong as when you came here, child. Don't look surprised—I heard the Bradfords talking over the decision to have you live with them."

What had he heard? I had no reply but just sat on the stoop, embarrassed into silence. *He had called me a child!*

"Ah, I can see I have wounded you. Pay me no mind. I will admit you have matured in many ways and are now quite proper, except for your insatiable curiosity."

I remained silent.

"All right, I'll tell you what happened, if only to win back your friendship. There were various thoughts expressed about the moving away of our citizens. Some present were for staying, saying we should be content with the way things are, especially since there is no real necessity to move. These men believed the real motive for leaving was the idea of personal enrichment. Ohers were resolute about leaving to build farms on their land, even if they would not have a church nearby. They argued if a settlement grew up around them, a church could be built there."

"What did Governor Bradford say?"

"That they were leaving our church, which is like an old mother forsaken by her children. Her oldest members are being taken by death, and her children are moving away..."

His words made me think of myself, of moving to the Bradford house. It was not such a bad thing.

"...leaving the church like a widow, with only trust in God remaining. She made many rich but now has become poor herself."

I shook my head at these words. I would indeed miss many in our settlement after they left, chief among them the Aldens, who were determined to build a house on the Blue Fish River to the north. Even though my father's family had already left, we still saw them for our Sunday meetings, and I presumed I would see the Aldens, too. "And what of you, Thomas? Will you leave?"

"No, I'll remain. I plan to continue to work the governor's land and mine and to assist him in any way I can. The expansion of this township will require the building of roads, and someone will have to survey for them. I'd like to take on that job, as well as continuing my studies with Elder Brewster."

"Your future seems well-planned, Thomas. Will you stay living with the Bradfords?" My question was self-serving and selfish—I enjoyed his companionship, however infrequent.

"Yes, for now. Perhaps I will build a home of my own someday."

His plans reassured me we would still have such conversations. The present one ended when I heard, "Mary! No time for idling. William must be put to bed."

ꙮ ꙮ

Remember occasionally stopped to visit me Sundays, when everyone sailed from their farms to attend services in the settlement.

"Is Mistress Allerton any easier with you?" I asked Remember during one of these brief visits.

"No, Mary, she rides me like an angry man rides a horse, threatening to thrash me if I don't do as she wants."

"Do you take care of young Isaac?"

"Since the day he was born. He is a peevish and fretful child, and I've come to believe she either dislikes babes or just dislikes him. I think she would like to be with child again to please Father, but that is unlikely to happen, given his long absences. Perhaps that is why her tongue is as sharp as a needle."

"I'm sorry to hear that, sister." I placed my hand on her arm in sympathy.

"I do look forward to Father's return, when I'll have some measure of relief. My step-mother is honey-tongued when he is around."

I smiled at her, thinking of my difficulties minding young William. The one good thing about her troubles was that they brought us closer together.

Chapter 21

An Execution Takes Place and the Bradfords Move

Mary Allerton, Plymouth 1629

Soon after I had joined the Bradford household, my mistress had warned me not to speak or ask questions when the men were talking about colony business, since it was generally believed that women were incapable of rational thought on such matters. Boys were likewise discouraged from saying anything until they were of age. Thus when Constant and Thomas Southworth first spoke out of turn with questions, they were silenced by a thunderous look from the governor. He then told them that impertinent young boys should not interrupt adults. Nathaniel, already aware of his place, later reinforced what the governor had said by telling them they would be thrashed if they did.

The governor frequently talked to Thomas over our evening meals, and although everyone else had to remain silent, all of us were privy to news of recent developments in the colony.

One of great interest occurred on the night after the return of my father in August of 1629. He had sailed on a ship called the *Mayflower,* which also brought thirty-five more of our faith from Leiden. A short time later, a smaller ship arrived —the *Talbot*— from which a group of single men disembarked. The arrival of more unmarried men dismayed our governor. "James Shirley, one of the London merchants with whom I'm more than well acquainted, sent these people without notifying me in advance they were coming," the governor began calmly enough.

I had heard the name Shirley so often that I knew this man was a thorn in the governor's side.

"In truth," Bradford continued, "these men are poorer and less capable than many who have come before. Worse yet, neither Master Shirley nor the other merchants paid the cost of their voyage, maintenance, and clothing, making it clear we must assume this financial burden." With this, his voice rose, but then lowered when Mistress Bradford shook her head at him.

"How much will this add to our debt?" Thomas asked.

"A good question, and one you might ask, since you're now a shareholder in the debt. The answer is hundreds of pounds. Will we ever be free of our debts? I can only hope this is the last time we are burdened like this."

He paused in a long moment of silence, as if in prayer, then said in a resigned and quiet voice, "Since the Lord in His goodness has preserved us, then our people here in this wilderness will find a way to repay these debts—even though they were levied on us by others from afar. In the meantime, we must be thankful that through God's mercy, we have prospered."

To which Thomas added a fervent, "Amen."

Having always been curious and somewhat indulged by my father in terms of conversation, I had more difficulty holding my tongue than even the boys. Mistress Bradford could often answer my questions, since she knew a great deal about her husband's business, most of which she also shared with the members of her gossip.

Isaac Allerton, Plymouth 1630

Upon my return from this last London trip, when I had purchased more goods for my own trade, I found Bradford had been re-elected governor for the fourth or fifth time—God's truth, I'd forgotten how many. He now worried about the establishment of the growing colony to the north—the Massachusetts Bay colony, founded on the shores of the large bay we had explored early in our years here and where we now had a trading post.

We gathered in the meeting house one evening because Bradford wished to tell us of a matter that had just come to his attention concerning the Massachusetts Bay colony.

"You may be unaware that a fleet of five ships, including the *Mayflower* and the *Talbot,* recently arrived on our shores. These ships first landed on the coast at Cape Ann, at the site of Roger Conant's fishing village, which is now a town called Salem. According to Master Allerton, who was on the *Mayflower*, three hundred and fifty men, women and children disembarked along with some," and here he consulted a piece of paper, "two hundred and forty cows, sixty horses, plus oxen, goats and armaments for settlement in that area."

As I had anticipated, there occurred a great gasp at the mention of so many new settlers, not to mention the cows and horses.

"They will populate an area on the north side of the Charles River, an extension of the Massachusetts Bay colony. The governor there is John Endecott, a minister who arrived in Salem last year. He's now written me that there is an infectious fever, which came with those ships and is now spreading to others. Many are dying and they're in need of food. I propose to send them our physick, Samuel Fuller, and supplies of food. Are you in agreement?"

"Ayes" were all we heard.

"There is one other matter to consider. With the number of people settled in that area, it's inevitable they will spread southward toward us. Thus the wish of some of us to leave our settlement and occupy their lands in the northern part of our colony now seems reasonable, so we can further define our boundaries. For this reason, although still with a heavy heart, I now encourage you to move to your lands.

"The establishment of this large Puritan colony has caused me to think about our own settlement. The Massachusetts Bay colony has some distinct advantages we don't have—a royal charter for one, whereas we only have a patent—a patent which the king could revoke at his pleasure. Second, their seat of governance does not reside in England, as ours did at the beginning. Their governors now reside in the colony and this allows them to maintain their independence from the Crown.

"We must also consider that these Puritans have arrived well-equipped for settlement. I expect many more will soon arrive, as Puritans flee the rule of the king and his church."

"How many do you think will come?" Edward Winslow asked.

"Hundred, if not thousands," replied Bradford. "I believe this puts us in a precarious position, because with the rapid growth of the Massachusetts Bay colony, I think the king will look to his colonies for revenue. I can only hope we are yet too small for him to see profit in taxing us, or worse, to eliminate our patent."

Those present immediately started talking amongst themselves, and most of us left the meeting sharing the governor's apprehension. Taking the governor's advice, those who had hesitated now proceeded with plans to build farms on their land.

☙ ❧

My family would soon expand again, as Fear again carried a child. I hoped for another son. She had an easier relationship with Remember now, for which I thanked God daily. As my oldest daughter was now sixteen, I reasoned that she had matured in her views or, with God's help, had accepted her role in my household.

To my regret, Bartholomew didn't change in his decision to return to England, and I booked him passage on the return voyage of the *Mayflower*. He walked to the pier along with such poor possessions as he owned and a letter of introduction to my family. As I stood next to the shallop that would take him to the boat, I blinked to hold back the tears that threatened to escape my eyes.

Both Mary and Remember had said their good-byes earlier that morning, with much crying and embracing of their brother. Despite their differences, they had been through much together and their ties ran deep.

"You must write," I told him, "so I'll know you arrived safely. With my letter to our relatives, you should have a place to live, and also their support, while you determine your future. You should let me know of your decision." Since I had been counseling him on his expected behavior and social manners for the past several days, there was little more I could say.

"I will, Father," and here Bartholomew's voice broke, "and I hope to see you all again in a few years. Perhaps if you come to London again as agent."

"I hope that, too, my son."

I hugged his shoulders, and he turned and got into the shallop. I watched until he had boarded the *Mayflower*, then waited until it set sail, finally allowing my tears to flow. I hoped I would see him again, but I doubted his sisters ever would.

Mary Allerton, Plymouth, 1630

One evening, as Mistress Bradford told Mercy a story and I readied little William for bed, the governor and Thomas, who had become something of his secretary and aide, sat at the hearth. Bradford enjoyed his pipe, from which rose a fragrant stream of smoke. The big-eared boys were outside in the dark, but I swore I heard some whispering near the door.

Bradford waved a letter in the air. "News from Governor Endecott, Thomas. Our good physick and surgeon, whom we sent to help with their contagious fever, has healed the bodies of many in that settlement and has also given them a new vision of religious life.

Endecott expresses some surprise that we aren't what he thought we were, from what he heard from England."

"And what was that, sir?"

"That we were overly pious and insensitive devils," replied Bradford.

"That bodes well for our relationship, does it not?"

"Yes, it's reassuring, but I suspect that with many more people arriving on each ship, our neighboring colony to the north will expand southward, possibly causing friction between us. Conversely, until their colony is firmly established, they'll be a great source of trade for us."

The governor was correct, for I learned that our colony prospered in the following months by trading up and down the coast at our various posts. The Puritans eagerly bought our surplus of pigs, cows, and lumber. *Perhaps that's why the governor regained his even temper?*

ꕤ ꕤ

"I think we'll finally have a minister, my good wife," I heard the governor tell Mistress Bradford one day over our morning meal.

"After so long and so many mistakes," she said dryly.

Bradford ignored her. "His name is Ralph Smith and he came with his family to Massachusetts Bay, hoping to lead a church there. Apparently, his beliefs have proven too radical, even for the Puritans. I have offered him a place here. He wrote back most eagerly, mentioning he had been given an ill-maintained house in a poor area, so we will provide him suitable housing for his family and some financial support…at least until we see how he preaches and tends to our flock."

At fourteen, I should have been attentive to sermons and prayers, but in fact, I found one pastor much like another. With great interest the Bradfords attended the Sunday service when Smith first preached. I was, as usual, bored.

Nevertheless, over our evening meal that day, the governor pronounced Smith's words well-spoken, articulate and thoughtful, but most importantly, he found Smith well-suited to our beliefs. After a subsequent recommendation from Elder Brewster, Reverend Smith stayed. We had a pastor at last, and just in time. Elder Brewster, who had been our religious leader for so many years, had become too frail to bear all the burdens of his responsibilities.

That year, my stepmother gave birth to a daughter named Sarah. Remember, although not overjoyed at the prospect of having two children to mind, didn't complain. My father seemed indifferent, as the baby was a girl, but perhaps what I knew of his current poor relations with the Council distracted him.

"Have you heard about Father's problems?" asked Remember in a whisper one Sunday, when she came to visit. Our new half-sister, Sarah, relaxed sleepily in her arms as we sat by the hearth.

"Only the barest news. Can you tell me more?"

"Apparently he returned from London this last time with many things he now sells to our neighbors at high prices."

"How do you know that?" I couldn't comprehend my father doing anything wrong.

"I hear them complaining."

Apparently Remember's skills at listening now rivaled mine, and her words brought me shame. A conversation I overheard between Thomas and the governor not long afterward only deepened this feeling.

"Did you know Allerton has set up a trading post to compete with ours on the Kennebec River?" Bradford asked Thomas.

There was silence, which I took to mean this was news to Thomas.

"He has a man there named Ashley to run it for him, and that man is a crafty pate and utterly disreputable. He sent a large number of beaver pelts directly to England to Allerton's benefit, with no repayment of the goods Allerton took from our colony to set up his trading post. At least not yet. I cannot help but think our English partners are also sending supplies to him."

"What do you plan to do about it, sir?"

"I'm sending Allerton once more to England to purchase supplies for us and to settle whatever quarrels may yet exist."

"Do you trust Master Allerton to do what is needed for the colony?"

"The outcome of Allerton's trip should make his ambitions clear."

My face burned. I could only hope my father's return to England and his business dealings there would restore his good name with Bradford and the Council.

ᘐ ᘓ

In my father's absence, tensions between the colony and one of its citizens, John Billington, increased. I had been frightened of Billington on the *Mayflower* and recalled how his mouse-like wife had been the bane of my early childhood. What I didn't know, until a discussion one evening between Thomas and Bradford, was that Billington had been a troublemaker in the colony since we first arrived. And now he'd committed murder.

"Murder?" asked Thomas. "Is it proven?"

"Yes, someone saw it," replied the governor. "Billington's had a long-standing feud with the owner of the fields neighboring his land, John Newcomen. Billington waylaid him in the woods some days ago and attacked him. The poor fellow, aware of his neighbor's intent, sheltered behind a tree, but Billington had his fowling piece and is a good enough marksman to hit his target. Newcomen was struck in the shoulder."

"Surely not a mortal blow?"

"No, but Newcomen developed an infection and died yesterday, after some days of suffering."

I uttered a gasp from the corner, where I sat rocking Mercy. Nathaniel and Mistress Bradford's two sons approached the governor and began asking questions. The governor gifted all of us with a glare. "This is none of your business, any of you," he said. "Boys, if your chores are completed—but I see there isn't sufficient firewood on the hearth—then it's time you were abed."

After some discussion amongst them about who had the responsibility, Constant went out, dragging his feet, while Nathanial climbed to the loft with his brother.

"Is there some reason for Billington shooting him?" asked Thomas.

"None," replied Bradford, "except for ill will and a long history of disagreements between them. Billington has been quarrelsome from the start. He is a member of the Church of England, but he came here with us because he and his family were very poor and looking for a better life. Hence his strong relationship with John Lyford. We should have banished him along with Lyford and Oldham."

"Is there nothing at all to explain his actions?"

"Perhaps. Billington was hit hard by the death of his son two years ago and became even more bitter in his dealings with me and Council members thereafter. He has often complained he'd been given the least amount of acreage in 1623 and again in our division of land three years ago. As someone who came on the *Mayflower*, he thought he deserved more."

"What did he receive?"

"A house in the center of Plymouth, sixty acres of land, and a share in the colony's livestock and rights in any future distribution of land."

After a pause, Thomas asked, "Did the Council feel this fair?"

"When I asked the members for reassurance, they agreed we'd been fair. I spoke with Billington this morning, and he explained he'd not meant to kill Newcomen, that it was an accident.

"I believe his lack of social status is the basis of his ill feelings. Over time, they have grown and now have led to this. He wants to be chosen for public office, but he isn't a member of our church, and his constant ill temper engenders conflict. Further, because he lacks financial resources, he cannot be one of the undertakers of our debt. This would have elevated him and allowed him to participate in our trading ventures. I don't know what to do at this point."

"What will happen to him?"

"He will be arraigned and the evidence examined by a grand jury to determine if a crime has been committed."

As I later learned from Thomas, the grand jury did indict him, and then a petty jury of citizens found him guilty of willful murder by reason of the evidence. This verdict badly affected Bradford, who had used every means he had to ensure the fairness of the trial. He'd even contacted the new governor of the Massachusetts Bay colony, John Winthrop, asking for advice. When Winthrop concurred with the jury's verdict, the governor ordered Billington's execution with great sorrow.

Billington hanged in September, and neither I nor Mistress Bradford chose to be there when he did. Thomas told me Billington's wife sobbed and cried aloud and his surviving son issued dire threats to those present. Although certainly old enough to see the hanging, I had had enough of death. The boys went with Thomas, but never spoke about what they'd seen and afterward were noticeably subdued.

ꙮ ꙮ

That year saw some good things, as well. Myles Standish built a more spacious home near his land in a place called Duxborough, and then the governor went against his own initial decision and moved our crowded household to his land north of the settlement. He chose a site some five miles away, on his land adjacent to the Jones River, named for Captain Jones of the *Mayflower*. The area where he built was called Stony Brook.

On the day we all visited the site, the governor told us the land around the Jones River had been one of the three sites considered by the men of the *Mayflower* for the original settlement. Since it was not far from where my father now lived, this move made me happy. I could now see Remember more regularly.

Carpenters newly arrived from England built the new house, a spacious residence with a large central fireplace.

A kitchen, the place for cooking and taking our meals, was on the right side of the entrance and a parlor for the governor's writing and greeting of visitors on the other. It housed the Bradford's bed, which could be raised against the wall. Mistress Bradford insisted on a lean-to at the rear and a cellar hole for storing vegetable and fruits under the kitchen.

Since broad beams supported the roof, the governor had had a storage and sleeping area constructed beneath them, reached by a ladder from the entry. The floors were planked with wood and best of all, there was a window in each room. The windows had real glass, little panes set into a lattice of lead, brought from England in casements, ready to put in place. Visitors approached the heavy front door with its iron latch by entering through a palisade that surrounded the entire site.

We now truly lived on a working farm. Mistress Bradford had a large garden at the rear of the house, a more spacious pen for the chickens, and since we hoped to soon have a cow, the governor had built an enclosure for it when it would not be grazing. I would have to adapt my goat milking talents to the cow, a chore I would happily teach the boys, but soon we would have milk, butter and cheese. The pigs Master Bradford now owned had a large enclosure of their own, and other outbuildings would soon arise to house the various activities of the farm. I had never known such wonderful place to live!

The governor still kept his house in the Plymouth settlement, since when the river froze over in winter, we had to move back there so that we could attend church on Sunday. For most of the year, however, church was but a brisk sail away.

Mistress Bradford expressed hope that the distance of this spacious farm from the village would somehow lessen the governor's duties and worries with the colony, but they followed him relentlessly.

Chapter 22

Isaac Allerton Falls into Disfavor

Mary Allerton, Stony Brook, 1630-31

At fifteen, I was accomplished enough in the work of a household to be a goodwife myself. My days in the Bradford home were full of work, and like any goodwife, there were chores I liked and some I hated.

Unlike my sister, I enjoyed minding the children. William at six looked like his father—dark hair, a bit curly, and dark brown eyes. Recently breeched, he now accompanied his father, with Thomas Cushman and the other boys, to the work in the fields most days. He had gone hunting for the first time and returned home very excited, bearing a rabbit. He also had been admitted into the company of Nathaniel Morton and Constant and Thomas Southworth, the boys having judged him old enough to consort with—to a limited extent.

Mercy at three toddled here and there in the house and yard in her long gown. She had progressed from her walking stool at an early age, and I had sewn the leading strings into the shoulders of all her gowns, so if she stumbled, we could pull the strings to keep her upright. Her light hair escaped her biggen on a regular basis, and because of her tendency to topple over, she had a pudding wrapped around her forehead for safety, like her brother before her. Mercy had the sweet and calm temperament of her mother, was easy to entertain and was not a mischief-maker like young William.

Mistress Bradford now carried a third child, and Elizabeth Bryan, an indentured servant, had joined the household. Elizabeth was the wife of Thomas Bryan, himself indentured to Samuel Eddy. A round, cheerful woman, she worked hard, laughed often, and doted on the children. With so many people in the household, Mistress Bradford was happy to have her assistance.

One day my sister Remember came for a visit, the distance between our homes now but a long walk. We sat in the yard behind the house. It was a lovely sunny day in early autumn, with a hint of color to the trees. The garden was lush with green and the colors of flowers and the air scented with wood smoke and the smells of our animals. Mercy wandered here and there, toddling about the garden but never far, entranced by whatever flowers she came upon, which she would tear up with glee. Knowing her mother would not be pleased at the destruction, I picked some late-blooming dandelions for her to wreak havoc on and sat her at my feet. I could hear Elizabeth humming a psalm under her breath while stirring clothes in a kettle over a fire, not far from the garden.

I was grinding corn with a mortar and pestle. The mortar was a large tree stump whose center had been burned out and the pestle was a log with a flattened end. I was expending a lot of energy doing it, and sweat trickled down my neck. Remember sat nearby mending one of young Isaac's gowns. "What do you hear from Governor Bradford about our father, Mary?"

"Nothing. Why do you ask?" I stopped grinding.

"There is news," Remember replied, "and it isn't good."

My stomach fell. I knew that his initial trading ventures had not been accepted by the governor, but I'd hoped all that was in the past. "What has he done?"

"Well," and here she leaned in and her voice fell almost to a whisper, "you know on an earlier trip to England, Father was instructed to bring back fifty pounds worth of shoes, stockings and linen, and a similar value in trading goods. Those purchases were to be marked for the colony so there would be no mingling of them with what he bought for his own trading ventures. It seems he didn't do that. He didn't make the ordered purchases, saying he had to pay his expenses in England, but he brought back many goods to sell himself."

"Yes, yes, I know all that. He is in such high standing in the colony that the governor didn't complain. I thought all that had been resolved."

"Not so, dear sister. Did you know that man Ashley, who was running Father's trading post on the Kennebec, is being sent back to England for selling powder and shot to the Indians?"

"No, I hadn't heard anything about that. Is there more?"

"Yes," Remember replied, frowning. "On this latest trip, Father was to hire a ship to bring trading goods here, with a plan for the ship to be used for fishing to increase the colony's profits. The ship—it's named the *Friendship*—was delayed by bad weather and only arrived a short while ago. The problem is that she wasn't constructed for fishing and, furthermore, she didn't hold many supplies."

"Where is Father?"

"He didn't arrive with the ship and no one knows."

Oh, Father, what have you done? "How do you know all this?"

"We both know women don't just sit about in their homes, keeping to themselves and never speaking to each other." She smiled slyly.

"Mayhap it's not true." I held tightly to my belief that my father was an honest and godly man.

ꟼ ꟼ

Later that day, a man arrived on our doorstep unannounced and asked to speak to the governor. Elizabeth Bryan greeted him and ushered him into the parlor, where Bradford met guests. She later told me the governor seemed to know he would be coming, and the two men stayed closeted, talking for some hours. The stranger then left as inconspicuously as he had arrived.

There was little talk at our evening meal that night. I could tell the governor had something on his mind, but with Thomas Cushman absent, Bradford would not discuss his work. The following evening, when Thomas returned, the two men spoke in the governor's room after our meal. The boys were all outside, playing noisily in the dimming light, while we women stayed in the kitchen with Mercy, cleaning away the remains of the meal and preparing food for the next day. How I longed to know what was being said in that room. I made an excuse to go to the door off the entry way but only heard snippets.

"Allerton…mismanage…disreputable…" I fled in shame.

When the children and the boys were in bed that night, I took myself to the garden and sat on the bench there. I loved the peace in the darkness. An owl hooted in the distance, and I could catch wisps of the wood smoke from the banked fire. Late blooming flowers added their perfume. *What would happen to Father?* Even this quiet night couldn't dispel my anxiety, and I startled as a dark figure sat beside me on the bench.

"Mistress Allerton, it's me, Thomas. I know you overheard some of what the governor said this evening. I could see your shadow in the entryway."

"I beg your forgiveness. I shouldn't have listened in to your conversation. It was improper of me."

I could sense a smile on his face when he said, "Yes, it was, but I've come to expect it."

"I find it odd that you address me as Mistress Allerton, while I call you Thomas. You may call me Mary."

"I call you mistress because you're now of age. But if you prefer, Mary it is. I suspect you want to know why we were discussing your father."

I didn't answer but he knew I did.

"How much has your sister told you? I know she would share whatever she knew."

"She told me about the *Friendship*, and that it came with few goods. She doesn't know where Father is now."

"News has come that he sailed on another ship, the *White Angel*. A man named Timothy Hatherly, who is one of our London partners, came on the *Friendship* and brought this news."

"That must be the man who came here yesterday to speak with the governor."

"It was, and he carried a letter from James Shirley—you know he is one of the London partners—and in it, he explained what your father had done."

"I pray to God in heaven that whatever he's done isn't unlawful."

Thomas stopped for a moment, as if measuring his next words. "It seems the *White Angel* came loaded with goods for the Massachusetts Bay Colony. The profit from these supplies will mainly go to your father and some of the London men. For us, as you heard, the *Friendship* carried next to nothing. The London partners had spent a considerable amount of money buying and provisioning the two ships and have added that cost to what our colony owes them."

And our debt grows bigger because of my father's greed."

"How do you know of such things as our debt, Mistress…er… Mary?"

"I have ears and I can think, Thomas. You must think me an empty-headed poppet."

"I've never thought that, but such matters should not concern women."

"Of course they should, and he's my father. I hope you'll tell me what happens with him from here on."

"Er...."

I got up and flounced into the house, where Nathaniel accused me of having a tryst in the garden. The boy was everywhere and heard everything.

"I saw you. I'm going to tell Master Bradford," he whispered.

The governor was very strict when it came to the interactions between young men and women, and he would quickly put a stop to my meetings with Thomas. "No, you won't, Nathaniel," I said. "I saw you spill that bucket of goat's milk last week, and I know you didn't tell Mistress Bradford. If you say one word about what you saw tonight, she'll find out about the milk."

Thomas and I continued meeting.

Early the next day, Master Hatherly reappeared on our doorstep, arriving out of breath from his climb up the hill from the river. I answered his knock. As we made introductions, I noted he was extravagantly dressed in an embroidered coat with breeches of rich wool, silk stockings, and fancy shoes now wet and muddy. His clothes hung on him, and I suspected he had lost weight on his voyage. Hatherly had a thin face and a pointed chin, covered with what had probably been an elaborately trimmed beard at the time he left London. Now he had a scraggle of brown and gray to match his hair, in sharp contrast to our clean-shaven governor, who had only a dark, well-trimmed mustache.

I held the door open for Hatherly to enter and ushered him into the parlor. Bradford looked up from his writing when I said, "Timothy Hatherly, sir." The governor squinted in surprise that I knew his name.

I dawdled in the entryway long enough to hear Hatherly say, "As agreed, I'm here to examine the colony's accounts."

Oh dear. My father took care of the accounts for the governor, who was not skilled at keeping books. I could only hope Father had left them in good order.

There followed many hours of silence, punctuated by requests from Hatherly for clarification. Mistress Bradford soon drove me from near the parlor door, clucking at my nosiness, but I knew she would ask me what I'd heard. When she sent me in with beer about halfway through the morning, I heard nothing more. Hatherly joined us for the midday meal, commenting on the moist and tasty roast fowl we had prepared and the sweetness of the corn cake. He left late in the afternoon, before the sun set.

Tension thickened the air during our evening meal, and I sensed the governor was anxious to talk with Thomas. He said nothing to us of Hatherly's visit but told Mistress Bradford he would be traveling to Plymouth the next day to meet with his Council and would be gone for two days.

"I'll gather up some food for you to take, husband…what do you think of Mr. Hatherly? He seems quite the fine London gentleman."

I knew something was boiling beneath his calm appearance, but he replied, "Yes, he is a fine gentleman. William, did you work on your letters today?"

"Yes, Father."

"And did you complete all your chores?"

"Mary showed me how to milk the cow. I'm practicing. And I fed the chickens and gathered kindling. When can I go to the fields to work?"

"When I return from Plymouth and can instruct you."

"What did *you* do, Nathaniel?"

"Elizabeth taught me a new gliffe. Do you want to hear it?" When Bradford nodded, he said slowly, "Dick drunk drink in a dish; where is the dish Dick drunk drink in?"

His father smiled for the first time that evening and looked around at all the boys. "Anything else to tell?"

Little William replied, "Mary showed me a toss and catch game. You tie a rope to a stick and at the other end of the rope, you tie a circle of vine…"

"Yes, yes, I know this game. I saw some of the Wanpanoag children playing at it. Can you catch the circle on the stick?"

"Not yet, Father, but I'm going to! When are we going to get a horse? It would be fun to ride out to the fields, instead of walking."

Bradford gave him another smile. "When there are good roads on which to ride and money enough to buy one, my son. A horse is still an indulgence and costs good money to keep. You can consider the benefits of walking in the meantime. And what of you, Thomas and Constant? Have you done your chores?"

"Yes, sir," they said in unison.

"We worked in the fields as you instructed. When we came home, we chopped wood, fed the pigs and gathered nuts for Mother." said Constant.

Bradford turned to his wife. "Is there anything you need from the settlement?"

His wife blushed and replied, "I'm in need of some extra linen for…" She patted the large swelling of her stomach. Little Mercy began babbling in her highchair, which drew Mistress Bradford's attention.

"I'll find some, but you'll need to give me some eggs and butter for trade. Do you need any seeds?"

"No, only the linen."

Almost everything we needed, we obtained by trading. Some people paid in pounds and shillings, but I'd never seen any real money. I also knew of a currency called wampum, something made by the Indians and much prized. Thomas once showed me a string of it—tubular white and purple beads made from the shell of a clam the Indians called a quahog.

"If you see Master Alden, please give my greetings to his wife. Tell him I'll visit her soon."

The governor grumbled. He wasn't one for passing time with social pleasantries. The Aldens now had four children underfoot, two girls and two boys, and lived not far from our new house here, a short sail away to the Herring River.

After our meal, the governor retired with Thomas to his study. From the loft where I slept, I could hear his raised voice but couldn't make out his words. Hoping that Thomas would share with me the contents of their conversation, I waited until the rest of the house was quiet, except for Elizabeth's snores from her bed beside mine, then headed to the garden. On the way, I checked on nosy Nathaniel, who for once slept soundly, drooling from his open mouth.

I sat on the garden bench for a long time, wondering if I would see Thomas, but eventually he joined me.

"I'm reluctant to talk to you, Mary. It's unseemly."

"No, it isn't. Do you think women are without curiosity, without a wish to learn? That we're content with a life of hard work, childbearing and death?"

He sat quietly and finally said, "I don't think I've ever considered what women might think."

"Well, if you wish my friendship, you might begin. I only hope to hear news of my father."

"Well...the governor thinks it's a good thing Hatherly looked at our accounts. Hatherly taught him how to examine them in detail. Bradford's very angry that we, as the undertakers of our debt, are expected to pay for the costs of those ships your father ordered and the goods he purchased. We didn't agreed to any of it."

"I don't understand what my father does, but this shames me. I only see him as conscientious and hard-working."

"Tomorrow the governor will share what he's learned about this new debt with the Council, along with anything else that is discovered in the accounts." He placed his hand on my shoulder. "Don't be afraid, Mary. I'm certain all of this will work out."

His touch comforted me, and in truth, I had come to appreciate his friendship, his conversation, and his calming presence.

The governor left early the next morning for Plymouth, carrying a large basket with eggs and butter wrapped in a cloth chilled with cold water. There was also smoked meat and corn bread for the governor's meals.

Some hours after his departure, Mistress Bradford began to feel the first pains of labor. She asked me to send for her gossip—my stepmother, Fear, and Mistress Alden— and also for Mistress Fuller, who lived nearby. I sent our servant Elizabeth to fetch the gossip and the three boys—Isaac, Constant and Thomas—to fetch Mistress Fuller, since they could run faster than I could. Soon after they all arrived, Mistress Bradford delivered another son, named Joseph.

Governor Bradford returned home a day later than expected. I wondered if he'd delayed because he felt overwhelmed with the children already underfoot. Mistress Bradford stood at the hearth when he came in. He embraced her and asked if she felt well, then went to the cradle to see the baby.

"So this is Joseph," he said. "He seems to be the smallest of all our babes."

"He is, husband, but he has the mightiest of cries. You chose his name well, and I wonder if, like the youngest son of Jacob and Rachel, he'll become your favorite."

The governor gave his wife a smile and replied, "All of my sons are my favorites."

I knew immediately he thought of his first son, John, whom he had not seen since leaving Leiden in 1620. Mistress Bradford had told me John would now be thirteen years old.

Thomas Cushman told us a few days after Joseph's birth that his staying with the family now overburdened my mistress. Although Mistress Bradford asked him to stay, he found lodgings of his own nearby. Thus, although I yearned to know what had transpired in the council meeting about the colony's expenses, it was several weeks before I had the opportunity to ask Thomas about it. I found that I missed his presence every day.

One evening Thomas came to visit, I think hoping for a well-prepared evening meal. God's truth, our table was now crowded. Bradford read for some time from the Bible, interspersing his reading with prayers, while the baby Joseph burbled in his cradle, rocked by his mother's foot. William tried his hardest not to squirm in the place where he stood alongside Mercy, who sat in a highchair. Constant and Thomas Southworth, Nathaniel Morton and I now sat on stools.

The governor and Thomas talked over the meal, discussing the crops, the forecast for the harvest, and snippets of gossip about various citizens of Plymouth. Neither Mistress Bradford nor I engaged in these discussion, since such matters were deemed of interest only to the men, but we stored everything we heard. The boys longed to be included, but they had finally learned to keep their place. Nathaniel, now fourteen, was occasionally allowed to participate.

I learned much from these discussions of the frequent suits and countersuits, along with the petty crimes, the governor was required to resolve. Sometimes he did this with his Council, sometimes with the body of freemen in Plymouth called the General Court, and sometimes on his own. Most often he resolved these on his own, based on the number of petitioners who appeared unannounced at our door. The governor and his Council presided over the General Court, but as yet, I didn't understand what constituted a freeman of the General Court.

That night the governor did say one thing of interest to me. "The letter Master Hatherly brought with him was very blunt. The London merchants will take it most unkindly if Hatherly, when God pleases he returns to England, does not give them a satisfactory accounting of our business. This worries me because of what was discussed at the last Council meeting."

More than that, he didn't share at the table but retired with Thomas to the parlor after the meal. The conversation continued at a low murmur, and I was certain they talked of my father. Thomas left well after dark, and the children being in bed, I slipped out of the house to catch him. I found him waiting by the gate in the palisade surrounding the house and its yard.

"Thank you, Thomas, for waiting for me. I'd hoped you would."

"It's good to see you, Mary. I've missed our conversations."

He did? I felt the heat creeping to my cheeks, which thankfully he couldn't see in the dark.

"How unsavory is the news of my father's doings?"

"It's not entirely bad. As one of the undertakers of the colony's debts, I attended the meeting of the Council in Plymouth, where his activities were discussed. It is now generally known that the *White Angel*, the ship on which your father returned, carried only some crude wool rugs made in Barnstable, and two hogsheads of metheglin..."

"What's metheglin?"

"It's a fermented beverage made with honey and many different herbs. It's said to be well-favored in England, but I've had some and found it vile-tasting. Although there were two full hogsheads of metheglin on board the *White Angel*, on arrival there were only six gallons left. We were told the rest was lost to 'leakage.'" He chuckled.

"Did the ship carry anything else?"

"Quite a lot, but she and the *Friendship* were unloaded of all these goods in the Massachusetts Bay colony before sailing here. The profits from the sale of those goods will go to James Shirley and his partners and to your father."

"Oh." I didn't know what to say, I was so stunned.

"Hatherly also found the colony's accounts kept by your father very hard to decipher, with many seemingly unorganized entries and intricate notations. From his initial review, with some work by the governor, it seems we have been charged exorbitant interest rates, charged for things we didn't order, and charged double for some purchases. The Council, and in particular the governor, are quite angry."

"What will happen to my father?"

"Despite their misgivings, the Council recognized the good deeds and hard work your father has done for us, and they seemed inclined to overlook these problems for the time being. But a more thorough examination of the books will occur."

My sigh must have been audible, because Thomas placed his hand on my arm to comfort me.

"Don't worry about what may not happen, Mary." He removed his hand.

"And now I have to leave…it's dark and I have some distance to walk."

I stayed at the gate, listening to his footsteps fade, and found his leaving made me sadder than the news of my father's misdeeds.

Chapter 23

A Smallpox Epidemic and Isaac Allerton Leaves the Colony

Mary Allerton, Stony Brook, 1633

During the next year, the children grew like weeds, the boys joined Master Bradford in working the fields, and Mistress Bradford and I toiled endlessly to keep them fed and clothed, while minding the youngest.

The governor continued to struggle with the wide range of his duties for the colony. He maintained a voluminous correspondence, and after seeing him at his desk, writing night after night, I asked him one morning what he wrote about.

"I'm writing the history of Plymouth Plantation, Mary."

"The story of the people who came on the *Mayflower*?"

"In part, but much more."

"Why would you do this?"

"So that people who follow us will know why we came to this wild and empty place and how we overcame adversity and prospered. It's a testament to our faith and resilience. I only hope what I write will be worthy of remembrance."

I had nothing to reply, and the governor hungrily attacked the bread and cheese I had brought for his breakfast.

For many years, a candle burned each night as he wrote, and I eventually learned he had entitled his book *Of Plymouth Plantation.*

ꙮ ꙮ

That year, some of the colonists in Duxborough asked to be dismissed from the Plymouth church to form their own. The governor and the Council agreed, but even though he recognized this action was inevitable, the governor was morose for weeks afterward when the subject came up. One evening, after he'd offered some long and heartfelt prayers, he made an announcement to the family gathered for our meal. "My dear wife and family, I have decided to ask the Council to elect another governor. I don't know how they'll respond, but my burden has become so heavy as to be unsupportable."

Mistress Bradford reached across the table and placed her hand on his. "If this is what you want, then I support you."

I noticed the small upturn of the corners of her mouth and knew she was pleased. Her husband needed to tend to the family's well-being. And indeed, not long afterward, he announced that Edward Winslow had been chosen to replace him as governor. His argument to the Council must have been very convincing. We did indeed see more of Master Bradford, but the business of the colony never ceased, as Master Winslow and Council members often came to the farm to discuss ongoing problems.

ꕥ ꕥ

Elizabeth, servant to the family, became ensnared in one of these problems. She came crying to Mistress Bradford one morning, while Mercy was helping me mix and bake the day's corn bread.

"Good mistress, I fear that my husband has broken the law."

"Shush, Elizabeth, you'll wake little Joseph. Let's sit down and talk about this quietly."

An active three year old, Joseph was exactly like his older brother William, always running from one thing to another. When he finally tired, he sat down and fell asleep. Currently, he leaned against the chest in the corner, snoring softly, and his nap brought some blessed peace.

Both women sat and Mistress Bradford asked, "What is your husband's trouble?"

"My husband, as you know, is indentured to Master Samuel Eddy. He still owes some four years of service, but he has run away. I just saw him outside the gate. He told me his master worked him hard and he was exhausted. He left because he wanted a few days of rest, which Master Eddy would not give him. But once he ran away, he didn't know where he could go. He became lost in the woods. Thanks be to God, an Indian found him and brought him here."

"Is he still outside?"

"Yes."

"Then ask him to come in. We'll feed him and give him something to drink. Perhaps I can persuade him to surrender to my husband."

"What do you think will happen to him?" asked Elizabeth. "He's a good man, just not diligent in his chores. He told me he finds it hard not to be working for himself."

"I don't know what will happen, Elizabeth, but there will have to be some punishment. The law requires him to obey the terms of his indenture. "

Elizabeth's normally jolly expression was now one of fear and worry, but she did as Mistress Bradford had instructed, and soon her husband, a short, wiry man in dirty clothes with a dirtier face, appeared at the door. "Good morrow, Mistress Bradford." He stayed just outside.

"Good morrow, Goodman Brian. Please wash yourself with the water in the bucket by the door. Be thorough, as your goodwife keeps this house clean. When you have finished, you may come in. Elizabeth, get your husband some food."

Elizabeth put some bread on the table, along with jam. She also poured him a mug of beer, which Mistress Bradford now made since hops were available.

Brian came in silently and slid onto the bench at the table. The food disappeared in a moment, and he looked around expectantly for more.

Mistress Bradford regarded him sternly, saying, "You may eat with us for our midday meal. In the meantime, make yourself of use and clean the goat enclosure. Put the goat manure in a bucket with water, then pour it on the garden and muck it into the soil."

Brian left and we soon heard sounds of him drawing water from our well, followed by the bleating of the goats and then mucking in the garden.

Elizabeth scurried around for the rest of the morning, trying not to catch Mistress Bradford's eye, and Goodman Brian stayed outside. When Master Bradford returned for our meal, we discovered he'd already heard about Elizabeth's husband. Before we ate, he read from his Bible of Philemon's runaway slave, Onesimus. "Onesimus was wrong to run away, and his punishment was severe," he said when he finished reading. "However, he ultimately became the bishop of Ephesus. Like him, I hope you will raise yourself up. While I may forgive you, you've broken the law and you must face the General Court. The members may not be so forgiving. Well, Goodman Brian, what do you have to say for yourself?"

"I'm truly sorry, Master Bradford. Master Eddy does work me excessively and hard. I just had to have some time to rest."

"Were you a freeman before coming here?"

"Yes, both me and my wife. We hoped to earn a better life here."

"We'll pray for that after our meal."

With that, we ate heartily of an onion sop with bread, pickled cucumbers, roast rabbit, and dried fruit.

ꕥ ꕥ

Master Bradford left for the Plymouth settlement with Goodman Brian the following morning, and when he returned a day later, his face told us the outcome hadn't been good. Elizabeth had been very quiet and subdued in the master's absence, but when she saw his face, she collapsed, crying, "What's happened to my husband, Master Bradford?"

My mistress led her to their table, where she sat Elizabeth down, then sat herself, with her husband across the table. I took the all children outside at their mother's direction, and so I didn't hear what was said, except for a piecing wail from Elizabeth. She suddenly rushed by me to the far end of the garden, where she stood, shoulders shaking with her sobs. Mistress Bradford appeared in the doorway and shook her head when I started toward Elizabeth to comfort her.

Later that afternoon, while Elizabeth worked in the house and we were outside—I was mending clothes and Mistress Bradford sat beside me, grinding some herbs in a small stone mortar and pestle—the governor's wife told me what happened.

In a quiet voice she said, "Goodman Brian was judged guilty and whipped before being returned to Mr. Eddy. The punishment seems cruel, but the whipping didn't occur in a public place and Goodman Brian accepted the judgment. According to my husband, he has vowed not to run away again and will be obedient to Master Eddy in all things. The governor spoke kindly of him to the Court, hence the whipping was done in private."

"I think the punishment was overly harsh, given that Goodman Brian was not previously a servant."

"The Court felt it was justly applied."

Naturally, the boys came to me that evening to learn about Brian's fate, since they were used to getting news from me. They had grown tall and strong these past years, their voices had deepened, and they nurtured the beginnings of facial hair. Best of all, they now treated me with some respect and seldom made me the object of their pranks.

Knowing it was past time they stopped consulting me, I put my hands on my hips and said, "Nathaniel, Constant and Thomas, you're old enough to sit with the men at the Sunday service. You do men's work in the fields and also here within the confines of the farm. It's time you asked the governor directly about such things."

Their faces brightened and after the evening meal, all three went with the governor into the parlor. It was the beginning of a confidential relationship between them that lasted many years.

ꕤ ꕤ

My father remained a bane to the Council, which I learned during an evening meal which Thomas Cushman shared with us, not long after Master Hatherly's visit.

"See this letter from Mr. Shirley of London." Master Bradford pointed to a page in front of him on the table. "In it he writes, 'Oh, the grief and trouble that man Mr. Allerton has brought to you and us!'"

Mistress Bradford's head reared up and she said, frowning, "This isn't a good conversation now, husband," indicating me with a nod of her head.

Bradford pressed his lips together at the admonition from his wife but said no more on the topic. I stared at Thomas to let him know he would have to tell me later. He and Bradford sat together a long time that night, without the company of the boys. We were all abed when I heard the front door close, and I had to wait some minutes before I could creep down the ladder and slip out of the house. As usual, Thomas waited for me by the gate.

"So what of my father?" I asked him, without even a greeting.

"What, have you no 'good evening' for me?" When I didn't answer, he said, "It isn't all bad news, Mary."

"But he's my father! What has he done?"

Thomas waited a moment or two, then began. "Our debt to London three years ago was 2200 pounds, but now it's 6000 pounds, even though we have paid 600 and sent many beaver pelts to London.

Unfortunately, much of the increase is due to your father's dealings."

I couldn't comprehend these amounts, but his words weighed heavily on my mind. "Is there any good news at all?"

"If there is anything good, it derived from his brother-in-law's death."

Godbert Godbertson, whose wife Sarah I remembered with guilty irritation, had died of an infectious fever a few months earlier along with Sarah. Although they had lived in my father's house following their arrival on the *Anne*, I'd never grown close to them, but still, I felt sad for my father's loss. Remember was the one who told me of their deaths, and she had heard it from Fear. Such was the goodwives' network.

"Godbertson owed more in debts than he had in assets, and he owed the greatest part of his debt to your father. Your father decided the other creditors should be paid before he received anything. This will bring some money to the colony. And he pledged that what he received after they were paid could be applied to our debt. There is only their young son, Samuel, remaining to inherit, and your father has taken him into his family."

Remember had told me about Samuel's arrival. She remembered him as the fussy baby she'd cared for when his parents first arrived, but now he was well-schooled in hard work by his father and a pious and quiet boy. He had become withdrawn in grief at the loss of both parents, but my sister hoped he would find some happiness in the companionship of her half-brother Isaac, now six.

Thomas placed his hands on my shoulders, and I felt a jolt of emotion at his touch. *Why do I feel this?*

"So you see, my dear Mary, it isn't all bad news."

"No, and I thank you sincerely for the gentle telling. You're a kind man, Thomas."

"Only because I enjoy your company. You're very intelligent for a woman, if a bit forward," I heard a chuckle, "and I often find your questions to me challenging."

While I should have felt offended, his words pleased me.

ॐ ॐ

Not long after that evening, Master Bradford kept everyone at the table after a mid-day meal. "I have serious news for all of you. Smallpox has visited our Indian neighbors, causing terrible suffering and death. I've received word that those Indians living near our trading post at Aptucxet have fallen sick of this disease and have died miserably. As those afflicted by the pox lay on their hard mats, the pox would rupture, and the contents would leak out. They died like rotten sheep, covered with blood.

"They weren't able to help one another, not even to make a fire or fetch water to drink or bury the dead. When they couldn't gather wood to make a fire, they burned the dishes they ate from and then their very bows and arrows. Some would crawl out on all fours to get a little water and sometimes die on the way.

"Those of our faith at the trading post, though at first afraid of the infection, heard their pitiful cries and had compassion. Each day they fetched them wood and water, made them fires, got them food and fed them whilst they lived, and buried them when they died. Very few of the Indians survived, but by the marvelous goodness and providence of God, not one of those caring for them became sick, even though they did these chores daily for many weeks.

"Now this disease has made its way to our colony and some here are afflicted."

With that, we all knelt while Master Bradford prayed for us to be spared from this disease. When we rose, we looked at each other in fear. What he had told us sickened me, and I could see this in the faces of the family. "You all must remain here for now," he told us, "within the palisade of our farm, as all our neighbors will keep to theirs, to avoid exposure to the pox. No one will travel to the Plymouth settlement."

Despite precautions, twenty of our congregation died before the spread of this terrible disease ended, and it took the life of our physick, Samuel Fuller. He had tended ceaselessly to the afflicted and dying, before catching the disease himself.

One day we heard a banging on our gate, sometime after the disease had ended in the settlement. Since Master Bradford was away visiting our neighbor, Thomas Prence, Mistress Bradford went to the gate to discover the source of the noise. I followed right behind, warning the children to stay at the house.

A Wampanoag family stood outside our gate, a young man, his wife large with child, and two young children—one boy, one girl. The father gestured with his hands, begging for food. Indeed, his two children were as thin as twigs. I knew their crops had been poor the past year—with all the deaths, there had been no one to work their fields. Mistress Bradford looked the family over carefully. She found no sign of the pox, nor could I see any.

"I think they left their village to escape the disease. God has clearly not provided for them, but we will," she said to me. Without opening the gate, she held up her hand to signal them to wait, then turned back to the house.

Once inside, she gathered up most of what we had on hand for food at the time —two loaves of bread, smoked meat, turnips, parsnips, and all of our eggs, placing everything carefully in a large cloth, the ends of which she tied tightly.

"Won't Master Bradford notice the poorness of our evening meal?" I asked.

"Probably, but we will make bread immediately and surely there are more eggs in the chicken house." She lifted the bundle of food carefully and carried it out to the gate. "Open the gate, Mary," she told me. I opened the gate, and the family retreated, probably more afraid of us than we of them. Mistress Bradford stepped out, placed the bundle carefully on the ground, then retreated into the yard, closing the gate.

I watched as the woman squatted and carefully untied the cloth to see the contents of the bundle. Her eyes widened and she looked up at us with a shy smile and some glistening of tears in her eyes. She immediately tore off chunks of bread to hand to her children, before retying the cloth and lifting it carefully. The children were busy stuffing bread in their mouths but stopped long enough to give us a smile. Then the family left, taking the path running into the woods behind our house.

With a soft look on her face, Mistress Bradford watched the family walk away, then said, "We need to hurry to make sure we have food for tonight. Mary, can you pull some onions and parsnips from the garden? I'll make a sop and Elizabeth can get a loaf of bread ready for the oven. This must be our secret, child, for as much as my good husband practices charity, I fear he will consider ours most uncharitably. He cares only for our well-being and will see this as a risk not worth taking."

We never spoke of this in Master Bradford's presence, but some months later, unseen hands left a brace of rabbits outside our gate.

Later we learned that more than half the Wampanoags had died, along with many of the Massachusetts and Narragansett nations.

ဢ ဢ

The death of our physick from smallpox devastated those in our colony. This kind and caring man had not only provided services and comfort through his calling but was a godly man and a deacon in our church. The Bradfords, their children and I sailed to Plymouth to attend Master Fuller's burial service on the hill overlooking the bay, where so many had been buried. Being there brought back memories of my mother, and I missed her anew. She had receded in my memory as the years passed, but on that bright summer day, I felt her closer to me than I had in a long time.

We hadn't planned to stay, and since the weather was fine, the sail home in the afternoon was easy. Mercy and Joseph were tired and leaned against William, now a gangly but strong nine-year-old. Our boat was not overcrowded—Thomas and Constant Southworth had stayed home since the motion of the waves nauseated them. As I watched Master Bradford and Nathaniel manage the sails and the tiller, I enjoyed the fresh smell of the air, the salty spray and the slap of waves against the hull. I thought how nice it would be if I could sail, but I was sure it would be considered unseemly for a girl.

At some point as we sped along, I asked Mistress Bradford what would happen now to Mistress Fuller and her son and daughter.

"I'm certain Master Fuller's wife and children will inherit the house and his belongings. Since the children are still young, it's good that Bridget will be able to raise them in the only home they've known."

I further learned from Mistress Bradford that the goods of all who died were inventoried either before or after their death, and their inheritors were named either in a written will or by testament to the Plymouth Court. In many cases, the inheritors were the wives, and in this way the women of the colony became the heads of their households and the managers of their husband's properties…at least until they remarried.

ॐ ॐ

On the afternoon of a hot summer day, there came a loud knock at our door. The door was open for the air, and when I approached it, I saw a young man whose looks reminded me vaguely of William Bradford. He also had the governor's thick black hair, some glued to his forehead with sweat, and dark eyes. When he asked politely after Master Bradford, I welcomed him in, saying, "He isn't at home this afternoon, but Mistress Bradford is. Whom should I tell her comes to call?"

"John Bradford, Mistress."

John Bradford! William Bradford's son from England!

"Who is it, Mary?" Mistress Bradford called from the parlor.

"A surprise, Mistress Bradford." I led John to meet her.

Alice Bradford was indeed surprised and also very delighted at the arrival of her stepson. She knew how her husband had missed him. After introducing me, she gathered the younger children to meet their half-brother. John was much taken with Joseph, ruffling his hair, and he gave a little bow to Mercy.

"Both my husband and our son William are in the fields today with my sons Thomas and Constant Southworth. Would you care to rest after your journey? Are you hungry or thirsty?"

"Some small beer only, please. After that, if you could give me directions, I'll go to meet my father."

When Master Bradford returned with John that evening, his face was alight with happiness. He couldn't stop looking at his grown son, as if in disbelief he was actually there. At his father's asking, John led the prayers that evening and then Bradford read from the Bible the story of the lost son. They talked energetically at the table that night, the joy between them evident. John would spend some time with us but eventually moved to the house Master Bradford still owned on First Street in Plymouth. From there, he worked lands owned by his father and later some of his own.

That year my father left the colony. His business dealings with the London merchants and his self-enrichment had finally created such a cloud of doubt about his honesty that he decided to move north to Marblehead Neck, near Salem. I believed he thought he might be expelled from the colony. I only learned of this decision during a visit from Remember, and, after she'd told me, my sister and I shared a long embrace and wept together. The passing years had worked to bring us close.

One warm late summer day, the family and the Bradford's tenant farmers were all in the fields for the harvest. Now we not only grew the Indian corn, but also barley, wheat, and hops. I was tasked with gathering the ripe corn, the husks still green but the silk at the top brown. After twisting and removing the ears, I placed them in my apron and carried them to a basket by the side of the field. The younger William came behind me, gathering the husks and stems to use as fodder for our goats and sheep. What corn we didn't cut that week, while it was still sweet, we would later take for drying or for making succotash, an Indian dish I liked.

As I worked, I wondered if my father had already left for Gloucester and felt hurt that he might have done so without saying good-by. Just then I heard someone call my name from the side of the field and looked up to see my father waving. I left my work and walked over to him. "I'm happy to see you, Father."

"It's good to see you as well, Mary. I see you're in good health. I've come to tell you I'm moving the family to the Massachusetts when the harvest is in."

"Yes, Remember told me." My eyes teared up. "I'll miss you all. Will you return?"

"Yes, of course, when business and the crops require my presence. I'm not renting the house, so I'll have a place to stay when I do."

"Will you bring Remember to visit me sometime? I'm sad to think I might not see her again."

"Yes, yes," he replied impatiently. "But I imagine she will marry and then she can decide to come or not, with her husband."

He placed his hands on my shoulders. "You have become a proper woman, Mary, although not…" and he smiled, "…without some difficulty."

I had to return the smile, although there were still tears on my cheeks.

"I'm ever your devoted father." He embraced me, then turned and strode away.

As I watched him, I wondered if I would see him again. Some part of my life felt over.

One evening not long after, I was in the parlor, looking for one of Joseph's toys, when I happened to see a page of Master Bradford's history of the colony. I did snoop, and what I read shamed me: "Mr. Allerton had deserted us but not before having brought us into the briars. He leaves us to set up his own trading house in Maine, which will cut off our trade there as well."

From that time on, I would occasionally get letters from my father. Owing to Mistress Bradford's teaching, I could read them myself. Since it was unseemly for a girl to write a letter, I wasn't able to send him my news, but Master Bradford would still communicate with him from time to time. My father's letters to me were now my only tie to my past.

Chapter 24

A Death in the Family and the Hocking Misadventure

Mary Allerton, Stony Brook, 1634

That year Master Bradford had the house enlarged, with the addition of a second floor to provide sleeping space for the crowded household members. The work disrupted the family with constant noise and planks of wood everywhere, but to my mind this change was long overdue.

I thought the casement windows with glass diamond panes were quite a luxury, and there was now a trimmed slab of stone below the front door. The entire farm was surrounded with a secure wooden palisade that also kept out the wild animals attracted by Mistress Bradford's lettuces and other vegetables. With the addition of two actual rooms above the main floor, instead of a loft, I now slept with Mercy and the servant Elizabeth in one, while the boys kept to the other. It was difficult to judge which room had the noisier snores.

ℌ ℌ

The Bradfords now had a few sheep, kept in their own enclosure and overseen by one of the boys when they were put out to pasture. I soon discovered these were sheep for eating, not for wool, and I asked Mistress Bradford why their wool couldn't be used for weaving.

"Their wool is made of short, coarse and weak fibers, Mary."

"What kind of sheep have good wool, then?"

"Merino sheep. They have an especially long, soft coat and have been bred with our English sheep for vigor. Master Bradford looks to purchase some, but for now, we still have to purchase our clothes or fabric from England."

Mistress Bradford wove her own linen, however. Her flax seed had grown well, and she now had a small spinning wheel to spin the flax, along with a loom for weaving it. She began by showing me how to harvest the flax stalks, which she did before the plants even flowered, explaining I must pull the plants out by their roots.

"Why by the roots?"

"To get the longest fibers, but we won't take them all. We need to leave some to mature for their seeds." After tying the stalks in bundles, she said, "Come with me, Mary, and I'll show you how to ret the flax." She lifted two bundles and I took another two, and I followed her down the hill to the bank of the Jones River.

"What does ret mean?" I asked as we walked, wondering what we would be doing at the riverbank.

"It means soaking in water. We'll set these bundles in the river water, which will soften and remove some of the bark from the fibers. But mind you—when we come back for them, they will give off a terrible odor."

She weighed the bundles down and tied them to shore, and when we came back for them a week later, the bundles gave off the most horrible rotting stench, almost as bad as a chamber pot.

"What do we do now, mistress?" I asked, trying to keep the water from the bundles off my clothes as we walked back to the house.

"We unbundle the stalks and lay them out to dry. Once they're dry, we will scotch them."

I learned that scotching meant scraping a wooden knife down the length of the fibers to remove any bark that had not fallen away. It was difficult, and the dried bark cut my fingers. Next, we heckled the fibers by combing them through a bed of nails on a piece of board, something Governor Bradford had made his wife.

Mistress Bradford then showed me how to spin the fibers into a yarn using the distaff pole attached to her spinning wheel, a task I failed at utterly for some time, wasting the fiber and more than once eliciting some chiding from my mistress. She then wound the flax thread around a bobbin, ready to weave into linen. Using the small loom was my favorite task, as I found the repetitive movement of the shuttle relaxing.

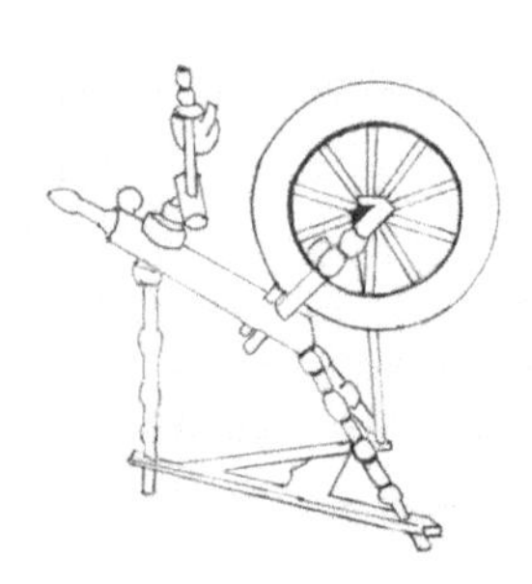

Flax Spinning Wheel

ꕤ ꕤ

Early that year, I was surprised to receive a letter from my father.

To my dearest Daughter Mary,

I regret not to have returned to Plymouth to check on your welfare, but our life here in Marblehead Neck is very busy, as I'm much occupied by my trading business at posts I have established at Pentagoet and Machias. I unfortunately lost the Machias post when the King ceded most of this northern coastline to the French.

I'd heard the Governor using some colorful language when talking about the Pentagoet post because it was close to the one the colony had built at Cushnoc, which was overseen by Master Winslow. The proximity of the two trading posts meant they would be competing for trade with the Indians, which would only serve to increase Winslow's longstanding vexation with my father.

This next news weighs heavily on my heart. As you know, disease has lately traveled though in our colony. I'm deeply sorry to tell you of the death of my dear wife, Fear.

I nearly dropped the letter after reading this and sat down on a bench, overcome with the thought of losing my stepmother. Fear and I had never established a warm relationship, but she was not much older than I. I wondered how my sister felt.

Disease had come back to the Plymouth colony as well, but I hadn't thought it reached the Massachusetts colony. By God's grace, we'd had been spared by our isolation on the farm, but it struck close by. Mistress Prence, daughter of Elder Brewster and wife of the man who was now governor, had succumbed not long before. Tears finally came for my father and Fear's children, and I sobbed quietly until Mistress Bradford sat beside me and gave me the comfort of her arm around me. She took the letter and read it, then understanding my grief.

Finally, I took the letter back to read the rest.

When he is old enough, I plan to send young Isaac to live with Elder Brewster and be taught by him, so that he will grow up to be learned.

Your sister Remember is well and will soon marry Master Moses Maverick, a righteous and godly young man. His father is the minister in Dorchester, and Master Maverick became a freeman this year. I believe your sister and he are well suited.

You are ever in my thoughts, and I beseech God daily to favor you with His love, to the praise and glory of his name,

I remain your loving Father,
Isaac Allerton

I turned to Mistress Bradford, who said, "So there is some happiness to leaven the sad, my dear daughter. We should thank God for taking Fear into his loving arms and pray for the continued health and joy of your sister in her coming marriage." We knelt and prayed, but memories of Fear still occupied my mind, and I knew her death would affect the Brewsters deeply.

At the evening meal that night, Master Bradford asked about my father, and I told him the contents of the letter. I detected a small upward turn of his mouth when I mentioned the loss of the Machias trading post, but he said nothing, except to tender his sympathy at the death of my stepmother. I asked him to explain what it meant when my father wrote Master Maverick had become a freeman.

"It means Master Maverick is a land holder and now possesses all the rights and privileges of a citizen, Mary. Being a freeman gives you the right to vote. To become a freeman here in Plymouth Colony, you need to be elected by the court. You don't need to be a member of the church, but in the Massachusetts Bay colony you do have to be a Puritan."

"Are you a freeman?"

Bradford sighed at my impertinence. "Yes, for many years now. Eventually, I hope Constant and Thomas Southworth, Nathaniel and young Thomas will all become freemen."

We prayed again after our meal, this time about the virtues of obedience and respect.

Now I now knew what he meant when Thomas had told me he had become a freeman and would now serve on various juries. I hadn't seen him much recently, since he worked his land grant and also surveyed for highways. As our colony grew, so did the need for roads between townships.

One morning, as Mistress Bradford and I were making bread from cornmeal, I asked her, "Is there anything other than corn for making bread, Mistress?"

She snorted at that. "I'd forgotten you would never have had bread made from anything but corn! There is bread made from wheat, which is most common in England, and also from rye. We've had little luck with wheat—my husband tells me the soil is too poor and rocky for this crop. I myself prefer rye and I hope soon to have rye flour, but until then, corn we have aplenty. I hear Master Jenney has received permission to build a grist mill in Plymouth. Won't it be wonderful when we no longer need to use a mortar to grind our corn flour?"

"Indeed." Since Elizabeth or I normally did the grinding, a mill would be most welcome.

ꟲ ꟲ

Master Bradford often discussed the situations with our trading posts with Nathaniel, who now served informally as his secretary, and with Thomas Cushman, whenever he came to visit.

One evening, I couldn't help but overhear some of this from my room above the parlor below. Bradford, Nathaniel, and Thomas sat there talking well after dark, their words reaching me through the floorboards. To tell the truth, I lay with my ear to the floor, listening through the cracks.

Master Bradford had just returned from a long stay in Boston, weary and somewhat depressed. "It seems we are now challenged on all sides by others wishing to do trade near our own trading posts," I heard him say. "And now, after a murder on the Kennebec River, Master Alden, our old friend and a righteous man, was arrested in Boston for that murder."

"I hadn't heard, sir. Why was he arrested?" I heard Thomas ask.

"It seems a man named John Hocking, of the Massachusetts settlement of Piscataqua, sailed up the Kennebec River with goods to trade with the Indians. When he reached our trading post there, Master Howland, who oversees our business with the Indians, told Hocking to return home, that we had a patent for the post. He knew Hocking wanted to take our profit by sailing further upriver to intercept the Indians coming to trade.

When Hocking and his crew continued on, Howland followed him and asked him again to leave. When Hocking refused, Howland sent two men in a canoe to cut the mooring cable of Hocking's boat. Hocking then shot one of our men in the head, killing him. A friend of the dead man then shot at Hocking and killed him."

"How was Master Alden involved?" asked Thomas.

"Master Alden had just arrived at our post with a load of supplies and, after the incident, he returned south, stopping in Boston. Word of the murder reached the authorities in Boston before he did, and they had him arrested and put in jail."

"Why would they do that without hearing both sides of the story?"

"I believe, being Puritans, they were more inclined to take the word of other Puritans."

I clapped my hand over my mouth to keep from blurting out, "But that isn't fair!" I'd known Master Alden from our first year here. He had lived with us for a while before marrying Priscilla Mullins, and a gentler and kinder man I'd never met.

Thomas spoke my mind. "I cannot imagine why this would happen to such a good man."

Bradford replied, "When we first heard of this, Captain Standish was determined to leave immediately for Boston to demand Alden's release. To smooth his way, I gave Standish a letter to their governor, stating we considered Alden's arrest an unfriendly and unfair act. Standish also took a certified copy of our patent, showing our rights on the Kennebec."

"Did Standish obtain his release?"

"Yes, but not at first. The colony leaders feared that without taking action against us, the king might send a general governor to adjudicate the situation, something they wanted to avoid. So I traveled north with Governor Prence to attend a conference with the Massachusetts governor, some colonists of Piscataqua, and other leaders from Boston. In the end, the Massachusetts representatives decided the case fairly and laid the blame and guilt on Hocking. Thanks be to God, Master Alden is now home. But the seriousness of this event cannot be underestimated. Both governors decided to send Edward Winslow to England to ensure no harm comes to either colony as a result of this incident."

Their voices lowered as they talked of this and that. I fell asleep there on the floor, enveloped in the smoky smell of Bradford's pipe tobacco penetrating through the spaces between the floorboards.

ꟷ ꟷ

Later that year, I approached Master Bradford with a question which had long nagged me. He would think me forward in asking it, but if I worded it correctly, he would see it as a religious lesson.

I waited until an evening meal, when he usually expounded on various topics with Nathaniel and Mistress Bradford's sons. At a pause in their conversation, I asked, "Master Bradford, I'm hoping you can tell me of the difference between our beliefs and those of the Puritans. Do we believe differently? Are their practices of faith much different from ours?"

Bradford's thick eyebrows rose, and I noticed a small shake of Mistress Bradford's head, in response to my impertinence.

The tension in my shoulders relaxed when he smiled and replied, "Mistress Allerton, I'm surprised such issues are of interest to you, but perhaps this is an instructive moment for Nathaniel and the other boys."

I doubted that Joseph, at four years of age and still sitting in a highchair, would understand anything, but I was pleased he decided to answer me.

Bradford speared a piece of chicken with his knife and chewed on a bite before beginning. "Both Puritans and Separatists follow the teachings of John Calvin, but we differ from the Puritans in that we have formed our own church, apart from the Church of England. The Puritan church is still aligned with the Church of England with some of its idolatry and celebrations and we are not. In our church, the congregation can choose and ordain our own ministers. The Bible is our only doctrine. We recognize no importance to Christmas, Easter and other days celebrated by the Church of England, only the sanctity of our services on Sunday and the truth of the Bible. Our church and our community are one and the same."

My ignorance must have concerned him, because Master Bradford continued, "The Puritans want to reform the Church of

England from within. Their worship therefore follows that of the Anglicans in most of its trappings. But there is a clear line in their society—their church is tied to our government whereas ours is not. Does this answer your question?" He probably assumed that as a young woman, I would not be able to grasp these ideas.

"Thank you, Master Bradford, for this explanation. But is Puritan marriage civil or religious?"

I believe he was surprised I'd understood what he'd told us. "We believe since our Scripture does not identify marriage as a religious rite, it must therefore be a civil function. For Puritans, marriage remains a religious rite." With that, he resumed eating and asked the children about what they had learned that day.

It seemed to me the differences between Separatists and Puritans were very blurry.

ঌ ঌ

That winter, we moved back to the Plymouth settlement before the Jones River froze over. How tight and cramped the little one room house seemed to us all! I wondered when a church would be established near our new home in Stony Brook, as more Separatist families had moved to that area. It would be so much easier to overwinter there.

Thomas Cushman came frequently to share meals with us that winter. He often spoke at our Sunday services, reminding us of the lessons of the Bible with gentle and intelligent comments. I was quite taken with him as he spoke, thinking him rather handsome. My thoughts wandered to our secret conversations and the touch of his hand on my arm or my shoulder. I had to force myself to pay attention to his words, since he later liked to ask me what I thought of his chosen subject. Perhaps I imagined it, but I felt his eyes on me even when he discussed some issue with the governor at our evening meals.

Occasionally we had time to speak alone, although in the noisy and boisterous house, not as often as I would have liked. One evening before he left, he asked me to accompany him to the gate on some pretext or other—I don't remember now—so I donned my cape and followed him outside.

"You look very comely today, Mary. I found it hard to keep my mind on my words as I spoke at our afternoon service."

My heart raced and I bowed my head so he wouldn't see the flame in my cheeks. After a rather long silence, during which I struggled to find the right reply, I finally said, "And I found it equally hard to pay attention to you."

"Why? Because of Joseph squirming in his seat beside you? I couldn't help notice he slipped off the bench more than once."

"No, because of you." I whispered these words, embarrassed at my forwardness.

I heard his quick intake of breath, then he stepped closer and wrapped his arms around me, speaking softly in my ear. "I think of you constantly. I regret I've had so little time to spend in your company."

I felt a soft kiss on my cheek, interrupted by the sound of the door opening. I jumped back, startled by Master Bradford saying, "Thomas, if you wish to court Mistress Allerton, you have only to say so."

"Indeed, sir, that is my intent."

A surge of happiness nearly lifted me off the ground.

"I'll see you soon, Mary," Thomas said, stroking my cheek with his fingers before turning to go.

We did spend more time together after that, although largely overseen by Master Bradford, who felt there was too much inappropriate consorting between young men and women.

Chapter 25

Illness in the Family and a Great Storm

Mary Allerton, Stony Brook, 1635

The freemen reelected Master Bradford as governor this year—in truth I had lost count of the number of times he had served in this capacity—and anxiety about the colony replaced his easier demeanor of the past year. Its business once again revolved around him. Members of the Council, in particular Thomas Prence, visited frequently, and the governor kept on with his copious letter-writing and his history of the colony.

Bradford often debated the question of our debt with his visitors. These nearly daily discussions could become loud and boisterous as the men drank beer and smoked their pipes. Since Mistress Bradford and I were in and out with chores, between us we were usually able to piece together what had been discussed.

On a day following one such an evening, we were both in the garden, weeding. The piercingly bright spring sun warmed our shoulders and backs, as Mistress Bradford and I pulled unwanted visitors from around the herbs. Some of the herbs we would later cut, dry and grind—mint, sage, parsley, thyme, marjoram, pennyroyal, and rosemary. This chore let me enjoy the young green of the new growth surrounding us and the muted sounds of newly born pigs, sheep and goats, all enjoying the day as much as I did.

"So what did you hear of the discussion yesterday, Mistress? Was it about the usual topic?"

"Yes, but our debt is plaguing the governor's Council more than ever. Edward Winslow, as you know, went to England as our agent. My husband told me Winslow was a good choice because he is well-regarded and felt to be honest. With him went a large amount of trade goods from the colony that should have sold for a good price." My mistress knew her words would affect me. At this point, we moved on to pull weeds from amongst her flowers. These were something of an extravagance because they'd been obtained from England: Eglantine roses, hollyhocks and peonies.

"I'm ashamed my father is thought so ill of," I replied, "but since none of it was my doing, I'm pleased Master Winslow has taken his place. But I overheard last night that Winslow is now imprisoned in a place called the Fleet. What is that? Why is he there?"

"It's the Fleet Street Prison, a terrible place so I'm told. He's there because he apparently ruffled some feathers with a petition he made to the colony's Lord Commissioners." She suddenly looked up and asked, "Where is Joseph? I don't see him."

I stood and looked around the yard. "He's over there, near the palisade, doing as he was told." Joseph, soon to be breeched, was gathering twigs for kindling. "William's in the pasture, herding the goats in for milking, and Mercy is feeding the chickens."

'Good," she said, as I once again bent to my task.

Resuming our conversation, I asked, "I also heard Master Winslow was to partition parliament for some relief from the French and Dutch raids on our trading posts." I brushed back some curls escaping from my coif.

She nodded, yanking on a deeply embedded weed.

"How could just writing a petition send him to a prison?"

"Well, it seems two other men had received patents for the Kennebec River area, theirs coming from the king's Council for New England. In order to pursue their rights to that land, they had to eliminate ours." The hardy weed finally came free and Mistress Bradford fell backward.

I had to laugh before I offered her my hand to right her. Laughing at herself, she took my hand, pulled herself up and brushed the dirt from her apron.

The situation seemed fundamentally unfair, so I said, "The king and his representative seem to grant patents to everyone."

"You're exactly right, Mary. To answer your question as to how Master Winslow came to be in prison, the two men who had received the patents asked the Archbishop of Canterbury to block Winslow and our claim. The archbishop questioned Winslow about his faith. When he discovered Winslow had solemnized marriages in civil ceremonies, he committed him to the Fleet Prison. To the archbishop's mind, only an ordained minister can perform a marriage." Mistress Bradford pulled on another weed, saying, "It seems to me the undertakers of our debt in London should arrange his release. As long as he's imprisoned, they don't get paid."

The perception of my mistress often impressed me. "Did you mention this to Master Bradford?" I asked, putting the weeds I'd pulled in a pile.

"No, I doubt he'd consider my opinion of any import." Weeding finished, we both stood and wiped the dirt off our clothes. "I wonder if Mistress Winslow knows anything about this?" she added.

ꟸ ꟸ

Before we heard more, sickness struck the family. Master Bradford had been to several meetings, and I thought someone there had passed on the illness. Soon everyone in the household but my mistress and I suffered from a high fever, sore throat, coughing and severe aching. Mistress Bradford worried it could be smallpox, but when no spots appeared, she was relieved. Now we just had to deal with the fever, aches and coughing.

With everyone confined to their beds, she sat me down at the table with her receipt book to determine how to treat her sick family. I'd already begun such a book for myself, detailing the various nostrums I'd seen her administer over the years, but I didn't understand why and how they worked. So, I asked her.

"I'll tell you what our family physick taught me when I lived in England, probably condescending to a young, inquisitive girl. He told me that there are four humors or fluids found in the body that influence a person's health and temperament. These are blood, phlegm, yellow bile and black bile."

"I understand phlegm and blood, but what are yellow bile and black bile?"

"I cannot tell you exactly what they are," she replied, "but I do know what organs they're associated with: blood with the liver, phlegm with the brain and lungs, yellow bile with the gall bladder, and black bile with the spleen."

Of course, I knew these organs, having dressed many a wild animal for meat.

"Later I'll teach you how each humor is related to a season and an element…"

"You mean air, water, earth and fire?"

"What a quick young woman you are, Mary! For now, we need to consider that the family is suffering from a severe imbalance of their humors."

"But what caused this?" I could hear the deep, fluid coughs of the children, the boys, Master Bradford and our servant, Elizabeth.

"I don't know—it might be excessive heat, foul air, digestive troubles, an affliction of the devil—in this case I think it is foul air, much like you experienced living on the *Mayflower* that first winter.

We must keep the doors and windows open so fresh air can circulate, and I need some leeches to bleed our patients."

"I saw Master Fuller use them once on my sister. But where can you find them?" The thought of using leeches excited me, though I didn't want to handle them.

"Get our bottle with the narrow mouth and put some chicken meat in it. Then go down to the river and find a place with weeds and leaf litter in the mud on the bottom. Sink the bottle there but tie some string around the neck. Then attach the other end of the string to something on the bank. We'll have leeches in the bottle by this evening."

I ran to do her bidding. The day bathed me in heavy warmth, so walking in the water without my shoes and stockings was pleasant, and I like squishing the mud between my toes. My skirt dragged in the water, despite my efforts to tuck it up, before I found a perfect spot out of the run of the river. Once the bottle sank, I anchored it to a small sapling close to the water's edge, then dawdled a while, enjoying the cool water. The sudden thought of why I was there brought my pleasure to an end, and I ran back to the house, carrying my shoes and stockings and flapping my skirt to dry it.

Mistress Bradford was steeping something fragrant in the small iron kettle over the fire as I came in. "I'm boiling some willow bark, rosemary and yarrow for a tea, because the children refuse to chew the bark to drop their fever," she explained.

I pointed to another, smaller kettle in the coals. "And that?"

"The bark of the slippery elm. I'll show you where it's found the next time we are out gathering things in the woods."

"What does slippery elm do?"

"It should help with the sore throat. Have you noticed that my husband often takes a concoction of slippery elm after eating an overlarge meal? It calms the stomach, as well. Hopefully I can barter for some honey, because it's good administered with honey."

Late that afternoon, when I retrieved the bottle from the river, there were quite a few leeches inside it. I watched in horrified fascination as Mistress Bradford applied some leeches to the inner arm of each of our patients. When they were full of blood, they rolled up and fell off. After letting their attachment sites bleed for a while, my mistress treated them with some strong alcohol the governor had purchased.

Within two days, everyone in the household felt better, although Mistress Bradford herself soon gave evidence of the same unbalance in her humors. I was pleased to think I knew how to treat her.

After this sickness had passed, I noticed a bit of gray had crept into Master Bradford's hair at the temples, and careworn lines marked his face. My mistress, too, had some gray in her hair, and time had also etched her features. I found it hard to imagine the Bradfords growing old.

ꕤ ꕤ

A great storm buffeted Plymouth in late August of that year. It began with a darkening of the sky with huge clouds rolling by at great speed, followed by steadily increasing winds. In anticipation of the storm, we drew buckets of water from the well to drink and brought our goats and the chickens inside along with their feed. We left the pigs and our new cow to fend for themselves. Soon the fierceness of the wind confined us within the house. We gathered by the hearth as the noise of the wind increased to where we couldn't hear each other speak, and streams of air blew in through cracks and under the door.

How was Thomas? Where was he? I feared for his life with each buffet of wind that shook the house. We heard the splintering of wood as the clapboards of our roof tore off. I wondered if the thatched roofs of some of our neighbors would survive at all.

Joseph cried out with the quakes of the house, and I tried to distract the children with stories from the Bible. We took turns praying for salvation. After some hours of terror, when the winds had calmed a little, Master Bradford ventured out, even as his wife implored him not to.

He returned visibly shaken by what he had seen. "The air is very heavy and filled with a strange orange light. I had to pick my way to the ocean shore, so many trees have fallen. When I got there, I found the water many meters higher than normal, with enormous waves, larger than I've ever seen, crashing on the sand and spraying me with water, even though I stood well back from ocean's edge."

This exited the boys and they pleaded to see for themselves, but Master Bradford settled them with a thunderous, "No!"

The winds then increased again, and until the storm passed, there was little to do but milk the goats and make sure the chickens were fed. Eventually, after a hasty meal of cornbread and dried meat, the children fell asleep, and eventually the rest of us did as well. During the night, we heard a crash when part of our chimney fell into the fireplace, wind sweeping from the chimney hole into the house along with some rain. Master Bradford told us there was nothing we could do about it and to go back to sleep. Still, I slept fitfully, waking often with the noise of the wind and fearful that Thomas may not have survived.

When we arose the next morning, we walked out into a new world. No longer did a palisade surround the farm, and the chicken house and lean-to for the goats, along with most of the fencing, had disappeared. The cow and the pigs were gone. Mistress Bradford's garden lay flattened, and in the distance we saw the naked roots of many overturned trees. Pine trees had broken off at various heights. The roof had sustained serious damage with the loss of clapboards, and of course most of the chimney was missing. Viewing this destruction made us even more grateful for our survival. Before breaking our fast, we knelt and gave thanks to God for keeping us all safe.

Mistress Bradford expressed some unease about cooking over the hearth with the chimney gone, but her husband assured her it was possible. After the boys removed what had fallen into the hearth, she lit a fire, but it generated so much smoke in the house that we all fled outside, coughing violently. After that, she had the boys build a fire-bed in the yard. Thomas and Constant brought out the iron tripod from which to hang a large kettle, along with the smaller kettle with legs and a flat fry pan to place on the coals. For the next few weeks, rain or shine, this is where Mistress Bradford cooked, until the chimney was rebuilt.

Thomas Cushman arrived right after we ate our first meal cooked outside. He was out of breath and anxious but broke into a smile when he saw me unhurt. He wrapped me tightly in his arms, right in front of Mistress Bradford, telling me, "Thank God. I prayed you were unharmed and came as soon as I could."

"Tsk," I heard from my mistress. "Did you not pray for us too, Thomas?" She smiled broadly as she said this. "And you should be more reserved in your affections in public."

"I'm glad to see you all are well," Thomas quickly replied. "And I will."

"Have some food. You must have set out early to be here so soon."

"Thank you, Mistress Bradford. I've not eaten since yesterday morning." Taking me aside, he brought me close to his chest and whispered, "I feared for you, Mary. I didn't sleep for worrying."

His words had my emotions soaring. "I was worried for you as well, Thomas. But thanks be to God, we both survived." I reached up and touched his cheek in affection.

After Thomas had eaten, the governor announced he was going to the Plymouth settlement to see how it had fared. Thomas proposed to go with him and promised they would return before nightfall. The governor had dragged the boat far up the bank when the storm first began, and it and its sail had survived, so we all went to the river bank to watch as Thomas rowed down the swollen river and raised the sail.

Nathaniel, young William, and Constant and Thomas Southworth then left in search of remains of the palisade, fencing, and chicken shed. When they returned with some of it, they told us the wood had been scattered over a half mile. Nathaniel then looked for the cow while the Southworths looked for pigs, and after some hours they returned, herding the spooked and dirty animals into the yard. I couldn't imagine how and where they had survived. Mistress Bradford, Mercy, Elizabeth, and I spent the day cleaning the garden and yard of smaller branches and twigs to the tune of Elizabeth's fretting over having no place to bake bread. The larger branches we encountered would need the strength of Master Bradford and Thomas to be cleared.

When the men came home that evening, they appeared much shaken. As we ate our evening meal, the governor told us, "The town has suffered terrible damage. Many houses have been destroyed and the roofs are gone from others. The power of this storm left a long stretch where all the trees are down, like a wide-open road."

We realized again how good God had been to us. We could rebuild, and no lives were lost.

Thomas stayed by my side that evening, occasionally squeezing my hand and looking at me with such love in his eyes that I longed to be alone with him. When he finally took his leave, we walked out into the growing darkness with his arm around me. Before he headed down to the river and his boat, he took my face in his hands and kissed me long and deeply. His kiss ignited my passion, and I longed for more.

ꕥ ꕥ

We now had plenty of firewood, and I overheard Master Bradford say, "God has given us one good thing from this tragedy. We have a great supply of hardwood trees already down, ready to cut for trade with London and the Massachusetts colony."

Over the next weeks and months, when not in the fields, he and the boys were occupied with cutting wood—some for our fires and rebuilding but most for trade. Mistress Bradford had to remind him several times until he found some men to help him rebuild our chimney. The boys worked on replacing the palisade and the animal pens. In the meantime, the goats helped themselves to Mistress Bradford's garden, until she gave Joseph the chore of minding them. Young William took it upon himself to make the new chicken shed and lean-to, and I thought he did a good job of it.

It seemed his father did too, because one evening afterward, Master Bradford said, "It seems our Lord has given my son His gift of carpentry. I've inspected what he's built and they are well-made. Let us give thanks to God."

It was as near to a fair blessing as I'd ever heard the father give the boy, and young William's face beamed with pride as we dropped our heads to pray.

Letters began to reach Bradford from the Massachusetts Bay colony, describing the wreckage of buildings and ships and the loss of life. Not two weeks later, I received a letter from my father, an unexpected occurrence. Taking the letter outside with shaking hands and fearing what it would say, I sat down on an upturned stump.

To my dearest daughter Mary,

I send you my warmest greetings and the love of a father. All of us here are well. I pray to God each day that you survived the great storm. If you would take the occasion to have the Governor reply to me, I would be most grateful.

Whilst I still grieve for my wife Fear, I have remarried. My new wife is Joanna Swinnerton of Marblehead and you should know that she is a kind woman who cares much for the children. We will continue to live in Marblehead, since I now have a shipping business here.

My small barque, the Watch and Wait, didn't fare well in the storm of last month. It sailed from Ipswich, England and was to land here, but the winds tore it apart on the rocks near Cape Anne. One of its passengers, a Reverend Avery, came to answer a pastoral call from our community. Accompanying him were his wife and nine children, and his cousin Thomas Thacher with his wife and six children. I'm sad to tell you only two of these passengers survived, Master Thacher and his wife. All the others were swept into the sea. Thacher found a plank which upheld him until he reached the shore of an island. There he found his wife entangled in some wreckage. With goods from the ship blown ashore, they were able to sustain themselves until they were rescued, some three days later. The loss of twenty-one lives and my ship has affected me most grievously.

Remember and her husband are well and prospering, and my children send you their most heart-deep greetings.

Be you lovingly saluted together with all the Bradfords. The Lord Jesus bless you.

Your devoted and afflicted father, etc.
Isaac Allerton

Relief flooded me when I read that my father and the family had survived the storm, but I felt surprise that he had remarried so soon after Fear's death. Then again, he'd had little time for the care of children since arriving on these shores.

ജ ഇ

When Reverend Ralph Smith suddenly left our church, the governor seemed even more annoyed than by the wreckage of the storm. He would expound on our inability to procure a pastor who would stay longer than a year of two at our evening meals, his frustration evident.

"Will we never have another minister? One who stays?" he asked loudly one evening, seizing the loaf of bread and violently tearing a piece from its end.

"My dear husband…" ventured Mistress Bradford in a soothing tone.

"I don't want any nostrums, wife. We've failed again."

The children shrank back from where they stood. Mistress Bradford offered him a platter of lamb meat, and he stabbed at the meat with his knife twice before securing a portion. She remained silent, hoping his foul humor would ebb.

Indeed, after a few mouthfuls of food, it did. "I apologize. I have allowed this matter to vex me over much. The Council ordered Master Winslow to bring back some able man to be our minister, and I should be patient."

ꟹ ꟹ

The governor's temperament didn't improve upon receipt of a letter from Mr. Shirley, the colony's main financial person in London, a short while later. After reading it, he left hurriedly to consult with his Council, returning the next day to discuss its contents with Master Prence, who'd been unable to attend.

With the smoke from their pipes collecting under the ceiling, the men reclined in chairs at the hearth, warming themselves from the chill air of late fall that seeped into the house. Mistress Bradford had Mercy read from the Bible, while I attempted to improve my knitting by working on a cap for Joseph, so of course we were privy to his conversation.

"My friend, we face yet another blow to the colony's finances. Mr. Shirley, it seems, will not take any money off the debt the colony owes him until he receives yet more goods from us. In addition, he fails to provide us with any account of the sale of the trade goods Winslow brought with him this last time, which were substantial. More rudely, he reminded me that we still owe money to pay for the *White Angel*—the ship that scoundrel Allerton bought for our trading business and then usurped its use. And now Winslow still sits in Fleet Prison, unable to do any business for us."

His choler got the best of him, because with this last sentence, he pounded the arms of his chair. My own face grew heated with the reference to my father.

Master Prence leaned in and said something which I couldn't hear, but I knew whatever his words were, they didn't soothe, because for some time afterward, the governor remained like kindling ready to be lit.

ꕥ ꕥ

I only learned the Edward Winslow had been freed and had returned home because of something Mistress Bradford had overheard. She shared this news as we sat outside, wrapped in our cloaks to enjoy a brisk fall day, mending clothes. The children seemed to rip their clothes daily, clothes already worn thin from use and handing down.

Young William sat nearby making a new broom, something we often needed because the children broke them in play, despite Mistress Bradford's frequent threats. His father had scraped the bark from a straight, thin, tree limb, of which we had plenty following the great storm, and had cut it to a useful length. To one end of it, young William bound a handful of strong twigs as tightly as he could manage, using twine his mother had given him.

"Mistress, I gather that Master Winslow was released from prison, based on last evening's discussion of the arrival our new minister."

"Yes, and this is the second one Master Winslow found for us. The first fell ill and died while Master Winslow was in jail. Just before he sailed from London, Winslow met John Norton and hastily procured his services."

"Is the governor not happy with this choice?" I asked.

Mistress Bradford smiled, recalling what she'd heard. "While I know my husband is relieved that Master Winslow has returned safely, the arrival of Pastor Norton has not improved his temper.

He's worried because Reverend Norton has made no commitment to stay here, lest he like somewhere else better. Plus the Council had to lay out seventy pounds—imagine that, seventy pounds!—so our new pastor could purchase things he needs for living in Plymouth. Yet more debt to irritate my husband."

The size of the debt was beyond my comprehension. "So, what have you heard about Master Winslow? Did he languish long in that terrible jail?"

"Seventeen weeks."

"Seventeen weeks!" This from Young William, who was clearly listening to us.

Mistress Bradford clucked. "Yes, a long time in a foul place."

"How was his release made, Mistress?"

"Master Winslow made it clear to James Shirley he would not be paid, as long as he, Winslow, remained in the Fleet. The authorities released him shortly thereafter."

We looked at each other and smiled knowingly.

"Money," she said. "It always comes to the money."

ꙮ ꙮ

Reverend Norton was well-liked. He joined us on occasion for meals, and I found him to be a gentle man whose presence had a calming effect on Master Bradford. His sermons were learned and interesting, and I hoped he would stay.

That trying year ended on a happy note. Nathaniel Morton, the Bradford's adopted son, married Lydia Cooper in December, a joyous occasion which we celebrated with a great meal. Visitors came from all over Plymouth, along with Massasoit and his three sons, plus some Wampanoag warriors and Hobomok and his family, who lived in a Wampanoag village not far from Plymouth.

While Thomas had not yet asked me to marry him, I felt certain he would. When we married, I hoped our celebration would be a bit quieter, but Mistress Bradford enjoyed company and never seemed to lack the energy to cook all the food.

Chapter 26

The Plymouth Court Is Busy and Another Marriage Is Celebrated

Mary Allerton, Rocky Nook, 1636

Thomas Cushman now came often to the Bradford house. My love for him and his for me grew in intensity, and it seemed I couldn't get enough of his touches and kisses during those rare times when we were alone. In fine weather, we would take long walks, arm in arm, and talk of all sorts of things, some instructive for me but a lot of them inconsequential. Our physical yearning for each other often became intense, but Thomas was ever mindful of the Bible and its teachings. The first time this happened, he stood back and quoted Hebrews 16:34: "Let marriage be held in honor among all, and let the marriage bed be undefiled." Thereafter, he would pull away, take a deep breath and say, "Hebrews 16:34." Although I longed to be with him in that way, I honored his wish, but not always in good humor.

On one of our walks in late spring, he drifted into a consideration of where we might live.

"Thomas Cushman!" I said, removing my arm from him and standing back. "How can you think about where we might live when you haven't yet asked me to marry you?"

I swore his face became as red as the maple leaves of fall.

"I just assumed..."

"A woman prefers to be asked, not just presumed."

He stood there, shifting from foot to foot. I'd never seen him this way, like a young boy and he eight years my senior.

Finally he took my hand, and looking into my eyes, he asked, "Mistress Allerton, I find you a most pleasing woman in every way. I hope to be your devoted husband. Would you consent to be my wife?"

At last! "Yes, Master Cushman, I do consent."

He took me into his arms and kissed me with passion. I hoped we would be like this forever, and I walked back to the Bradford house some inches above the ground.

When we entered the house, Mistress Bradford looked up from her sewing and, recognizing the happiness filling our faces, called the governor from his paperwork. "My good husband, I do believe Thomas has something to tell us."

ജ ഇ

We decided to marry at the end of the year. I would miss living with the Bradfords in Rocky Nook, since so many of the original *Mayflower* passengers—the Old Comers —were making a small community there.

The presence of so many from the original settlement now in Rocky Nook had led to the discussion of having a meeting house there for Sunday services. I believed the Bradfords grew tired of the winter move to their original house. Mistress Bradford often complained about the work involved in the yearly move and the cramped space of the original house.

Edward Winslow, now governor, appointed ten men, including Thomas, to examine the land around the Jones River for a suitable building site. In March, these men met at the Bradford's house, and I caught enough of their conversation to know they had made up their minds.

I overheard Governor Winslow say, "Master Bradford, in the opinion of these men, the Jones River land is a good place for a new meeting house. Do we agree to ask the members of the churches in Duxborough and Plymouth to consider it?"

A chorus of "ayes" followed, and thus within a short time, a meeting house was built in Rocky Nook, and Elder Brewster became our pastor. But it soon seemed we would need another one. While Reverend Norton was well-liked by the Plymouth community, he soon left for Ipswich, despite Governor Winslow's entreaties that he stay.

"I do believe it's because there are many rich men of his acquaintance in that settlement, Alice," Master Bradford said one evening. "He is ambitious and wants a better life."

Mistress Bradford nodded her head to this, hoping to keep his anger in check.

"We are now faced with finding a new pastor for our mother church and a pastor to lead the services at our new one, as Elder Brewster is frail. Will we never solve this problem?"

We were all grateful when the conversation ended there.

Despite the construction of the meeting house near Rocky Nook, our travels to the Plymouth settlement didn't cease. With Jenny's grist mill now fully working, the men took our corn and rye there for grinding. Our need for trade goods from London, Boston, and the Dutch didn't diminish, and I welcomed a trip with the Bradfords to Plymouth so I could see the progress on the house Thomas was building for us. I knew Thomas wanted to live close to his fields, and I'd hoped we would be able to move into my father's house, not far from the Bradfords. However, Thomas Prence had purchased it. Instead, Thomas bought land for a house on New Street in Plymouth and constructed, with the help of a carpenter, a simple one room house with a loft. It had several acres of land around it for a garden and animal pens, and I thought it would suit us well. I spent time after each visit imagining what my life would be like when I lived there.

ꙮ ꙮ

The year brought our colony more worries. The most serious concerned a conflict stewing in the colony named Connecticut. My first knowledge of the depth of Bradford's worry came during a discussion at a mid-day meal, when both Nathaniel Morton and Thomas Cushman were present.

"You may not know, but at least sixty men, women and children from the Massachusetts Bay colony now live in settlements in Connecticut. Our trading post is in Windsor, run under the direction of Master Winslow," Master Bradford said. "It seems that John Winthrop, son of the Massachusetts governor, came from London with a commission naming him governor of Connecticut. He was given the authority to seize land and to build a structure at the mouth of the Connecticut River they call Fort Saybrook. It was placed there to safeguard the river valley, which is a rich place for farming, from incursions by the Pequot tribe. The Pequots have been aggressively extending their lands, impacting the settlers, the Wampanoags, and other tribes, according to Massasoit."

"Does the Council expect trouble here?" asked Thomas.

"Possibly. It could spread."

In late August, I heard raised voices in Bradford's room, where he met with Governor Winslow and Thomas Prence. The heat of the day didn't help. "A pox on Governor Vane! Does he not realize what a threat he's created to our colony?" I heard a thump on the table, which had to be Bradford's fist.

"Calm yourself, William," I heard Master Winslow say. I knew he would not use Master Bradford's first name except in the most private and dire of circumstances. "What exactly have you heard from Governor Vane?"

"He had the temerity to write and tell me he'd sent a large party of men to Block Island, where they attacked a Niantic village. He did this in revenge for the killing of a trader and his crew by Niantics. Most of the Indians living there escaped, but the Puritans burned their village to the ground and carried away crops stored for the winter. The Niantics are our neighbors. What did he think, doing this?"

The voices tapered off to a level I couldn't hear, but Thomas later told me Pequots had begun to besiege Fort Saybrook and there were no signs of the siege lifting. Mistress Bradford became anxious on hearing this, since we lived far from the protection of the fort in the palisaded Plymouth settlement. Master Bradford kept his musket by the door, and he made shutters for the windows, which could be barred on the inside.

Although everyone remained alert, no warnings came and the colony remained peaceful.

ꙮ ꙮ

One evening in early October, Thomas and I sat outside. He had just returned from the Plymouth settlement, where as a freeman, he sat as a member of the General Court. Master Bradford had missed the court session with a rasping cough and painful chest, so after the evening meal, Thomas had told him privately what had transpired.

Now Thomas and I sat outside, alone, our arms entwined. With our marriage sworn, we were allowed to meet privately. *If only Master*

Bradford knew how often we had met in the past and what intimacies we'd shared!

We each had an apple, which had come from the Massachusetts Bay colony in trade and which Thomas had purchased. "These are so sweet and tasty," I said. "Thank you for this! Where can we get more?"

"I'm not sure, but I'll ask the trader from Boston the next time I see him."

"Better if we grow our own. Are there apple trees?"

Thomas chuckled. "Yes, and it seems former Governor Winthrop of Massachusetts is interested in having whole areas there planted with apple and pear trees. Perhaps I can find some seeds for us to grow. We'll also have to get some bees, though, for without them the trees won't bear fruit."

"Why is that?"

"I don't know. But there must be honey bees."

"What is a bee? Do they really make honey?"

"Bees are like wasps and they do indeed make honey, along with wax. There are none here naturally, so they were brought to the Virginia colony and then carried north in their hives. But I've been told they naturally migrate far afield."

"Perhaps we might be the first to have them here. Then we'd have honey—I never knew from where it came." Planning our future delighted me, but I saw Thomas' face become somber. "Is there bad news, Thomas? What's happening in the colony?"

"The Billington family is once more a source of irritation," he replied, placing the cores of our apples in his handkerchief for the seeds.

"Frances Billington?"

"No, Eleanor, Billington's wife. We found her guilty of slander against John Doane."

"What did she say about him?"

"If I repeat what she said, I fear God's retribution, Mary. I won't say more."

"How was she punished?"

"She was whipped and sentenced to time in the stocks."

"That poor woman. She's had a difficult life with that husband and sons of hers, all of them rough men. I often wondered if they mistreated her in some way, which led to her sharp tongue. Did you not notice how neat and clean her house always appeared, compared to others? Do you think she feared her husband?"

"Possibly. Many in the settlement have commented on how poorly her husband treated her while he lived," replied Thomas.

"She didn't deserve such treatment. She was one of the few women who kept our colony alive that first winter and spring," I said, thinking of that terrible time of death and deprivation. "She deserves our gratitude, not punishment."

Both of us sat lost in thought for a few moments. I remembered Mistress Billington's harsh treatment of me as a child, so long ago. Older now, I saw how hard she'd worked for all of us and knew I'd deserved my punishment.

"What else faced the court?"

"Well, a number of men and women were brought before the court for drunkenness."

"Is this a problem now?" I asked.

"Increasingly so. The owners of the ordinaries don't pass judgement on how much their patrons drink, even when they are loud and staggering about. The Court has always been lenient in its treatment of drunkards, but now I think its members are taking the problem seriously. John Holmes was censured for drunkenness, made to sit in the stocks, and fined twenty shillings."

Thomas leaned in and whispered in a conspiratorial way, "Did you overhear? ..." and here he pulled back and laughed because he knew I listened to everything.

After I struck him lightly on the arm for teasing me, he hugged me to him and kissed me with passion. I swear I heard him mutter 'Hebrews sixteen.'"

ꟸ ꟸ

Mistress Bradford sat me down by the hearth on the day before my wedding. When I looked at her face, which had become so dear to me over the years, I saw tears in her eyes.

"My treasured daughter, while I'm joyous on the occasion of your marriage, I'm also sad that you'll no longer be living with us and sharing our lives."

"I'll see you when you come to Plymouth, mistress. I'll always be your daughter, and I'll never stop needing your advice and wisdom."

More tears came, and she wiped them away with the hem of her apron. "I have a gift for you to mark your marriage." She stood and went to a chest, opened a drawer and withdrew a lovely platter, made of blue and white pottery in the Dutch way. "This will brighten your house."

My own tears flowed as I accepted her lovely gift, which would grace our home for many years.

"I would like you to call me Alice. If you're my daughter, then it's quite acceptable."

"Thank you, dear...Alice. I've come to consider you my true mother for many years, and I know my real mother would be pleased. I'll miss being here with you..."

We both wept at that, our hands clasped together.

I would still spend time with her, but as the children were now contributing members of the household—William at twelve, Mercy, nine, and Joseph, six—I was really no longer needed. And I knew in my heart our relationship would never be quite the same.

ഗ ഉ

The celebration of our marriage, despite my wishes for a quiet recognition, was still a somewhat raucous event. Thomas and I were joined in a civil ceremony in late December at the Bradford home in the Plymouth settlement. The singing of psalms and feasting, much like what had happened at Nathaniel's marriage the year before, went on for some hours. At times Governor Bradford seemed glum, because now both of his 'sons,' as he liked to call Nathaniel and Thomas, had left for lives of their own. But I knew him happy for us, not only for our love for each other but also for the fact we would add a second generation of Separatists to the colony.

Thomas and I left toward twilight to walk to our new home. The cold air and wind had us tightly wrapping our thick woolen cloaks around us. We both wore woolen mittens I'd knitted, so our hands kept warm. I linked my arm in his for stability as we walked from East Street, as the main street of the colony was now called, along the highway of flattened dirt that stretched between the former north and south gates of the village. We turned to the right at New Street, where Thomas had built our home during the past year. I saw a wisp of smoke coming from the chimney, slowly rising in the cold winter air.

"Is someone there, Thomas?"

"No, wife. You worry too much. I started a good fire this morning then banked it down—one of Mistress Warren's sons came to stoke it a while ago, so it would be warm inside."

The thick wooden door had iron hinges and a sturdy iron latch, which he opened to welcome me to my new home. Inside the light from the fire revealed the single, cozy room to which I had moved my belongings over several trips to Plymouth. The glowing hearth held iron pots, kettles and a skillet, some hung from a metal crane, all of which we had accumulated during the past year. I'd been happily surprised, on a visit to survey the progress on the house, to discover the walls had been lined with marsh grass and covered with daub and wattle, over which planks had been nailed to give us more respite from the cold. Our floors were of wood, and I remembered the cold earthen floor of my first home in Plymouth. That floor was forever torn up and constantly needing more soil packed down to fill the depressions. A small window in our new house had been placed to one side of the front door, its diamond-shaped panes reflecting the red and yellow of the fire.

Thomas had built or traded for some furnishings—a chest, a table and chairs, and a bedstead in the corner. On the bed lay a colorful blanket I had had woven with a flax warp and a woolen weft—called linsey-woolsey—thinking how it would keep us both warm. The chest held my clothes and some linen, lovingly woven over a year or more.

The Bradford's plate stood in a place of honor on a shelf Thomas had hung. Its sight filled me with happiness at the thought of the years I had spent in that household and sadness at the end of that part of my life.

A pewter candlestick, a gift from Master Prence, stood on the table, and after we had removed our cloaks and hung them on pegs set into the wall, Thomas lit the candle it held.

Thomas turned and held open his arms, into which I walked, the propriety of the past year forgotten in his caresses. Suddenly, I became shy and pulled slightly away.

"Does the prospect of our coming together frighten you, Mary?"

"Mistress Bradford told me that to be a good wife, I should lie down and let you have your will with me. She said there was no pleasure in it with her first husband but smiled when she talked about her first night with Master Bradford."

"Then I'll try to make sure there is pleasure in it for you, dearest, so you're not afraid."

Thomas touched me gently with kisses and caresses, which I returned, until my passion built with his. Then we undressed each other and lay in our bed, letting the pleasure of our first time together as man and wife overcome us. After, as I lay encircled in his arms, I felt complete in his love, in my own dear home, and hoped I might feel that way forever.

Chapter 27

A Witch, a Massacre, and a Birth

Mary Cushman, Plymouth Colony, 1637

The year after my marriage flew by, as I assumed the many duties of mistress of my own home, duties which I had mastered during my years with Alice Bradford. I cooked meals and baked bread, swept and cleaned, washed and mended clothes, knit stockings for us with wool from London, and planted the beginnings of a productive garden of vegetables, herbs and flowers. I fed the chickens we kept in a penned coop near the house and milked the goat Thomas had purchased. We vowed to have a cow as soon as we could afford to purchase one, so I would not have to buy or barter for cheese and butter. Later in the year, I hung a string of onions by the fire and fresh herbs from my garden from the rafters.

I think I fell even more deeply in love with Thomas that year. I missed his presence when he was working and eagerly looked forward to our evenings together and our nights even more. Thomas' lovemaking had me soon with child, and when Mistress Fuller confirmed my suspicions, I couldn't wait to tell him, meeting him at the harbor that evening when he sailed home from a meeting with Governor Bradford at Rocky Nook.

He looked surprised to see me waiting for him by the water. "Why are you here, Mary? Isn't there enough work to keep you at home?" he teased, as put his arm around me.

"Aye, there is, but I just thought I would walk home with you. How are the Bradfords?

"They are all well except for the governor, who again suffers from congestion of the lungs. Mistress Bradford clucks over him like a mother hen."

I smiled at that vision, as we walked up the street to our house, wrapping our cloaks around us against the wind. Thomas took my arm as he paused to look back on the blue expanse of the harbor, where several tall-masted ships rode at anchor a good way out.

"From Boston?" I asked, indicating the ships.

"One from Boston, the other from Virginia. There will be trading goods aplenty soon. Is there anything we need?"

"Some tobacco for your pipe? And also some soft wool for knitting and some fine wool fabric."

"And why would we need that? It seems to me we have enough clothing."

I stopped again, just outside our door. "Because there will be someone else needing clothes."

Thomas looked puzzled for a moment, then caught my meaning. His eyes opened wide in surprise, and he smiled broadly. "Are we to have a child?"

"Yes, in the fall."

He opened the door and pulled me inside, wrapping me in his arms and giving me a long, deep kiss. Then he whispered, "I couldn't be happier," in my ear.

Our union that night was tender and slow and joyful. I wondered if other women experienced such love.

ꙮ ꙮ

Until spring planting, Thomas attended to colony business. Now the surveyor for future roads that would link Plymouth with its northern and southern townships, he left me nearly every day on some job or other. During the evenings, he finished a high-backed bench to place alongside our hearth, the better to bask in its warmth on cold evenings, and then began work on a cradle.

Thomas and I would occasionally join the Bradfords for the midday meal, either at their home in Plymouth or at Rocky Nook. We would travel by boat, leaving early in the morning, and while I helped Alice with the cooking, Thomas spent time in conversation with Master Bradford, once again governor. I'd stopped trying to overhear what they talked about, except over our meal, of course. With some prompting, Thomas would tell me later.

Alice, well aware of my past attempts to hear what was discussed, said to me one day, "I notice you're not so attentive to the discussions of our husbands as you once were."

I felt my face heat at her meaning. "I just wished to know what was happening around us. Was I so obvious?"

"Yes, and I thank you for your undue influence," she replied, giving me a smile. "Mercy is adept at listening now, and we share what we learn as you and I once did." She looked lovingly at her daughter, who was kneading bread at the table. Her voice dropped and she whispered to me, "Have you heard of the witch brought to trial in the Massachusetts colony?"

"No, Thomas hasn't mentioned it." I shivered at the thought of witches. Our pastor warned us several times a year about cunning men and women who offered healing, conjuring and divining, all with malevolent purposes. "Who is this witch?"

"From what I've learned, her name is Anne Hutchinson. She is the wife of a prosperous man and has ten living children, and she also serves as a midwife."

"What is her sin?"

"She's been holding meetings of women in her home to discuss religious matters, which is most unseemly for a woman, and she doesn't believe a good life necessarily leads to salvation."

"What possible difference can she have with that belief?" I asked.

"She believes the grace of God comes from faith, not from doing good deeds, and she thinks only a few Puritan ministers preach the word of God correctly."

I gasped. This was blasphemous, even for a man. "But how is this witchcraft? It seems to me more like heresy."

"I believe that's the real reason for her trial, rather than actual witchcraft. She was large with child during the trial and spoke up without governing her tongue in reply to questions from the colony's lawyer, John Winthrop. He suspected her of using the devil's powers to subjugate men though her community of women. He charged her with fostering wickedness."

"What happened to her?" I asked, breathless with curiosity.

"As you suggested, the court judged her guilty of heresy, not witchcraft. She and her family have been banished from the colony. I think she received God's blessing in that the punishment was not more severe."

"Where will she go?"

"I heard," and here Alice looked around to make sure none of the family were close, "that Roger Williams invited her and many other families who supported her to settle in his Providence Plantation."

"And who is Roger Williams?"

"I believe he's a Separatist…I hear our husbands." And with that, she directed Mercy to set plates, napkins and spoons on the table for our meal.

ꕥ ꕥ

I burst with questions once Thomas and I returned home. We had hardly entered the door when I asked him, "Who is Roger Williams?'

"Where does this question come from, wife?"

I'm caught out in my curiosity! How can I avoid mentioning Alice Bradford? I paused, then said, "Oh, I heard something of him today." I gave him a half-smile, and he nodded, knowing its source all too well.

"Indeed. Well, Roger Williams is a minister, originally of the Church of England, but he became Puritan, believing that church to be irredeemably corrupt. But he also believes the church should not have a role in governance…in that he is more like us than the Puritans. Unfortunately, he went further, calling the king a liar and questioning our right to take land from the Indians without paying for it. The general court in Boston found him guilty of heresy and sedition…"

Had I not used that word heresy, just this day?

"…and banished him. He spent the past two winters in the Wampanaoag camp of Massasoit."

"Our Massasoit?"

"The same. A year ago, Williams and some of his followers bought unchartered land from the Narragansett Indians. They call their settlement Providence, and he welcomes anyone prosecuted because of their conscience to move there. Why do you want to know?"

"Oh, just something Mistress Bradford mentioned in passing."

Thomas' forehead furrowed as it did when he was puzzled, but he asked me no more.

ꙮ ꙮ

One morning that summer, I heard the unexpected sound of banging outside and went out to find Thomas working on what looked to be wooden shutters, like those I had seen at the Bradfords.

"What are you making, Thomas?" I walked by him, carrying corn in my apron to feed the chickens. "Is that a shutter?"

"Yes," he said, grunting as he pounded in the iron nails.

"Why do we need them? I thought the danger of attack feared by Master Bradford had lessened. And you need to tend to the fields," I said over my shoulder, as I threw the corn into the chicken coop to the sound of hungry squawks.

"War has broken out in the Connecticut River valley. There is some thought it could spread here. Standish has left with a contingent of men to protect our trading post there."

I sat down abruptly on an upended tree stump serving as a chair. "Why didn't you tell me this earlier?"

"Because I knew it would make you anxious and fearful for our child. And I want him to be healthy." He gave me his special smile to let me know he teased me. He wanted a boy.

"What more can you tell me?"

"I need to finish, my good wife, so you'll have to wait until our midday meal." He returned to pounding nails.

Before coming in to eat, Thomas washed away the sweat from his hands and face, using English soap and the water in the bucket by the side door. He smelled pleasantly of the soap and fresh air as we sat down to our prayers and a sturdy meal of samp, bread and goat cheese, along with some deer meat I had fried on the fire. The day was surprisingly warm, and it was hot in the house. Beads of sweat stood out on our foreheads and ran down our necks, even though the window and door were open to let in a breeze.

"Why don't we talk outside?" I asked when we finished, wiping my forehead with my napkin.

After I had moved our dishes to the hearth for later rinsing and covered the food with scraps of cloth to keep off the ever-present flies, we retreated to the far side of the garden, to a bench Thomas had made with wood left over from the construction of our house. The pleasant breeze coming off the harbor cooled us.

"I'll try to explain what's happening in the Connecticut River valley as best I can, Mary, but it's complicated by the various factions and Indian tribes warring against each other as well as the settlers.

"From the communications the Governor has shared with the Council, I've learned the Pequots have continued their siege of Fort Saybrook. Last month, the Pequots attacked the settlement at Wethersfield, killing nine and kidnapping two girls."

One hand dropped unbidden to my stomach. "What happened to the girls?"

"I don't know, but the leaders of the surrounding settlements met to plan a campaign against the Pequot. A force of nearly one hundred militiamen was assembled, and they were joined by a nearly equal number of Mohegans."

"Are the Mohegans enemies of the Pequot?"

"Yes, because the Pequots took their lands. The militia forced the Pequots from the land they'd taken and then thought to attack their village. But they didn't have a sufficient force…"

"How many more would they need? Two hundred to fight is a large number."

"Apparently there was a strong force of Pequots in that village, so the militia leaders sailed east to the Providence colony where they were joined by Narragansetts. They had also been attacked by the Pequots. Can you see how confusing this is? This combined force returned to attack the Pequot village." Here he paused, shaking his head. "This isn't our way, Mary, but it had to be done."

"What isn't our way?"

"The leader of the force ordered the village set on fire and had anyone trying to escape over the palisade shot. At the end, only a handful of Pequots remained alive."

"The women and children, too?"

Thomas nodded.

"Is the Pequot tribe completely gone now?"

'No, their sachem was absent from the village, along with many of his men. That's why we're concerned."

I shivered despite the warmth of the day and later felt more secure when the shutter was built and hung. I imagined the horror of an Indian attack and told myself to be more cautious with the Wampanoags I encountered. I never did listen to my own advice because my interactions with them continued to be friendly.

Although the settlement and our militia prepared for an attack, it never came, and we never needed that shutter. The remaining Pequots were killed by Mohawk Indians when they sought refuge with them, and there were no further Indian attacks on settlements in the expanding colonies for many years.

ဢ ဢ

I had discovered early in my time with Mistress Bradford that I truly disliked soap-making. When we could afford it, we had good soap from England for washing our hands and faces and bathing perhaps once or twice a year, but I used lye soap for washing our clothes and household linens. Since we had only a few changes of clothing, I needed to wash them only once a month—but the supply of soap seemed to run out quickly. I anticipated making more with dread, hoping I'd not forgotten what she taught me.

I remembered to start by accumulating ashes from a hardwood fire, which I placed in a small iron pot. To that I added rain water—for some reason well water or water from the brook was unsuitable, and Alice had not known why. After much stirring and the addition of more water, I boiled the mixture over a fire outside because of its noxious smell. After the ashes settled for a day, I poured the water into another pot, leaving the ashes behind.

One thing I discovered when I had first made soap was that this boiled water was caustic. Alice had cautioned me, but that first time, I'd found small holes in my apron from where the water splashed. She'd just shaken her head when I showed her the holes. I made sure to wear on old apron this time.

After boiling more water with the ashes and combining the lye water, I then boiled it down until an egg could float on it. While it boiled, I put scraps of fat from meats we'd eaten in another pot over the fire and cooked them until the fat rendered. After picking out any solid scraps, I added the liquid fat to the bubbling lye water.

The next part meant hard work, because I had to stir the mixture for a long time, until it thickened to the likes of a pottage. When my arms grew tired, I took some short rests on the bench in the garden and then pulled weeds. When it finally thickened, I poured the mixture into a tightly-seamed wooden box Thomas had made. Then I let the soap sit for several days to harden. Thomas absented himself during soap-making, complaining the smell hurt his nose and eyes.

This soap was excellent for washing, and when we'd begun to get the blue, paper-wrapped cones of sugar from the Dutch, Alice had told me to add the paper to the wash because it whitened the clothes and helped remove stains. We couldn't use this soap for washing ourselves because of its harshness. As a result, my hands were rough, red and cracked after I washed our clothes, boiling them outside in a large kettle over an open fire. I found that a salve of animal fat infused with mint was very soothing and helped my hands heal.

ꙮ ꙮ

By the middle of September, I had grown large with child, making some tasks difficult, but Thomas would often help me. My back hurt and my ankles swelled, but I was happy—until the ache in my back turned to pains in my belly, which grew stronger and more rhythmic.

My time had come, and despite having been present for the birth of Alice Bradford's three children, I didn't really know what it would feel like. *Certainly not this*? As the pains grew stronger, I walked to relieve the building pressure and panted with each contraction, as I had seen Alice do. Thomas had sailed to Rocky Nook early in the morning to ask her to come and had then gone on to Mistress Fuller's house, not far away. All three returned mid-afternoon, along with Mercy Bradford, whose wide eyes made me think of how I must have looked when her mother gave birth to young William—scared and anxious. In the meantime, Elizabeth Warren had stayed with me. She had born five daughters and two sons, and now oversaw the estate of her husband —truly a formidable woman on whom I knew I could rely. With this group of women, I now had my own gossip, but I missed Priscilla Mullins. She lived in Duxborough with her seven children and now carried her eighth, so she remained at home.

The periods of contraction and pain made me fear for my life, and I felt as though I was being cleaved in two. Mistress Warren spent much of her time calming my fears, while Alice Bradford made a meal for Thomas. When he came in, he just grabbed some smoked meat and bread and left the house. Mercy milked our goat and her mother gave me warm goat's milk to drink and held my arm as I walked around the garden between the pains.

Midwife Fuller had brought her birthing stool and had me sit in it so she could examine me from beneath. She mumbled under her breath each time but said the birthing progressed well. She had me drink broth, wine with cinnamon, and some water with mugwort and feverfew during that day, to keep up my strength, and had me sit in a warm bath and hold a bag containing a concoction of herbs to my navel. I found the bath soothing. Then she applied a warm ointment to my back, belly and lower parts. She had compounded it from hollyhock root, fennel seed, quince kernels and butter, boiled in rainwater and then mixed with the oil of sweet almonds along with duck's and hen's grease—its fragrance filled the room. By that night, I had been laboring for some twelve hours and wore only my linen shift which was drenched in sweat.

I am ashamed to admit I cried out as the pains grew closer together. My groans and moans certainly drove Thomas elsewhere for his evening meal and perhaps out of the settlement. "Will this never end?" I asked with a gasp, as one particularly strong pain subsided.

"Let me check you again," answered Mistress Fuller. She motioned for me to sit in her chair and lowered herself to look beneath. "You're nearly there. Not much longer and all will be well."

Just then, I felt a great need to push down, and Mistress Fuller said, "Push again! I can see the head. She massaged me below with an oil containing what smelled like chamomile, rose and lavender, saying, "This will ease the baby's passage and prevent any tearing of the flesh."

Tearing of the flesh? At that point I hardly cared. I gasped and pushed again…and again. After a final scream, I felt a great release and there in Mistress Fuller's hands lay a red, crying mite. I fell back, caught by Mistress Warren.

"You have a fine boy, Mistress Cushman," my midwife told me. "I need to tie off his birth string, then you can hold him." She did this and then, taking clean linen from Mercy Bradford's hands, wrapped him well and gently placed him, still bawling, in my arms. "You need to deliver the after-burden, Mistress. Here, drink this."

Mistress Fuller told me later that she'd had Mercy boil the juice of mugwart, tansy and featherfew down to a syrup. She'd then added a bit of sugar to make it more palatable, but it still had an unpleasant taste. Soon after I drank it, the pain of a contraction occurred again—*I thought they were over!*—and the after-burden was delivered into a bowl.

Mistress Fuller wrapped me below in a napkin and helped me into a dry shift before I gratefully went to my bed, where I lay cradling my newborn until he finally slept. The members of my gossip gave me many instructions about taking him to the breast, although I heard them as if through a fog. Before I slept, Mistress Fuller gave me something to quicken the coming of my milk.

When Thomas returned and heard the news, he came to my side and kissed me, then stood back, wordless, in awe of his son, Thomas.

Chapter 28

A Serious Illness and Our Family Grows

Mary Cushman, Plymouth, 1638-1640

I recall that next year as a blur, as caring for our son now added to the daily work. We were fortunate in that young Thomas was generally good-humored, and he amused us with his babblings. He took after his father, with his dark hair and rusty brown eyes, and I must admit his father was smitten, spending time with him in the evenings, making him laugh. Thomas made him a walking chair well before his son even stood and carved him toys from wood. I loved hearing my little boy's noises during the day. So many children died during their first years, but despite my fears he would fall ill, he seemed resiliently healthy. I loved it when he had grown ready for soft food and I could sit and feed him, and I took as much time as possible from my daily tasks to play with him. I often carried him around the yard, while I told him the names of everything we encountered. He especially like the animals and I thought his first word might be 'goat.'

Living in the old settlement, I found I missed sharing my days with Alice Bradford and hearing her advice. I had countless questions for her, and while Elizabeth Warren provided sound counsel and information, Alice and I had enjoyed a special and comforting relationship. I knew despite the ignorance of my questions, she would smile and indulge me with answers.

ꕥ ꕥ

Thomas came home from the Plymouth Court one day, sorely troubled. He hardly spoke to me over our evening meal and paid scarce attention to our noisy year-old son, who sat in his highchair and banged on the table with a spoon. Once the baby had been nursed and put in his cradle, I asked, "What troubles you so, Thomas? Can you share it with me?"

"I don't want to discuss it now, Mary. Please leave me with my thoughts." When we were in bed, he lay on his side, apart from me. I waited for him to fall asleep but finally drifted off myself. Early the next morning, barely stopping to break his fast, he left for the Court again, returning for the midday meal.

Thomas remained silent as he ate his carrot sop, bread, goat cheese, and a portion of salted fish, pausing only to use bread to take up the remains of the sop. When we had both finished, I set little Thomas on the floor, where he grabbed at some wooden blocks, and then I cleared the food and our plates. Thomas had remained at the table, seemingly deep in thought.

After changing little Thomas' breech cloth, I placed him in his highchair, putting the wooden blocks on the table and sat down again. "Can you now tell me what's wrong, Thomas?" I asked. "Has it to do with Court business?"

Finally my husband replied. "Today we condemned three men to death. It's not something for which we have any enthusiasm."

"What had they done to warrant such a punishment?"

"They robbed and murdered an Indian."

"Had they any reason to kill him?"

"None whatever, other than to profit from the sale of what little their victim had on him."

Little by little, Thomas told me of the men. Their leader had been an indentured servant of Edward Winslow, a strong and desperate young man by the name of Arthur Peach, a former soldier in the Pequot War. Loath to work and in debt, Peach had gotten a maid with child. The other three were servants who had run away from their masters. Thinking to take trails to the Dutch colony to the south, the men had come upon a Nipmuc Indian carrying bolts of cloth and wampum to the sachem of the Narragansetts. They decided to rob him. Peach stabbed the Indian with his rapier several times and the injured man staggered away into the woods, leaving his goods behind.

Three Narragansets came across the victim near the site of his attack and sent word ahead to Roger Williams, who came with two physicks, who, despite their efforts, were unable to save him. Before the victim died, Williams listened carefully to his tale as well as to the sachem of the Narragansetts, who feared attacks against his tribe in retribution if the murderers were punished. Considering everything, Williams decided justice had to be meted out to the offenders, who were soon captured by Narragansett warriors.

"But why would the Plymouth Court be involved?" I asked Thomas.

"Because the attack occurred in this jurisdiction and the government of the Massachusetts colony didn't want to involve the Crown in the trial. The Massachusetts court felt the actions of these men might cause attacks against their colony."

"So everyone is afraid. Are we?"

"No, I think not. Our governor and our court are known for fairness and a willingness to apply justice. With the testimony of Master Williams and that of some Indians, the accused freely confessed to their crime and were sentenced."

"But you said only three would hang."

"One escaped before the trial and is now in Maine. The people there will not send him back."

I thought for a moment, then asked, "But weren't some of our own men guilty of killing Indian women and children during the Pequot War? They weren't tried."

Thomas frowned at my statement. "That was war, Mary. I don't want to discuss this further."

ꟷ ꟷ

The summer had truly begun by June. The sun burned hot, the crops in the fields thrived, and little Thomas now sat firmly in his walking chair. Anything within reach he put in his mouth, and I had to watch him constantly, especially in the garden, where he liked to pull out plants and try to eat them.

My own garden now produced vegetables and herbs for our table, and the apple seeds Thomas had planted in our yard had grown into small saplings. One day at the beginning of June, I was mucking goat dung in water into the garden soil to enrich it. My son sat in his walking chair nearby. I heard a low rumble, much like the growl of a cat, and stood up to find its source. Suddenly, the earth beneath us began to shake violently. I heard platters and dishes clatter to the floor in the house, and I fell to the ground, reaching out for my little one.

This must be God, showing signs of his displeasure.

The shaking seemed to last forever, but in truth it lasted only a matter of moments. Little Thomas appeared unhurt but seemed puzzled that the walking chair, with him in it, had fallen on its side. Shortly thereafter, there came another noise with more shaking, but it passed quickly. I knelt and thanked God when the shaking stopped. That night, I asked my husband, who had met with leaders of the town that evening, why this happened.

"We decided it had to be the mighty hand of God, Who can make both earth and sea shake when it pleases Him. Does it not say in the Bible, 'Who can stay his hand?'"

That night we prayed long from our Bible, the one sent to him from Robert Cushman's estate, one of the few things my husband had of his father.

ꕥ ꕥ

In the summer of 1638, I knew I was again with child. This time I thought to surprise Thomas and not speak of it until he saw the evidence with his own eyes. Days passed. I hid my sickness in the morning by telling him I was not hungry and would eat later. Still, he didn't seem to notice anything amiss, despite the fact I tired easily. Finally, one night, as we lay in bed, his hands roaming over my stomach and breasts, his breath quick with need, he stopped. Then he gently cupped my breasts and then followed the line of the swelling of my womb beneath the skin.

"Mary, are you…?"

"I wondered when you would notice. Are you happy?"

I couldn't see his smile in the dark but sensed it, as he stroked my face. "Very much so. Do you think it might be a daughter this time?"

"I don't know. But it took you long enough to see it!"

He laughed and lay back, but I touched him to continue our lovemaking.

ꕥ ꕥ

Our daughter Mary came in 1639, after an easier pregnancy than that with little Thomas.

Even the birthing went quickly, and I was less tired thereafter. The household became more chaotic with two babies, and I found it frustrating when I had to delay the more laborious of my chores, such as making soap, to tend to their needs.

The expansion of our colony exceeded that of our family. In two years, the townships of Taunton and Sandwich, plus Yarmouth on Cape Cod, were settled. All were within the Plymouth land grant but were populated by people coming from the Massachusetts Bay colony, since no more Separatists arrived from England or the Netherlands. Thomas had more work, surveying for new roads to connect these towns with the others.

For the most part, these roads would follow old Indian paths running from north to south and east to west, but the colony needed connections at places of crossing, such as at the Jones River. Joseph Rogers, who had come on the Mayflower, lived on the south side of the river at Rocky Nook and ran a ferry across it. He asked a penny or some goods in trade for each passenger. I had often heard Master Bradford complain of this price, since he crossed the river often on business, but it provided Goodman Rogers his income, as granted by the Council.

A highway north was now planned, continuing from a place near my father's former house in Rocky Nook and across the Jones River. It would follow the Indian path that led to the Boston area, and would link Plymouth with the settlements of Duxborough, Marshfield, and Scituate.

As our population continued to grow and founded more settlements, there would be a need for even more roads to keep Thomas busy with his surveys.

ᘓ ᘐ

Early in 1640, I received a letter from Remember, written by her husband Moses Maverick. I couldn't imagine how she'd persuaded him to write it for her, but perhaps out of love.

To my dearest sister, Mary,

I write with love and kind remembrance of our time together to tell you all that has transpired in the past few years. I know our father wrote you that I married Moses Maverick, and I'm happy to tell you we now have a daughter named Rebecca. She is like her father in many ways. I'm awaiting the birth of our second child now.

Do you hear often from Father? All I can relate to you is that he is selling corn in New Amsterdam, although he appears to have settled in the New Haven colony. I know from my husband there is still much discourse, not altogether without rancor, between him and the leaders in Plymouth over what he still owes for those two trading ships he bought. We pray this situation will be soon resolved.

I hope that we may meet sometime, not too long in the future. Perhaps our husbands can arrange a visit. You have never been away from Plymouth, and I think you would be quite amazed at the business and wealth in the Massachusetts Bay colony.

Your loving sister,
Remember Allerton Maverick

Although happy to read her news, my worries about my father's financial difficulties returned. I knew that but for the forbearance of Governor Bradford, he might have been dealt with harshly for his mishandling of the colony's trade goods and money, which left the colony with more debt than it originally had. And this debt had not yet been completely repaid.

༄ ༄

Thomas was constant in his loving making, and I became pregnant again in the summer of 1640. Early in that winter, Thomas became very ill with the flux and a fever. I sent a message to Alice to ask if she knew of anything I might use to treat him. She came to

Plymouth that same day with her husband, who regarded Thomas as a son and had a father's concern for his well-being. After taking one look at Thomas, by now feverish, pale, and groaning at times from the pain in his insides, Alice shook her head.

"How long has he had looseness of his bowels?"

"Two days, but increasingly worse."

"And of what color are they?"

"A little red today. I'm certain it's blood."

She nodded and turned to her husband, who sat at Thomas' side and held his hand with great concern written on his face. "William, I believe Thomas is seriously ill, and I don't know what can be done for him. He needs the care of a trained physick because he might have the bloody flux."

Alice's words caused my knees to wobble, they carried such fear. The bloody flux often proved fatal. *What if he died?* How could I go on living without him? He was my sun and the children, my moons.

The governor kept silent in thought for a minute, then said "I'll send a messenger to John Winthrop to ask for a physick." I knew from the years I lived in the Bradford household that the governor knew Winthrop well. Winthrop had been the governor of the Massachusetts Bay colony for four years, and the two governors had exchanged a copious correspondence during that time and even thereafter.

"But he's not a physick," I said.

"No, Mary, but Master Winthrop has actively sought more trained physicks for the Massachusetts colony, and he may know someone with the medical training and experience to treat your husband. Don't be afraid. I have hope that your husband will recover."

I was encouraged by his words, but Thomas didn't improve over the next few days, so weak he remained in bed, soiling the linen regularly because he had little control of his bowels. Despite his travails, my husband remained calm and uncomplaining, expressing gratefulness for his care and praying from his Bible. It was all I could do to keep broth in him, as advised by Alice, who remained with me to nurse him. I don't know what I would have done without her comforting presence, and she calmed my fear that Thomas would die.

Three days after the governor sent his message to Master Winthrop, a man arrived at our door, introducing himself as Master Giles Fermin, a deacon in the Puritan church and a practitioner of medicine in Ipswich. He looked tired and disheveled from his rapid voyage, a middle-aged man with shoulder length hair and eyes that dominated his face with their intensity. With him was an apprentice, a boy of no more than twelve, carrying a heavy travel case.

"Mistress Cushman? Where is the patient?" he asked abruptly, entering without waiting for an answer.

"This way, Master Fermin," I replied, indicating the bed in the corner where my husband lay. Fortuitously, I'd just changed the linen on the bed and dressed Thomas in a fresh shirt. He now passed blood constantly and seemed to have shriveled in his appearance.

I walked to the hearth where the midday meal cooked, to occupy my thoughts and ease my anxiety. The smell of cornbread baking in the oven at the back of the hearth and the slow bubble of a thick pottage in a kettle on the coals soothed me somewhat. Young Thomas was playing with some blocks whilst standing in his walker, and little Mary cooed from her cradle. It was a picture of perfect peace, except for my husband, groaning softly from the bed. I tried to keep this fragile shell of comfort around me but listened carefully to what Master Fermin said, knowing his words might crack the shell.

The physick sat in a chair I had dragged to the bedside, and his apprentice stood at his shoulder. "I don't believe in bleeding patients with the flux," I heard Master Fermin say to Thomas, "because when treating dysentery, I believe a physick must be cautious lest the patient become too weak. But we must cast out the choleric humors and counter the malign presence in your blood, Master Cushman. Then we need to heal and consolidate the ulcerations in your intestines."

I shuddered to think what that meant.

"Mistress Cushman, I'll need new milk with the cream on it, three well beaten egg yolks, some sugar and some fat from a pig. Also, I need you to heat some pebbles in the fire."

I knew that Mistress Warren had a cow, and Master Fermin sent his apprentice with my instructions on how to find her and relay my request. We had plenty of eggs, and I had just brined fresh pig meat in a barrel outside, so the fat was readily available

"Are there dogs in the village?" Fermin asked.

Puzzled, I nodded yes.

"Where can they be found?"

"Two houses down the street."

"Good." He took a glass vial from his bag and strode out the door, returning in a short time with some white powder in the vial, which I later learned came from the drying edges of dog excrement. In his absence, I had found some small pebbles outside in the yard and washed them of dirt before placing them in the fire to heat.

When the apprentice returned with the milk and I had brought the eggs from the chicken enclosure, Master Fermin asked for a bowl and while I watched, began to mix the various ingredients—first beating the egg yolks, then adding a small handful of sugar, the white powder he'd collected and the fat. Finally, he added the hot pebbles, which melted the fat and made the whole concoction frothy. From his bag he removed an elongated cylinder with a tapered end, placed his finger on the tapered end and filled the cylinder with the mixture in the bowl. I knew he had created a clyster, to be injected into my husband's intestines.

Alice took me and the children outside into the garden, remaining by my side, holding my hand. I had wrapped myself in my cloak, but despite holding Mary close under its folds, I shivered uncontrollably. Thomas moaned loudly as the clyster was given, frightening little Thomas, who clung to my legs.

"It will be alright," Alice said over and over, and we paced up and down in the garden, startling with each noise from the house. "Look," she said to little Thomas, offering him a pine cone she'd found on the ground in order to distract him.

After a while, the apprentice, to whom I had not been introduced, appeared in the doorway with an ashen countenance.

"Mistress Bradford, may I ask you for a cup of water?" His throat seemed constricted, as he choked out these words.

I gave Mary to Alice and filled a wooden cup with fresh water from a bucket, handing it to him. He drained it in three gulps, so I filled it again and he drank more. When his thirst was sated, he said more clearly, "Master Fermin must tell you what he now needs."

Leaving little Thomas with Alice, I went back to my husband's bedside without even removing my cloak. "What help can I give you?" I asked Master Fermin.

"We'll need to repeat this treatment several times a day, and as well, he needs to drink some warm broth from chicken meat between each purge. You must understand your husband is very sick."

His words and demeanor confirmed that Thomas might die, and my world swam around me. Alice appeared and took my arm, helping me to the table where I sat down heavily. Master Fermin came and sat beside me, placing one hand on my head and the other on my stomach.

"How long are you with child?"

"Some five months."

After examining my face and using his hand to push on my stomach, he told me, "You're quite well. Your husband's illness has created a strain on your body, so you must rest regularly. Know that I'll use all of my abilities to cure him."

After changing the bed linens once again and heating water outside to boil those that were rancid, I washed my hands and face and removed the bread from the oven. Then Alice and I set the table for the midday meal.

Thomas lay within the bed curtains, and when I checked on him, he seemed to sleep, curled up with his back to the room. Mistress Warren arrived in the afternoon with her daughters Mary and Anna and took in hand in the running of the household —milking our goat, gathering more eggs, making the chicken broth, and washing the dirty linens.

Alice continued to tend to me and the children, exhorting me to walk outside with my son, then sit by the fire and rest. In truth, I felt unneeded, but I was very grateful for all their help. After our evening meal—roast chicken and boiled parsnips with fresh bread and jam—Anna Warren brought mattresses down from our loft for Master Fermin and his apprentice. After ensuring all was in order, including a supply of the ingredients Master Fermin would need, the Warrens left for home, promising to return the next day.

Alice Bradford and I climbed the ladder with my children to the loft to sleep. I lay on a mattress and kept the baby beside me so I could nurse her during the night. I was so tired, I slept as if dead and only awakened at dawn when Mary cried in hunger and little Thomas needed to use the chamber pot.

The physick and his apprentice had clearly been up all night with Thomas' care, but he greeted us with a wide smile. "Your husband will live," he said. "My treatment has proven effective, and by the end of this day, he should be rid of the flux."

I wondered how he had affected this miracle, but Alice and I fell on our knees to thank God for his blessing.

Master Fermin stayed one further day, maintaining treatment, but by the third day Thomas was completely well, sitting up in bed and eating pieces of bread dipped in an onion sop. This time, when he talked with his caregiver, I did listen in.

"How did you heal me?" he asked with wonder in his voice.

"The milk washes the bowels," Fermin replied, "and clears them of the sharp humors that irritate them. It's also healing and repairing. The sugar cleanses and washes away impurities from the injured places, while the fat sticks to those parts, so they can defend themselves from further injury. Running over the fat, the humors can find no place to stick."

All of this I wrote in my own receipt book, which I would pass on to my daughter. I paid Master Fermin with what money we had at hand, plus a large bundle of eggs, carefully wrapped, and soap. I couldn't pay him enough for the life of my husband, and I prayed that this physick would live long and heal many others.

Chapter 29

A Girl Joins the Household and A Contentious Preacher Arrives

Mary Cushman, Plymouth, 1641

Carrying my third child seemed more difficult than with the previous two. With young Thomas only three, and little Mary not yet walking, my days were over full. Mistress Bradford often sent her daughter Mercy to help me, since she was now fourteen, but I confess some of my chores were left undone because I was continually tired.

We often visited the Aldens. I missed Priscilla's company, and with nine children now, she couldn't really leave home. They had built a long, three-room house, set on a sturdy fieldstone foundation and accessible by water from the bay and the Blue Fish River, which ran along one edge of their farm. Our last visit had been just after little Mary's birth. Priscilla had wanted to see her, and our son had many playmates in the Alden household. We always enjoyed this change of scenery because their home was set in pleasant woods, and with the river close by, the children could wade in the water. Their large numbers created a somewhat chaotic household, but Priscilla kept them firmly in hand. The older boys, John Jr. and Jonathan, had grown into strapping young men, able to work with their father in the fields.

We welcomed any opportunity to return their hospitality, even if only Master Alden visited. One late Sunday afternoon, after traveling to the Plymouth meeting house for our services, he came to our house to talk with Thomas. He and my husband sat with their heads together in chairs by the hearth, chatting quietly. I heard the name Sarah—one of the Alden daughters—over the cracking of the fire. Then, "Would you consider it?" Soon after, Master Alden left, but not before inviting us for a visit the following Sunday.

That night at our meal, young Thomas stood beside his father, gobbling down pieces of roasted duck as fast as his chubby fingers could grab them and being admonished to use his napkin and not wipe his hands on his shift. Our son pointedly avoided taking any of the boiled carrots until his father ordered him to eat them. I had nursed little Mary and had given her some corn porridge, which she loved, and she now dozed in the trundle bed. With another baby on the way, I was planning to wean her and free up the cradle for its new occupant.

"Dear wife," began Thomas, laying down his knife and wiping his hands on his napkin. "I have something to ask you."

"Does it have to do with Master Alden's visit?"

"I'm surprised you don't already know what I'll tell you." He looked at me from under his eyebrows.

I made a face at him in reply, which got a smile.

"Master Alden would like us to accept his daughter Sarah into our household, so that she may grow in righteousness and knowledge with strict guidance and teaching. With four other daughters, Mistress Alden feels Sarah has been somewhat overlooked."

This surprised me, and he had to wait a few moments for my response. It seemed only yesterday my father had put me with the Bradfords, and memories of that earlier time came flooding back.

Am I capable of giving this girl the teaching and supervision Alice Bradford afforded me? Have I learned enough myself? However, with another child coming, I welcomed the idea of someone to share my work, even if she might need constant instruction. "She's almost six now," I finally said.

"Yes, old enough to be of help to you."

"Tell the Aldens I'm happy to have Sarah here. You can school her in our faith and teach her how to read, if she doesn't already, and I'd welcome her assistance." I rubbed my stomach, almost without realizing it. Thomas reached over and placed his hand on mine, with love in his eyes. Despite our daily challenges and the interruptions of the children, we still enjoyed conversation each night, relating amusing things little Thomas and Mary did each day and the activities in the colony, finding comfort in our love for each other.

Sarah arrived a week later, hand in hand with her father, her eyes red from crying. My heart went out to her. I knew her emotion, and I felt mine from so many years earlier all over again. I greeted them at the door and bent down to talk to Sarah. She was small for her age, with a narrow face and straight hair that fell out of her coif, but her large, bright hazel eyes were captivating. "Sarah, welcome to our home." I put my hands on her shoulders. "I hope you'll be happy here."

Master Alden, somber in his gray cape and black felt hat, handed me the parcel of Sarah's clothes saying, "Sarah, you must listen to Mistress Cushman, and be respectful in all things. Your mother and I will see you soon." There were the glistenings of moisture in his eyes as he turned away and walked down the hill, back to the harbor.

I took Sarah's hand and led her inside, placing her bundle at the bottom of the ladder leading up to the loft. "Would you like some goat's milk?" *I could hear Alice Bradford's first words to me.*

Sarah nodded silently and sat quietly at our table while I fetched her some in a wooden cup and sat down beside her. "Sarah, you and

I are going to become good friends. I understand how you feel—my father put me with another family at your age."

"Really?" Her voice was high but soft.

"Yes. I joined Governor Bradford's household, where I learned much from Mistress Bradford. She was strict, but kind, and I came to love her as my mother. The Bradfords lived across the street from my father's house, so I saw him most days. With your family living in Duxburough, you'll be lonely, but I'll keep you busy and will endeavor to be a good teacher to you. Do you know how to read?"

"No."

"Master Cushman and I will school you in your letters and reading, and I'll teach you how to write. Would you like that?"

Sarah looked up at me, a bit of milk on her upper lip, and nodded with a smile. I knew now how I must have seemed to Alice Bradford.

Watching Sarah drink her milk, I considered how fortunate my dear friend Priscilla Alden had been in the births of so many children—myself also with the births of my first two. Childbirth was a great risk to the life of the mother, and many women I knew had succumbed to fever, loss of blood, or a malaise of the mind after giving birth. My survival and that of Priscilla Alden, Alice Bradford, and many others I attributed to Mistress Fuller's care.

I returned from these deep thoughts to find Sarah had finished her milk and now regarded me with interest. *My thoughts have taken me away!* I stood up, saying, "Well, child, we must get to work. Come see young Thomas and Mary. I'm happy they already know you." I smiled at her. "We may have a problem because I'm determined to name this new child Sarah, if it's a girl." I placed my hands on my stomach. "So Sarah, we may have to find a way to distinguish between you, don't you think?"

ഇ ഇ

Would we ever be rid of contentiousness with our ministers? Charles Chauncy had arrived here in 1637 to take the position of pastor of our church. He had been a vicar at two churches in England, and as Thomas learned later, probably came to the Plymouth colony because he had been censured for his pronouncements on the issue of ceremonies. We found his sermons marked by a studious simplicity of speech that at first was rather jarring, compared to what we had experienced from others. But gradually the members of the church came to accept, if not enjoy, the fact that his thoughts were easily understood.

Lately, however, he'd been in heated debates with various leaders—Elder Brewster and my husband, as well as secular leaders of the colony—over the issue of baptism, the one rite celebrated in our church.

One evening, while Sarah cleared the table of the remains of our meal and washed the platters, knives and spoons, I asked Thomas why this had become such a problem. Young Thomas stood beside me as I picked lice from his hair and then combed them out. My son's head was a welcome home to lice, and I hoped to keep them from little Mary's.

"I think there's been some doubt of him from the start because he's really of the Puritan faith," replied Thomas.

"But our religion is just an offshoot of Puritanism, isn't it? We've had Puritan pastors before—not that any of them have stayed."

"Chauncy believes that only baptism with full immersion in water is valid. You know from the baptisms of Thomas and Mary that sprinkling of water is just as good."

"But it has be done by sprinkling water! Our weather can be cold and harsh—the babies might take sick from the cold or even worse if they are submerged."

"We've told him this, but he remains unconvinced."

'What do the church leaders plan to do?"

"We'll hold public debates on the subject, but in the meantime Elder Brewster, Master Bradford and others will write to religious leaders in Boston and New Haven for their views on the subject."

These debates failed to change the view of Pastor Chauncy, but the letters received from Boston and New Haven stated that both forms of baptism were valid. Still unwilling to bend, Pastor Chauncy left us for Scituate. We would hear of him again, though.

God then blessed us with another minister, John Raynor, who would be our teacher and spiritual leader for some years. He'd been relegated to associate minister during the term of Charles Chauncy, and his humility during this time reflected an able and godly man. He came to be much loved in our community.

ᜭ ᜮ

There occurred a major change in our family's life that year—we sold our house and acreage on North Street to Master William Lettice and moved to Duxborough, where we would live on a larger farm nearer Thomas' land grant. Part of the reason for the move was that we needed to raise as much corn and other crops as possible due to the weaker economic footing of the colony. Our profitable cattle trade with the Massachusetts Bay colony had dwindled to almost nothing, as the immigration to that colony had slowed and fewer newcomers needed our cows.

It fell to me to pack our belongings, furnishings and household goods and see that they were carried safely by water to our new home. The furnishings we had acquired during our years in Plymouth made the moving difficult: iron pots and kettles, a sturdy bed with rope to support our mattress, a tall carved chest, a finished table with a bench and two chairs with backs, and various other things that Thomas had acquired or made.

Sarah provided me with help, although she hadn't the strength to carry much. Thomas helped when he could. With my growing belly, bending and lifting were difficult and my back hurt constantly and my feet swelled in my shoes each day. I felt blessed when the members of my gossip came to help me.

We then had to carry our belongings to our new home from the landing on the Blue Fish River in Duxborough. This settlement already had members of our church: the Standish, Brewster and Alden families lived there. So we had more help with transporting our loads. Duxborough now had its own meetinghouse and had been formally incorporated as a township. I looked forward to having Priscilla Alden nearby, as did Sarah.

Our house was still only one room, but Thomas had strived to make it as comfortable as possible, from the stone hearth and wood plank floors, to the oven in the rear wall of the fireplace, a spacious loft above for sleeping quarters, and a small root cellar accessed from one side of the room. He had also tilled a considerable expanse of land behind the house for my garden, and we now had two windows for light.

ꙮ ꙮ

Not long after we'd settled into the house, I began to feel the first pains of childbirth. Knowing what to expect, I delayed for nearly a whole day before sending Sarah, first to Bridget Fuller and then to her mother's house. Priscilla Alden, now expecting yet another child, soon arrived, along with Alice Bradford.

History seemed to repeat itself with Sarah Alden there, much as I had been with Alice for the birth of young William. Like me at William's delivery, Sarah spent her time with the children in the garden. Occasionally she would tuck her head inside to check my progress, and with her mother, she prepared our evening meal to the music of my moans. I gave thanks to God that Bridget Fuller lived not far away. As for my previous two births, she had me sit in a warm bath then applied the fragrant ointment to my back, belly and lower parts.

This birth was difficult for reasons only God knew. The pains were slow to progress, and I spent much time walking in the garden. Mistress Fuller told me that in her experience, girls took longer to birth than boys. I thus wondered if my child would be a girl. When it came time for me to push down, and I made no progress, Mistress Fuller had me sit on the birthing stool and after anointing her hand with fresh butter, felt inside me.

"Mistress Cushman, your child is presenting with its buttocks. I must turn it around. This will be painful, but it must be done."

At this point I didn't really care; I'd labored for so many hours. She gave me more of a tea she'd brewed of pennyroyal and featherfew to help with the pain, but the agony of turning the baby left me without reason for some minutes. When I became aware again, Priscilla Alden was holding me upright on the birthing stool.

"Mistress Cushman, push again."

I looked at my midwife in despair, not knowing where I would find the strength.

"You must, now, as quickly as you can, because your water broke many hours ago."

I gritted my teeth and pushed and soon I delivered a tiny girl, who despite my long travail, blessed our ears with a lusty cry. I inhaled the smoke of marigold flowers to hasten the release of my after-burden, and then Mistress Fuller cleaned me, swathed me in clean cloths and helped me to bed, where I fell asleep immediately.

Alice Bradford gently shook me awake to feed my new daughter, and I saw Thomas had come to sit by the bed and hold my hand. His eyes were filled with tears. "I was never so afraid for your life, Mary.

I thank God you're delivered, and our little girl is healthy. Will we name her Sarah?"

I smiled at him and looked down at my daughter. "Yes, and how is our other Sarah doing? This must have been hard for her to witness."

"With all her brothers and sisters, I think she's accustomed to birthing and is taking great care of Thomas and little Mary. Her cooking is nearly as good as yours."

That got a smile from me. I needed to return to my normal energy in just a few days, because although Sarah had become adept at many of the household chores, I couldn't expect her to do everything—even with the help of two of her sisters, whom her mother also spared.

I thought Thomas had been hoping for another son, but he seemed happy with little Sarah. She quieted well and smiled at him when he held her, which was not nearly often enough. I hoped I would soon give Thomas the son he'd wanted.

ꕥ ꕥ

One day, as dusk fell, Sarah and I were preparing an evening meal of boiled bread, curd fritters, and left-over rabbit meat from our mid-day meal. Four-year-old Thomas occupied himself building something from pieces of wood in a corner, talking to an unknown person, and Mary sat quite contently in her walker, playing with a poppet. My youngest daughter slept blissfully in her cradle. She'd been born so small we had begun to call her 'Button,' which helped with distinguishing the two Sarahs in the household.

I told Sarah to set the table for our meal, but that night, for no reason, I decided to use our earthenware plates, called redware. They were much nicer than our wooden ones, but unfortunately had a tendency to chip. I set them out anyway, just so I could admire them.

I'd heard from my gossip that a craftsman named Drinker, in the Massachusetts Bay colony, made the redware, and I hoped to some day visit his place of business. I'd also heard he now imported better clays. It would be nice to have sturdier plates.

Just after Sarah had laid out the napkins and spoons, Thomas burst in the door, clearly excited from a meeting of the freemen in the Plymouth village that day. "Something smells wondrous, and I'm past hungry, my dear wife. Can we eat? Then I'll tell you what I learned today." Spying the redware, he asked "What is the occasion for such an elegant table?"

I shrugged my shoulders. "No real reason—just to welcome you home."

We gathered to eat, Mary in a highchair beside me, Sarah sitting opposite from me, with young Thomas standing at the end of the table. My husband first offered up prayers to God, thanking him for his gifts to us and for our survival in this bountiful land. Sarah then served bowls and platters of the food, along with butter for the bread. How I loved butter! And I could now barter for it. I longed for the day when we would own a cow and would have milk along with cheese and butter.

Thomas only paused in his meal to cut some meat for little Thomas, then he leaned back in his chair with a contented look. I ate more slowly, helping Mary with her food, but could barely contain my interest. "So what happened at this meeting?"

Thomas paused to drink some beer, then said, "A legal code called the Body of Liberties has been established by the Massachusetts General Court."

"And why does this make you so excited?"

"Well, it establishes our individual rights here in the new world."

"I thought we already had rights."

"This legal code specifically enumerates them, Mary. It gives everyone freedom of speech, a right against the uncompensated taking of one's property, and if accused of a crime, the right to notice and hearing before the court and a jury trial. It also states we have a right against cruel and unusual punishment."

"Isn't this our law already?"

"It is. This Body of Liberties is very much like the codification of our laws that Bradford instituted some four years ago. It's just reassuring to see the Massachusetts colony is agreement with that, so that justice and freedoms throughout this area are consistent. This meal can celebrate it."

I shook my head, having difficulty seeing how over-joyed my husband had become over some rules that just seemed logical.

Chapter 30

Turmoil and Sin in the Colony

Mary Cushman, Duxborough, 1642

I always looked forward to a Sunday afternoon visit with Priscilla Alden, now a neighbor and forever a dear friend. With so many of her children and my three, there were plenty of possibilities for them to play and older ones to look after the younger. This gave us an opportunity to engage in sharing news. Sarah sat close to her mother on the bench, rocking Button in the Alden cradle with her foot. I knew she missed her mother and made sure she had every opportunity to visit.

"So, Sarah," Priscilla asked, "are you being helpful to Mistress Cushman? Are you learning?"

Sarah looked a bit puzzled. "Learning what, Mother? Do you mean reading and writing? Yes, the Cushmans teach me in the evenings. I can write my name and read some passages from the Bible." Pride filled her words.

Her mother looked at me for confirmation.

"She's an eager student," I replied. "She's also now quite skilled in the preparation of our food, milking the goat, gathering eggs, and we have lately made soap. Soon I'll show her how to make linen from flax—we have a good crop this year. I cannot thank you enough for sending her to me."

Sarah's mother now beamed with pride, although she tried to hide it. "I'm just pleased you're growing up in a straight path, daughter. Please see you continue.

Now go join the other children down by the stream." She watched her until she was out of earshot. "Mary, I have a request of you." Here she looked down in her lap at her folded hands and seemed to be reluctant to put her request to words.

"How can I help you?"

"Would you teach me to write?" Her cheeks reddened. "I know my letters but cannot read, and no one ever taught me to write my name or any words."

"Of course! You had only to ask. Would you like to start today?"

"Right now, if you would."

I looked around for a stick, and we found a place in her yard covered with a fine dust. I used the stick to write the letters 'A, l, d, e and n' in the dust. "There! That's your last name. Can you copy the letters?"

My friend frowned and with great concentration, wrote the letters over and over. Then I wrote her first name in the dust, and she copied me. Finally, we returned to our seats on the bench.

"Next time you can show me how you write your name and we'll practice reading and writing from the Bible."

"Thank you, Mary. I'm ashamed to be illiterate and not be able to teach my daughters."

"Well, soon you will be able to." I knew her sons would be schooled by either their father or a traveling teacher to ensure their position in the colony. Girls were mostly ignored.

Button awoke from her nap in the cradle at my feet and started to fuss. I picked her up and rocked her in my arms, then put her to my breast. She may have been small, but she had a bottomless appetite. As I did so, Priscilla asked, "Have you heard the news of our Reverend Chauncy? It's humorous—at least I think so."

"Tell me!"

"You know he now practices his faith in Scituate. His wife gave birth to twin sons this past year, and he sought to baptize them by full immersion in water, to show the members of his church he would practice what he preached. One of his sons fell senseless after being dunked."

"Is the child well? I cannot imagine what worry this caused his mother."

"Yes, the boy survived, but the mother of a child who was to be baptized at the same time refused to let Reverend Chauncy immerse the baby and grabbed the reverend, nearly pulling him into the water himself."

The vision of the reverend being pulled into baptismal water by an angry woman set us both to laughing.

"How did you learn this?"

"The usual way—I overheard my husband talking with Governor Bradford, who had it in a letter from Governor John Winthrop of the Massachusetts colony."

I saw my first walking spinning wheel at the Aldens that day. I knew what it was, of course—a very large wheel, also called a wool wheel, for the long, drawn-out spinning of wool yarns. The sheep Thomas owned had coats of poor quality, not suitable for spinning, but the Aldens now had two sheep that had been bred with merinos, prized for their wool. With the spun wool, Pricilla could have the product woven into cloth. This was done by a group of formerly indentured servants who had learned weaving and now traveled about as itinerant weavers. With our children wearing clothes being used one after another as they grew, we found it costly to purchase clothes from England when the old ones wore out.

"We'll clip the sheep in a few weeks," Priscilla told me, "and I invite you to visit so I can show you how to spin the wool. Perhaps I can have another lesson in writing then?"

"I'll be here!"

ꟾ ꟾ

Sin beset our colony that year. For more than a month, Ralph Partridge, who had become pastor of the Duxborough church when Elder Brewster stepped down, spent our Sunday meetings lecturing on the wages of sin. These lectures, unlike his usual sermons, were long and loud and led to squirming children. Keeping my two oldest in hand while he spoke on and on had become a continuous struggle, something I noticed many of the other mothers faced as well. I came to dread the long Sunday sermons.

William Bradford, once again governor, also spoke on this topic at one of our meetings. "Wickedness has broken out in the colony—notorious sins including incontinency between unmarried people, and between some married to others, as well as drunkenness and uncleanliness, sodomy and buggery," he said in a solemn voice. "There are good reasons for this—the devil is more spiteful against our church and the gospel because of how much we've endeavored to preserve holiness and purity and punish those who transgress. I believe Satan is more powerful in heathen lands, and that here evil is more public."

I shuddered at his words and pulled my children closer to me, hoping young Thomas would not ask me the meaning of sodomy and buggery. I had no idea where Satan lurked and didn't wish to know, and Thomas and I prayed hard that the devil would not touch our lives.

Not long after, there occurred another hanging in the colony, one of great tragedy and undoubtedly the devil's work. Thomas refrained from speaking of it until we were in bed that night, when he could whisper to me. Even then, he didn't want to give me much detail, clearly feeling it inappropriate to a women's nature.

"So what deserved the sentence of death, husband?"

"God's teeth, it was buggery."

I took a deep gulp of breath at the thought, then considered my husband's words. "Thomas! Don't be a muckspout. Your words could curdle my milk and sour your beer."

"Forgive me, Mary, but this is a situation with no other resolution."

"Who is the person?"

"Thomas Granger."

"Why, I know him—he's the servant of Love Brewster. But he's so young, only sixteen!"

I shuddered because Love Brewster, the son of Elder Brewster, lived not far from us, next door to his father. "What of his parents?"

"They've come from Scituate, where they live, for the trial. They are overcome with grief and shame. But there is no other option to the verdict, as he freely admitted to the crime."

"When will the hanging take place?"

"Tomorrow."

"And who will do the deed?" I shuddered as I asked.

"Master Holmes, the Messenger of the Court. This is especially hard for him since he's a good man with a kind heart. Did you know he bought out the contract of a servant indentured to Stephen Hopkins?"

"Why would he to do that?"

"Master Hopkins refused to honor her contract after a convicted murderer made her pregnant. The murderer had taken her against her will."

"Then Master Holmes is indeed kind."

I tossed and turned in my sleep that night, beset by dreams of sin and punishment. I woke early, feeling anxiety for my children because we were so surrounded by deadly sin. Adding to my worries was young Thomas, who seemed listless and feverish that day. I gave him the inner bark of the willow tree to chew, in the hopes of cooling his heat. He soon developed a cough, and his nose ran with fluid from some imbalance of his humors. I wondered if his illness came from the preaching at the Sunday meeting.

Because this sickness might spread to little Mary and Button, I kept him apart and treated his cough with horehound steeped in hot water. The colony had imported horehound from England, and it was quite effective in treating coughs, a recipe I'd added to my book. I fretted most of the day, both from the thought of the hanging and worry for my son. Although I'd had much personal experience with death, losing my son was unimaginable, and I couldn't envision the depth of shame and grief experienced by Thomas Granger's parents.

I decided to confine young Thomas to bed under layers of blankets, in the hopes he would sweat out his affliction. Once he'd managed a good sweat, I bathed him in cold water from our well. Thereafter he fell into a deep sleep, not waking until the next day. With his fever gone and his cough much less, he began to object to the horehound tea, but I made him drink it. For the next several days I watched my other two children closely, praying they wouldn't fall ill. God answered me because little Mary and Button remained healthy.

ꙮ ꙮ

The execution of Thomas Granger had been attended by my husband, and he returned home unwilling to talk about what he'd seen. This made my imagining all the worse, and I wasn't soothed when Governor Bradford continued to expound on the wages of sin at another Sunday meeting. His talk that day followed a long, colorful sermon by our pastor, during which my children drifted off into sleep, slumping beside me on the bench. My own eyes grew heavy.

"You have often heard me talk about the godlessness from which we suffer. Let me say that some men who transported people to our colony didn't care who the people were, only that they could pay their transport. This is the source of many of our problems. I think that where the Lord begins to sow good seed, the envious man will sow noxious weeds. There are noxious weeds growing amongst us."

I knew the source of his words 'some men,' as I had frequently heard him speaking with Thomas about one of the original underwriters of our debt, a man named James Shirley. The root of much of Governor Bradford's frustration and anger was Shirley's inability to understand our life here and the challenges faced by our colony. Shirley had sent more than a few poor and useless men to Plymouth, charging us for their transport. During the years I'd lived with the Bradfords, I'd often heard the governor expound on this cost and the distaste of these 'noxious weeds' for real work, sometimes using words that couldn't be repeated in public.

We had suffered more than our share of them in the past few years. Although Thomas and I seldom spoke about them, the members of my gossip did. One of these 'weeds', a resident of Duxborough by the name of Goodwife Mendame, had been convicted of uncleanliness with an Indian and sentenced to be whipped while tied to a cart driven though the town streets. Thereafter, she had to wear a badge on her clothing with the letters 'AD', signifying her adultery. I'd seen her, and although I felt some pity for her for her continuing punishment, I still avoided her. I also learned two men, well known in the colony, had been charged and convicted of lewd behavior and unclean carriage one with another, to which they'd confessed. The Court had one whipped, burned on the shoulder with a hot iron, and banished from Plymouth. For some reason, the court didn't order banishment of the other, but had him whipped and prohibited from ever owning land in the colony, at least until he evidenced better conduct.

ꟿ ꟿ

One evening Governor Bradford visited our home to share a pipe and some conversation about colony affairs with my husband. As Bradford rose to leave, still puffing on his pipe, Thomas said, "Pray you put out your pipe, Governor. You know you could be fined for smoking more than a mile from your home, and your path home is rather long." They both smiled at what seemed to be a secret joke.

Naturally, as soon as the governor was out the door, I had to ask Thomas why what he'd said was humorous.

"Did you know we have a law against smoking in certain places, Mary?"

"No. Where?"

"In any street, barn, outhouse or highway, or further than one mile from your house, lest the pipe smoker set the woods or a building on fire."

"And what if he's caught?"

"A twelve pence fine, which is increased to two shillings for a second offense."

That drew a gasp from me. Coinage was still rather rare in the colony, basically coming from England via the Massachusetts Bay colony or from New Amsterdam. Twelve pence was a very harsh fine. "Well, best you leave your pipe at home, husband. We could scarcely afford that!"

ഗ ଊ

Late that year, Thomas returned from Plymouth with a heavy package and letter from my father, and for once the letter bore good news.

To my dearest daughter Mary and her husband Thomas Cushman,

I'm happy to write you the news that my legal issues over boats and some other business adventures have been successfully concluded by the sale of a barque I possessed, as well as a piece of property in New Amsterdam.

My good wife Joanna and I are in good health. I now have residences in both New Haven and New Amsterdam, but will, with God's grace, be completely moved to New Amsterdam within a year. I have a shop on Pearl Street there, and I'm blessed with a prosperous trading company. I'm not without influence in this city and will be appointed soon to the council of Eight Men, a citizen's advisory board.

I send you a very belated gift on the occasion of your marriage. I hope to see my grandchildren next year, when I plan to visit.

Commending you and yours unto the guidance and protections of the Almighty, I ever remain,

Your faithful and loving father,
Isaac Allerton

With great excitement I unwrapped the bulky package, which had been transported by ship from New Amsterdam. Nestled within the packaging was a set of Delft plates, bowls, mugs and an albarello pot for holding ointments. All were tin-glazed white with a beautiful blue pattern. I had seen Delftware in the colony but only in some of the better houses. My gossip would be envious.

"We'll eat from these plates tonight," my husband announced.

"Not for a crown," I replied. "These are too nice and too fragile to use every day. They are still made of clay, and the children are likely to break them."

He frowned but helped me put them away in the chest by the side of the room, where we kept some of our best possessions.

Chapter 31

An Encounter with a Wild Cat and the Colony Loses a Leader

Mary Cushman, Duxborough, 1643-1644

Young Thomas at six, Mary, four, and Button—little Sarah—barely two, entertained us daily with their antics. Button waddled here and there in her shift, following either Mary or young Thomas, much to his irritation. When Button fell, she just somersaulted like a small tumbler and got back up on her feet to continue in the same direction. Her pudding frequently saved her from serious harm. She would climb anything, and I had to watch her carefully, as she was quick as an eel. Both Mary and Button liked to feed the chickens, but I'm not sure how much corn they spread since both girls chased the poor birds around, to the shedding of feathers and the noise of squawking. The hens laid fewer eggs on the day following such a chase. Most days, Sarah Alden had little time to do anything more than run after them.

Young Thomas now went to the fields with his father but not before milking our goats, at which he had become quite skilled. He plagued his father and me with questions about everything. How do only certain goats have babies? Where does snow come from? When will I have a mustache like Father's?

Despite Sarah's extra hands to share the daily work, I was more than busy tending to my family's health, cooking and baking, and keeping the house clean and neat.

I greeted the bed gratefully each night. Sarah Alden would make an excellent goodwife —she'd already learned to make soap, spin flax, and cook nearly everything I had learned from Alice Bradford. She most liked sewing and knitting, at which she had become skilled, but she struggled with the names of the plants in my garden and the use of herbs in cooking.

I myself was still learning the uses of plants for treating ailments, from goodwives in the colony and especially from Bridget Fuller whose knowledge was endless.

ல ல

On a cold autumn day in 1643, with the harvest in, I took my basket and went with young Thomas to walk in the woods. There I picked such wild herbs and greens as still grew and gathered nuts. Thomas, with his untamed imagination, hid behind trees, playing hunter and pretending to shoot game. The woods were magical during that time of year. Many leaves had already fallen, creating a soft, colorful carpet under our feet, while the sun bathed us in golden light as it passed through the yellow leaves remaining on the beech and larch trees.

Ever mindful of wild animals, I always brought a knife, thinking it would be enough protection should we encounter anything dangerous. Up until then, I had only seen deer and skunks, but just days before, we had heard the call of lions in the night. Even thus forewarned, my heart nearly stopped when I saw a large tawny cat at the far edge of the clearing where I stood. As it stalked something, I followed its line of sight and felt a surge of terror when I spotted its intended victim, my son. I yelled out to distract it, dropped the basket and took my knife from my waist, running toward young Thomas, getting to him just as the cat leapt. They went down in a flash of his russet coat and the cat's golden fur. Thomas' screams blended with my yells, echoing in the woods, and he fought at the claws. With one hand I grabbed the cat by its scruff, as I would a kitten, to keep its teeth from Thomas' neck. With the other, I stabbed at it, a hard thing to do as they tumbled. I felt the knife penetrate the cat, and giving a hiss and a wail, it released my son and ran off, disappearing into the trees.

I knelt to examine what damage the wild thing had done, while Thomas moaned, his eyes fixed on something in the distance. The cat's claws had rent the front and sleeves of his waistcoat and blood seeped through the slashes. Deep scratches covered his hands. The most worrisome was the bite mark on his neck, dribbling blood, where the cat's jaws had seized him. I believed my yelling had distracted the animal from breaking his neck.

"Can you walk, Thomas?" I asked him, but the shock of the attack had rendered him nearly senseless. I would have to carry him.

My son weighed several stones, and I pulled him up with great difficulty. Then I bent and lifted him over my shoulder and began the long walk back to the house, staggering under his weight. By the time I reached our gate, I'd almost dropped him several times and with great relief, finally let him slip to the ground as I reached the palisade.

"Sarah, come help me!" I couldn't hear my words for the ringing in my ears, but Sarah ran out of the house, carrying Button, whom she set down as soon as she saw us. "Help me drag Thomas into the house."

Together, we got him on a mattress, and I stripped off his clothes. First, I examined his neck, where I thankfully found only shallow punctures—I'd kept the cat from far worse. I ran my hand over his head, checking for further blood and found none. However, Thomas' arms and chest were badly clawed, but not very deeply because of the layers he wore. Only a few of the slashes would need sewing, thanks be to God.

He finally appeared to recognize where he was and began to shiver with shock. I had Sarah warm some of the whiskey that my husband made from corn and kept for his guests and forced some of it into my son's mouth. He coughed violently, but the color returned to his cheeks and his eyes finally focused on my face.

"Mother, was that a wild cat?" he asked.

"Yes, and you're a lucky young man, because I think it was immature, based on its size. Thomas…it's going to hurt, what I must do to treat your wounds. Are you brave enough to stand some pain?"

"I can do it," he said, but I saw fear in his eyes.

I swabbed each slash with soap and water to wash away the dirt and blood, then poured a little whiskey on them, which one of my gossip members had recommended. I knew full well how much it stung him, and he took it bravely. Finally, I told him I would need to stitch two of the slashes on his chest, the worst part.

While I did the sewing, he gripped Sarah's hand until she groaned in pain, and while he cried quietly, he never screamed. I sat back, pleased with my work. "This is the sweet part," I told him with a smile, packing honey into his wounds before wrapping them all in clean linen. When I had finished, he looked as if he were covered in a shroud from the waist up. Then his eyes closed, and I thought he'd fainted, but he'd just fallen asleep.

Sometime later, when my son sat up and said, "I'm hungry. What is there to eat?" I had to turn my head to hide the tears. The experience had shaken me to my roots, and it was the hand of God that had helped me save him. I knew he would bear the scars of the cat for many years, and I hoped they would remind him of God's love.

When my husband returned for his midday meal and saw his son, I allowed young Thomas to tell the story of our encounter with the cat, only adding a few details. After a heartfelt prayer of thanksgiving for his son's delivery, to which we all added our voices, Thomas took his musket and left to retrieve my basket and follow the wounded cat. He didn't find it, so perhaps I hadn't wounded it mortally.

In bed that night, Thomas whispered to me, "You were very brave today, my dear wife. With God's power flowing through you, you saved our son. I hope such a terrible thing will never happen to you again, but this new world presents us all with unforeseen dangers."

Warm, drowsy and feeling safe in his arms, I struggled to listen to him. As my eyes closed, I murmured, "I should have had a bigger knife."

ᘓ ᘐ

One early spring afternoon the following year, just before planting time, Thomas and I sat for a while at our table. He'd just returned from the Plymouth settlement where he'd bartered for some goods we needed: sugar, wool, a new pipe, and some cowcumber seeds for the garden. I was determined to have a crop of those to pickle this year. I gave him a mug of beer to enjoy before he went off to work on repairs to our palisade.

"Is there any news you can share with me?" I asked him.

"Well, it seems I'm now named with some other men of the colony on the 'Able to Bear Arms List.'"

"What does that mean, Thomas?" I felt a nubbin of worry in the pit of my stomach.

Mary toddled over to him and lifted her arms to be picked up and placed in his lap. He sighed but raised her up and tickled her, so she giggled. Button followed her, begging a turn. "It means I'll be called to bear arms if defense of the colony is required or if men from the colony are called to fight elsewhere."

"Please God, that day will never come. We must pray on that tonight. Is there any other news?"

"Lydia Morton expects another child next year—this would be what? Their fourth?"

Nathaniel Morton had grown up with Thomas and me as members of the Bradford household. I always thought of him as the small imp who played tricks on me when I lived there. He and his wife Lydia were close friends to both of us, and I worried for her health with each child. As months had gone by and my own womb hadn't quickened, I fought the sin of envy I felt at hearing this news.

Love didn't lack betwixt Thomas and me, and Thomas didn't seem to mind, since the children we had were more than a handful. *Did Thomas feel me to be at fault, not bearing another child? Did the difficulty of my last birthing affect my ability to carry?* Though I was older now, at twenty-seven, age didn't seem to deter other women.

Button fussed in her father's lap as Thomas talked, so I took her up and placed her in mine. Although she'd been weaned, she still nuzzled my breasts.

Thomas watched in amusement, then, to my relief, changed to a much sadder topic. "Captain Standish's old friend Hobomok has died," he said with a sigh.

I recalled hearing of Hobomok's kindness and help to our settlement when I lived with the Bradford's, and I'd often seen this elite Wampanoag warrior in the village, although I'd never spoken to him. He had lived amongst us near the Standish farm for many years, probably because of his friendship with the captain, and I'd heard he had converted to Christianity. "How did he die?"

"He contracted some illness, probably from an English visitor to the Standish household. Standish buried him on his farm in Duxborough."

"He and Standish indeed had a long and lasting friendship. The captain must feel deep grief at his loss. I'm sorry he's gone—he was so much a part of our history."

Thomas nodded. "There is more to tell, but I must get to my afternoon's work." I looked at him, and the expectation for more must have been clear on my face, because he added, "Tonight, when the children are abed."

He drained his beer and then left to make repairs to our fencing. This palisade, surrounding the house and its acreage, served as a barrier to wild animals, many of which continued to find ways to dig under it and ravage my garden from time to time.

I sat Button down and went to get her the last of our goat's milk. My own milk had now dried up, but I frequently longed to unfasten my waistcoat and loosen my stays as I had when I nursed her. On the days when I found my work particularly burdensome, I didn't wear the stays at all—days of comfort when my movements were free. Remembering what still waited to be done that afternoon, I called to Sarah Alden, who had been playing outside with young Thomas. Since he'd had gone off to help his father, I asked her, "Sarah, could you please milk the goats?"

"I'm going to do that right now."

ഇ ഈ

That night, when the fire had grown low, Thomas and I sat in chairs by the hearth. Thomas smoked his pipe—I did love the smell of it—and the children were at last in their beds. My son slept above in the loft, while Sarah Alden slept on a mattress in the far corner of our one room, the better to awaken and soothe Mary or the baby should they stir in the night. We kept our voices low, but I knew Sarah would listen until sleep overtook her.

"What couldn't you tell me earlier, Thomas?"

"There have been two more hangings in the colony. I know you will probably hear it from your gossip, but I thought it might be better coming from me."

I leaned over and grasped his hand. "What wickedness was there to warrant the punishment of death?"

"Adultery."

"Adultery? Who?"

"I don't know if you have made the woman's acquaintance. Her name is Mary Latham. The Court ordered her to be hung, along with her consort, James Britton."

"Mary Latham? The wife of William Latham who used to live here in Duxborough? I haven't met her, but I heard she's very young." I shook my head in sorrow. "What could possibly have led her to this end?"

"Apparently a young man whom she loved rejected her, and as a result, she vowed to marry the next man who asked. Unfortunately, it was Mr. Latham. She told her gossip that she considered him ancient and she had no love nor even liking for him."

"But he cannot be that old—I would guess no more than thirty-five or forty. He's still in his prime." Here I smiled at my thirty-five-year-old husband. "But my gossip told me Master Latham is both dishonest and lazy, so perhaps that's the reason for Mary Latham's contempt for her husband. Wasn't he brought before the Plymouth Court several times?"

"For slanderous speeches and failure to pay his fines."

"What did Mary Latham do?"

"Soon after she married, several sought pleasure with her, offering wine and other gifts. Britton was amongst them, and he was the one to whom she succumbed."

"Who's James Britton?"

"A professor from England, who, when he came here, opposed our church and government and became dissolute and ungodly."

"How could Mistress Latham consort with such a man?" I asked.

"We don't know her reasons, but Mary Latham openly confessed to abusing her husband, once putting a knife to his breast and threatening to kill him. We heard testimony that she called him an old rogue and a cuckold and threatened to make him wear horns as big as a bull."

I gasped. I couldn't imagine such vileness in a woman. "I assume Governor Winslow oversaw the court proceedings?"

"He did, and I'm glad Master Bradford didn't preside. He takes such things deeply to heart and deals with them very harshly."

"Hanging would seem as harsh a punishment as possible."

We sat quietly, listening to the soothing snap and crackle of the fire and basking in its warmth—the March night was cold, with a threat of a late season snowfall. Finally, I asked, "More news? Perhaps of a less wicked nature?"

Thomas chuckled. "Well, our Governor Winslow will now represent our colony in Boston, along with men from the Connecticut, New Haven and Massachusetts Bay colonies. They'll form a confederation called the United Colonies of New England."

"Well, it's about time the colonies began to talk to each other!"

At this Thomas laughed out loud, but quickly stopped when I put a finger to my lips and nodded toward the trundle bed, where Mary and Button were sleeping. "I don't think it was formed for just talking, Mary," he whispered.

"For what then?"

"For mutual defense. The ability of our various militias to co-ordinate was clearly lacking during the war with the Pequots. With this confederation, we'll have a common military."

"And just who will pay for this common military? Soldiering costs money." I could see from the surprise on Thomas' face that he'd not expected the depth of my understanding.

"Since you ask, dear wife, the cost for military operations will be distributed proportionally amongst the colonies."

"What is pro...proportion...?"

"Proportionally," he replied. "It means the cost levied on a colony will depend on how many men from sixteen to sixty years of age live in that colony and are thus able to bear arms."

The words 'bear arms' registered in my mind. "So that's why you're on the Able to Bear Arms list."

He nodded. "The confederation's commissioners will also have the authority to declare war, search for fugitives from the law and settle disputes between colonies."

I nodded, more from tiredness than in agreement. "This is more than enough to fill my head for tonight, Thomas. Why don't we retire? I can ask more about this later."

"I know you will," he said with a smile.

I left to undress and crawl under the blankets. Thomas sat for a few minutes more —I thought to allow time for me to warm his bed—then put out his pipe and banked the fire. I was already asleep before he joined me.

ᘓ ᘓ

We experienced another loss the following year, 1644. Elder Brewster, the godly and pious man who had led the religious life of our colony since its beginning, died in April, just as the flowers started to bloom and warm breezes danced over the fields where the corn sprouted green. He was nearly eighty years old, and, as he remarked before his death, he'd lived a good long life. Along with his increasing frailty, a sadness had stayed with him following the deaths of his two daughters, Patience Prence and Fear Allerton, from smallpox and influenza.

We heard he was active until his last day and died peacefully surrounded by his sons Jonathan, Love, and Wrestling, and his dearest friend, William Bradford.

Many members of the colony, including Thomas, the children, and I attended his burial on the high hill above Plymouth. Scudding clouds overcast the day, with the heavy air promising a spring rain. The wind off the ocean whipped our capes around us, almost carrying away the words of William Bradford.

"Elder Brewster was wise and discreet and well-spoken. He had a very cheerful spirit, a humble and modest mind, and a peaceful disposition. He gained the love of those both within and without this place." Here the governor's voice wavered, and he stopped for a moment. "He was tenderhearted and compassionate with those in misery. He had a singular gift of prayer and always begged that God in his mercy would pardon us of our sins. Accordingly, God blessed his endeavors all his days, and he saw the fruit of his labors before he died. We shall not know such a man again."

More than a few of us wept, remembering this good man, knowing in our hearts no one could replace him.

Sadly, Elder Brewster's son Wrestling soon followed him in death, yet unmarried and even before the settlement of his father's estate. I'd always wondered about his name until I was told that it came from the phrase 'wrestling with the devil.' His name lived on, as his brother, Love, named his newborn son Wrestling.

ഇ ഈ

In the summer of 1644, having still not conceived, I thought to consult with Mistress Fuller. "Your situation isn't uncommon, mistress," she told me after I had, with a hot face, blurted out my problem. "It may possibly come from overwork or perhaps from your diet."

"Do you have something for food or drink that might help me conceive?"

Mistress Fuller's wrinkled face bloomed with a smile, revealing several missing teeth. "There are several things I believe might help."

She took me into her garden, where she showed me a bush with lovely purple flowers that gave a sweetness to the air. "This is called a chasteberry or monk's pepper. The berry is brown with a peppery flavor, and it helps regulate your monthly flow. I'll give you some." She then led me to another flowering bush. "This is garden angelica. It has many uses—for example, it's particularly good for the treatment of dysentery and cholera—but it will improve the flow of blood to your womb…and this is black cohosh," she said, indicating a plant with white and yellow blooms. The root of this plant is also used to regulate your monthly flow and help fertility. I'll give you what you need of these and the receipts for their use."

I went home with a lighter heart and waited.

Chapter 32

Thomas Is Called to Fight and My Father Asks a Favor

Mary Cushman, Duxborough, 1645-1646

Early in 1645 I received another letter, addressed by my father to both Thomas and me. Thomas brought it from the village when he went there to trade for sugar, but with this thing and that, we had no time to sit and read it together until evening. We sat at the table with the light from a candle, after the children were asleep and the fire was banked.

To my beloved daughter Mary and her husband, Thomas Cushman,

I write to tell you I'm in good health and that I prosper. As you may have heard from others, I was chosen as a member of the Council of Eight for New Amsterdam when the number was reduced from twelve to eight. Thus I have a great interest in the business of the city, although I have extended my trading ventures to a new settlement south of New Amsterdam called Fort Cristina, where the colony of New Sweden has been established.

Dearest Mary, I have heard from your sister Remember and her husband Moses Maverick that they are now parents to a third daughter. Her name is Abigail. They live still on the outskirts of Salem, in an area Mr. Maverick hopes to have incorporated as a separate township. I landed in that very same area a few years after we founded our colony at Plymouth and had hoped to establish a trading post there.

I made good to visit your brother, Bartholomew, on one of my voyages to England. He is a minister in Bramfield, England. His first wife, Margaret, died without issue soon after their marriage, and he married again, to Sarah Fairfax. They have been blessed with two daughters and two sons. I had never ceased hoping he might return here with his family, but he seems to have grown roots in England.

Thomas, I must ask a boon of you. I have money owed me in the colony, namely from the estate of John Coombs. I learned recently he has died, without paying his debt to me of £100 silver. This was originally owed to my brother-in-law, Godbert Godbertson, who then turned it to me. This letter serves as a legal document assigning you the collection of this debt on my behalf.

You have sufficient standing in the Plymouth Court to make a motion to this end and in this way assure I can collect. I pray that you can achieve a good result.

God's blessing upon you both. Yours truly loving,
Isaac Allerton

"It seems we'll never be free of your father's business," Thomas said with a deep sigh. "I'll do what he asks, but I doubt he'll ever come here to collect what's owed him, given the nature of his leaving the colony. This is undoubtedly why his debtors haven't willingly paid what they owe—they know he'll never demand it in person."

"Perhaps once you've made this an issue, they'll come forward," I replied.

"Perhaps when water flows uphill."

I reached over and grasped his hand in silent thanks for doing this.

ꕥ ꕥ

Thomas went to Plymouth with the burden of recovering what was owed to my father and presented the letter to the Plymouth Court. The court assigned him the debt, and while he was there, he sought advice on how to collect it. As he told me later, this could be done—but not without some difficulty, as he explained in a letter to my father.

To my esteemed father-in-law Isaac Allerton,

I have this day come from the Plymouth Court, where I presented your letter asking that I collect the debt owed to you by John Coombs, now the estate of said John Coombs. Mistress Coombs left Plymouth for England soon after his death and gave her sons, John and Francis, into the care of one William Spooner. Goodman Spooner was until recently the Combs' indentured servant. He is now the guardian of Coombs' sons, enjoined by the Court to maintain them unless there are further requirements from their mother. He is also the administrator of the Coombs estate, for unknown reasons. Having received permission from the Court to collect your debt, I spoke with Goodman Spooner. He informed me that I must wait for repayment until the sale of the Coombs' corn crop, one third of which is Mistress Combs' dower share. Thus it will be some time before all of this is settled.

With affection as the husband of your daughter, Mary,
I commend you to God's mercy.
Thomas Cushman

ꕥ ꕥ

Soon thereafter, I received a letter from my sister, Remember, asking that I come visit her. I had not seen her in more than fifteen years. I wondered what changes time had wrought but had no idea of how I could manage such a visit. Work filled my life from sunrise to dark and beyond, but my curiosity about my sister's life in the Massachusetts colony and my desire to see her again became an itch.

One morning, as we broke our fast over bread, butter and jam, I asked Thomas, "Do you think I might travel to Boston to see my sister? Perhaps all of us we could make the trip."

Thomas' forehead rose in surprise. "Why? Who would care for the children and the house while you were gone? Or our farm, if we all went?"

"I haven't seen her for so long, husband, and I dearly wish to see her again and meet her husband."

"Our place is here," he replied, the harshness of his voice attracting the attention of the children. "I'll not consider it." He placed both hands on the table, rose and left the house.

It was the first time Thomas had denied me anything without the usual give and take, and his curt decision was hurtful. I'd never asked to leave the farm before, and he knew I hadn't seen Remember in many years and that Bartholomew was lost to me. His obstinence was unexpected and brought tears to my eyes. I'd bide my time, but I knew the longing to see her would not diminish.

ꕥ ꕥ

William Bradford became governor again in June. Although other men served as governor from time to time—Edward Winslow frequently and Thomas Prence occasionally—everyone considered Bradford our true leader because of his intelligence, fairness, and skill at overseeing the business of the colony.

One Sunday after our morning services, Thomas and the children and I ate our midday meal at the Bradfords. The heat of the day, with just the slightest of breezes from the nearby river, had us eating outside, at a table hastily arranged of planks set on barrels. This set me to thinking of our early days in our crude home in the Plymouth settlement and the first feast of thanksgiving we'd celebrated.

When we were all seated, with my daughters standing and ready to serve the food, Governor Bradford invoked the blessing. "God, we recognize your marvelous providence, not only of the food before us but also for our long lives. You have supported us in the face of the perils of nature, of heathens, of the sea, of false brethren, of weariness and painfulness, and in hunger and thirst." He opened his Bible and continued for several minutes before Mistress Bradford laid her hand on his arm as a signal he overtaxed the attention of the children. He ended by saying, "We must thank Almighty God also for the payment of the last of our debt, so this colony is now free to grow and prosper. Without His sustenance, we would not have seen this day."

In this way, I learned the colony had finally paid off its last creditor. When we returned home, Thomas told me, "You and I both know the governor has long been vexed with our debt—twenty-five years! I'm glad he'll no longer have that worry."

"How was it paid?"

"Governor Bradford and the Council agreed to offer John Beauchamp, who held the last of that debt, colony lands with a value of nearly three hundred pounds."

"Didn't you owe some of that debt, along with others?"

"I did, and I'm relieved to have this resolved without any further lien on our farm's profits."

ꕥ ꕥ

In July, we received news that Thomas would be amongst the men sent by the United Colonies to deal with the Narragansett Indians, possibly in some conflict. The affairs of the various Indian tribes were complex, and Thomas did his best to explain why this was necessary, after he read the notice to me.

"This is hard news, Mary, but I'm listed as able to bear arms for the colony and must go when I'm conscripted."

"Why is this so urgent?"

"Because the Narragansett Indians threaten the Rhode Island colony. They've been in constant conflict with the settlers and Mohegans over territory there, and now, with the death of their sachem at the hands of the Mohegans, the Narragansetts have vowed revenge. They've already fought one serious battle with the Mohegans with the loss of many lives on both sides. Roger Williams— one of Rhode Island's leaders—has received information that the Narragansetts now plan to move against the United Colonies. The commissioners have decided to send a combined militia to confront them."

"How many men will go?"

"Three hundred have been conscripted, with forty from the Plymouth Colony," he replied.

"You have to go." My words came out in a whisper.

"Aye." He kissed me on the cheek. "I've work to do now to prepare."

My heart sank, and I watched Thomas until he disappeared, on his way to visit our tenants and indentured men. They'd be needed to continue working our farm in his absence, and he'd have to name an overseer. I covered my face with my hands, unable to imagine life without him, even for a short time.

On the morning of Thomas' departure, I organized a knapsack with bread, cheese, smoked meat and such food as might sustain him for at least a few days, a clean shirt, plus soap, a razor and flint. "How long will you be gone?" I couldn't help it—tears ran down my cheeks.

He looked at me long and hard, with sadness written on his face, then replied with great patience, "I don't know, my dear wife, as I have told you many times." With that, he stooped to place his hands on the shoulders of each of our children, who had gathered to see him off. He wished them each God's grace and admonished them to be good, then embraced me one last time, blessing me and whispering to me he had faith I could manage.

I handed him his battered felt hat.

After tying bags of powder and bullets to his belt along with a container of water, he shouldered the knapsack and his bedroll, seized his musket and walked resolutely to our gate, turning to wave as he left.

I'd long dreaded a day such as this—the possibility of losing Thomas, my empty life without him, and the challenges of being a widow with three young children.

Thomas had gone hunting before he left, to supply us with venison, plus we had salted pork from the slaughter of one of our pigs. Young Thomas, now nearly eight, was an accomplished fisherman and could be relied on to split wood and milk our cow and goats. Mary, at six, was beginning to be helpful with small things. She had proven adept at weeding the garden once I'd shown her the difference between flowers and weeds, and she pulled them out with the same enthusiasm with which she'd previously destroyed my flowers. And I had Sarah Alden. I sighed deeply, thinking the fields would also need weeding.

Mary took my hand and asked, "Where did Father go? When will he come back?"

I looked down at her. "You mustn't worry, daughter. He will be back soon enough. We'll pray for him every day until he returns."

Young Thomas placed his hand on my arm. "Don't be distressed, Mother. I'll stand in Father's place."

I ruffled his hair in affection at his determination to be a man.

ꟗ ꟗ

Several weeks passed during which we received no word, and the children never stopped asking me if I'd heard anything, where their father was, and when would he be home. Their questions pained me, like picking at a wound. I kept myself busy, moving from one task to another, trying not to think about Thomas. I couldn't sleep without his comforting bulk in the bed next to me, and I stopped many times during the day, thinking to call out to him with a question.

Before the month ended, I saw Thomas come through the gate and approach the garden where Mary and I were weeding, Button playing at our feet. I stood up, waved, and started toward him, but Thomas put his finger to his lips and snuck up on Mary and little Sarah and hugged them. They squealed in delight, which brought young Thomas from the cow's lean-to.

After father and son had embraced, I held my husband at an arm's length before wrapping him in my arms. He looked weary and dusty from the road. "I'm so glad to see you home and uninjured, Thomas," I said, with tears of joy. He hugged me closer, muffling my face into his shoulder. That lasted only a moment before I had to pull away. "Your odor repels me," I said with a smile and a wrinkle of my nose. "Go wash yourself and put on clean clothes while I put something on the table for you. Are you hungry?"

He nodded vigorously and headed to the tub of water we kept by the front door. Sarah herded the children inside, while he stripped off his shirt and washed himself vigorously with soap. He looked thinner than when he'd left, but the sight of him shirtless still made my heart leap, even after so many years. He smiled when he saw my admiring look. I went to get him pants and a shirt, which he donned after washing the rest of his body and drying himself in the air.

When he came inside, he sat at the table, where young Thomas had placed a mug of beer to slake his thirst. The children danced around him, Mary begging to be lifted to his lap and young Thomas peppering him with questions about what had happened. "Restrain yourself, son. There'll be time for answers after I have eaten. Is that rabbit stew I smell?"

"Yes, young Thomas snared one yesterday." I brought him a bowl of the stew, full of carrots, onions and parsnips. Mary got down from his lap and carried bread and butter precariously to the table.

Several black and white kittens wound their way around his legs, and he looked down at them. "It seems we have more than just one cat, Mary. Did Pearl have a litter while I was gone?"

"Yes, she did, and the kittens are already spoken for. It seems our neighbors have as much of a problem with vermin as we used to. Pearl has become an excellent mouser, and they hope the kittens will have her skills."

I sat down across the table from him, while Mary and young Thomas remained at his elbows. Although clearly famished, Thomas offered a long and heartfelt prayer, thanking God for his safe return and the health and well-being of his family. Then he tucked into his food.

I couldn't wait for him to finish, and as he buttered a slice of bread, I asked, "Now can you tell us of your adventure?"

"I'd not call it an adventure, wife," he said between mouthfuls. "We had an arduous journey, which thankfully saw no one killed. In fact, there were no confrontations at all with the Narragansetts."

I offered a silent prayer. "Did the militiamen find this situation frustrating?"

"Not at all. One benefit of having little to do is that I met men from the other colonies and learned much from them." He paused to finish his stew, while we waited patiently for him to continue.

"Our contingent first sailed to the Seekonk River and camped there for nine days, waiting for the arrival of the men from the Connecticut and Massachusetts colonies. Since Captain Standish led us, we were drilled constantly."

I went to refill his bowl.

"Then what happened?" asked young Thomas.

"It was more like what didn't happen, son." He stopped to take a drought of beer. "It seems the Narragansetts had sent a gift—I don't know exactly what it was—to the governor of Massachusetts. He'd refused to accept it. The United Colony commissioners, hoping to delay any hostilities, decided to return it, along with a message that if the Narragansetts were desirous of peace and wished security for their future, their sachems should come without delay to Boston. The commissioners guaranteed their safety."

I buttered Thomas another a slice of bread and handed it to him quickly, seeing a tiny hand come up over the edge of the table to try to snatch it. "Sarah! That isn't for you. If you wish some bread, you must ask for it. Otherwise, you will be punished." I turned my attention back to my husband. "Then what happened?"

"Their three principal sachems and a large train of their men went hastily to Boston and concluded an agreement and treaty. When word of this reached us, we left for home."

"God be praised." I gave a small bit of bread to little Sarah, who remained lurking under the table, then leaned across and took his hand. "I'm glad you're home, Thomas."

"As am I. Now would you mind if I slept for a while?"

"You may try, but I'm not sure the children and cats will allow it."

They did their best, but Thomas still managed to sleep soundly through the rest of the day, kittens and their fleas curled up next to him.

ഇ ര

I found myself with child soon after Thomas' return. Scarcely a week after discovering this, I felt sharp pains, almost worse than childbirth itself, and soon passed blood. Mistress Fuller advised me I'd miscarried. Since I hadn't told Tomas I was carrying, neither did I tell him about this.

I'd followed Mistress Fuller's remedies for barrenness: prayer, eating meats and vegetables, and I tried not work to exhaustion. All of this, except for less work, was how I lived already. I had eaten chaste berries and concoctions of angelica and black cohosh until my mind and stomach rebelled. Nothing had led to conception until now, and I had lost the baby. Following the miscarriage, I had to fight a deep sense of sadness. My daily chores seemed more endless than usual and I had a sharp tongue with the children. It was several months before I felt right again, and still I didn't conceive.

ഇ ര

One day in May of the following year, I was in the yard, using a paddle Thomas had carved for me to stir our dirty clothes in a cauldron filled with hot water and lye soap. Washing was a chore I disliked, especially as it now had to be done every other week because of the children. I always washed on a Monday, a tradition from the day my mother and the other Separatist women had come ashore on Cape Cod.

Just then, Thomas walked through the gate, returning from a trip to the Plymouth settlement, where he had attended a meeting called by Governor Bradford.

"What news, Thomas?" I asked when he approached.

When he didn't answer straightaway—he did like to tease me—so I asked, "Could you bring the kettle of hot water from the hearth and add it to the wash?"

Once done, he sat down on a stump we used for a seat. He remained silent for a bit more, watching me rub lye soap into the stains on the clothes, then pound them with the paddle. It was hot and sweaty work, and I paused to wipe the sweat from my forehead with the end of my apron.

"What news?" I asked again. "Are you trying to irritate me with your silence?" I wrinkled my face in fun as I said it.

"Some pirates have sailed into Plymouth's harbor."

"Pirates?" I dropped the paddle into the water.

"Yes, three ships with their captain, one Thomas Cromwell. They came from the West Indies, where they'd taken booty from the Spaniards. It seems they had a commission from the Earl of Warwick."

"Did they come ashore?"

"They did, and I heard from Governor Bradford, who went to meet with the captain, that the crew—some eighty or more—drank immoderately in various ordinaries and behaved like madmen in the village. After some were punished and confined in the fort, their behavior moderated somewhat. Our governor dislikes their actions more than he welcomes the gold the men scatter about."

Young Thomas, who was chopping firewood, and Sarah Alden, who had been inside and had come out to help with the wash, had caught some words of the story. Our son was quick to ask, "Real pirates? Where?"

My husband repeated it again, focusing more on the sins of drinking and carousing.

That wasn't the end of the problems with these pirates. I learned from my gossip they'd stayed in the settlement for more than a month, mistreating some women and spoiling for fights, before they finally sailed to Boston, where they continued to spend their booty and practice their sinful ways.

After dinner that night, my husband told us something more he had heard about the pirates. Young Thomas, Sarah Alden and little Mary sat on the floor at his feet with rapt attention, reminding me of the days below deck on *Mayflower*, when my father would tell us about what he was doing on shore. "While their boat was moored in Plymouth harbor, one of the pirate company, a quarrelsome fellow chained many times below deck for fighting, was ordered by the captain to moderate his behavior or be dismissed." He paused for effect, and the children squirmed with anticipation.

"Then what happened?" asked young Thomas, as we knew he would.

"The man turned on the captain, using vile language, and he drew his rapier. The captain grabbed the rapier and hit him soundly on the forehead with its hilt."

"Was he hurt badly?" I asked.

"He died a few days later, but the Plymouth Court found the captain not guilty of willful murder, as his crew testified on his behalf."

Outside the next day, I spied young Thomas wave a long thin stick around and then lunge, saying, "Take that, you villainous cur!"

I took the stick at once, telling him what he did was sinful behavior, but he would have to be reminded many times in the coming months. I also scolded my husband for telling the children such tales.

ꕤ ꕤ

Later that year, we gathered at the Bradford's house on a Sunday to say our farewells to Edward Winslow, a man who had served us ably as governor from time to time and also as a commissioner to the United Colonies. While in London as our agent, he had caught the eye of a man named Oliver Cromwell, because of his eloquent representation before parliament of the colonies' situations and businesses. Master Winslow left now to work for him.

After our Sunday services and on our way to the Bradford's, I asked Thomas. "Who exactly is this Oliver Cromwell?"

"He is a member of the English parliament, and one of the men who want a constitutional monarchy." He held up his hand to forestall what he knew would be another question. "That means the king would rule according to a constitution. Because King Charles is unwilling to cede his God-given authority, many from the parliament are now waging a war against the crown."

"And Cromwell?"

"He leads the war on the side of the parliament."

"So what will Master Winslow do?"

"I imagine he'll represent the interests of both the Plymouth and Massachusetts colonies on various parliamentary committees, to ensure we are dealt with fairly, despite the war."

"Will Master Winslow be in any danger?'"

"I don't think so," Thomas answered. "He isn't a soldier."

When we reached the Bradford's, we met with many of those who had traveled with Edward Winslow on the *Mayflower*: John and Priscilla Alden, Myles Standish, Mary Brewster and her son, Love, John Howland, and Stephen Hopkins. Susanna White Winslow attended with their two children, Josiah and Elizabeth. Most surprising was the appearance of Massasoit and his family. Massasoit was a close friend of Master Winslow, beginning soon after the *Mayflower's* arrival, when he had saved Massasoit's life during a near fatal illness by feeding him fruit preserves and sassafras tea. Although now very elderly, Massasoit remained chief sachem of the Wampanoags, and he was still a remarkable figure in his bearing and dress.

Perhaps sensing that he would never again see his dear friend, Governor Bradford intoned a long prayer for Winslow's health and well-being and a safe voyage to England. Then we enjoyed a feast such as we had not seen since the harvest of our first year in Plymouth. Alice had arranged tables outside to accommodate the many adults and children and had assigned guests to oversee the roasting of a deer and a pig over open fires. Women carried unending platters of root vegetables from the house, along with countless loaves of bread. We had brought butter, jam and cheese, as had many others. There were pottages and samp, and the men consumed beer in copious quantities. The smell of roasting meat, onions and garlic filled the air, along with the high-pitched voices of the children, who took advantage of their time together to play noisy games.

We returned home that night with very tired children.

ꟸ ꟸ

In October, Thomas and I received another letter from my father, sent from New Amsterdam, with some brief family news.

My greetings and love to my beloved daughter Mary Cushman and her husband Thomas Cushman,

I hope this finds you in good health. Some brief news of the family. I'm happy to relate that last year, Remember gave birth to a daughter named Elizabeth. Mother and child are well, although her husband, Master Maverick, complains of having four daughters underfoot and the eventual difficulty of finding good husbands for them. Remember is with child again, and he prays daily for a son.

My deepest gratitude, Thomas, for your efforts to resolve the situation of the debt owed by the estate of John Coombs.

Commending you and yours to God's grace and with deepest affection,

I remain,
Isaac Allerton

"The debt hasn't yet been settled, has it?" I asked my husband.

"Not yet, although I'm hopeful it will be soon, when the money from Coombs' crop is accounted."

"How fares Goodman Spooner as the overseer of that land?"

"He appears to be good in that position, and I hope he will be more diligent than his former master in the repayment of debt."

"Goodman Spooner has certainly risen in status from being an indentured servant," I said as I folded Father's letter and put it away in a drawer in one of our chests. "How did he come to work for John Coombs?"

"He was first the servant of John Holmes, but Holmes assigned him to John Coombs for the remainder of his indenture. Coombs must have been well pleased with him, to make him guardian of the children and administrator of his estate."

"Will Mistress Coombs return to the colony for her sons?"

"I have no idea."

"I find her leaving them most strange…you do know she is related to us," I told him.

"By what means?"

"The widow Coombs is Sarah Priest, daughter of my father's brother-in-law, Degory, who died that first winter."

"Mary, my head spins with these relationships, but it does explain why Combs sought to borrow from Master Godbertson—he was family."

Chapter 33

A Debt Is Paid and Another Hanging

Mary Cushman, Duxborough, 1647-1649

In June of 1647, William Bradford became governor of Plymouth for his twentieth one-year term. As I told Priscilla Mullins on one of our Sunday visits, "Mistress Bradford did complain of it the last time we met."

"The burden of the many things he is asked to do?"

I laughed. "No, the short temper they cause!"

She laughed, too.

We sat outside, enjoying one of many delightful early summer days. Flowers were blooming in her garden, attended to by foraging bees, and a light, refreshing breeze tickled my neck below my coif.

"Would you like to see my writing?" Priscilla asked. Taking a stick, she wrote, 'The Lord is my shepherd, I shall not want' in the dirt of her yard.

"I'm so proud of your skill in reading and writing, Priscilla. You're now a literate woman!"

Whenever we'd visited with each other, I'd worked with her—first on common words, then on short readings in the Bible. While she'd struggled with some of the longer words, her reading had now become slow but smooth. I couldn't imagine how she'd accomplished this with so many children underfoot.

"Even my husband has complimented me on it. Now I'm teaching my older daughters to write their names."

"Did you know your daughter Sarah is very quick to learn? She asks me questions for which I have no answers, such as how do chickens make eggs? Or what makes rain? I would ask Thomas, but he feels time shouldn't be wasted teaching girls anything beyond basic reading." I sighed.

Priscilla nodded her head. "John has taken lengths to ensure the boys are learned, but Priscilla, Ruth, Mary and Rebecca must rely on me to school them."

Priscilla sat back on the bench and reached around to rub her back. She had grown thick in the middle from bearing nine children, and the reaching was difficult for her, so I rubbed her back for her.

I looked her over carefully. "Are you with child again?" I asked.

"No. I think David was my last. He is now five, and with no babes since, my childbearing years are surely over. Every one of my forty-five years weighs on me, and there are now pains in my knees and hands, and especially in my back. My back now troubles me when I bend."

"Have you been drinking willow bark tea?"

"Yes, and it seems to help, but I grow tired of its taste." Priscilla turned to me and made a face.

"Might I suggest yarrow or boneset instead? Both grow wild here. I'll bring you some next time I visit. Even though you may feel old, dear friend, you're always young in my mind. I was certainly blessed by God to have had you in my life when I first came to Plymouth. Those early years were hard, and I was without friends, except for you."

"But you had Remember!"

"Yes, but she was occupied trying to keep the house without anyone, except for you, to teach her. She hadn't time for me, and I didn't think of her as I should have, as my sister. I resented her directives and threats when I disobeyed her. I thought because she was only two years older than I, she had no right to rule me. Only when I had been with the Bradfords for some time did I see she also suffered, and then we began to share things."

Priscilla looked off in the distance, perhaps thinking about her brother Joseph, who died with her parents during the first winter. "You're blessed to have a sister. Do you hear often from her?"

"Not from her directly, but through my father's letters, since she isn't literate. She has five children now, four girls and a boy. I hope to see them all one day. But when I asked Thomas if I could visit her, he looked as if I had asked for the moon in a bucket!"

Priscilla laughed. "After that long, dreadful voyage we've become quite fixed in place, have we not?" She gave my stomach a thoughtful look. "Are *you* with child, Mary?"

I flushed, because after so many years, I could answer yes. When my courses stopped, I'd worried about another miscarriage, so I'd said nothing to Thomas until my body began to round. "I am! Thomas seemed pleased when I told him, but he grumbled about having yet another baby in the house." I shared a smile with Priscilla.

She took my hand and gave me a look of such joy that her face lit up into a thing of beauty, the years falling away. "When will the baby come?"

"Next winter, possibly in January."

"Then it's a good thing Reverend Chauncy is no longer preaching here. He would plunge your babe into icy water for its baptism."

"And I would surely prevent him from doing that." I laughed, thinking of the brave mother who had confronted him in Boston.

"What news does Thomas bring from Plymouth?" Like me, Priscilla had an interest in the business of the colony.

"Well, our governor and his Council have given permission for the building of what will be called the First Parish Church. We've all seen the dreadful condition of the fort as a place for our services—the wind blowing in during the winter months, boards cracked or missing and the smell of rot. After all these years, it will finally be torn down and replaced by a real church."

"I do remember the endless sermons by Elder Brewster and that dreadful cold in the winter! It pierced us to our bones, and we all sat there shivering and longing for our warm hearths. I look forward to seeing what will be built." Priscilla stood and offered me her hand to rise. "You told me the last time we met that you now have sheep with good wool for spinning. Come inside and see what colors I've used for dying."

Her offer was timely, as I hadn't yet learned to dye wool. It was dim inside the house after the brightness of the sun in the yard, but cooler with the thick walls. When my eyes adjusted, I saw the contents of her knitting basket—piled with skeins of wool in different colors. "How beautiful! What did you use for this red?" I asked, picking up one skein.

"I used madder roots. There is another dye that yields a brighter red, something called cochineal. But you have to purchase it at some cost because it comes from a beetle."

"A beetle? Can we not find this beetle here? There are certainly many in my garden."

Priscilla chuckled. "No, this dye must be imported from England."

I pulled up two more skeins, one pink and one yellow. "And what did you use for these?"

"The pink comes from pokeberries—they grow wild as weeds and I have often seen you pulling them out. The yellow is from the petals and buds of tansy, which I know you have in your garden."

We spent some time discussing where I might find easily find sources of dye, such as black walnut husks for dark brown.

"I have to tell you something quite humorous," Priscilla said with a twinkle in her eyes. "When I first washed a garment I'd knitted with the dyed wool, all the color came out!"

"No! Why?"

"I didn't know that before you dye the wool, you have to use a binder."

"What's that?"

"It's something that binds the color to the wool. I have no idea how it works, but you need to soak the wool in it first, before dying."

"So what do you have for a binder?"

"In most cases, I use something called alum. It comes from England—I'll give you some of mine. I've been told vinegar and salt can be used as binders, as well as water from boiled nails. I've tried them but not with much success. Someone also told me it's better to dye your wool in an iron pot. Here, let me write this down for you..." and here she turned and gave me a knowing smile, "...so you will know which of these binders is best for each dye I've tried."

She took out some paper, ink and a quill pen from a chest in the room and laboriously wrote down several directives. When she finished, she turned to me. "Do you have a spinning wheel now, Mary?"

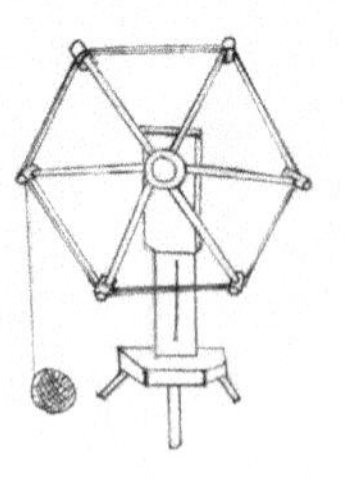

Spinning Weasel

"Thomas bought me a walking wheel made in the Massachusetts colony, not long ago. Mistress Bradford taught me how to spin the wool on one of her visits, but I haven't yet mastered this skill to my satisfaction. You would laugh at what I first spun —all thick and thin and breaking apart. Sarah now learns as well, and God's truth, she is a better spinner than I."

Walking Spinning Wheel

"Have you a spinner's weasel to measure a skein?" Priscilla asked.

"Aye, but its use needed some explanation for Sarah. She had some interesting ideas of what the knobs on the wheel were used for," I replied with a laugh, "including the hanging of wet clothes or the attachment of annoying children. What will you do with all this lovely spun wool?"

"I'll pay a weaver to weave it for me. I'm not skilled in weaving and the cost of a loom is beyond our means. I'll use one of the journeymen weavers who come to your home with a loom and weave your wool. I know there's a weaving business in the Massachusetts colony, where you can send your yarn to be woven. But just for cloth that doesn't need to be fulled." Priscilla's forehead furrowed as she said this. "I'm not sure what fulling means, but I've been told if you want better cloth, it should be fulled."

"Let me ask Thomas, perhaps he will know."

"He does tell you most things, doesn't he?"

"Only because I'm persistent with my questions."

ꟿ ꟿ

That evening, Thomas laughed when I asked him what fulling was. He shook his head, saying, "I never know what you will ask me next, Mary, but this a question I can answer. A fuller cleanses wool cloth of oil and dirt, using hot water containing some type of clay. The cloth is then pounded in the hot water, and it shrinks and thickens. It becomes so thick from this treatment that it almost repels the rain."

"And how do you know this?"

"I learned about it from a man from Scituate, whom I met when I visited the church there. A fuller now works in that township and he has a machine to do the pounding. The hammers are attached to a water wheel which pushes them up and down."

"I cannot imagine this, Thomas. It must be a marvel!"

ꟿ ꟿ

A week later, Priscilla came to oversee how I spun my wool. I had some fleece from which Sarah Alden and I had removed odd bits and bobs, at the same time pulling it apart to separate the fibers. I enjoyed this because the oil from the wool made my roughened hands feel soft. We'd washed the wool in warm, soapy water to rid it of its oil and dirt, then rinsed and dried it.

"When I first learned about preparing wool for spinning, I wondered what those paddles were," Priscilla said, as I took out my carders and grabbed a handful of wool. "I thought they were used to discipline the children."

The carders did indeed look like they might inflict serious punishment: two wooden paddles, each with metal teeth embedded on one side. I picked them up and began combing the wool, brushing it between the paddles to separate and straighten the fibers. While I did this, Priscilla took some wool that had already been thoroughly carded and rolled it in her lap into a long cord, the thickness of a finger.

As she did so, I noticed something. "Why are your fingers purple? Is it some medicine?"

"No," she laughed, "I used blackberries to get a purple color. Unfortunately, when you boil them for the dye, the color stains everything. My good husband feared when I touched him, he would turn purple!"

While she told me this, she took the roll of wool from her lap and attached it to the spindle that projected from the side of my spinning wheel, then turned the wheel as she walked backward, pulling on the attached wool. The action of the turning spindle twisted the wool into yarn, which Priscilla wound around the turning spindle by walking forward. "Have you another roll for me to attach?" she asked.

I handed her one which she deftly blended into the end of the yarn, turned the wheel and walked backward again to continue the strand. "The new roll just seems to grab onto the yarn, doesn't it?" she said as she spun more.

I held up a skein of yarn that looked somewhat ragged. "I can see I'm not nearly as skilled as you. How long have you been working with the wheel?"

"A few months," she replied. "Don't worry about your first yarn. Spinning will soon become as natural as walking."

I had been standing next to her as she spun, watching what she did with her hands, when I suddenly felt faint.

I must have wavered because Priscilla said, "Mary, you're pale. How goes the carrying of this baby? Why don't we sit for a while?"

I gratefully collapsed on the bench at the side of the table. "I'm tired, but otherwise well," I told her. "But I do think we need some refreshment." I turned to Sarah, who had been watching us and asked, "Can you please me bring the sassafras tea and also some of the corn cake you made for your mother? For yourself, too, if you're of a mind." Sarah loved sweetened corn cake. "But please check on the children first. Young Thomas is supposed to be minding them, but I wonder what they have gotten into. It's too quiet in the yard."

Over tea and cake, I tried to explain the work of a fuller, but Priscilla, like me, couldn't envision the machine.

ꟸ ꟸ

Our son Isaac, whom we named after my father, arrived in early February of 1648. It was bitterly cold, and I sat on Mistress Fuller's birthing chair near the hearth, as the house was freezing with drafts that found their way around the doors and windows and in under the roof.

My gossip was present, and this time the birth was easy—my squalling son came into the world rather quickly. The baptism, done at our meeting house, was most certainly accomplished without immersion.

Isaac was a colicky baby, and neither I nor Thomas got much sleep, as I had to rise often to try to calm his cries. My husband would grumble each time I left the bed, letting cold air slip under the covers. Wrapping Isaac warmly and rocking him by the fire seemed to help his distress, as did giving him a few spoonfuls of cool water in which fennel seeds had been boiled.

Our two daughters now had distinct personalities. Little Sarah, who disliked being called Button, was now seven and Mary was two years older, both of them sufficiently responsible to share in the work of the household. Isaac's smiles and small grabbing hands delighted both girls, and they often left their chores to watch him in his cradle. Mary in particular liked to carry him around. While Mary was light-hearted and reasonable in nature, little Sarah was demanding and frequently peevish. Thomas thrashed her nearly every week for being disrespectful, although neither I nor Thomas punished our children as much as we had been.

Both my daughters were readily distracted by games, little Sarah often leading Mary into mischief, and Sarah Alden had had to become expert at keeping them on their tasks. Now thirteen years, Sarah had become an indispensable part of our household. Although older in temperament than her years, she still laughed frequently and liked to prank the children. I had to remember to allow her time for herself, recalling how I enjoyed some freedom at that age.

ꕤ ꕤ

In August of the following year, income from the Coombs estate finally settled the debt to my father. Thomas received one third of the corn harvested from the Coombs land by the caretaker, William Spooner, who had proven a faithful and competent steward. Thomas sold the corn and notified my father, who wrote back telling my husband to keep the profit for the trouble he'd taken in collecting it. Given our four children, the money was welcome. My father may have been less than honest in trying to enrich himself, but he was generous with his family. I couldn't understand how these two sides of him existed in harmony.

ꕤ ꕤ

As the seasons passed, watching our children grow in God's goodness and grace became one of our greatest pleasures. They didn't always grow in thoughtfulness, though. One morning, my daughter Sarah offered to mind the baby and I agreed, as long as Mary stayed by her side. She and Mary took little Isaac out into the yard where they loved to show him the animals, naming them for him. At mid-day, when my husband and young Thomas came home for their meal, I called to Mary and little Sarah to come in from the yard. After some time, they came in laughing and winded, with burs and straw sticking to their clothes—but without baby Isaac.

My heart pounded in my chest, and I found I couldn't draw breath. "Where is the baby?" I finally gasped out.

My girls looked at each other with alarm growing in their faces. Clearly, they had forgotten him while they engaged in play.

"Where did you leave him?"

Thomas rose from the table and joined me, glaring at his daughters. "Show me where you left him," he said, pushing both girls out the door ahead of him.

Both girls were crying as their father pulled them by their hands out through the gate, heading for the nearby trees. I fell into a chair with Sarah Alden holding my hand and didn't move until I heard a baby's wail coming closer. Running out the door, I found Thomas gently cradling Isaac, who was no worse than hungry. Two woebegone girls trailed at a distance. I took him at once to nurse, praising God he had not been taken by wild animals. The look in Thomas' eyes told me that Sarah and Mary were due for serious punishment.

Indeed, Thomas immediately thrashed them both soundly and set them on their knees to pray for God's forgiveness while we ate our mid-day meal. We sent them to bed that night without food. Whispered recriminations and crying came from the loft.

"This is your fault with your silly game. You told me to set him down, and I just forgot him."

"But you were the one told to mind him!"

"I know, but you distracted me. You're always getting me into trouble."

"Father is truly angry with us. What would he have done if something had happened to Isaac?"

"I cannot imagine it, and it would have been all your fault."

"No, yours."

"Mother will never forgive us!"

They slept at last, bringing quiet to the house.

When the sun came up the next morning, I could hear them whispering to each other again. When we had all risen and dressed, Sarah and Mary made heartfelt apologies. We accepted their words, but Thomas' face remained stony during our morning prayers, and he glared at them as they hungrily ate their bread and cheese. Each night for a week, they were made to pray for an hour on their knees before they went to bed. Still, I didn't trust them with the care of Isaac for a long time.

ꕥ ꕥ

In addition to working his fields, Thomas often attended to various matters in Plymouth with the governor's Council and the Court. He had also assumed Elder Brewster's work, visiting members of our church and occasionally preaching on Sunday. His calm and reassuring presence, which had first attracted me, now blessed other people.

Returning from one of these trips in early October, he didn't immediately answer when I asked him how matters were with the Court.

"I'll tell you tonight when the children are in bed," he finally replied.

I knew the news was not good. That night, as we sat near the hearth, I said, "Something unfortunate has occurred, hasn't it?"

He didn't answer at first but sat deep in thought. The house was quiet except for the crackling of the fire and the thump of logs as they burned through and fell into the ashes. Finally, he said, "Another woman has been hanged. I know you will hear it from your gossip but thought to tell you before that."

"Another hanging! What a terrible thing. What did she do to deserve this?"

"Murdered her child."

His words struck me silent, and for once he continued without my asking. "Alice Bishop stabbed to death her four-year-old daughter."

I spoke without thinking, "Oh blessed God, take that innocent child into your arms." The thought of what the child had known—at the hands of her own mother!—made me cry.

Thomas took my hands in his. "The coroner's jury reported that when they came into the house of Richard Bishop, her husband, they saw blood at the foot of a ladder leading to the upper chamber of the house. When they climbed the ladder they found the child, still in her shift, lying on her side with her throat cut through. A bloody knife was on the floor beside her."

"Why would a mother to do such an evil thing?"

"No one knows. Mistress Bishop had no recollection of doing it. She concluded she must have done it when she went to look for the child. So she confessed she had murdered her daughter and said she was sorry for it."

"Would no one vouchsafe for her innocence?" I asked, leaning forward in my chair, wiping the tears from my cheeks with my apron.

"Only Mistress Ramsden was about. She said she'd last seen the child lying in bed asleep and had been sent out by Mistress Bishop to fetch some buttermilk from the Winslows. When she returned, she noticed some blood at the foot of the ladder leading to the upper chamber and went to find Alice Bishop for an explanation. Mistress Bishop said nothing but just sat silently and unseeing by the hearth. After Mistress Ramsden mounted the ladder and saw the child, she ran to find Master Bishop."

"Has the sentence been carried out?" I asked.

"Yesterday. I ministered to her before the hanging."

"Oh, Thomas." What a burden for my husband to bear. I reached across and placed my hand on his. With his other hand, he grasped mine tightly, like a drowning man grabs the hand of a rescuer.

ℌ ℌ

In April of 1649, the members of our church, recognizing Thomas' godliness and goodness, chose him to be Ruling Elder of the church, the first Ruling Elder to succeed our beloved William Brewster. It was a great honor but came with many responsibilities, which often took him far from home. Young Thomas, by now eleven, readily took on some of his father's chores, from the non-stop gathering and splitting of wood for the fire to working in our fields. My husband was also able to hire men to help him, since he now received a small income from the church.

Again that year, the colony re-elected William Bradford governor. On learning this, I said to Thomas one evening, "Quite honestly, husband, I don't know why the colony goes through the motions of an election each year, when it's foregone that Master Bradford will be our governor as long as God gives him breath."

Thomas smiled. "Perhaps you will get your wish, Mary. The freemen of the colony have suspended further elections because of the tension prevailing in England."

"What tension is this? Why have you not told me?"

"We've only just learned of it ourselves, in news from the Massachusetts Bay colony. Because of the ongoing civil war between parliament and King Charles, the decision has been made to suspend political activity until the nature of the British government is resolved."

"Do they have the constitutional monarchy now?" I remembered him telling me about this.

Thomas grimaced. "No, unfortunately. Parliament put King Charles to trial for treason and found him guilty."

"Did they banish him?"

"No, they beheaded him."

A feather could have knocked me over, and my hand flew to my mouth. I couldn't imagine how ordinary people would decide to behead their king, who ruled by divine right. "So who rules as the king now?"

"Oliver Cromwell, in a way. He named himself the Lord Protector of England, Ireland and Scotland. It was he who signed the king's death warrant."

"Then will Master Winslow come home, since the civil war is over?"

"I think not, Mary. He has written Governor Bradford that Cromwell still has need of him."

A discussion of a different Cromwell took place over our midday meal the following day.

As Thomas helped himself to slabs of roast pork and tore bread from the fresh loaf, he asked me, "Do you remember the pirate Thomas Cromwell, whose crew ran rampant in the colony for some months?"

"I do, indeed. Many women still talk of their unsavory meetings with his men. What news of him?" I could see the ears of my oldest son and his two sisters veritably twitching with interest. *Pirates.*

"It seems he and his crew sailed again to the West Indies and eventually returned to the Massachusetts colony with valuable prizes, making him a rich man."

"Humph." *Why is evil ever rewarded?*

As if in answer to my unspoken question, Thomas said, "I believe God has punished him for his sins, wife. He fell from his horse not long after arriving, landing on the hilt of his rapier. It damaged his body badly and a fever then took him, leading to his death. Governor Bradford thinks there might be something of the hand of God in this outcome."

"I recall Cromwell caused the death of one of his men by hitting him on the head with the hilt of a rapier."

"Exactly. I do believe God at times exacts his punishment on the living, rather than in the hereafter."

To belay the intensity of the children's curiosity, I replied, "Then after our meal, we will pray to the Lord for the forgiveness of Captain Cromwell's sins and the redemption of his soul."

Chapter 34

News from My Father and an Addition to the Family

Mary Cushman, Duxborough, 1650-1651

Early in 1650, I received a letter from my father. Fearing the worst, I was relieved to find it short, containing only good news of the family.

To my dearest daughter Mary,

I'm happy to tell you that your scattered family is faring well. Young Isaac is an exceptional scholar and will graduate from Harvard College this year.

Remember's husband, Moses Maverick, has been successful in the recognition of Marblehead as a township. He was elected last year as one of its first Selectmen, and I am assured he will be re-elected to this position, as he is recognized as an important leader.

Remember was safely delivered of another daughter, named Elizabeth. I'm honored that you would name your youngest son after his grandfather and trust that God keeps the children well.

I take my leave of you in all love and affection, and remain your father,
Isaac Allerton

This letter brought me joy with its good news, and we immediately replied, telling my father of our desire to have my brother stop to see us on his trip home to New Haven, after graduation. We also sent a letter to Harvard, in the hopes Isaac would receive our request in time. Sending and receiving letters was largely random and haphazard, depending on ships to bring the letters to the closest port, and then on soldiers or travelers to take them to their destination. The General Court of Massachusetts had many years ago designated the tavern of Richard Fairbanks in Boston as the as the official repository of mail going to other countries. This certainly made the delivery a little more certain, but I knew the governor often sent duplicate letters on different ships.

ꙮ ꙮ

Later that year, Thomas told me he planned to petition the General Court of Plymouth for more land. With our growing family, we had a great need for more income. The petition was granted, but when Thomas returned from the Court with the good news, he seemed discouraged rather than happy.

"Why aren't you glad at this outcome?" I asked.

"It has to do with the state of the Plymouth Township. Perhaps I saw it through different eyes whilst I was there. I observed it hasn't grown in recent years. So many of its citizens have left to move closer to their land, creating other towns. Look at how many of them now comprise our colony. Even last year some of our brethren bought land from Massasoit to build a new town called Bridgewater.

"In trade, we have nothing to offer to England but pelts, lumber, and corn, and Plymouth is hampered in this exchange by the shallowness of its harbor. Boats with a shallow draft are required to bring in goods from the ships having to anchor at a distance. Salem and Boston now have ship-building sites, ones which employ carpenters, joiners, sailmakers, and blacksmiths. We have few of these tradespeople. It's clear to me our colony will never become as prominent as the Massachusetts colony, and I worry what that means for our future."

I turned to face him from the hearth, where I fried some pork for our evening meal. "We must have faith in God, Thomas. He'll not desert us. Our people are in your care now, and you must trust in the Almighty to sustain and support us."

My husband reddened at my words, to be so reminded by a woman, but he took what I said to heart, for our prayers that evening were long and heartfelt, asking for God's grace upon our endeavors and offering thanks for all we'd been given.

ꟷ

Early on a June afternoon, a young man opened the gate to our house and strode toward me in the garden, where I gathered vegetables with the smaller children at my feet. I looked at him carefully for a moment.

"Do you not recognize me, sister?" he asked.

"Isaac! How you have grown!" *My brother!* I had not seen him since several years before he left for college. Now an adult, Isaac looked more like my father, especially in some features of his face.

"I've come for a day's visit before sailing to New Haven."

"This is a wonderful surprise! You must have gotten our letter." Smiling, I crossed the distance between us and embraced him. Looking up into his face, I said, "You've become a man since last we met. Come into the house. You must be thirsty after your journey."

I had Isaac sit at the table, and Mary brought him a mug of beer. I decided to make a feast to celebrate his visit—I had Sarah Alden kill a chicken, and when Isaac had finished his beer, I asked him to chop some wood for the fire. After all, he was a member of the family. Mary made fresh bread and boiled onions with parsnips, and our little Sarah was tasked with churning fresh butter.

I thought to cook chicken in verjuice, something I had learned from Alice Bradford. After Sarah Alden plucked the chicken and cleaned out the innards, I washed the bird, filled the belly with parsley, and trussed it. The liver, kidneys and neck were used to make a broth in which I boiled the chicken. In a shallower pot, I heated the juice of some crab-apples with butter and salt—what we called verjuice.

Mary retrieved a late harvested pumpkin from the cellar hole below the kitchen. Somewhat wizened, but not rotted, it would do for stewing. After hollowing out the pumpkin, I put inside it milk, honey and spices, along with the pumpkin pulp without its seeds. Mary set it over the hot coals to bake.

While all this whirled around him. Isaac played with my younger children, amusing them with tales, giffes, and a game of fox and geese until my husband and oldest son returned for the evening meal. Both were surprised to see my brother and joined him at the table for beer.

As they drank, I set the table with the delftware my father had sent us and went back to the hearth to finish the chicken. After removing the cooked chicken from the broth, I took the parsley from the belly, minced it small and added it to the verjuice.

When we finally gathered at the table, Thomas offered a lengthy prayer, praising God for the health of our family and the presence of my brother. At a signal from me, Sarah Alden brought us the chicken covered in the verjuice, along with sippets —slices of fried bread. Everyone helped themselves to the chicken and sippets, the boiled parsnips with onions and the stewed pumpkin.

My oldest son had forgotten his uncle, and as we ate, his face lit with interest as Isaac told us about Boston and Harvard College.

We learned that attending Harvard was not a goal easily achieved.

"I arrived in July to be examined for admission. My grandfather Brewster had to prepare me well, as I would be tested in my ability to read, understand, and write in Latin and Greek. Our books and much of the instruction at Harvard is conducted in Latin."

"Where did you live?" asked my son.

"In the buildings where we were taught and had our meals. We slept there as well, with three men to a room. One of the three is always an upper classman. All the new students must run errands and do the bidding of all upperclassmen and the faculty, which is a huge inconvenience. But it evens out when you become an upperclassman."

"Who prepares your food and washes your clothes?" I had to ask.

"Our meals are cooked and our beds prepared by the college stewards, but, in fact, slaves do most of the work."

"Slaves?" Thomas frowned, because he didn't condone slavery.

"Oh, yes, there are many slaves at the college. In fact, many of our professors and even the college president own slaves. Slavery is legal in Massachusetts, as I'm sure you know."

"Are these slaves from Africa?" asked Thomas.

"Some, but not all. A few are from England, and some are displaced Indians."

I could tell from Isaac's frank and open answers that he had no difficulty with their condition. "What subjects did you study, brother?" I asked, to change the topic.

"Many different ones—Logic, Rhetoric, Greek, Hebrew, Ethics and Metaphysics mainly. For some, we translated works and delivered the translations to the class and professors. With others, we learned by rote, and the tutors and faculty constantly drilled us. They were very strict."

"Did you ever get in trouble?" asked young Thomas, a subject close to his heart.

"Well, very rigorous rules exist, and you're fined if you break them. For example, you cannot be late or absent from prayers or lectures or go out into Harvard Yard without a coat or hat." He took a deep breath before continuing, "And you cannot fight, lie, drink distilled spirits, swear, play cards, pick locks, or fire a gun in the Yard. Those are just a few."

By this time, we had all ceased to eat and just listened.

"And were you ever fined?" I asked.

"I'm ashamed to say yes," he answered with a big smile. "For roughhousing in the meeting house, drinking, and playing cards. Oh, and missing classes."

"Was there no corporal punishment?" My husband was ever the disciplinarian.

"The faculty boxed me several times." My brother paused, waiting for someone to ask what boxing was. When young Thomas obliged, he continued, "You have to kneel in front of the faculty, then they hit you with their hand on your ear. You might be publicly beaten for a very serious transgression. Before I came there, one of the faculty had been dismissed for a particularly savage beating of a student." As my brother recounted more of his days at Harvard, it became clear he was a natural mimic, and he made us laugh with imitations of his teachers.

Once Sarah and I had cleared away the remains of the meal, I brought out a special treat—curds with sugar. Little fingers had interrupted me several times in its preparation, trying grab some sugar from the paper-wrapped cone.

"And what will you do now, Master Allerton?" asked my ever-practical husband, watching as his children devoured their sweet like suckling pigs.

"I'm going to work with my father. I'll join him in his enterprises in New Haven and New Amsterdam. I'm particularly interested in commerce with Virginia and the West Indies."

"Did you not find contentment in farming with your Uncle Brewster?" I asked.

"No," he replied, scrunching up his face. "I didn't like it at all… although clearly Uncle Brewster is much drawn to it."

With tears, prayers and many heartfelt words between us, Isaac left the next day, carrying greetings to my father and his wife. I hoped I would see him again, as I needed his light in my life.

ஐ ஐ

Our daily food had much improved with the acquisition of our cow. I now had milk for the children, churned butter, and soon made cheese. With our pigs, we had pork, fresh and salted, to add to our diet of fish, eels, clams, wild game and fowl. My garden overflowed in the summer with squash, pumpkin, beans, peas, turnips, carrots, lettuce and spinach. I smoked or salted fish and meat for the winter months and pickled vegetables with vinegar.

Best of all, we now had a tree which bore apples, which we stored in our cellar hole for later use in cakes and puddings—if the children didn't steal them all from the tree. Of course, this bounty added to daily and seasonal chores, but I had the children, willing and, at times, not so willing, plus Sarah Alden to share in the work.

That year William Bradford kept his position as our governor. When we saw him at one of our Sunday services, we couldn't help but overhear him speaking loudly to Master Prence, clearly in an ill temper.

"I see our faith declining, my friend, as many have become comfortable with a prosperous lifestyle. Most have seen a good harvest, and I say hallelujah and rejoice! But we must not fail to spend Sunday in thanks to God. We must be diligent in attending our church services and not be distracted by work or amusement!"

His face was flushed, and Thomas remarked to me on our way home that he suspected new laws would be enacted as a result of this outburst.

His words proved prophetic, for later that year our government passed a law forbidding servile work on Sundays, as well non-essential travels, hunting, and the sale of alcoholic beverages. Thomas, as Ruling Elder, was tasked with noting transgressions and counseling those who broke the law. This created some conflicts in his mind. "I find it troubling that I have to name those whom I find in contradiction of these laws, for didn't God say to forgive the sinner? These aren't crimes like theft or assault," he told me. "They hurt no one, only the church. I wish to bring them back to the church, not see them placed in the stocks or fined to the detriment of their families."

And yet this task, as distasteful as it was, he had to undertake.

ꙮ ꙮ

In October, I missed my courses again. Another addition to our family would arrive in the early summer of the next year. I didn't know how my husband would react when I told him, since we now had four children in the house, with Isaac still in his walking chair.

I waited until we had finished a mid-day meal consisting of many of his favorites: bread made from oatmeal; a roast turkey with onions inside; eels Mary had collected from the river; jams from summer raspberries; and stewed pumpkin. When my husband leaned back in his chair, sated, I gave him the news.

"Another child, Mary? Are you sure?"

I nodded.

He sighed but smiled at the same time—contradiction clouded his face. "I'm happy for us. Another child…it's surely God's grace, is it not? Do you feel well?"

I stood and gathered the napkins from each place and signaled to both Sarahs that they could clear off the table. "For the most part. I'm overly tired, husband, and my stomach is in flux." In truth, I had eaten little of the meal but for bread.

"I'll make sure the children pay attention to your needs, then."

I wanted to tell him I could use his help more than that of the children, but it was not my place.

ꙮ ꙮ

Our third son, Elkanah, came in June of the following year. By now, I knew the birthing process well, and my gossip came only for support. The importance of Bridget Fuller's presence was immeasurable, since I still harbored some fear of my mortality from the difficult birthing of little Sarah.

Mistress Fuller had introduced the use of red berries, called cranberries, to the pregnant women in the colony. Indians, from whom she had learned about them, prized their use. She told me cranberries grew in salt marshes overgrown with moss, and she warned me of their sourness. Mistress Fuller swore they eased the pregnancy and childbirth and instructed me to grind them up and steep the grindings in water, then drink the water like a tea. I confess I had to add some honey to the pot, so bitter were the berries. She also applied a poultice of stewed cranberries to my womanly parts after the birth, and I must admit it did soothe me and seemed to speed my healing.

Our honey came from a honey bee colony in our woods, and my two Thomases would gather the comb and the honey each fall, although not without a number of burning stings from the occupants. I wondered where they came from. Thomas told me that several of Plymouth's citizens had bought bee colonies for their property. He believed our bees had escaped from one of them, and they were the reason we now had apples on our tree. We planned to make a straw skep in which to keep our own colony the next year.

Later that year, with Elkanah already teething, I visited Alice Bradford. We had not spent time together for a while, since I was fully occupied in a home overflowing with children. Even with Sarah Alden to keep the children and set them to their chores, I rarely went anywhere without one or the other. That day I decided to take with me my bright-eyed and curious Isaac.

The cold weather had turned the leaves, giving wondrous colors of russet, red, orange and yellow first to the trees, and then to the forest floor where those leaves now lay. When Mistress Bradford greeted me with a smile and invited us to warm by the hearth, I felt a pang of regret that we spent so little time together now. Her presence always soothed my spirit.

As soon as he'd shed his cloak, Isaac immediately walked to the first thing that drew his interest in the room, asking, "What is this?" Without waiting for an answer, he toddled off to the next item, grabbing it for a closer look. Alice looked on, smiling, unbothered by what he touched.

"How old is he now, Mary?"

"Almost four," I replied, following him here and there as he walked around, "but he thinks he is older. He is unhappy that he still wears the shift of a child and oft whines about wanting breeches."

"He looks more like you than Thomas, with his lighter hair and hazel eyes. I think I know the source of his curiosity, too."

"You would certainly know," I replied with a smile. "How fares young William?" In truth, he was not 'young' anymore, having married the year before, an event which delighted both parents. I still thought of him as the child I had minded in the Bradford household in Plymouth.

"Very well, indeed. I'll soon be a grandmother—can you imagine that? Despite my misgivings, William is drawn to the military. He is now third in command of the Plymouth militia company." Her face was suffused with pride.

"And Mercy? I've seen her in Plymouth."

"She also prospers. Her marriage to Benjamin Vermayes is a happy one, although they don't yet have children. Her health is a concern of mine. She is thin and eats little."

"And Joseph?"

"Oh, he's still here, helping us with the farm."

I marveled at how quickly the time had passed and that those dear children who had been in my care were now grown with lives of their own. "I need to ask you something, Alice. Elkanah has teethed early and is always fretful. He chews on anything he can place in his mouth and at night cries more than my other children did. Do you have anything in your receipt book that might help?"

Alice got up and retrieved Isaac from under their bed. He was delighted to be held in her lap. "I know teething can be a source of illness, and I have heard some babies die suddenly during teething. Has he been well?"

"Yes, he hasn't had a fever and eats with energy."

"The only thing I can think to recommend is an anodyne necklace. You place it around his neck, and it will prevent him from dying while he is teething."

"How do you make this necklace?"

"Do you have henbane in your garden?" When I nodded, she continued, "Just string some henbane roots for the necklace."

"What if he chews on them?" I knew that henbane could be poisonous in some circumstances, soothing for pain in others.

"I would not let him chew on them, if you can…although my own babes seemed to be soothed when they gummed the roots. It was so long ago, you've forgotten, haven't you?" She smiled.

"I must have!" I leaned toward her as if we were conspirators. "What hear you from the governor? What happens in the colony?"

Alice laughed. She knew I enjoyed a good discussion of issues not normally of interest to women. Then she shook her head. "There is little to tell. My husband works hard on his book of our history and continues his communications with the other colonies. One thing of concern to him is something called the Navigation Act. He learned of it from John Endecott, who is once again governor of the Massachusetts colony."

"Like our governor…What is this Navigation Act? Does it regulate where our ships may sail?"

"No, something much worse. It prohibits the shipment of colonial goods to England on non-English ships."

I thought for a moment. "I see an unfairness in this law. It's a boon for the English ships, certainly, but a constraint on our trade with England with fewer ships available to take what we have in trade."

"Exactly. The governor has been irate, especially since shipping from Plymouth harbor is already limited by the ships having to moor far from our docks."

Just then, the door opened, and sunlight entered, along with a gust of cold air. I noticed in the harsh light how my dear friend had aged, her face now lined with many wrinkles, and missing and blackened teeth were visible when she smiled. With the cold air came a handsome youth.

"Joseph!" I said. "It's good to see you."

"And I, you, Mistress Cushman. And who is this young man?" he asked, spying Isaac.

"Isaac, please offer greetings to Master Bradford." I was persistent in teaching my children to be respectful of their elders.

In answer, Isaac jumped down from Mistress Bradford's lap and ran to Joseph, hugging him around his knees.

"Isaac! That is unseemly!" I said.

But Joseph just leaned down, took Isaac by his arms and swung him up on his shoulders, where my son laughed in delight.

Chapter 35

More Children and the Family Moves Again

Mary Cushman, Duxborough and Rocky Nook, 1652-1654

In early autumn, when the leaves had just begun to brighten with color and the air turned dry and cool with inviting, sunny days, I received a brief letter from my father.

My dearest daughter Mary,

I write you with heavy heart. God has seen it in his infinite wisdom to take my daughter, your sister Remember, into his arms. She went with the many prayers of her husband and children, soon after the birth of her daughter. At the babe's christening, Master Maverick named her Remember in honor of his wife.

Offer up prayers for her soul, and think of her with love and kindness. You shared much anxiety, fear and anguish together, but God has provided for you both, with good marriages and kind husbands.

There is yet some joy. Your brother Isaac, who has been working at my side, will marry next month to a God-fearing and respectable young woman.

Hold the memory of your sister deep in your heart and say prayers for the health and welfare of Isaac and his new wife.

I remain with God's grace, your truly loving father,
Isaac Allerton

My stomach fell and I sagged down on the bench where I sat. A coldness seized me that the sun couldn't dispel, and I cried out in grief. I had never thought to lose Remember, especially at such an early age. She was only two years older than I! I shivered, dropped the letter and placed my hands over my face, crying.

"What is it, Mary?" Thomas paused in chopping wood.

Struck by the news, I couldn't answer for a moment. Then, looking up, I replied, "It's Remember. She's died."

Thomas came to the bench and sat beside me, wrapping his arms around me. I heard his deep sigh. He had not known Remember well but knew she was often in my prayers.

Despite the distractions of my children, I hardly remembered the rest of the day, and Thomas prayed long and fervently for the soul of my sister that evening.

I couldn't sleep that night, thinking of her—of our fractious early days when we fought with each other almost as much as for survival and together endured hardships almost beyond imagining…and of the days when we became friends, sharing our lives and confidences, sitting in the sunshine of Alice Bradford's garden.

I'd been certain I would see her again, to share our lives and that of our children, to laugh together over the tiny things we found humorous. My mind wandered to the risk of death a woman faced every time she carried a child and to the anxious days after childbirth, worrying an infection would strike the womb. I then thought of the re-marriages of the widowed men, sometimes when their wives were not yet cold in their graves. Did these men come to love their new wives? Or were the women just the means for producing a larger family to work for their husbands' prosperity or for caring for the children left behind by the previous wife? And yet...there were some long and seemingly happy marriages. Governor Bradford and his wife, Priscilla and John Alden, and even Thomas and me. *If I died with our next baby, would Thomas remarry? And if so, who?*

Remember's husband, Moses Maverick, now had seven children, one a newborn babe. *How would he manage? Would he soon remarry?* Perhaps the oldest girls, now thirteen and twelve, could assume the care of the house and their siblings.

With these thoughts, I tossed and turned. When Thomas grumbled, I got up to sit by the still warm hearth with a blanket around me, wrapped in memories and sorrow.

My unhappiness only abated when my courses stopped yet again in October. Although Thomas grumbled at the addition of yet another mouth to feed, I sensed his secret pleasure at having so many children filling our house. My prayers for Remember's happiness in her heavenly home left me wondering if she had sent me this child to raise my spirits.

ഗ ഇ

I presented my husband with a daughter, whom we named Feare, in June of the following year, with little fuss. I had worried more with this birth than I had of those before, so perhaps her name was fitting, although Thomas said he chose it as in 'Fear the Lord thy God.' But Midwife Fuller tended to my health, and I soon rose from my bed and to resume the work of the household. Compared to her brother Elkanah, a fitful child, especially with his teething, Feare proved calm and smiled often. She was particularly taken with my husband, who in turn was enchanted by his new daughter. She babbled in delight at the faces of her older brothers and sisters, her dark, bright eyes taking in everything around her.

That same year, my husband bought the house of my father in Rocky Nook, which lay on the other side of the Jones River from our good friends, the Bradfords. Built around 1628, it sat on a small rise with a pleasant view overlooking the river to the north, some six miles from Plymouth itself. It had one room, of the size of the original houses in Plymouth, with a fireplace and wooden chimney at one end.

Over the years, one of the house's owners had been Thomas Prence, who had added to the land around it by buying an adjacent meadow owned by Bridget Fuller. Our immediate neighbors would now be Mistress Fuller and John and Elizabeth Howland and their ten children.

My husband decided that the age and decrepit condition of the house made it uninhabitable and had it torn down. Over the site, he built a two room house with a stone fireplace on the north side of the main room, where it acted as a windbreak to the cold winds, and a large cellar, walled with dry-laid stone, was created beneath the kitchen. The entrance to the house remained on the south side and opened both into the parlor, in which we placed our bed, and into the kitchen. My father had begun to build a palisade around the house, which Thomas continued, enlarging the yard to contain a substantial garden. He knew I loved my garden, and now I had more hands to help grow vegetables and herbs. He also planted the saplings of two apple trees, since he knew we would miss the tree at our old home and the bounty of its fruit each fall. We also had a buttery, an outbuilding for the making and storage of beer.

Not long after we had made the move, requiring moving many loads of household furnishings, Thomas, who had been to Plymouth, came into the house with a smile on his face.

"I've brought you a gift, Mary. Can you guess what it might be?" Thomas loved to surprise me.

"I cannot imagine." I followed him eagerly outside, where he proudly showed me two skeps.

Bee Skep

"I had these made by a woman in Plymouth skilled in the braiding of them," he told me. "They're made of oat straw and neatly done."

"Yes, I think the bees will be most appreciative of her skill," I replied with a chuckle. "Where will you mount them?"

"I'm going to build two platforms against the palisade, in the shade of that oak tree."

"Perhaps the bees will like the shade." I teased him again.

Thomas frowned, then finally understood my humor and laughed. "You'll find the next thing to be done with them very unpleasant, my good wife."

I continued smiling and I asked, "What is that?"

"The skeps need to be covered in cow dung to prevent the sun from rotting the straw."

At that, I made a face, then we both laughed out loud, which drew the children from the house to see what made their parents so merry. "I think that's a task Isaac might enjoy," I finally managed to say, "since he loves playing in dirt and mud." I directed Isaac to bring a bucket of clean water from the well and the lye soap, so he could wash his hands well afterward, and Thomas told him what needed to be done with the cow dung. God's truth, I'd never seen a happier boy.

ꙮ ꙮ

In midsummer, with the weather at its hottest, I decided we all needed to bathe. We bathed several times a year, but never in the winter as it would bring on illness. Sarah drew water from our well to fill a large wooden tub John Alden had made for us, along with as many buckets as we had, and I left the water to warm in the sun for a few hours.

I washed the two babies, Feare and Elkanah, first, with Sarah holding them one at a time in the water so I could scrub them. Feare gurgled with delight at the water, while Elkanah howled at the experience, loud enough for my husband to hear him in the fields, or so he told me. While Sarah Alden dried them and dressed them in clean shifts, I had to chase Isaac. When I finally grabbed him, I led him by the ear to the bath. "You will get the rod tonight from your father for your resistance, Isaac. And don't tell me you don't need a bath! You're so dirty I can hardly see you."

After I'd scrubbed him vigorously from head to toe, the water had turned so brown that Sarah and I had to dump it into the garden and refill the tub. Little Sarah and Mary were but a few years apart, so they bathed together, washing themselves and their hair without my help. Sarah and I then washed ourselves with clean water, and later that afternoon, when my two Thomases returned, they each took their turn in the tub. We all smelled sweetly at the table that evening, although Isaac was dirty again.

He had a tear-stained but resolute face after his father applied the rod. He was our most rebellious child, and I do believe he gave us more trouble than all the other children together, although the others were far from angels.

ꙮ ꙮ

Early that fall, Thomas and I both suffered with tooth aches. I remembered the disease we now knew as scurvy, which we'd suffered from during the *Mayflower's* voyage. At that time, many of my teeth had become loose and fallen out, but as they were the teeth of a child, replacements grew. Those new teeth I had scrubbed daily with a rag and scoured out bits of food with a frayed willow twig, as directed by Alice Bradford. But still some of my teeth had blackened, despite my care. Thomas often suffered from toothaches, with some of his teeth now so decayed they were past keeping. I gave him brine to rinse his teeth with and yarrow root to chew, to ease his pain.

I admonished the children each morning to scrub their teeth as Alice had taught me. Sarah kept an eye on them to make sure they obeyed, but more than once I'd had to apply the rod to a chorus of "But I just forgot!" I also made a paste of ground sage and salt, which we rubbed on our teeth occasionally to keep them white. And in the winter, we all drank a freshly steeped brew of green pine needles daily to ward off scurvy, something I'd learned from my gossip. I think this bit of lore came from the Indians. The smell of the brew was unpleasant, but the taste, with a touch of honey, proved acceptable to everyone.

There came a time when brine and yarrow would not abate the pain of one of Thomas' teeth. "You must pull the tooth, Mary."

"I'm no physick, husband. How can I do that? We must find someone else."

"Master Fuller pulled two of my teeth many years ago. Did you not watch?"

"I did, but he had a special tool for it."

Thomas groaned and held his cheek. "Talk to Mistress Fuller. Perhaps she still has the instrument."

Leaving Sarah to oversee the children and their chores, I walked the short trip south to the Fuller home, calling out to her as I entered her gate. She emerged from the house, wiping her hands on her apron and smiling when she saw me. Always a small woman, Bridget was now slightly stooped, but I didn't think it was caused by age but more by her bending to deliver babies.

"Mary, how wonderful to see you. Please come inside and I'll make you some tea."

"Would that were possible, Bridget, but I've come to ask you what I might do about my husband's toothache. He's in great pain and wishes me to pull the offending tooth. I have no instrument to do that, but I recall that your husband did."

"I know this piece. Let me find it."

I had barely a chance to admire the herbs in her garden before she returned with an ugly metal instrument.

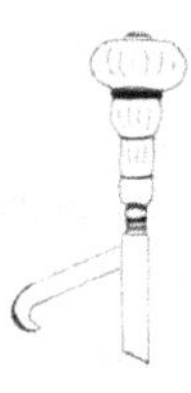

Dental Pelican

"This is called a dental pelican, or so my good husband told me." She held it out for me to look at. "The claw mounted on the shaft can be adjusted to meet the head of the shaft and tightened, pinching the tooth between the claw and head. Then you just pull."

I recalled seeing it and still thought it looked like an instrument of torture. "Why is it called a pelican?"

"Well, I've never seen one, but my husband told me it resembles a pelican's beak."

"Oh." I took the instrument and nearly dropped it. Made of iron, it was not a light tool.

My fear at having to use such a thing must have been visible, because my friend said, "Let me go with you. Together we can remove that tooth. But first, let me get something to deaden your husband's pain." She went back into the house and came out with her leather bag, then we set out north to our farm.

The day had become quite warm, and the heaviness of our clothing made the heat worse. Sweat dripped from my forehead, despite the straw hat I wore, and ran in runnels down the sides of Bridget's face. Trickles of sweat ran down my sides and back and my heavy skirts caught in brambles. I longed for cooler weather, or at least the relief of wearing only a shift at night, without my stays.

We found Thomas on the bench near the garden, bent over and holding his head in his hands.

"Master Cushman," Bridget said, on nearing him.

He looked up with only a slight flicker of recognition, such was his distress.

"Come with me into the house." She took my husband's hand and drew him upright. "Mary, would you draw fresh water and place it on the hearth to heat. Then pour some beer for your husband."

I did as told, and when I came inside with the bucket of water and a mug of beer from the buttery, I saw Thomas sitting up on our bed. Bridget took a brown bottle from her bag, uncorked it and put just two drops of its contents into the beer. "Here, drink all of this." She handed the mug to Thomas and waited while he drank it.

I poured water into a kettle over the flames, and to it, Bridget added a handful of willow bark. "The willow bark tea should keep any resulting fever at bay and ease the pain. Don't let it boil overlong."

"What did you add to the beer?" I asked her.

"A tincture of laudanum. I purchased it from London—I learned a physick there has proclaimed its benefits in deadening pain. It will also make Master Cushman drowsy."

"How did you come by it?"

"Governor Bradford kindly wrote a letter to obtain it for me."

In a few minutes, Thomas fell back on the bed, saying he felt sleepy and wondering at the reduction of his pain.

"Now, Mary, open his mouth as wide as possible and show me the tooth." Once I had done so, she took the dental pelican, and with me holding his mouth wide, gripped the offending tooth between its ends and yanked with all her strength. The tooth came out with a moan from Thomas and a popping sound, leaving behind a bloody hole. "Please get me some sugar."

By now Sarah and the children had gathered round, watching the procedure and making unsuitable noises. I shushed them out of the house and got the sugar cone from the high shelf where it was stored. Using a knife, I scraped the cone until there was enough to satisfy Bridget. Taking some in her fingers, she blotted blood from the hole with a rag and packed the sugar into it. "This should promote healing and prevent infection, but you'll need to pack that hole often. It will cost you in sugar." She smiled. "I have used honey to pack external wounds, but the honey doesn't stick as well in the mouth."

I heard loud whispers from just outside.

"Father gets to have his mouth packed with sugar."

"I wish I had a tooth to be removed."

"Will he leave any sugar for us?"

Bridget left us and Thomas slept on for a while longer. When he awoke, still somewhat drowsy, he proclaimed himself much improved. Still, I made him drink the willow bark decoction and over the next several days, repacked sugar in the hole where his tooth had been.

There would be more tooth-pulling as the years passed, even some of mine.

Chapter 36

Another Child, a Dutch War and Quakers Arrive

Mary Cushman, Rocky Nook, 1655-1656

In the early summer of 1655, Thomas, the children and I visited the Aldens, as we frequently did when the days lengthened, with pleasant weather and ripening fields. The children would have the chance to play with the Aldens' youngest, and Thomas and Master Alden would always find a private corner where they could sit down to discuss civic and religious matters. This time, Thomas would order some barrels for water and for our buttery. Alden had been a cooper his entire life and kept busy, particularly in the winter months, with orders from his neighbors. Of course, the visit would also give Priscilla and me a chance to catch up on any news of which we'd only heard tidbits.

Master Alden, with the help of his grown sons, had built a new house for his family the previous year. This one had two spacious rooms and was just down a wooded path from the old, elongated house where they'd all lived since 1627. Master Alden had incorporated some of the wood and beams from the old house into the new one and its buttery, both of which stood on a knoll above the Bluefish River in a cool and shaded clearing. Priscilla's happiness with her new house was evident from the smile with which she greeted me.

"Good morrow, Mistress Cushman!" she called out, spotting us coming through the woods from the river.

I was somewhat winded when we reached her sunny, south-facing doorstep. "Good morrow, Mistress Alden," my husband replied, handing her a basket containing some jams and a container of butter. We would not stay for a meal, since between us we numbered so many, but the children could share bread and jam.

When everyone had dispersed—Thomas and Master Alden to the parlor, the children into the woods or down to the river—Priscilla and I chatted about our families, as we always did. Priscilla then had her fifteen-year-old daughter Rebecca use a stick to script some words in the dust to show me newly acquired abilities. As we watched her, Priscilla asked, "Have you heard the fate of Edward Winslow?"

"No, I'd thought we would see him one day soon, returned from England." I leaned back on the bench where I sat, the playful cries of children reaching us from the creek.

"Master Bradford came to visit my husband some days ago, and I overheard them talking. Master Winslow has died."

"Oh dear. Thomas must not have heard, because he would have been stricken by the news. The governor must have taken it badly."

"Indeed, he did. He became quite emotional in telling of it."

"What happened to Master Winslow?"

"Oliver Cromwell sent him as a commissioner to someplace called the West Indies to fight against the Spanish. He became ill with a fever and died at sea."

"I'm indeed sorry to hear this." I recalled the last time I'd seen Edward Winslow, his round and congenial face, ruddy cheeks, mouth framed by a mustache and trimmed beard. He laughed readily and often. Another Old Comer gone. I didn't know Master Winslow well, but felt an emptiness at the loss of another of the founding pillars of our colony. Governor Bradford must feel so lonely.

Regarding Priscilla and thinking about Master Winslow, I saw clearly how we were all aging, the surviving Mayflower passengers, now called the Old Comers. I was now nearly forty years of age, while my good husband was almost fifty. Priscilla was the age of Thomas. Her face had wrinkled early, careworn by hard years and her many children. But her soft words and kindness and the twinkle in her eyes over the slightest mischief persisted. My gossip was growing old!

That night, when we were abed, I whispered, "John Alden must have told you of Edward Winslow's death."

"He did and said the governor was struck hard by the news because he'd expected Winslow to return after the death of King Charles. After Cromwell defeated the royalists, Bradford assumed there was nothing to keep Winslow there, but then Cromwell sent him to the West Indies. Did you know Winslow lived for some time with a number of the Separatist merchants? One of them was James Shirley."

"The one who vexed the governor for so long," I whispered.

"At the persistence of Master Winslow, these merchants provided money to send missionaries to the Indians. Winslow wrote a book about it, and another book called *New England's Salamander*."

I yawned. The long day had tired me. *A salamander?* I dozed off, wondering what he meant.

ꕥ ꕥ

As it happened, Governor Bradford had a copy of *New England's Salamander.* At a Sunday meeting led by my husband as our Elder, we mourned the passing of its author, and Bradford read from the book, which Winslow had written in response to a widely-disseminated pamphlet full of hypocrisy about us. Bradford declared the book was a fine defense of our colonies, laws and government. Perhaps out of his grief, the governor talked on and on about the controversy, during which even some men dozed, and the children grew increasingly fretful. Although I felt deep sadness at the loss of Edward Winslow, I was relieved when our services ended.

ꕥ ꕥ

The March day blew bitterly cold when Thomas returned from a meeting of the General Court of Plymouth. Young Thomas was outside chopping wood for the fire, which Isaac carried in to stack by the hearth. My girls, Mary and Sarah, concentrated on mending clothes. They also minded Elkanah and his sister, Feare, who toddled here and there in her wool shift, over which I had pinned a small wool blanket because of the cold. A turkey Thomas had shot the day before roasted on a spit over the fire, providing our noses with something else to smell besides the smoke of the fire, which, as usual, made my eyes water.

"This is a most pleasant domestic scene," said Thomas as he entered. His nose shone red from the cold as he removed his wet boots and wool gloves and placed them by the fire to dry. Feare immediately lurched over to him and grabbed him about the legs.

"And what have you been up to today, my daughter?" He picked her up and sat down in the chair near the hearth, with her in his lap.

"She's trying me, husband. If Sarah or I aren't watching her, everything within reach goes into her mouth. Isaac, go out to the buttery with that pitcher and bring in some beer for your father." Another draft of cold air filled the room as he left. *At least it abates the smoke.* "How went the meeting of the court?"

"I'll talk of it later." He looked around at the children. Mary and Sarah were always curious. It had become harder and harder for us to talk privately with all the children around and their big ears. "Has Isaac behaved today?"

At seven, Isaac was a child with definite ideas of his own and was not spared the rod. "Today was quite calm," I replied, but added no more because just then Isaac and the cold wind came back into the house.

Isaac placed the pitcher in front of his father and brought him a mug, then poured him some of the aromatic brew. When he sat down next to Thomas, I knew a request of some sort was coming.

"Father, I'm now old enough—when will you or Thomas take me hunting?"

My husband pulled back and looked at Isaac in surprise. "You are not."

"I am! And you took Thomas when he was six. *I'm* seven."

"Don't speak disrespectfully to you father or you will get the rod from me, Isaac!" No one challenged Thomas like my second son, but often as not, I dispensed the punishment.

Thomas looked at Isaac as if seeing him for the first time. "You're right, Isaac, and you may accompany us the next time. But your disrespect will be punished."

I swore I saw a slight smile on Isaac's face, and he took the rod that night without a sound.

When all the children were in bed, along with their parents, Thomas turned to me for one of our nightly conversations.

He groaned as he turned over, because at forty-eight years, his joints had begun to complain, and he drank willow bark tea daily to ease his aches.

"What happened today?" I asked.

"A sad case. Do you know Robert Latham?"

"The man married to Susannah Winslow, Edward Winslow's daughter?"

"He is…he appeared before the Court today, accused of beating to death his servant, John Walker. The boy was only fourteen. You'll certainly hear of this from your friends, and I want to prepare you."

I knew this news would spread like fire through the colony.

"I have sought to spare you much of what I hear of violence in Plymouth's households, even though it's often seen in the Court… but never before to this extent. We have laws to punish those who do violence to a family member, but the physical abuse of servants is rare. We've never had to deal with it before."

"I've heard that a servant's remaining time in service can be bought by another to remove them from the abuse."

"You hear right, dear heart."

I felt some solace when he called me dear heart. "But usually the abuse is just a complaint of overwork or failure to provide clothing. How could Robert Latham do this? Surely Mistress Latham didn't participate." It was difficult to keep my voice calm and quiet.

"Regrettably, she did, and she may be called before the Court later in the year."

"I cannot believe it. She's always seemed a kind person and from a God-fearing family."

"Be that as it may, the abuse of the boy was clearly seen. His body was bruised severely, and his skin was broken in many places. He had suffered a bloody blow to his head, and this blow was probably fatal. Stripes from Latham's beatings covered his back. We heard evidence that Latham had forced him to carry a large log, well beyond his strength. When the log fell on him and he was down, Latham whipped him."

"Please, Thomas, say no more. We must pray to God that nothing like this happens again. I cannot bear the image of that boy." Tears came to my eyes. "No one deserves such treatment."

"It's too late for me to do anything but preside over his burial and provide moral stricture concerning this at our Sunday meeting. Would that I had known earlier." I could hear him grinding his teeth in frustration.

"How did the Court decide to punish Latham? Did they condemn him to hang?"

"No," Thomas replied, grinding his teeth again. "The grand jury found him guilty of manslaughter, which isn't punishable by hanging. However, they sentenced him to have his hand burned and all his belongings confiscated. I don't know how he and his family will survive...perhaps on the largesse of the Winslow family."

"As harsh as it is, the punishment seems fair to me," I whispered back. "But the beating of the boy was willful, not unintended. Willful murder is punished by hanging." Silence. I knew Thomas agreed with me. "What will happen to his wife?"

"I know not, but the punishment of her husband will affect her as well, with the loss of all they own."

I lay awake a long time, trying to contemplate such abuse of another human being. I felt lucky to be married to a godly man, who while stern, was always fair.

ഇ ഇ

In the hottest part of the summer, my courses stopped again. When I told Priscilla Mullins, she said perhaps they had stopped for good, as nature intended. She had welcomed this after her last child was born some seven years earlier. However, when my breasts swelled, I knew I was with child. This time I didn't feel the fear preceding my previous birthing and was comforted by the fact my older daughters were now sixteen and fourteen and much help to me in raising our babes. Nevertheless, this one's growing made me more tired than before and I felt the kicking early and intensely.

Sarah Alden remained with us and often took over the management of the household so I could rest. She had become an extension of myself on whom I depended. Thomas and I had asked her more than once if she wished to return to her family, but she had always said she was happy living here. She was now nearly thirty years of age, well past the time of marrying, but had yet met no man who expressed interest in her, nor she in him. I worried, but Sarah seemed content.

ꙮ ꙮ

The threat of an Indian attack was never far from our minds, and later that year I learned from Alice Bradford, at whose home the leading men of the colony often met, that Indians had burned farms in New Amsterdam. This news served to increase my anxiety about the safety of my father and his family—only relieved when I received a letter from him.

To my dearest Daughter and her Husband, Thomas Cushman,

I imagine news has reached you of the recent Indian uprising in New Amsterdam, and I'm writing to assure you we are all well.

The Council of New Amsterdam, of which I'm a member, negotiated the withdrawal from our city of the members of the diverse tribes involved in the attacks.

The reason for these hostilities is thought to be the murder of a young Indian woman by a former city prosecutor, who caught her stealing his peaches. The prosecutor subsequently received an arrow to the back, and the Mayor was determined to act against these savages.

Despite this negotiation, the Indian raids have continued, most recently on Staten Island, with the killing of about fifty settlers and the burning of forty farms. The savages held one man and his family for several weeks, then moved on to Paulus Hook, taking captive over one hundred women and children and stealing six hundred head of cattle, before leaving the area.

It's my belief that the war against the Indians led by the Dutch ten years ago, in which many men, women and children were massacred, fomented terrible resentment that led to the Indian uprising. The murder of the young Indian woman was but a trigger.

I pray that you maintain peaceful relations with your native neighbors, helping them with God's grace in their times of need. If Massasoit is still the sachem of the Wampanoags, then you have some measure of safety.

May God watch over you and the children and hold you in His hands. I keep you in my prayers daily.

I remain your loving father,
Isaac Allerton

We passed his letter along to Governor Bradford and later learned that the Dutch governor, Peter Stuyvesant, ransomed the release of seventy of the hostages but had a fort built on the western shore of the Hudson River to prevent future attacks.

ꟷ ꟷ

Not long after the death of Robert Latham's servant, Thomas told me the General Court of Massachusetts had enacted a law to reduce violence in the home. We had retired for the night but lay with the curtains around our bed pulled aside, due to the heat of the day. Thomas whispered, "The Massachusetts Court has ruled that no man can strike his wife nor can any woman strike her husband. The penalty is a fine not exceeding ten pounds. Either that or such corporal punishment as determined by the Court."

"It sounds like a good law, Thomas, but will it be enforced?"

"I suspect the men may complain of being struck by their wives, but few women would come forth to complain." He chuckled.

"I agree. Their complaints would do much damage to their husbands' reputations. Would the Plymouth colony enact such a law?"

"In my counseling of our church members, I've frequently heard stories of the abuse of a spouse, so I think this law would come as a relief to some. Perhaps I'll suggest it to the governor."

so cs

The following February I gave birth to a boy we named Eleazar. Mistress Fuller came with my gossip, including Alice Bradford, who loved newborn babes. I thought the reason for this was that she'd had but three, and the last many years ago. But now her son, young William and his wife had a son, making Alice a grandmother.

The birthing of Eleazar came as easily as that of Elkanah, and I much enjoyed the company of Alice, Bridget, Sarah and Priscilla Alden, and my two oldest daughters, despite the pain. We chattered aimlessly, which helped pass the time and took my mind from my labors.

Thomas had chosen the name Eleazar, telling me it meant 'God is my help.' I hoped my new son would follow the original Eleazar, son of the brother of Moses, in godliness. Indeed, Eleazar had a calm disposition and didn't fuss with either colic or teething. His hair remained golden brown during his first year, later darkening, but his eyes stayed a rusty gray-green.

Elkanah, nearest to Feare in age at four years, grew particularly fond of his new brother, often watching him for hours while he rocked the cradle. Even Isaac showed interest, carrying Eleazar around the yard, pointing out this or that. God had blessed Eleazar with his brothers.

Before we sat down for our midday meal one day late in February, Thomas first offered prayers for God's grace on our new son and then read from the Bible. I was surprised when he asked God for wisdom in his interactions with members of the Religious Society of Friends, whom I knew as Quakers. The children looked puzzled at the name and, Isaac, ever outspoken, held his tongue and didn't ask anything. He'd been punished the week before for complaining to his father about still having to stand for his meals. Since then he'd been silent at the table, even when I could see he itched to ask a question.

Sarah and Mary brought our food—salted pork, which I had cooked with stored vegetables in a stew, slices of bread browned on the hearth to put under the stew in our bowls, pickled onions, along with butter and more bread. Elkanah stood at the end of the table with Isaac, while young Thomas, the two Sarahs and Mary joined us in sitting. Feare, now two, sat in her highchair.

We felt the chill at the table, despite its closeness to the hearth, and February fingers of cold air seeped into the room, causing steam to rise from the food. Thomas helped himself first, as was his custom, followed by me and our children in order of age, except for Eleazar, who was in his cradle. Sarah Alden and our Sarah fed small portions of food to Elkanah and Feare.

"Tell us more about these Quakers, Father," said young Thomas, after we'd begun to eat. "Do they really quake?"

My husband chuckled. "In truth, I don't know where their name comes from, son."

"How are they different from us?" Isaac, always the curious, spoke at last.

"They are perhaps not so different, as they are another sect split from the Church of England. However, they don't believe in any sacraments, and we have the sacrament of baptism. We and our brethren, the Puritans, feel this country needs to be Christian, while the Quakers believe in religious freedom for everyone. They also believe in nonviolence."

"As we all should," I muttered under my breath.

"What is that, Mary?" Thomas still didn't like my input into non-private discussions, other than those concerning the family.

I had taught my daughters to maintain silence at the table, although even after all these years, I myself still found it difficult. I just shook my head as if I had said nothing, or at least nothing of importance.

"Are they welcome here?" asked young Thomas.

"Yes, because we are more tolerant than our northern brethren," replied my husband.

"What do the Puritans think?" asked Isaac.

Thomas tolerated questions from the older boys, if they dealt with matters of faith. "They consider them heretics and have passed a law to expel them from the Massachusetts colony. Anyone who transports them to the colonies is heavily fined. Many of the Quaker missionaries are women…" he paused when he heard a sharp intake of breath from me. "…and two of their women preachers had their books burned, their property confiscated, and then were imprisoned. I heard their condition in the jail was terrible. Perhaps it was God's blessing when these women were finally deported."

I later learned from Alice Bradford that the commissioners of the United Colonies had decided to support the Puritan laws against the Quakers. And yet their existence in our own colony remained tolerated.

I never did make the acquaintance of a Quaker, nor did I understand why laws had been enacted against them, since it appeared to me we all worshiped the same God.

ᘓ ᘓ

In October, our military leader Myles Standish died of strangury, which Bridget Fuller explained had something to do with stones in the kidneys. He'd had a painful death and had suffered greatly. He left behind his wife Barbara—his second wife, since we had buried his other wife Rose during that first horrible winter—and seven children. He had been one of the strengths of the colony as it grew roots and spread, and many of us attended his burial in the cemetery in Duxburough. These included some of our Indian neighbors, with whom Standish had maintained cordial relations. At his request, he was buried beside his daughter Loara, who had died the year before.

Soon after his death, Alice Bradford came to visit, I think to enjoy my babes, whom she alternated between rocking and holding. October days on our farm were some of the best—still warm and sunny and noisy with the hum of bees preparing for over-wintering in our skeps. We sat in the garden on a new bench, which young Thomas and Isaac had crafted for me.

"Captain Standish did seek a quieter life many years ago by moving to Duxborough. He was your neighbor there, was he not?" Alice asked.

"Yes, although we didn't see much of him except at our meetings. He kept to the fields of his farm and cared for his livestock." I ground herbs with a mortar and pestle as we talked, unable to be doing nothing.

"For all his being years older than his wife, Captain Standish fathered many children." Alice chuckled, as she held a sleeping Eleazar, rocking him gently.

I smiled at the thought of the feisty and dour Captain Shrimp, as I knew he was called behind his back, being surrounded and pestered by young children...and of how afraid I'd been when we first met.

"I think it's remarkable that he didn't sit around in his dotage," said Alice. "I know after he moved to his farm, he yielded the leadership of our militia to others, but he served as the colony's treasurer and in other positions, working with my husband." She paused, then said with sadness, "I don't think we will see his like again."

I nodded in agreement.

ஒ ஐ

At the end of the year, a letter arrived from my father, sending his good wishes and relaying a piece of news that brightened a gloomy and cold day: my brother-in-law, Moses Maverick, had married a widow, Eunice Cole. She brought one child to the marriage and already carried a Maverick child. I rejoiced that Remember's children had a new mother and would soon have another sibling.

Chapter 37

We Lose More Old Comers

Mary Cushman, Rocky Nook, 1657-1659

The Bradfords' daughter Mercy, whom I'd cared for when she was a child, had married nearly ten years before and now lived in Boston with her husband, Benjamin Vermayes, a sea captain. Mercy at last carried her first child, and I worried because, at thirty years of age, she was rather old for a first babe. Nevertheless, this news gave Alice much joy, and she spent her time during our visits knitting tiny wool garments and blankets.

In February, Thomas returned from a visit to Governor Bradford, who ailed, with sad news: Mercy had died in childbirth, along with her child. While I knew the governor had undoubtedly taken the news with his usual stoicism and prayers, her death would certainly affect his already poor health. As for Alice, I knew the weight of Mercy's death would crush her. I left immediately to offer her what comfort I could.

I found my second mother sitting in front of her hearth, staring at nothing. She looked aged and hunched, her gray hair lank upon her forehead where it had escaped her coif. When I touched her shoulder, she looked up, not recognizing me for a moment, so deep was her grief.

"Mary, how good of you to come," she finally said. Tears filled her eyes.

I knelt beside her and put my arms around her. "Mercy was perhaps my favorite of your children," I told her, my eyes glistening. "Light of heart as a child, respectful and intelligent. She grew into a lovely, caring woman—so much like her mother. You and Master Bradford should be proud of how you molded her."

She leaned into me with a deep sigh, perhaps drawing some comfort from my words. Then she asked plaintively, "How could God let this happen?" I knew she would never voice this to her husband.

"I know not, Alice. His workings often seem both confusing and hurtful. Perhaps He measured Mercy's time on earth to be short, wanting her and her babe to be with Him. I know your faith is sorely tried, as is mine. Will you let me take some of the burden of your grief?"

She sobbed then, but after a while straightened up, blew her nose on her apron and rose, pulling me up beside her. She hugged me and said, looking into my eyes, "You're my remaining daughter."

Tears then came as I replied, "As I'll ever be, until time separates us."

ꙮ ꙮ

One day in May, with soft rain showers and the deep, rich odor of newly turned earth, the world turned dark for us with terrible news. William Bradford, the man who had been our governor for nearly all our years here, had died. He was the beating heart and founding soul of Plymouth, and our grief at his loss pierced Thomas and me as a sword. Having lived with him for so long when we were young, we saw him as a father figure both to us and the colony. We had expected his death, since his health had been in decline for some time, and he had relinquished his office to Thomas Prence a few months earlier. Still, we were not prepared for how deeply we felt the pain.

I had visited Alice Bradford many times during his last days. His sickness and her daughter's death had shrunk her, and she moved about the house doing her work without thinking. Their marriage had been long and rich, and although she knew and accepted his passing as imminent, sadness overcame her at times. We saw the vestiges of tears on her face when she was in our company, but in her husband's presence she strove to remain cheerful and loving.

His mind remained active even in his last days; he wrote poetry and continued his correspondence with far distant friends. Thomas, as the ruling Elder of our church, but mainly as Braford's adopted son, spent much time with him talking of future plans for the colony, as well as recollecting the early days of the colony.

Thomas told me Bradford's main disappointment was that his hope to build an ideal society, based on our religious principles, had been diluted by the realities of our harsh existence. He had despaired as he saw fertile lands draw people away from the original settlement, even while knowing it had to be. He saw Plymouth as left in a widow's state—sad, alone and poor.

William Bradford was buried on a rainy day on the high hillside cemetery overlooking his beloved Plymouth and its wide blue bay, where he had arrived so long ago. Raindrops pattered on the newly fledged leaves over our heads. Even the songbirds were silent, as if to honor this great man. Throngs of people attended, Indians and colonists alike, all come to pay tribute to him, and tears flowed as freely as the rain.

My husband offered the prayers and Bible reading, then John Bradford read something his father had written.

"Thus, out of small beginnings, great things have been produced by His hand that made all things out of nothing. One small candle may light a thousand, so the light here kindled has shone to many. May God be praised."

ꟸ ꟸ

Many people came to visit the Bradford family after the governor's burial, a day-long celebration of his life. Although there were offerings of food and other gifts, Alice kept busy preparing meals, greeting and talking to the wives of visitors, seeing to their sons John, William and Joseph, and doting on her grandchildren. The activity held her grief in abeyance, at least for the present. The Bradford sons heard many recollections of their father, both serious and humorous, judging by the laughter. I helped Alice as much as possible, along with Priscilla Alden, the indomitable Elizabeth Warren, and Barbara Standish, Captain Standish's widow. Alice loved company, but I knew her unprepared for the sadness that would follow when everyone had left.

A few days later, I brought Elkanah and Sarah Alden to visit with Alice, leaving my daughters, Mary and Sarah, and Isaac to tend Eleazar and Feare and do what work needed to be done.

"Why do I have to do this?" Isaac asked, as I left. "I'm nine and a man grown, and this isn't a suitable task for me."

I regarded my impertinent son, pursing my lips. "You're not yet mature, Isaac, despite your belief, and you may not disrespect my wishes." I regarded the poorly hidden resentment in his face, seeing a boy with a face still rounded like a child, but angular and thin with recent growth. *Why is he always like this?* I sighed. "You will help your sisters, and we will deal with your disrespect tonight."

Isaac's eyes flashed in anger, but he said no more.

As I had thought, the lack of people to distract Alice had diminished my dear friend even further. Even her grandchildren, who had stayed for a while, plus the sunny spring day, failed to alleviate her despair. We sat side by side on a bench in the garden, her place of respite, and I took her hand.

"I cannot imagine the grief you bear, my dear mother. I would share it with you, to ease your mind. Perhaps if we offer a prayer?"

We prayed simply, each in turn, for the soul of her husband, and for God's blessing upon him and upon us all for the days to come without him. When we'd finished, Alice's face had brightened a little.

"I hope I'll not lose you as my neighbor," I told her when we were done. "If you move away to be with one of your children, I couldn't bear it."

Alice squeezed my hand and replied, "Then have no fear, Mary—I remain here. My husband named me the executrix of his will and left the house to me, plus stock in the Kennebec trading post for my subsistence."

I knew this already because Thomas had been present when the governor made his will, in which, unusually, Bradford had described Alice as his dear and loving wife—a testament to their abiding bond.

"Governor Prence, Captain Thomas Willett and my son, Thomas Southworth, will oversee the disposing of the estate," she continued. "Our sons John and William have already received their portions of the land, so I only need to make provision for Joseph, when he leaves this home. I asked only that my husband's personal property remain in this house, and William decided to move his family here. That will be a great joy to me." She managed a half-smile, and that expression gave me hope her spirit would soon reassert itself.

That evening, Thomas thrashed Isaac for his disrespect. Glancing often at his second son, he then read from Proverbs, saying, "The eye that mocketh his father, and despiseth to obey his mother, the ravens of the valley shall pick it out, and the young eagles shall eat it" and "The rod and reproof give wisdom: but a child left to himself bringeth his mother to shame." By the time Thomas finished, Isaac's face had reddened, and he avoided my eyes. It was always thus with my second son, and at times I wondered whether Isaac would ever become an adult in God's image—respectful, godly, and willingly contributing to the family, the church and our society.

ꕤ ꕤ

Thomas remained at the center of colony affairs, often in conversation with the new governor, Thomas Prence, elected unanimously to succeed Bradford.

Governor Prence, a whip-thin man with a long face and nose and receding hair, was by nature solemn and judgmental. Yet I observed he could be friendly in informal situations, and a humorous tale would occasionally coax him to laugh. By contrast, his third wife Apphia, whom I'd met several times, was a large, pleasant woman with a ready smile. I knew she'd divorced her first husband after they had arrived from England, an unusual event about which I didn't inquire. Our conversations generally centered on her three daughters with the governor. They were now fourteen, sixteen and seventeen, and their mother already worried about the attention the two oldest attracted from young men in the village.

Thomas chuckled when I told him that. "I think Mistress Prence looks on her daughters through the spectacles of love. Plainer girls I've never seen." He paused and then said, "But of course, they are charming and intelligent."

Late on a cold afternoon in September, brought on by a brisk wind from the north, Thomas and I sat inside by the warmth of the hearth. The children had time to spend as they wished, and they went outside to play, except for our youngest two. Eleazar sat in his walking stool, grabbing at some blocks I'd placed in front of him and Feare prattled on the floor, bouncing her poppet up and down. I knitted, keeping a sharp eye on Feare, while Thomas read one of his many books, as he did daily. With the death of Bradford, I'd lost one of my main sources of information—Alice Bradford. I had to quietly annoy my husband to learn any news. I looked up at him with a question. "How go the affairs of the colony with Master Prence as our governor?"

"Well, my good but always inquiring wife…" and here he squinted one eye at me to see my reaction—of which I had none, keeping my eyes on my knitting needles, "… I have observed when he presides over the Plymouth court, he is strict and authoritarian, considering any oppositions to his views as evil. Quite a change from Bradford, who had always been willing to listen to both sides before making a decision."

"Does he make unfortunate decisions?"

Thomas put a finger in his book to mark his place and closed it on his lap, resigned to my inquiry. "No, at least I hope not. So far, he has been fair and humane in his dealings with the Indians. For example, he recently agreed to a seven-year embargo on the sale of Indian land in order to preserve what still exists of the Wampanoag territory."

"How does he manage his many tasks? Doesn't he live with his wife and children in Eastham? I believe that's a fair sail to Plymouth harbor and a long trip by road."

"For now, he remains there. He'll stay with one or the other of his Council when he comes to Plymouth."

"How does the governor deal with the Quakers? I've heard the Quakers have become a cankerous sore in the colony's side." I stopped my knitting, setting it in my lap. I saw Thomas becoming irritated by my questions, but since this one concerned religion, I knew he would take time to instruct me.

"I'll not ask where you heard that, but whoever told you, they're correct." Thomas frowned, which deepened the lines of his face. "The governor is harsh with them, seeing Quakers as a threat to our faith."

"This surprises me, husband, since I have neither seen nor heard any open animosity toward those living here."

"Your experience would be different if you lived in the Massachusetts colony. Two Quaker missionaries were discovered preaching in Salem, for which they were arrested, lashed and expelled. They then went to Martha's Vineyard, where they were ill-received, and finally decided to live in the town of Sandwich, which as you know, is home to some of our own brethren."

"Is it not peaceful for them in Sandwich?"

"Perhaps too much so. The Quakers are great advocates for their faith, and some fifteen families there have adopted their religious practices, meeting in secret. As you can imagine, Governor Prence is furious."

"But don't we have laws against the practice of their faith?"

"We do now. The Council has passed a series of laws designed to punish them and drive them out."

I was astounded at this news and leaned toward him. "Punish them how, husband?"

"Heavy fines and whipping, and fines for the captains of the ships which bring them here and any who harbor them."

I shook my head. "That seems uncommonly harsh, Thomas. And Governor Prence supports this?"

"He sees them as an instrument of Satan."

"What do you think?"

"I think them a dire threat to our church. While I do find their punishment harsh, they need to be removed from the colony." With that, he opened his book and resumed reading.

I thought he would never change this opinion, so I remained quiet.

ꕥ ꕥ

In December, Thomas told me a constable had been sent to Arthur Howland's house in Marshfield to arrest a Quaker harbored there. Master Howland, brother of *Mayflower* passenger John Howland, was known for his open and vociferous dislike of Governor Prence and his policies on Quakers. When the constable went to seize the Quaker, Howland protected the man with his body, saying, according to Thomas, "I would rather have either a sword or gun in the belly of me." No arrest was made.

I subsequently learned the Massachusetts colony had hanged four Quakers for openly practicing their faith, and I prayed such events would not come to pass in Plymouth. There were no hangings here, but the hatred of Quakers remained.

ꕥ ꕥ

The following year saw relative peace and a time of growth for my children. Their clothes never accommodated them for long and even though the younger children wore those of their older siblings, I continuously had to alter shifts, petticoats, bodices and skirts, along with breeches, shirts and coats to fit. The girls knitted socks as quickly as possible since they were subject to great wear, especially by the boys, and I taught them to use my walking wheel to spin wool into yarn and dye it. Weaving of the wool I left to a traveling weaver, who came to our house carrying his loom on a wagon. He would stay with us while he worked, and we paid him with such coinage as we had, plus surplus yarn and cheese. I hoped to have a loom of my own one day, but within the confines of our house, I didn't know where I might put it.

Each of my children, except for Eleazar, now had their own tasks. Young Thomas, Isaac and Elkanah were often in the fields with their father. The younger boys also had the responsibility of drawing water from the well and splitting wood for the fire. Isaac and Elkanah, now seven, cared for the goats, pigs and cow, while my daughters and I milked, churned butter, made cheese, cooked, gardened and ground herbs. No longer did we have to grind corn, oats or rye by hand, since Plymouth now had a busy mill for that, its wheel turned by the running water of the brook that emptied into the harbor.

Soon after we'd moved into our rebuilt house on my father's former land, we finally had sufficient hops to make beer. I remembered that time well.

Thomas began by telling me, "You now must become a brew master, Mary. Many of our women are expert at this, you know."

I shook my head, releasing laboriously captured curls from under my coif. "It's been a long time since Alice Bradford showed me how to brew. Do you not think I have enough to do each day?" Noting his scowl at my impertinent question, I added, "But it's probably time I learned the process again."

His face relaxed at my words, and I realized this was a task for which there would be no negotiation. It was women's work. "You may watch what I do today so you can later do it yourself," he said. "I'll oversee you, of course." Thomas already had water boiling in an iron kettle in the yard, and he showed me how much barley grain to add to it. "It must steep for a while," he explained. "I'll call you when it's ready."

After some time, which I'd profitably used with other tasks, I heard him call my name and went out to see him mashing the barley in the water with a thick stick. "This releases the sugar," he explained. When he finally stopped, he poured the mash from the kettle into a wooden barrel and quickly placed it on top of the empty kettle, now on the ground. "This is the leaky barrel made by Master Alden." I could hear the mash water dripping through the bottom of the barrel. "See, Mary—the grist remains in the barrel."

I looked in and saw the water slowly dropping as the leavings accumulated in the bottom.

"We call this strained liquid 'wort,'" he told me, "and I'll add hops to it, boiling it again. The more hops I add to the wort and the longer they boil, the sharper the taste."

There were hops that grew in the wild, but they'd proved hard to find and were limited in amount. Thus Thomas had ordered seeds from England, and I devoted a large area of my garden to their cultivation.

Later I watched as Thomas poured the wort into another barrel, water-tight, and added yeast. The yeast had first come from England, but we now obtained it from local sources—at a price. Thomas then sealed and stored the barrels, adding pine needles to those which would age over the winter. The content of other barrels, which Thomas stored for only a short time, made a less potent drink for me and the children. The deep yellow and foamy result of all this work became a staple at our table.

Unsure at that time that my beer-making skills would result in a good-tasting product, I approached this task with dread. However, with oversight from Thomas, I eventually became proficient enough to teach my daughters.

The evening when the first product of my brewery was served, beer-making was the dominant subject of our dinner conversation.

"When we first arrived here," I told my family, "we had no barley or hops, and I remember my father trying to make a beer from steeping red and black willow bark and using pumpkin for sugar. I snuck a taste one day and it was truly terrible." I made a face.

The children giggled.

"Once we had a sufficient harvest of corn, he used corn to make beer."

"Did you taste that, too, Mother?" asked Isaac.

"I did. I found it rather pleasant, and there are many in the colony who still prefer the corn-based beer to what I now make."

"Did they use anything else for beer?" asked young Thomas.

I suspected he might try to concoct on his own whatever I described. "We did make a persimmon beer. For this, I gathered ripe persimmons, and Mistress Bradford skinned and mashed them before working the fruit with wheat bran. After shaping the mixture into a large loaf, she baked it in the oven until it was dry and brown all through."

"How can you make beer with such a loaf?" Isaac shook his head in disbelief.

"Well, we broke the loaf into a coarse powder and added to it water, then left the mixture for two to three days. Mistress Bradford then drew off the liquid and boiled it, adding a small amount of the wild hops and finishing it as we would ordinary beer."

My husband had never made this and asked, "What did it taste like?"

"Children were not allowed to drink it…but I did sneak a taste once. It was rather sweet and tart, just like the fruit, but very strong. Perhaps that's why Mistress Bradford reserved it for the men." I doubted I would ever try to make this beer, since my children would swill anything called sweet.

I can hardly remember the time when beer was not our drink, but in those very early days of the colony, water was the only thing available. I can yet drink water, but my children will not.

ꕤ ꕤ

In the middle of the bleak and snowy February of 1659, I received a letter from my brother Isaac.

To my dear sister Mary and her husband Thomas Cushman,

It is with surpassing grief that I tell you of our father's death early this month. He remained vigorous right to his last day and was at one with God at the end. He was felled by the plague that swept through New Haven, and his children's names were on his lips when he died.

He will be sorely missed both here and in New Amsterdam, where he also has businesses. Since I have worked by his side for these several years, I can carry on these businesses, at least until his will is read.

I think of you and your family with love and wish you God's blessings.

I remain your brother,
Isaac Allerton

It had been many years since I'd seen my father and had still hoped he might visit Plymouth again, but I'd always felt his presence because of his letters. As I sat by the hearth, wrapped in warm shawls, bent over in my chair in deep sorrow, the letter clenched in my hands. Thomas took the letter from me to read.

My father had been my only source of support and even comfort during the early days here and had remained that to me, even though many years had passed with many miles between us. I grieved that I'd never seen him again and that I'd not been able to say good-bye. My thoughts went to the dark days in the hold of the *Mayflower*, where my father's stories and prayers had lightened the frightful journey, to his work to make a home for us and better us all, to his struggles—not without fault—with the colony's leaders, and finally to his leaving. I only hoped he would not be forgotten for all he had done: his intelligence, bravery, determination and hard work in the face of so many hardships, everything to ensure the survival of this colony. Despite the emptiness and grief I felt with his passing, I had few tears. I knew God had taken him into His heaven, and somehow I still felt close to him, living on the site of his house.

"Mary," Thomas said after reading the letter, "this is a bitter day for both of us. We will pray tonight and every day for his soul. It's the best we can do now." He came to squat beside my chair, groaning as he did so, because his knees betrayed him. Taking my hand, he said, "Our children knew him not, but as their grandfather, they are his best legacy. Let that be a comfort to you."

Chapter 38

Sarah Alden Leaves Us and Massasoit Dies

Mary Cushman, Rocky Nook, 1659-1663

Sarah Alden, who had spent so many years in our household, finally met a man to her standards and liking. I suspected something when I noticed her smiling as she worked, humming psalms and seemingly unperturbed by even the most egregious behavior of my children. One of their favorite games was launching rotten apples from sticks at any available target, and she only laughed and joined in when they threw them at her. Watching her carefully at our next Sunday meeting, I noted Alexander Standish, oldest son of Myles Standish, engaging her in a private conversation after we ended the morning's service.

That evening, in the warm nest of our bed, I asked Thomas, "Have you noticed the closeness of Sarah Alden and Alexander Standish?"

"Hmmph. You must be the last to know," he replied, turning on his side with his back to me.

I tapped him lightly on his shoulder. "When did you know of their courtship?"

"Perhaps two months ago. I would have thought your gossip had shared that news."

In truth, I felt lonely for my women friends, but I had been particularly busy with the usual chores—weaving flax and spinning wool, making beer, soap and candles, plus the unending washing and cooking. I'd just had no opportunities to visit with them. "So men talk about these things as well?"

"Oh, aye," I heard him rumble. "No more questions, wife. I need to sleep."

Not long afterward, Master Standish joined us for the Sunday mid-day meal, and I took the opportunity to examine him more closely. Standish stood somewhat taller than his father. He had a hint of his father's ruddiness in his hair, with green eyes, and a full beard in his father's style. We knew him to be well-educated, but unlike his father, he had a sense of humor. Master Standish had inherited all his father's house and lands, and his mother, now ailing, lived there with him.

Sarah watched him carefully during the meal, from beneath her lowered eyes, and blushed so often, I knew she was smitten. Thomas and I were overjoyed when we learned she'd promised to be his wife. Both Sarah and Alexander were in their thirties, old to begin a marriage, but we thought Master Standish fortunate to have found a woman of her mettle, skills, and even temperament, and Sarah likewise to marry a freeman of the colony and a land owner. Their marriage entwined two of the colony's first families.

The newly married couple took up residence in the Standish house in Duxborough, and Sarah left us to the accompaniment of many tears on both sides, along with happiness that she would now have a home of her own and soon, hopefully, children as well.

Sarah brought sunshine when she came to visit me, her face alight at seeing the children. While with us, she always offered a pair of hands to share the work, despite the fact my daughter Mary helped run the household. I saw real grief on Sarah's face when, in October, she told me Barbara Standish had died. I knew she'd been a great comfort to her husband's mother in her waning days. With her death, yet another Old Comer had left us, and I grieved with Sarah because we'd also lost her mother-in-law's sound advice and counsel.

ꕥ ꕥ

Early in the fall, after long hours of work in our fields harvesting corn, Thomas, the older children, and I stopped to slake our thirst with beer Mary had brought. Not even the large brims of our hats kept the warmth of the bright sunshine from our faces, and we all ran with sweat from the heat and labor. After we'd drunk greedily of beer, we sat down in the shade of a tree at the edge of the field. I lowered myself to the ground with an inward groan at the aches in my body. I knew my husband felt the same—the long years of daily labor and his frequent short nights, when he was called to tender solace or aid to a member of our church, had taken a toll. While still strong, he now stooped a little, and his gray hair had receded from his forehead.

We had received news not long before that Massasoit, the colony's valued friend and great sachem of the Wampanoag tribe, had died. An old man, he had outlived many of the founding members of our colony. I had not seen him since his appearance at the Bradford home after Governor Bradford's death, although I often saw Wampanoags when I visited the Plymouth settlement.

On the evening after we heard of his death, Thomas had told the children, "It's remarkable that since his first meeting with Governor Carver so many years ago, Massasoit kept to that first treaty he forged with us. The Wampanoags have largely existed in peace with both the Plymouth and Massachusetts colonies. I wonder what will happen now."

I'd been thinking much about Massasoit during the mindless work of the harvest, and I'd concluded it was fortunate he'd not died before Governor Bradford, for theirs had been a long and deep friendship. The grief from his passing might have hastened that of the governor. Despite not having seen Massasoit recently, I felt his passing keenly, seeing it as a hole in the fabric of the colony. Now, as we sat in the shade, I thought to ask Thomas, "What news is there of the Wampanoags, since the death of Massasoit?"

He stared at me in surprise, not expecting such an open question from me, even after our many years together. Our older children, who relaxed on the ground around us, turned in their father's direction, clearly interested in his answer. He frowned but replied, "Massasoit's oldest son, Wamsetta, has assumed leadership of the tribe. He appeared with his brother Metacom in the Plymouth court, not long after Massasoit's death, asking to have their names changed to an English form."

"So what are their names now?" young Thomas asked.

"Alexander and Philip Pokanoket," my husband replied. "Alexander—Wamsetta—has agreed to honor the treaty his father made with us, to keep the peace."

I dared to ask another question. "Do you think the peace will survive?"

"I don't know, dear wife, but yours is not the place to ask or worry."

My son Thomas now frequently led the family in prayer, read passages from the Bible, and expounded during our Sunday services. He also joined his father in visiting members of the church, who, my husband reported, seemed calmed by the presence of father and son bringing them God's word. I found myself looking at my son with wonder—now an adult at twenty-three, working alongside his father in the fields and doing more work than any other. He strongly resembled his father but was shorter and more muscular, with soft hazel eyes and lighter hair and a neat beard. *Where had the years gone?*

One evening, Thomas asked what his father had heard on his visit with church leaders and Plymouth Court members the day before. My son knew the Quaker issue would have been a major topic of concern.

"Our discussion of the Quakers continued for some hours, often with strong emotions," Thomas replied. "We concluded it was in the best interests of the colony and our church to reach an accommodation with them. We'll no longer support any punishment of them, and we'll tolerate their presence, as long as they don't disrupt our religious services. Of course, they cannot vote or participate in our civic affairs, and as members of our community, they must pay taxes to support the church."

I opened my mouth to say something, but young Thomas spoke first. "I think that's a fair and wise solution, Father. I hope this will settle the problem."

"I pray for that as well, my son."

Amen. The Quakers would now live peacefully in our community, but they would have to pay for it.

ꟷ ꟷ

That year Sarah and Alexander Standish became the parents of a daughter, named for Alexander's sister Loara, who had died unmarried five years before. When I went to see the new addition to their family, Sarah looked the picture of health, rounded and pink cheeked. As she held the baby in her arms, she told me with tears in her eyes she wished her mother-in-law, Barbara, had lived to see her new granddaughter. Many of my visits now seemed to involve deaths, marriages and births of the Old Comers and their children.

One night not long after, Thomas and I lay in bed, talking about the events of the day as we usually did. I whispered to Thomas, who had again attended a meeting of the Plymouth General Court, "Why were you smiling when you came home today?"

"It seems our governor is again at odds with Arthur Howland, still bearing him great animosity because of his former sheltering of the Quakers."

"Governor Prence still begrudges him for his action?"

"Not for that. It seems Howland is now seeking the affections of Prence's daughter, Elizabeth, and the governor's consideration of him as a possible son-in-law is warped by what Howland did. Master Prence was so enraged that he had Howland brought to court, where he accused Howland of endeavoring to obtain the affections of Elizabeth in unseemly ways."

"Can the governor use the court to punish Master Howland for a natural affection?"

"It seems he can—he has great standing. The Court fined Howland five pounds and put him under a bond of a further five pounds unless he refrains from interacting with Elizabeth."

"Do you think that will stop him?"

Thomas chuckled. "I doubt it. Would it have stopped us?"

Governor Prence indeed failed to control the forces of nature, because by spring of the following year, his daughter and Arthur Howland were wed.

ꕥ ꕥ

The next year, 1661, our daughter Sarah married John Hawkes from Essex County in the Massachusetts colony. John was eight years older, a righteous and godly man with a large land grant he actively farmed. I would miss my second daughter and her sunny disposition and competent housekeeping, but she was ready for a life and family of her own.

That same year, the horror of witchcraft revisited our lives. Long had Elder Brewster, and now my husband Thomas, lectured on Satan's work. Thomas expounded frequently on how malevolent spirits worked their evil through our misfortune. Following a Sunday when Thomas' prayers focused on the evil of witchcraft, I returned home feeling that an unseen malevolence swirled around our lives.

It wasn't far away, it seemed. On an evening soon thereafter, on a walk around our yard, Thomas said, "There appears to be witchcraft in Scituate, Mary. A goodwife named Dinah Sylvester claims to have seen her neighbor, Goodwife Homes, in conversation with the devil, who appeared in the form of a bear. No one would speak in support of the accused. Goodwife Sylvester, considered a godly woman, was generally believed, and the other neighbors feared being accused themselves."

"Really? She saw Goodwife Homes talking to a bear?" I had difficulty believing this.

"That's what she said."

Soon thereafter, this was brought to trial in the Plymouth General Court, which Thomas attended. When he returned home after the judgement had been rendered, he said, "It seems the court didn't try the woman Homes for witchcraft."

"Wasn't she seen talking to a bear? Then what was the trial about?"

"Goodwife Homes sued her accuser for slander," he replied.

"What is slander, Father?" asked Elkanah, who had replaced Isaac as our most inquisitive child.

"Slander, my son, is making a false statement damaging to a person's reputation. It's a crime and is so named in our laws."

"What was the judgement?" I asked.

My son Isaac, who had been there with his father, answered. "The court showed good common sense, judging Goodwife Sylvester guilty of slandering her neighbor. The Court gave her a choice of punishments—be publicly whipped and pay her neighbor five pounds, or openly confess her slander and pay the Homes' for their court costs and charges. She chose this latter option as less humiliating."

"Will anything further happen to these women?" I asked.

"We will pray that Goodwife Homes can forgive her neighbor for such a terrible falsehood and that her neighbor will beg God for forgiveness for her lie," replied Thomas. "We must also pray that this result will discourage any further false accusations of witchcraft."

Our prayers that night dwelt long on this subject, as did our meetings on subsequent Sundays.

ꕤ ꕤ

Later that year we were pleased to receive a letter from my brother.

To my dearest sister and her husband, Thomas Cushman,

I pray that you're well and blessed with God's goodness.

I send you the sad news of the death of my wife, Elizabeth, last year. After her death, I moved to Northumberland County in Virginia, where I own land and grow tobacco. I am now expanding my holdings, building a warehouse and a wharf, and of course I continue our late Father's trading businesses, which I now own. I hope eventually to embark on a career of public service.

My son Isaac is with me. Being unable to care properly for my daughter Elizabeth after the loss of my wife, I left her with her grandparents. I look forward to the prospect of marrying Mistress

Elizabeth Colclough early in the next year and reuniting with my daughter.

I pray you bless my endeavors, as I bless yours. Pray that my new marriage receives God's grace. You are ever in my prayers.

I remain your loving brother,
Isaac Allerton

I found Isaac's news both sad and joyous. Thomas, however, focused on the practical and said, "It seems your brother is indeed your father's son in his continued interest in the trading business. I'm sure we will hear more of him in the next years."

Perhaps my brother's blessing had some effect, because soon after his letter arrived, my courses stopped yet again. At forty-five years of age, I'd been certain my childbearing was over, but God must have had other plans. When I told the family I carried another child, their responses were mixed.

"I hadn't thought us capable of having another child, Mary," said Thomas.

I wondered if the half-smile on his face indicated he was secretly pleased that at the age of fifty-four, he'd sired an eighth child. I was not so pleased, as childbirth posed a great risk at my advanced age. I only hoped the carrying would be easy.

My son, Thomas, and daughter Mary looked at me curiously when I told them. As our oldest children, they could not have been expecting another sibling. I was certain they considered their parents too old for such a thing—and especially now, since their sister Sarah carried her own child. Happily, Isaac had always loved our babes, so he said nothing, but just smiled at the news, whilst Elkanah, Feare and Eleazar were too young to recognize there would be a change in the family's hierarchy.

ꕥ ꕥ

Lydia, my eighth child, came into the world without incident in 1662, assisted as usual by Bridget Fuller, our dear and valued midwife for such a long time, and to whom I owed my life many times over.

When I became a grandmother for the first time that same year, with the birth of a granddaughter named Sarah to my daughter Sarah, I thought it quite strange that my youngest would be the same age as my first grandchild.

I wondered what Lydia would think as she grew, having a mother with gray hair and missing teeth, when her cousin of the same age had a young and comely mother. Despite these thoughts, I gave thanks to God to have borne eight children and lived, when so many other women had been taken before their time.

Lydia, like Isaac, proved a fussy child who cried unless I paid her constant attention, either with nursing or rocking her, and I took to carrying her close to me in a sling to soothe her. I supposed after the sweet-tempered babes who had followed Isaac, God had decided to test us with this one. Mary and young Thomas had melted with Lydia's firsts coos, however, and happily paid her the attention she demanded.

I thought I would never regain my strength, weeks passing when I needed more rest than was possible with the demands of our large family. Mary did her best to oversee the work of the household with the help of Feare, now nine. I prayed to God for forgiveness when I found myself hoping Lydia would be my last child.

Even Isaac seemed concerned at my lack of strength, offering to do work not his own when he wasn't in the fields. At fourteen, he had at last managed to govern his impertinent tongue and worked hard alongside his older brother, enjoying traveling with his father to counsel, console and pray with the members of our church. He read from the Bible and frequently led our prayers, which pleased my husband, and frequently asked God to restore my good health. *Perhaps my prayers to God for His blessing on this rebellious child were heard?*

I sensed relief from all the children, even the littlest, when I finally resumed my normal tasks.

ꟷ ꟷ

By early autumn, harvest time, we worked together in the fields once more. The days were golden but warm, and our clothes were damp with the sweat as we cut weeds from the corn stalks before harvesting the corn. How I wished for lighter clothing! At least I didn't add petticoats under my skirt or wear my stays when I worked like this.

I'd always loved the change of seasons, especially when the days grew cooler and the russet, orange and red hues of the trees spattered the land like an artist's splash of oil colors. A sudden heat enveloped me, and after I deposited a load of corn into the wagon at the side of the field, I removed my hat and fanned my face. Exhaustion overcame me, and I sat with a thump on the ground by the wagon.

"Mother, are you well?" called Mary, approaching with a look of concern on her face.

"I'm fine, child, just a bit hot and tired. Perhaps I just need something cool to drink." In truth, I now often felt like I was baking in an oven, and sweat had soaked my shift at night. I looked around to check on Feare, who had been tasked with watching Lydia, tucked in a basket. Feare's scowl told me she wasn't happy with this chore.

As if on cue, Isaac appeared, bringing a bucket. "Here, Mother, drink this," he said, handing me a ladle.

I took a long draught of beer, then wrinkled my face at its taste. "This is the beer for your father! It's a bit strong…but refreshing."

Isaac laughed, as the other members of my family joined me in slaking their thirst, then sitting, removing their hats and fanning themselves as they did.

My husband took a long drink and asked, "Are you certain you are well, wife? Your face is as red as some of the wool you dye. Perhaps this work is too taxing for you, having just born a child."

Would he had thought of that earlier! "I'll be fine after a rest, but I need to return to the house shortly to prepare food for us. If my own hunger is a judge, you'll be wanting to eat soon."

Our conversations then drifted to the weather and the status of the harvest, and I slumped drowsily against the wagon. I snapped up, however, when I heard my oldest son ask Thomas about the colony's ongoing relationship with the Wampanoags. "Has Alexander Pokanoket kept his promises to maintain our treaty? Have we cause to worry?"

"There are rumors circulating amongst the governor's Council that the sachem is independently negotiating land sales. Also, that he conspires with the Narragansetts to attack various settlements in the Providence area," my husband replied.

"And you thought not to tell us?" I couldn't restrain my tongue, when all of us were now in peril.

Thomas looked at me and said, "It isn't your place to question me, wife. I'm responsible for our welfare and will see to it."

I put my hat back on my head to hide my shame at being chastised, but his words did nothing to stop my worrying.

ꟾ ꟾ

Some weeks later at a mid-day meal, Thomas informed us sachem Alexander had been called to the Plymouth Court to explain his actions and had been seized at gunpoint. After being imprisoned for three days, he was released.

"Will there be a trial?" asked young Thomas, helping himself to a stew of mussels and vegetables.

"Yesh...will...there be a trial, Fatha?" Elkanah mumbled the question, an impertinence at his age and worse yet, asked with a mouthful of bread.

"Elkanah, you're not to speak unless spoken to! And not with your mouth full!" Elkanah looked surprised because for once, these words came from me. Silence filled the room. I didn't often lose my temper, but the thought of war with the Wampanoags had frayed my disposition.

Finally Thomas answered, "No, there will be no further action taken. He died suddenly right after his release, before he returned to his people."

My three oldest sons looked around, as if daring each other to ask the cause of his sudden death.

Before they did, my husband spoke. "I don't know the manner of his death. The Pokanokets believe we poisoned him and bear us ill will."

"Who will be the sachem now?" asked Isaac.

"Massasoit's second son, Metacom, or King Philip as he now wishes to be known. He signed an agreement with the colony not to provoke or raise war unjustly with other natives or with us, and we have agreed to advise and support him."

Despite this indication that the peace established by Massasoit would continue, a small nugget of worry about the intentions of the new King Philip stayed with me, and I continued to have an uneasy feeling about the future safety of the colony.

Chapter 39

The Family in Turmoil

Mary Cushman, Rocky Nook, 1664-1668

John and Elizabeth Howland, who had both come to Plymouth on the *Mayflower*, lived nearby in Rocky Nook, and our children grew to know one another through the church and also as neighbors. Thomas and I observed that young Thomas had been a frequent visitor to the Howland home since the previous harvest, noting he often returned from these visits in the darkness of early morning. His father took him to task about the impropriety of these late hours. I doubted he listened, since the visits continued, albeit less frequently.

Master Howland visited our home unexpectedly one evening in early March. First alerted by outside noises from our animals, I responded to his knock on our door and welcomed him inside. His face told me this was not to be a pleasant visit, and seeing my husband, he immediately asked if they might meet in private. My husband and Master Howland remained in the parlor, while I shooed and shushed the family into our kitchen, where I sat everyone at the table and had the children read verses from the Bible.

Young Thomas, with apparent foreknowledge of this visit, sidled to the corner by the hearth. We were interrupted by a loud call from my husband. “Thomas. Come here!”

Although a grown man of twenty-six, my son could still be set to trembling in the presence of his father’s anger, and I noted he took a deep breath and squared his shoulders before joining my husband and Master Howland. Despite the raised voices from the parlor, I kept the children on task with their reading to avoid them overhearing anything. Isaac, of course, went to the door to listen, until I threatened him with the rod—*at his age!*—if he didn’t return to the table. Although I had some idea of what transpired, I actually heard very little, except for some long and sonorous prayers before Master Howland left.

There followed long discussion between my husband and son before they rejoined us in the kitchen. My husband’s face gave me no idea of what roiled in his thoughts, and my son refused to meet my eyes. Neither said more that evening, but Master Howland’s visit hung over us like a cloud of black smoke. Thomas, for once, rolled away in silence when we went to bed.

The next morning, before we broke our fast with bread, butter, and smoked meat, he spoke to the family. “You should know from me what you will undoubtedly hear from others. Your brother Thomas will be called to the Plymouth Court for having carnal knowledge of Ruth Howland. This is a shameful thing he has brought upon the family and is only mitigated by what Master Howland told me last night—that Thomas and Ruth made a contract to marry after last year’s harvest. This contract was made between them but not in the sight of God.”

He struggled to keep his voice even, but I knew from the deadness of his tone that he burned with fury. Although he would not say it, our son’s indiscretion greatly shamed Thomas, as Ruling Elder of our church.

“I will go with him to court tomorrow. We’ll speak no more of this, but let us pray for the soul of our son and your brother.”

My husband offered up a long, impassioned prayer on the sins of the flesh and atonement, during which young Thomas seemed to shrivel, never looking at any of us. He disappeared for the rest of the day, not returning until after our evening meal, the cold remains of which he ate in silence. Together, father and son set out for the court early the following morning.

Upon their return, I learned young Thomas had only been fined, since a verbal agreement to marry had existed between him and Ruth. In past years, the punishment had been much worse, but because charges of carnal knowledge prior to marriage were no longer rare in Plymouth, they now merited only a fine. My husband paid it, and I knew he blamed himself for not being more rigorous in overseeing his son's activities.

Master Howland visited us once more, the following month, to tell us we would be grandparents, yet another blow to my husband. Ruth came to visit us several times over the summer, already large with child. We had known Ruth since she was little, the youngest of the Howland's children, and now a pretty and gentle young woman with a soft, round face, light brown hair, and greenish-brown eyes. We had watched her grow into a well-spoken adult who didn't shirk hard work. I could easily see how she'd gained my son's affection.

Perhaps because of her shame, she worked hard to establish a cordial relationship with me and the rest of the family. I had long forgiven both her and my son, as God would have wished, and I did my best to ensure she would not be judged by my children.

My husband was another matter. He preached repeatedly of the sin entailed in the common practices of courting by young men and maidens and warned that keeping company until the small hours of the morning would only lead to unvirtuous intercourse. Despite his words on Sunday, he was civil to Ruth. He saved his disfavor for his oldest son.

One of her visits to us came in late September, on a day when I had planned to make candles for the winter. As she entered the house, I was gathering what I needed for the task, but stopped to welcome her. "What a fine surprise, Ruth! How fare your parents?"

"My mother is helping me prepare for the birthing. We pray that our two families will find some happiness in our marriage."

"As far as I'm concerned, my daughter-to-be, God has answered your prayers. I welcome you to our home and hope to be welcomed to yours when you and Thomas are married."

Ruth beamed. "Have you seen the house he builds for us near Plympton?"

"Not yet, but I'm happy my husband has offered to help him." Thomas' anger had lessened. "You came on a busy day, not that every day isn't busy. We're making candles —would you be willing to join us? I'll set some aside for you, for when you and Thomas are married."

She smiled. "Of course, just tell me where I'm needed."

Mary and Sarah emerged from the house and greeted her happily. They were all near in age and had spent time playing together when they were younger. At their age, they were not judgmental.

Elkanah had chopped wood for an outdoor fire and had hung an iron kettle containing water above the fire. Into the kettle, I put another pot containing beeswax we had taken from our hives and washed. I'd learned to use the smoke from a wet wood torch to calm the bees before we robbed them. Still, we all smelled of vinegar after some of them took revenge—my receipt for cooling the stings.

While the beeswax melted, Fear twisted together two cords to make a wick and attached it to a stick, with a small rock tied to the other end to keep the twisted cords from curling. The girls then took turns dipping their wicks into the melted beeswax.

Ordinarily, I would have simply let these wicks rest on a rack until the wax cooled and partially hardened before dipping them again. But to allow the girls to enjoy each other's company, I had them walk around my very large garden. Once around was enough to cool the wax, and the wicks could be dipped again and again, until the coating became thick enough to use as a candle. The chirping sounds of their conversation with occasional peals of laughter made the garden a happy place.

I still made tallow candles from animal fat in order to have enough for the winter, but they gave off smoke with an unpleasant smell and splattered as they burned. The beeswax candles burned with a pleasing odor.

From my gossip, I'd learned that a certain woody shrub bore berries, called bay berries, which would yield wax. For several autumns, I had gone with the children to the Jones River, to areas where creeks flowed in. In these swampy areas we found the shrubs and gathered as many berries as possible. Boiling the berries in water released their waxy coating, which floated to the surface. I skimmed it off and allowed it to harden for later re-melting and wick-dipping. The candles from this wax were not greasy nor did they melt in hot weather, like the beeswax candles. They also gave off a slightly bitter, woodsy odor and no smoke, far preferable to tallow candles. I discovered crushing the leaves of the shrub and adding them to the boiling water gave the berry wax a more pleasant odor.

The first time we went to gather the berries, we discovered we had to remove our shoes and socks to walk into the marshy areas.

"How long must we gather berries, Mother?" Eleazar had asked. "I cannot feel my feet."

"Until we have gathered all the berries there are," I replied. "Don't be disrespectful, my son. Your feet will survive." I saw the flash of a scowl before he turned away.

"How many berries do we need, Mother?" asked Feare.

“All that we can find.” I didn’t want to tell them that half a basketful would only yield enough wax for one candle. We harvested for two seasons before I made our first bayberry candles, but giving Elkanah and Eleazar the task of finding more of these shrubs provided them with a challenge to see who could harvest the most.

ꭍ ꭍ

Our second and third grandchildren arrived that year, a son Adam to my daughter Sarah and in early October, I numbered amongst the gossip who attended my daughter-in-law, Ruth, during her labor. Because Bridget Fuller oversaw the birth, I had little to do but keep Ruth calm and encourage her to push. She bore everything with largely silent equanimity, putting me to shame when I thought of the birth of her husband. The babe, named Robert, brought us joy with his frequent smiles and placid disposition, so much like that of his mother.

In November, Thomas and Ruth wed in a civil ceremony, and after a bountiful mid-day meal, the newly married couple set off with their month-old son for the seven-mile trip to their new home in Plympton.

My husband missed his eldest son, and his anger and disappointment at what young Thomas had done soon disappeared altogether. He began to include him again on his visits to see members of our church in the Plympton area, and eventually my son preached at our Sunday meetings. Thomas’ earlier misstep had apparently not hurt his standing in the church, but he told his father he had no ambition to become a minister.

ꭍ ꭍ

The freemen, having great confidence in Thomas Prence’s abilities, re-elected him governor each year, much like Governor Bradford before him. Thomas learned during his frequent trips to

Plymouth that the court had ordered that the governor be paid fifty pounds for each of his terms and provided him with the so-called Plain Dealing farm and its house, along with the means to support himself there.

"Why wasn't the same done for Governor Bradford?" I asked.

"Mary, you simply don't understand the politics of this."

Even chastised, I couldn't govern my tongue. "Governor Prence must have made clear this was a condition of his continuing to serve, whereas Governor Bradford would never have made such a request."

"Fie, woman, for your ignorance," my husband replied and stomped out of the room. I could see I'd seriously offended him with my impertinence about a matter in which he felt I had no business. It wasn't the first time, but he'd reached the limit of his tolerance. That night he read from Ephesians, "'Wives, submit to your own husbands, as to the Lord. For the husband is the head of the wife, even as Christ is the head of the church, his body, and is himself its Savior. Now as the church submits to Christ, so also wives should submit in everything to their husbands.'"

My children stared at me after hearing this rebuke, and I said not a word to anyone for several days, except to direct the work of the household. I knew I tried my husband's patience with my questions and pronouncements, and I found some quiet time each day to ask God to teach me humility. Although I had prayed for this for many years, God had not seen fit to hear me.

After nearly a week of my silence, Thomas finally began to ask me questions about this and that, to which I gave only short and direct answers. In bed that night, he said to me, "I believe I have nothing to apologize for, but I recall that Colossians says I must love my wife and not be harsh with her. I have been harsh, but I never need to be reminded to love you. You're my dearest heart, and I find life without your questions and comments to be dull indeed. So I ask your forgiveness."

"Oh, Thomas." I sighed softly. "We have such a good life together. You're always my loving and caring husband, and I promise you I will practice humility and constraint."

I could hear his chuckle in the darkness—he knew it would not always be so. We wrapped our arms around each other and fell asleep to the soothing sound of our breathing.

ꙮ ꙮ

My heart broke the following year when Bridget Fuller died. She had been a member of my gossip for so many years and had helped me birth eight healthy babes. I could hardly look to the south of our house without seeing my friend walking toward us, carrying this or that of a cure or a palliative for our aches and pains. She left behind six children of her own and a large second generation in the children of her friends and neighbors, healthy and delivered by her hands.

Even in death, Mistress Fuller provided for us, deeding a half acre garden plot to the town of Plymouth. The produce of this garden would generate income for our church.

Three days after Mistress Fuller's burial, my husband received a letter from our son-in-law Thomas Hawkes, who had married our daughter Sarah six years earlier.

Dear Reverend Cushman,

I'm happy to tell you of the birth of a second daughter, whom we have named Anna. Her mother is recovering well from the birth, no doubt due to the teachings of her own mother.

Susannah and Adam are healthy, for which we give thanks to God every day. I must admit that the household is noisy with three young children.

We look forward, as I'm sure do you, to a good harvest this year after so salubrious a spring.

We send you God's blessings with hopes to hear from you soon.

I remain,
John Hawkes

Despite my husband's opposition to leaving our farm, I still longed to see Sarah and her new babe, as indeed I wished to see all my scattered children.

ꟸ ꟸ

In April of 1667, Thomas returned from Plymouth, having attended a Council of War. The mere word 'war' filled me with dread.

Isaac had asked to go with him, and Thomas granted his request because at nineteen, Isaac was an adult. Then, wishing to be fair, my husband also agreed to bring Elkanah, now sixteen with a deep voice and the beginnings of a beard of sorts. On being told he was too young to go with his brothers, eleven-year-old Eleazar became incensed and stomped around the house, evidencing his displeasure. He was not spared the rod.

My two sons and husband returned after several days. Our older sons chattered excitedly to each other, excluding Eleazar, and my husband said absolutely nothing until the mid-day meal the following day.

Thomas first gave a long prayer of thanksgiving and hopes for peace. With the aroma of a rabbit stew with overwintered vegetables, garlic and onions permeating the room, my youngest children jiggled in place, anxious to eat. Finally he ended, and Feare brought the stew, bread, butter, and cheese sat to the table, along with a salad of fresh spring greens. She served everyone with help from Mary, and we all ate peaceably without words for several minutes.

When Thomas turned to the bread and cheese, he said, "I suppose you want to know what transpired at the Council of War." He looked pointedly at me, and doing my best to be humble, I simply nodded. "There are strong feelings amongst the colony leaders that there may be a war between the Dutch and the French, which would affect the colony. But there is more concern there will be troubles with the Wampanoags. Their leader, King Philip, has enriched himself by selling the land at Mattapoisett, Acushnet and Dartmouth. There is thought he may use these funds to finance a war against us."

I remained silent, but Eleazar rocked in his chair. "Were any decisions made for war?"

"Patience, Eleazar. You're unnaturally excited over such a serious matter."

Eleazar shrank down in his seat.

"No, but the Council decided that every military officer would now be formally commissioned. Townships, including our own here at Stony Brook, are ordered to maintain a military watch, with an alarm given by firing three muskets. Our arms and ammunition must be kept in a state of readiness, and we must formulate a plan to evacuate women and children if we are attacked."

My sons now all looked suitably solemn. Over the next weeks, our community established the order of military watch, with all but Eleazar included, which he again protested loudly. All of us were anxious for several months, none more than I. However, with no attacks materializing, we were eventually lulled into a false sense of security.

Chapter 40

A Time of Relative Peace and the Death of a Dear Friend

Mary Cushman, Rocky Nook, 1669-1674

By 1669, we had become grandparents again when Thomas and Ruth had a daughter named Desire, and our daughter Sarah and her husband, who lived in the Massachusetts colony, added another son to their family.

I watched my husband dote on little Desire when they visited with us. I wondered if he felt he had missed out on the milestones in our own children's lives, so busy had he been, working our land and tending to the members of our church. He now enjoyed each new grandchild—each first step, each new tooth—but he would quickly hand Desire to his mother at the faintest whiff of something in her breechcloth.

ꟷ ꟷ

John Raynor had been the pastor of our church in Plymouth for eighteen years when he abruptly resigned and left to be the pastor in Dover in the New Hampshire colony. Thomas told me he had resigned over doctrinal disputes, as it always seemed to be with our church leaders. We soon gained another pastor for our newly-named First Church of Plymouth—the Reverend John Cotton. He was the son of the famous John Cotton, pastor of the First Church in Boston. The older Reverend Cotton had gained a reputation for his record of religious conversions and his public battle with Roger Williams and others he deemed heretics. His son had preached to the Indians for two years and learned their tongue; thus, we saw him as a force for good in our relations with our native neighbors.

Reverend Cotton's installation took place during a Sunday meeting, where my husband, as Ruling Elder, gave the charge and Master John Howland gave our new pastor our blessing by placing his hands on Cotton's head. Shortly thereafter, Thomas and our new Pastor made it their special work to pass through the whole town and beyond, from family to family, enquiring after the state of their souls.

During this year, I often visited my dear friend, Alice Bradford. My old mistress was now nearly eighty, and those years had become a heavy weight. Her hair had thinned and gone completely white, and sagging skin and wrinkles scored her face. Yet her mind remained as lively as ever, and she still loved sharing interesting news. She alone had been my stalwart during the recent difficult time with my oldest son, counseling forbearance, love and acceptance.

I knew she looked forward to my visits with eagerness and I vowed that I or my daughters would be there more often for her. I usually brought her a pottage or a mash of some fruit or other to eat, since she'd lost so many teeth that chewing had become difficult. Her son's wife, also named Alice, cared deeply for her, but with the eight grandchildren now populating the house, her daughter-in-law had little time to spare for Alice's care. My former mistress helped with the care of the grandchildren and such household chores as she could manage, but clearly her strength was ebbing.

That late summer day we sat in the garden, while she supervised her granddaughters Alice, Mercy and Hannah in the pulling of weeds and harvesting of vegetables. In truth, I wondered if she saw what they were doing, since her once bright eyes were now clouded, and she used a cane to find her way. It mattered not, since Alice and Mercy were already wise in the growing herbs and vegetables, but, out of love, frequently came to their grandmother with questions about this or that.

When I grasped one of her hands and held it to my face, she said, "Don't be sad, Mary. My time will soon be ended, but this is the natural way of life. I'll join my beloved husband. I'm not afraid, for does the Bible not say, "Blessed are the dead who die in the Lord—they will rest from their labor, for their deeds will follow them.' I hope my deeds were sufficiently good."

"They were, dear friend. How could they not be? You had to raise me!"

That provoked a laugh and Alice recalled the time she'd taught me how to milk the goat.

"I remember getting the milk all over both us, trying to get it in the pail."

She laughed more, and her granddaughters looked at us, wondering at the source of our merriment.

In this way, we spent our time together with happy remembrances of times past.

The following March, I received a message from William Bradford, calling me to see his mother for the last time. The cold day spat snow, and my feet dragged as I approached the house, knowing Alice would soon be gone. She lay peacefully in her bed, shallow of breath and unseeing, and I whispered words of love and gratitude in her ear. Her mouth bent in a slight smile, but she said nothing in reply. I kissed her cheek in farewell and stayed at her side with her family, until her body at last stilled. Only then did I break into sobs of grief.

Our community buried her the next day, beside her husband on the burying hill overlooking Plymouth. Reverend Cotton and my husband read from the Bible, and then Thomas spoke about our dear friend and second mother.

"Alice Bradford was foremost of the women who ensured the survival of the Plymouth colony. She had courage, good sense, fidelity, determination and a vision of our future she shared with her husband. She was a godly matron, much loved while she lived, and we lament her passing. She has changed this life for the better and will be sorely missed."

Despite the comfort of my own children and Alice's daughters, several months passed before my spirits lifted with the birth of a grandson, named Thomas for my husband, to my oldest son and his wife Ruth.

ꙮ ꙮ

The next years ran by, as my youngest and my grandchildren all grew into their own. *Does time pass more quickly as we age?* We once again had some warnings that all was not well between the colony and King Philip Pokanoket. I heard of this from the members of my gossip, ever changing, as the older women left us and the younger generation spread its wings. Among them, I now counted Priscilla Alden, Mistress Bradford (my friend Alice's daughter-in-law), Sarah Alden Standish, and my daughter-in-law Ruth. News passed quickly amongst us from our visits and meetings on Sundays. I wondered if our husbands had any idea of how much we knew.

Mistress Bradford, wife of young William, was my nearest neighbor, and as her family grew rapidly, I attended her birthings and came often to share news and help with some of the heavier chores. William, still in my eyes a little boy, now held the rank of officer in the Plymouth militia and had become a bulwark of the colony. As such, he was often the source of news of the colony, much as his father had been.

One late fall day, cold with a hint of snow in the air, I visited the young Mistress Bradford, who was salting pork. I was not as close to her as I had been to her mother-in-law and thus didn't call her by her first name, although I often found myself slipping, since her name was also Alice. Her husband had killed one of their pigs that day and then prepared and cut the meat into large pieces. Since her sons were away with their father somewhere, she welcomed the addition of a pair of hands to help cut and treat the portions of raw pork.

"Have you news from Plymouth?" I asked, as I helped her slice the biggest pieces of meat into more manageable sizes.

"Most of what I hear from my husband are complaints about King Philip. He's been selling land to settlers, breaking his oath to have our court oversee all such transactions."

"Thomas told me he uses these sales to enrich himself and his tribe in order to buy weapons."

"William has also stated this, though not, of course, in conversation to me." She gave me a half-smile.

"So, Mistress Bradford, have you heard there will be conflict?"

At this point, we took salt peter from a barrel near where we were working and began rubbing the meat with it. It stung the cuts on my hands, and I winced as I rubbed.

"What I've heard is that our government is attempting to confiscate the weapons of the Pokanokets, meeting with little success and creating more animosity."

We switched to rubbing plain salt on the meat, taking it from another barrel. "I understand King Philip considers himself to be royalty, akin to King Charles."

As she continued rubbing, Mistress Bradford replied, "He has great physical strength and I've seen this myself when he parades with his followers through Plymouth."

At this point, she laid down salt on the bottom of a barrel and began to layer pieces of pork, with salt in between them.

I handed her the meat I'd salted and changed the subject, as the thought of King Philip waging war on us made me uneasy. "I heard some trouble occurred in Plymouth, involving Mary Churchill and Thomas Doty." Thomas Doty was the son of *Mayflower* passenger William Doty, whom I'd known, but not well.

"Has he strayed from the righteous path?" she asked.

"Yes, it seems he has. According to my husband, who attended the Court hearing, Mary Churchill confessed she'd become pregnant by him and the court fined him five pounds, which her father paid."

"And what of Doty?" Mistress Bradford stood straight, her hands massaging her lower back, and looked at me with interest.

"He left the colony. Mary has now sued him in court for having gotten her with child. The court awarded her all his property."

We both smiled and nodded at this carriage of justice. *Women are treated most fairly by our laws.*

After packing the remainder of the pork in the barrel and adding a thick layer of salt on top, Mistress Bradford covered it with a cloth, added a wooden top over the meat and weighted it with a heavy stone, which we lifted together.

After we both washed our hands, she asked, "Now may I offer you some refreshment? ... Have you heard of Jonathan Alden's forthcoming marriage?"

"Yes, Mistress Alden is quite happy with the match," I replied, as we entered the house that held so many memories for me.

ഇ ഇ

In 1673, Thomas presided at two more burials of Old Comers who had played major roles in our lives.

Thomas Prence, who had served the colony well as governor for fifteen years, died in March. He had arrived on the *Anne*, not the *Mayflower*, but had been so central to the development of the colony that his name often came in the same breath with Bradford, Winslow, Harlow, Alden and Howland.

I didn't go to Plymouth for Governor Prence's burial because our bees had stung me several times on the arm in retribution for taking their honey. My arm had swelled and throbbed, and I felt feverish. I had spread vinegar on the stings immediately to ease the pain, then applied a poultice of garlic to reduce the swelling. I drank willow bark tea for the fever, which abated, and by the time Thomas returned, the swelling had gone down somewhat. My arm remained hot and red, so I now wore a poultice of vinegar to cool the heat. I feared seeing deadly red streaks, indicating a serious and possibly fatal disruption of my humors.

"Who attended the burial?" I asked Thomas as we sat drinking beer at our table, the sharp smell of the vinegar overriding the more pleasant one of the beer. Our children, old and young, sat with us, listening in.

"Those of our generation able to make the journey did come," he replied, "but not nearly so many as for Governor Bradford. Prence was respected but not beloved—many found him strict and authoritarian and a terror to evil doers, traits which didn't endear him. But he had a gentle side as well, shown by his kindness in dealing with the Indians."

"What did you choose for your reading?'

"Psalm 94. 'Who will rise up for me against the wicked? Who will stand for me against those who practice iniquity?'"

I nodded my head in agreement with this choice. "How fared Mistress Prence?" Mary Prence was the governor's fourth wife.

"Well enough, I think. All seven of his daughters and their husbands were there in support. I believe she will now move to Yarmouth to live with her daughter Elizabeth."

The children soon became bored with our discussion and left the table to do their chores. "Who will succeed Governor Prence?" I asked. "We cannot be long without a governor."

"Josiah Winslow," Thomas replied. "It's already decided."

We both knew Josiah Winslow as the son of Old Comer Edward Winslow. "Is this a choice you support?"

"No, my dear wife. Master Winslow is no friend to the Indians, and I suspect there will be more trouble with them in the future because of it."

That month King Philip signed a new treaty promising comity with the Plymouth government, and yet Thomas' words would prove prescient.

ꟷ ꟷ

Later that year, in early October, Elizabeth Warren died. She had been a pillar of the colony during the forty-five years since her husband died, underwriting some of the colony's debt in his place. She had also been a source of strength for me when I lived in the village, and I, along with many others, considered her a most remarkable woman. Alone, she had raised five daughters and two small boys, managed her husband's farm, overseen good marriages for her daughters, and for the first time for a woman, had deeded land to her sons-in-law.

One evening many years before, Thomas had told me about that land.

"Did you know Elizabeth Warren's son, Nathaniel, and his grandmother-in-law, Jane Collier, went to the Plymouth Court to challenge her gift of land to her sons-in-law?" Thomas motioned me to move to the high-backed bench by the hearth, where he lit his pipe and leaned back in comfort. I joined him there, picking up my knitting. "Master Warren claimed he had the right, as his father's oldest son, to inherit all his land. I believe the devil spoke in his ear, encouraging his greed."

"I suspect the devil spoke to his mother-in-law," I said. "She's known to be a grasping woman. So how was the dispute settled?"

"An arbitration panel of four men decided the challenge. They allowed Master Warren to keep the land he currently owned and granted him two-thirds of those Warren lands which had not yet been assigned to anyone. When his mother died, he would get three acres of land near his current holdings. The lands given to his brothers-in-law remained with them.

"You should have seen his face when the decision was read! He'd clearly expected he'd be favored by law and custom. Instead, the panel smacked his hand as a father would a disrespectful son."

I had to smile at that. Elizabeth was truly a formidable woman.

Thus years later, at her burial on a warm and still October day, my husband read from Proverbs: "'A woman of valor, who can find? Far beyond pearls is her value... Give her the fruit of her hands, and she will be praised at the gates by her very own deeds.'"

Elizabeth Warren had lived more than ninety years, and as one of her sons said of her, "having lived a godly life, came to her grave as a shock of corn, fully ripe."

Chatting with my gossip after Elizabeth's burial, I learned Thomas Doty—the man who had fled after being charged with getting Mary Churchill with child outside of marriage—had returned to Plymouth.

No one knew the details of what had happened after his return, but we concluded Doty clearly knew what was good for him since he married Mistress Churchill, who had been given all his property. I prayed he would be a good father to their daughter, born during his absence.

ℬ ℬ

The following year, I was again blighted by sadness. The little girl who had grown up in our household, Sarah Alden Standish, died after a brief illness. Having had a child for almost each year of her marriage, Sarah had eight at the time of her death, the youngest but two years of age. I worried how her husband, Alexander, might manage with only his oldest daughters—Lorah, fourteen, Lydia, twelve, and Mercy, ten—left to run the household, but I consoled myself with the thought their mother would have raised them in knowledge and godliness.

Sarah had been part of our family for so many years, as dear to me as one of my own daughters. I bent with grief at her burial in Duxbury, close to where her father-in-law, Captain Standish, lay. Priscilla and John Alden quavered beside me, their faces gray and drawn in sadness, but stoic in the acceptance of her death.

Alexander Standish stood erect, his children gathered around him, the oldest carrying the youngest. He stared off in the distance as if reliving some memory known only to him.

My husband read first from Proverbs, "She looks well to the ways of her household and does not eat the bread of idleness. Her children rise up and bless her; her husband also, and he praises her.'" He ended, saying, "Sarah Alden Standish was the crown of her family. Her worth was far above jewels."

I wondered if Thomas would think of me this way, should I die before him. I never found courage in the face of death, which my husband bore with silent acceptance time and again. Deaths of the Old Comers, deaths of dear friends, deaths in the family.

Days passed before I again found simple joy in my life. I believed God had interceded for me when Alexander Standish, as his father-in-law before him, asked my husband if we would accept his daughter Sarah into our household. His oldest daughters were fully occupied with young Myles and the baby Ebenezer, and he thought Sarah, at the in-between age of eight, would be overlooked by her busy sisters and would need proper rearing in godliness—and, of course, in the tasks of a household.

Thomas, knowing my sadness, readily agreed, and thus did the daughter of Sarah Alden Standish become another Sarah in our home and granddaughter to me. I often saw a resemblance to her mother in her face, causing me to draw a quick breath, but having her with us provided a lightness and happiness that lifted my spirits.

Chapter 41

A Tragedy Strikes and King Philip's War Begins

Mary Cushman, Rocky Nook, 1675

Thomas and I enjoyed having little Sarah about. Our nearest grandchildren lived seven miles away, and although we did see them on those Sabbaths when young Thomas joined his father in the readings of prayers, their visits didn't compare to having a child in the house. Her laughter and giggles brightened our days and her little hands lent us help, although not without considerable direction. My daughters Mary, Feare and Lydia doted on her, chastising her with love and patience when she struggled to learn a new task. Truth be told, I worried little Sarah would become spoiled.

Early in 1675, my son Thomas rode into our yard in great haste from Plympton, where he and his wife, Ruth, resided. Ruth had cut her hand with a knife and her arm had become infected. He hoped I would have some means of curing her. Leaving little Sarah with my daughters, Thomas and I followed our son back to Plympton in our wagon, taking such nostrums as I thought might help.

Unfortunately, by the time I arrived and examined her, the wound site had become putrid and blackened, giving off a horrible stench. Swelling had extended with red streaks up her arm. I treated the wound with maggots, although it was clearly too late for them to be effective. Over the next days, Ruth's pain and suffering worsened, but she bore everything with God's grace. When she developed a fever, I gave her willow bark tea to drink and applied cold compresses to her forehead, trying to reduce it, plus laudanum for the pain. But her fever persisted, and she fell into raving incomprehensible things. She quieted only with the laudanum, and finally she fell into unconsciousness. Her breathing slowed and she died as I sat by her side, holding her hand. I wept with sorrow and frustration that I'd not been able to thwart her death and angry that God would take such a goodly and gentle woman. Thomas cried unashamedly, blaming himself for not bringing me earlier.

We buried her in Plymouth, in the place that had become so familiar over the years. I stayed with my son for a few days, to settle his three children and help organize the work of the household, as well as to provide him some comfort. Neighboring goodwives would help him with his youngest. When I returned home, nothing seemed to dispel my grief and I worried about my son. Gradually, little Sarah raised my spirits, as did visiting Thomas and his children.

ꕤ ꕤ

November that year arrived unusually cold and bleak. Everyone huddled around the hearth and went about with cloaks or woolen blankets over their shoulders. I was adding vegetables to a stew on the fire when Thomas returned with Isaac and Elkanah from visiting members of the church. They brought a blast of cold air into the house, and I wrapped my cloak more tightly around myself.

"Come in and shut the door, husband. It's so cold in here I can see my breath."

Before he shut the door, he turned and said to Eleazar, who sat at the table with a book, "Eleazar, please bring in more wood for the fire. Isaac, Elkanah, perhaps it's time for you and your brother to chop more."

All three sons frowned at this request, especially Isaac and Elkanah, who were red-cheeked from the cold and had headed directly to the fire to warm their hands. While Thomas removed his hat, coat, cape and gloves, the door opened once more to let the three boys out, and not a minute later, Eleazar staggered in with a large armful of split wood, and I heard someone wielding the axe.

"Put down that wood, son, and go out and help your brothers now," Thomas told Eleazar. "Mary, Feare, Lydia and little Sarah, will you go to the buttery and bring in beer? We have need of some refreshment. You don't need to hurry in this task, as I need to speak with your mother."

Why would he send everyone outside?

After everyone had dressed themselves warmly and left, the house was quiet. I squinted at Thomas. "You have something to tell me?"

"A letter, Mary, from our son-in-law, John. It bears unhappy news that I felt you should be alone to read." His voice quavered.

"Would you please read it to me?" I asked, trying to keep my heart from beating out of my chest.

Thomas' hands shook and he cleared his throat.

"Dear Reverend Cushman,

It is with great sorrow and endless grief that I write you of the death of our daughters Susannah, Anna and Rebecca..."

I clutched at my chest and drew in a sharp breath.

"There was a plague of scarlet fever, which we took far too lightly, as it is usually a childhood illness with no more than a red rash and fever. This time there were ulcerations of the throat and a swelling of the neck, such that the children died from strangulation within a short period of time.

We know not why God has chosen to smite us in this way. Certainly, we must have done something to occasion such punishment, and we pray constantly for his care of our girls in his heavenly abode, and for the health of our other children..."

I counted in my head. This meant that John, Ebenezer, Mercy, Adam and Thomas, their youngest, had survived. I felt their sorrow at losing their three lively daughters so quickly, and I hurt profoundly for their mother, our own daughter Sarah. I looked at Thomas and asked, "What is God's meaning in this? What have they possibly done to invoke his wrath?"

"I know not, Mary," and his voice cracked, "but I'll pray for them and for us. Perhaps in time, we can come to accept His judgement. We must."

From the look on his face and the glittering of moisture in his eyes, I knew it would take time for him, too. "You must write him immediately and let him know we are praying for them. Is there anything else in the letter?"

"Only that he asks us to pray for them all, living and dead. Would you like to tell the children of this?"

"No, I don't think I can bear it. Would you?"

He rose from his chair slowly, as if in great pain, put on his hat and cape and went outside. The gust of cold air as he left wrapped icicles around my already frozen heart.

ꕤ ꕤ

Our relations with our Indian neighbors worsened over the next months.

Thomas gave the family the first hint of this one evening in June, after our meal and the evening prayers. We all sat at the table, including Sarah Standish, who had, with Feare, cleaned away the remnants of the meal and returned to join us.

"I don't think you know of an Indian named John Sassamon. He was a convert to Christianity and highly intelligent—he even took classes at Harvard College."

Eleazar interrupted, earning a glare. "Why is he important?"

"He served the Plymouth Council and the governor for some time as an interpreter. He also warned Governor Winslow in January about an impending attack planned by King Philip. But our governor didn't feel the warning merited any concern."

"Why would the governor ignore him?" asked Isaac, waving his hand at the ever-present and annoying flies alighting on crumbs on the table.

"I wish I knew. Perhaps because Master Winslow is no friend to the Indians and would not take the word of any Indian seriously. We learned only recently that Sassamon's body was discovered in January in the Assawompsett Pond." He looked thoughtfully into the fire on the hearth.

Isaac asked the obvious. "How did he die, Father?"

Thomas replied softly, "Someone broke his neck."

"What has happened now, that you need to tell us of this?" I asked quietly, suspecting only the worst.

"Another Christian convert came to tell the governor he had seen three of King Philip's men kill Sassamon and push his body down in the icy pond water to hide it."

"Is the governor now sufficiently warned?" asked Elkanah, sarcasm dripping from his voice.

"Enough to have those men arrested and tried in the Plymouth Court for Sassamon's murder. It was a fair trial—twelve colonist and six Indian elders found the accused guilty and sentenced them to death by hanging."

"But why would King Philip have his men murder this man?" asked Isaac.

"I believe in revenge for Sassamon having told Winslow about Philip's plans to attack."

"What was King Philip's response to the hangings?" asked Isaac.

"We have received word he is outraged and is mobilizing his troops for war."

That statement sucked the air from the room.

"Now," said Thomas, "let us all pray that God will bless us with His grace and that we will not be attacked. And also that my youngest son learns respect and does not speak when not spoken to."

ꕤ ꕤ

Toward the end of June, an excited Eleazar returned home from the fields at midday with more news. He fairly threw himself through the open door and gasped between breaths, "The Wampanoags have attacked Swansea! They've murdered its citizens!"

I sat down with a thump. *Swansea is only two days away!*

Thomas followed behind him, panting from the exertion of keeping up. "No, Eleazar. Had you but waited to hear everything the rider said, you would know that Swansea's settlers went for safety to their stockade and most survived. But the raiders burned the entire town before leaving." He paused to take a deep breath. "There is more, unfortunately. The Nipmuc, Narragansett and some other tribes have joined the Wampanoags, and as we all now know, King Philip's sale of land has provided him with money to buy arms."

I couldn't speak. After more than fifty years of relative peace with our Wampanoag neighbors, overseen by Bradford, Prence and Massasoit, we were now clearly at war.

so ထ

Governor Winslow, enraged by the attack on Swansea, sent our militia, now led by William Bradford's son William, to Swansea, where they joined additional militia from the Massachusetts colony. They found the town in ruins, with bodies of men, women and children being buried by survivors. The combined militias then marched to Mt. Hope, where the Indians had a village, searching for Wampanoags. The inhabitants had fled but left a warning—the severed heads of some settlers mounted on wooden poles. Isaac, Elkanah and Eleazar, as members of the militia, had marched with the troops and returned home shaken by what they'd seen. My husband, a provisional member of the militia, remained behind. At sixty-eight years of age, Thomas couldn't have made that march, but he fretted constantly during his sons' absence, claiming he would have gone if called.

Over the next months, the news went from bad to worse. Indians destroyed Middleborough, fifteen miles to our west, and Dartmouth, on our southern coast. Men, women, and children were killed or taken prisoner to serve as slaves. Thomas gave us news almost daily of attacks on towns west of Boston, as well as on settlements in Rhode Island and the Connecticut River valley—miles away, but increasing the fear of those living in the Plymouth township and on outlying farms.

With all the local tribes now engaged in raids, burnings and killings, Thomas believed the uprising to be a bloody settlement of long-standing scores, and he knew the exacting of the tribes' revenge would not be over soon.

Thomas made our house ready. He affixed wooden shutters to the inside of the windows and reinforced the lock on the front door with a large wooden bar. When they were not being trained by the militia, Thomas repeatedly schooled Isaac, Elkanah, and Eleazar in the cleaning and use of muskets, and he moved our supply of powder, normally kept in an outbuilding, to the loft. My daughters and I gathered fruits and vegetables early for preserving and we salted and smoked additional venison and fish. Tension in the household reached such a level that any uncommon noise from outside caused us to jump.

ജ ഉ

Despite the daily tension, our son Isaac found love that year. Isaac had met Rebecca Harlow at the Sunday meetings in Plymouth, where he often presided with his father in prayer and Bible readings. The Harlow family was a backbone of the town —William, Rebecca's father, was a cooper by trade and a sergeant in the Plymouth militia. Her mother was Rebecca Bartlett, granddaughter of my old friend, Elizabeth Warren. Rebecca had the sparkling dark eyes of her grandmother as well as her wit and a charming smile. We were overjoyed to find her a godly woman, responsible and devoted to my son. Following their civil union in the early fall, they resided with us for some time—so they would have the protection of our home while King Philip's War raged on.

ജ ഉ

Isaac, Elkanah and Eleazar left us once again in November, when the Plymouth militia was called to assemble along with those of the other United Colonies of New England. The counselors representing the colonies finally decided to take the war in hand when the Narragansetts, in violation of a series of peace treaties, joined with King Philip and openly led attacks on colonial settlements in the Rhode Island area.

Before he left, Isaac told us James Cudworth would lead our militia, since Governor Winslow had been made Commander-in-Chief of the United Colonies forces. Master Cudworth had become one of the most important men in Plymouth Colony, serving both as assistant governor and also as commissioner to the New England confederation. Our sons thought him a fine leader, although he was rather elderly at sixty-three.

Plymouth's militia would rendezvous with the others in Rhode Island. I watched Isaac's wife Rebecca following him with her eyes as he packed his gear and prepared to leave. Rebecca already carried a child, and her face reflected the feelings I'd had when Thomas left during the Pequot War—love, fear and a sense of desperation. I embraced my sons with unchecked tears and then their father blessed them. After saying their farewells to their sisters, they walked to our palisade's gate, Isaac side by side with Rebecca, his arm around her. Elkanah and Eleazar turned to wave before leaving, and after a final embrace of Rebecca, Isaac followed them.

❧ ❧

We had a long wait for any word from our sons, made all the worse by the persistent cold, sleet and snow of the bitter season. We would have welcomed the distractions of our work in the spring and summer. Rebecca was often sick in the morning, adding to the miasma of smells from all of us living inside.

At the end of the following month, on a sunny day with no warmth, we heard a call from outside. Mary, milking our cow, saw Isaac first and called to us as he trudged wearily up the path to the house. We all rushed outside, with Rebecca embracing her husband, while his sisters all tried to pat him on the back at the same time. Thomas and I stood aside until the tumult had quieted.

"Welcome home, son. We have prayed for your safe return, and now God has blessed us," said his father. "How is it that you're released to travel? What of Elkanah and Eleazar?"

"It's a long story, Father..." he replied, leaning heavily on his musket, "but the short of it is that they are both alive and as well as can be expected." Exhaustion painted his pale face.

"Later, my good husband." I said to Thomas. "Can you not see he needs food and sleep? Sarah, bring beer from the buttery. Mary and Feare, will you find some food for our soldier? Lydia, please set him a place at the table."

Some minutes later, we sat around the table watching Isaac eat hungrily from a bowl of venison stew I had made two days earlier, to which I'd added vegetables and scraps of meat just that morning. Taking a breath, Isaac liberally buttered his bread. After cramming at least half the loaf into his mouth and washing it down with beer, he leaned back and belched. "I haven't had a decent meal in days. We had provisions, but not enough for the number of our militiamen, and we took to roasting squirrel or rabbit if we had the opportunity to hunt."

Rebecca got up to bring him more stew, then sat beside him again.

"So what can you tell us, Isaac? Did you have any success?"

"I honestly don't know if you'd call it success, Father. Our leaders told us we had to attack the Narragansetts before they could muster for a spring offensive. We burned every one of their villages we encountered, but most had already been abandoned. Some two weeks ago, we attacked the Indians' main fort. Unfortunately, a heavy snowstorm came that day. We couldn't see but a few feet in front of us, and we were quite a sight, covered in snow. Their fort sat in the middle of a swamp, requiring us to wade toward it, and we were soaked up to our knees in the icy water."

Each one of us around the table hung on his every word.

"Governor Winslow decided to attack their fortification with two companies, even before the rest of the army joined us. We were driven back with heavy losses, and I consider it a miracle I was spared death or injury."

I started to interrupt, but stopped as he continued, "I later found my brothers, both exhausted but unharmed. I'll not speak more about the savagery we endured, but Major Bradford proved a brave leader. I'm sorry to tell you he sustained terrible wounds, and we had to carry him to the rear of our forces for medical care, such as we had."

"Did he survive?" asked Thomas. Indeed, I felt most anxious to hear the answer to that question, since I had known him for so many years.

"He did, but he'll need a long time to recover from his wounds. That's why I'm here. I received orders from Major Cudworth to bring Major Bradford home and went to his house before I came here. Mistress Bradford is nearly overcome with joy and grief and asked that you attend her, Mother, as soon as possible. She needs your skills at healing."

Major Bradford's first wife, Alice, had died and the Major had quickly remarried a woman not much older than his daughters. I had spent time with her and saw she managed the household as best she could, but with some resentment from those young women. She now also carried a child. *She'll need help*, I thought. "Then I'll go as soon as possible," I replied. Yet I remained sitting to hear what else Isaac had to tell us.

"Did you succeed in conquering the fort?" his father asked.

Isaac grimaced. "We did, at the cost of some lives. Captain Benjamin Church led a second, coordinated assault that finally broke through the log palisade. Have you met Captain Church, Father?"

"Not personally, but I know he formed the first ranger company within the militia. I heard he's been successful at raiding those Indian camps in the forests and swamps."

"Probably because he's trained his rangers to emulate Indian practices of warfare," Isaac relied.

"What happened when Captain Church got through?" his sister Mary asked hesitantly, perhaps not really wanting to know.

"The Narragansetts put up a fierce resistance, but after Captain Church and the main body of the militia—which is where I was at the time—breached the palisade, we burned the fort. Many elderly Indians, women and children who were unable to flee were burned alive, and I hope never to hear or see such a thing again. It will haunt me all my days, although I know the fort had to be destroyed."

Silence ensued for several long moments as we all imagined the horror of that day.

"Did you capture King Philip?" Thomas asked.

"No, he escaped through the swamp. We followed him for a while and found many of his followers dead from exposure. We were near dead ourselves from the cold and wet. Church's rangers continued on, and we lost contact with them."

"Did you lose many men?" Feare asked.

"I'm not certain," he replied. "I heard maybe sixty or seventy died, with twice as many wounded."

"And Eleazar and Elkanah? Where are they?" I had to know.

Isaac shook his head, as if to clear his head, overcome with exhaustion.

"Still with the militia, I suppose," he replied. His eyes began to close. "But unharmed when I last saw them."

"Enough questions. I think it's time to let Isaac sleep. Mary, find a mattress we can place close to the hearth and some blankets. Sarah, clear the table. Rebecca, help your husband to bed."

ꟼ ꟼ

Soon thereafter, I took a basket containing some herbs, whiskey and honey, wrapped myself in my cape, hat and mittens, and left for the Bradfords. I was nearly frozen by the time I reached their home, where Mistress Bradford eagerly welcomed me. Great with child, she seemed at sixes and sevens, unsure of what she should do. Her husband lay on a bed pulled close to the hearth, and he was feverish and in pain. His wife had prepared willow bark tea, which I encouraged him to drink, then I set about examining his wounds.

He had a deep gash in one leg, down to the bone, and what looked like the wounds from several arrows on his torso, some of which had begun to fester. Mistress Bradford had washed away the blood and dead material, but pustulence persisted in his leg wound. Fortunately, I observed no red streaks running from the wound. "Mistress Bradford, your husband's mother taught me something about treating such an injury. Do you have a garbage pile?"

"We do, but what would you want of such waste?"

"You shall see. Have one of the children go outside and collect some maggots from deep in the pile. I need them."

She gasped in horror but nonetheless told her stepson Samuel to do as I requested. When the maggots were in hand, I placed them in the wound, covered them with a wet poultice of honey and bound the wound. "Remove the maggots in a day," I instructed her. "If the wound is clean, pack it with honey and bind it loosely. I'll stitch the gash then. If there is still pustulence, put new maggots on the wound, with the poultice."

Turning to the arrow wounds, I cleaned them with soapy water, removing dead skin. Then I took some crushed mandrake leaves from my basket and told Mistress Bradford to steep them in a little water, then apply poultices of this to the wounds. I left her with some dried juice of the mandrake root, which I instructed her to steep in wine for her husband to drink. "It will ease the pain and help him sleep," I said, "but don't give him too much. It's very potent."

By this time, Mistress Bradford had calmed and began to finally take charge, giving each of her stepdaughters, who had stood around looking on, a chore to do. I left her, promising to return the next day. When I arrived home, Isaac was still asleep, with the family trying to work quietly around him and failing at it. The noise had no effect—he slept as if dead until the following morning.

Major Bradford had improved the following day, but Mistress Bradford had had to pack the leg wound with fresh maggots. The wounds on his torso looked better but I cleaned them again, and I was finally able to close the gash to his leg after another four days. It would be several months before he was fully healed. Sadly, his young wife died not long after he had risen from his bed, subsequent to the birth of a son named Joseph. Once again, the Bradford household had no mother.

Chapter 42

A Long War Winds Down

Mary Cushman, Rocky Nook, 1675-1676

Throughout the rest of the year, Thomas kept us informed of where the raids occurred —I believed to keep us vigilant. I began to keep a list in my head of the towns attacked and destroyed by King Philip and his allies—Pawtuxet, Framingham, Lancaster, Weymouth, Medfield, Groton, Warwick, Providence, Marlboro—none of them protected by the colonies' militias. The militias were always a step behind in stopping the raids and capturing the leaders of the marauding bands. Fire and death consumed the Massachusetts and Plymouth colonies.

Isaac had returned to service, his time at home being just a short leave. I worried constantly about the conditions of my sons' wintering grounds, the availability of food, and especially the diseases which ran rampant through the camps. However, I was privy to the latest news since John Alden, the recovering William Bradford, and Governor Winslow, when he made a rare visit to Plymouth on business, would meet at our home to discuss the progress of the war.

In January, these men gathered at our hearth for warmth and conversation, smoking their pipes and enjoyed the fruits of my brewing. Cold air came in through the door, as the children worked around them on various chores inside and outside the house. I remained in the kitchen, knitting yet more socks and overseeing the making of succotash and brown bread with nuts. I tried hard not to appear interested in their discussion.

"The Narragansetts have sent envoys to me," Governor Winslow told the men. "They want to find common ground for a peace agreement. They promised to release a three-year-old child they'd captured near Warwick as a sign of good faith and evidence of their willingness to end hostilities."

"Did they release the child?" asked Thomas.

"I received word they did. Now they propose a one-month truce to work out a treaty."

"Did you accept their terms?" John Alden looked hopeful.

"No," replied Winslow, slapping the arm of his chair for emphasis. "I don't believe they would abide by the truce, and a pox on their treachery. I have heard that their younger generation of warriors would fight to the last rather than become, as they have stated, 'slaves to the English.' As if we have enslaved them!"

But Indians have been enslaved. My heart fell with the governor's words. There was a chance for peace, if only he would negotiate.

ℰ𝒪 ℰ𝒪

Governor Winslow persisted in his harsh dealings with the natives, and nothing came of the Narragansett offer. We went on with our daily lives, knowing we might be attacked at any minute. News came that Narragansetts had killed two residents of Norwich in the Connecticut colony as they sowed their fields with flax. They scalped and beheaded them, then threw their bodies into a nearby river. Thomas now didn't leave home unless necessary and always carried a musket and an axe.

News of bloody attacks continued to reach us weekly. In February, Narragansetts and Wampanoags burned houses in the town of Lancaster, killing four colonists who tried to resist them, and then carried off the minister's wife and three children.

In early March, as the raids and killings continued, even as I prayed for relief from constant anxiety and the tension of waiting.

I was cleaning the weeds and dead leaves from my garden, which still lay under a wispy blanket of snow, when my husband came through the palisade gate, returning from a trip to Plymouth in our wagon.

"Mary, you must have a lookout at all times when you and the children work in the yard," he said as he approached, getting down stiffly to unhitch our horse.

"Why, Thomas? What did you learn?"

"The fortified house of William Clark at Eel River has been attacked. The Indians planned their raid for when Master Clark had gone to church—they killed everyone in his family, women and children alike. Only his eight-year-old son survived, and he has a serious wound to his head."

"Oh, dear Lord in heaven!" I stood up too quickly and swayed a little.

Thomas caught my arm.

"How many died?" I heard myself ask, even though I didn't want to know.

"Eleven, and the Indians seized the family's provisions, guns, and ammunition before burning Clark's home to the ground. Since that house is just two miles from the town, there's general concern that we aren't sufficiently prepared."

"But we are prepared, Thomas, thanks to you. We've fortified the house, brought the ammunition inside and have stored food. What more can we do?"

"I think you and Mary need to learn how to shoot a musket."

I shook my head at the thought but saw the sense of it. "What do our neighbors think of the possibility of further raids on the town?"

"They consider it inevitable. The Indians are as exhausted as we are and are starving. They look for food and ammunition, so we must assume we'll be attacked."

"Then you must not stray very far from here," I said, placing my hand on his arm. We had little ears listening to our exchange at that point, so we delayed speaking further of it until that night. After the evening meal, Thomas and I sat together on our high-backed bench at the hearth and spoke quietly so as not to alarm our daughters and little Sarah.

"Mary, if the attacks on Plymouth continue, we will take the boat and sail north to your brother-in-law in Gloucester."

"How do we know that Gloucester won't be attacked?"

Thomas thought carefully before answering. "Thus far the raids have been on settlements in the south and west of the Plymouth settlement and to the west of Boston. I think Gloucester would offer us safe haven."

I had thought long and hard on whether we should leave. On several afternoons, outside on one task or another, I'd looked around at our farm and all we had built—the house, my garden, the buttery, the sheds and pens for the animals, and our fields. It was hard to imagine leaving the place that had become the foundation and center of our lives, especially not for some temporary lodging, which might also come under attack. I'd made my decision.

"No, Thomas. We must not desert our home. We've faced many hardships since we first landed on these shores, and I'm not going to leave everything we've built with our hard work and sweat. Our neighbors are staying…" for so said the members of my gossip, "… and we should stay as well, to defend our home and our lives. The Boston area cannot be guaranteed any safer than here. God will watch over us, as He always has in the past."

Thomas' face hardened—he never accepted any opposition to his decisions. I was thus surprised when, after a moment, it softened as my words worked into his thoughts.

"We will stay," I repeated. "And I pray we will not discuss this further." At this point, I expected loud objections from him, which I knew would precipitate anger between us, but instead he took my hand and kissed it.

"Then we shall face this danger together and pray that God will see us through."

At that, we both knelt in prayer, soon joined by the girls, who sensed something momentous had been decided.

The very next day, Thomas began teaching Mary, Feare and me how to shoot a musket. Lydia objected at being left out, but she was not yet strong enough to hold one. I was greatly startled by the flash of the powder, the noise of the firing and its painful recoil. I at least learned to fire a musket, but my daughters became quite adept at shooting.

The burnings and killings continued all around us—Bridgewater, Chelmsford, Marlboro, Sudbury and Scituate—even after one of the Narragansett leaders was captured and executed. We received an occasional word, largely through wounded militiamen returning home, that our sons were alive. But still we listened for unaccustomed noises, glanced frequently around the farm, worried about our friends and family. We spent hours each night praying for the dead and giving thanks to God for another day without an attack on our home.

I learned from the meetings at our house that the offensive by the United Colonies' militia now met with decreasing resistance, and in July we received some encouraging news: the Ningrit and Niantic tribes had signed a formal peace treaty with the Massachusetts colony, followed by the surrender of the Shoshoni and Nipmucs.

Late on a hot afternoon in August, Major William Bradford, healed but yet unable to endure the rigors of marching and battle, came to our home. He limped in, saying "Good morrow" to my husband and me with a smile on his face. He sat down heavily at our table, clearly exhausted from the exertion of walking so far. "I have good news," he said, as I placed a mug of beer in front of him. He paused to take a drink. "We must praise God, Thomas. The war is nearly over. King Philip is dead!'

We greeted his news with stunned silence as it sank in. Then the question "How?" came from everyone at the same time.

"Captain Church got word that King Philip was hiding in his original encampment in the New Hope swamp. Church marched his men there and killed him in their attack. King Philip's body was cut up, and his head was sent to the Plymouth Council. His hands were sent to Boston for display."

Mary and Feare both grimaced at this gruesome description, so I sent them outside along with Lydia and little Sarah, lest more unpleasant details were forthcoming. I kept my own thoughts to myself—grief at all that had been lost on both sides of this war, how it might have been avoided with different leaders, and underlying it all, a yearning for the more peaceful time of Bradford and Massasoit. Philip's head remained on display on a pole at the top for Fort Hill for many years, and we were reminded of the hostilities every time we saw it.

Even with the war winding down, I rose each morning worried about the fate of our sons, who had not yet returned home. Some raids continued and their presence in the militia was still needed.

☙ ❧

Not long after, Governor Josiah Winslow and the Plymouth Council of War were faced with a problem: what to do with more than one hundred captured natives, including women and children, left behind by Philip's retreating army. They decided to sell them to other countries as slaves. Thomas, as a member of the Council, but also as Elder of the church, didn't concur with this cruel decision, but the losses from the war had generated so much anger and pain, there was little he could do. The next month, Thomas brought news that the Plymouth Court planned to arrange for the orphaned Wampanoag children to be placed as servants in the colony's families until they reached the age of twenty-four or twenty-five.

In our bed that evening, with the curtains opened to let in some cooler air, Thomas whispered to me, "I should set a good example for our congregation and take one of the Indian children."

I'd been thinking much the same. "So we shall, husband, but not to be our servant. We can raise him or her in righteousness and make him a part of our family. I refuse to use a child as a servant."

The firmness of my words must have resonated because after a long moment, he replied, "I agree. This servitude is much the same as slavery, to which I don't subscribe."

༄ ༄

Samuel came to us in August, brought by Thomas. My first memories of him are of a small, stick thin, long-haired waif, hiding behind my husband's legs. I'd anticipated he would be unbearably dirty, but he was in fact quite clean. I later learned that the members of his tribe bathed nearly every day.

I walked over to Thomas, leaned around him and offered my hand. "Welcome."

To which he replied, "Welcome," without taking my hand.

Thomas then said, "He knows very little English, so for now we'll have to use our hands to communicate. I've given him the name we decided on—Samuel— and he knows that is what we will call him."

"What is his Wampanoag name? Do you know it?" I withdrew my hand.

"Yes, it's Sokanon."

"Does it have a meaning?"

Thomas smiled. "It pours, it rains."

While we were having this conversation, Samuel's dark eyes followed our faces, back and forth, his face lighting up when he heard 'Sokanon.'

"Then his name will be Samuel Sokanon," I decided.

Thomas turned and taking the boy by the shoulder, gestured to his stomach and mouth, something Samuel understood, because he nodded immediately. *Gestures for hunger are never misunderstood.*

Samuel, age five and orphaned, constantly followed my husband, whom he must have regarded as his rescuer. He proved to be an intelligent child, picking up English words rapidly, and, over the next few months, gradually relaxed his guard and accepted the chores given him. However, he slipped out often to bathe in the river, some habits of his old life remaining. He had an enormous appetite and came to like most of the food I served, but more than once I had to reprove him for stealing something to eat whenever he was hungry. Samuel ate using his fingers, as did we. However, using a napkin to wipe his hands was clearly strange—he wiped them often on his breeches, getting them soiled with grease.

ཉ ཉ

During the rest of August, the raiding and pillaging by the Wampanoags and their allies diminished to the point where most of the militia could come home. Young Thomas and Isaac returned in September to much jubilation and thanks to God. Their appearance at our house, accompanied by noisy greetings and the babble of excited voices, frightened Samuel, and he hid in the loft. Thomas explained to our sons why a Wampanoag boy now lived with us, then called Samuel down to meet them. God had blessed me with loving sons, for they made friendly overtures to the boy. Their uniforms, such that remained, were in rags, with shirts and coats replaced by whatever they'd been able to find, including animal skins. Thus I wondered if Samuel even recognized them as soldiers.

Thomas and I were grateful that our sons had stopped to see us first—they were thin and war-weary, and I knew they wanted to be at home with their families. They told us they'd become separated from Elkanah and Eleazar, but they should arrive soon. We fed them, and we noticed both young Thomas and Isaac were unusually quiet and often seemed to stare at nothing, perhaps thinking about what they had seen and experienced. Before they left, they spoke in private to my husband, a conversation Thomas did not repeat to me. Then he hitched up the wagon to take our sons home.

Elkanah and Eleazar arrived the following day, just as ragged and tired. How good it was to have my boys home again!

ꕥ ꕥ

After the harvest, all our family gathered for the first time since the hostilities ended. There were so many of us now that we had to sit in the yard to eat. The day was overcast and chilly, and I only hoped it wouldn't rain. Young Thomas came with Abigail and my three grandchildren: Robert, Desire and Thomas. Isaac came with Rebecca, already plump with child, and their little daughter Fear. Elkanah was now contracted to marry Elizabeth Cole, and she joined us as well.

William Bradford arrived with his new wife and eight children. He bowed gently to me, and said, "Let me introduce my new wife, Mary." At that point, we were interrupted by exclamations from some of his younger children. They had seen Samuel and wondered aloud why an Indian was in our home.

Captain Bradford turned to them and said "Hush! You are guests here and are being disrespectful. The boy Samuel lives here as a member of the family. Offer your apologies to the Cushmans!"

To their credit, or perhaps one of the three mothers they'd had, they politely begged our forgiveness. *May God protect Mary Bradford and her new family. These children have had so many mothers in so short a time.*

"How fare you, Mistress Bradford?" I asked, when I could at last reply to her husband's introduction. "You've taken on a challenge, it seems."

She smiled and looked at her husband. "One I find I'm well suited to."

I could see she already carried yet another Bradford child, and I only hoped she would survive the birth.

We'd brought our large table outside with as many seats as we had, and now the women brought out the fruits of our cooking: roasted pork and venison, stewed squash and boiled nettles, sops of onion and parsnip, a salad with herbs and parsley, bread, butter, jams and jellies of plums, raspberries, gooseberries, strawberries, and a large bowl of hasty pudding. My family especially liked hasty pudding, made with cornmeal mush stirred into thick milk and sweetened with honey and spices. I had also roasted several hollowed pumpkins containing the pumpkin flesh mixed with spices, milk and honey.

I suddenly recalled our first harvest feast, decades ago: the noise of children, the aroma of roasting venison and duck on spits over fires in the yard and of fish or eel stews with carrots and onions bubbling in the embers, the deeper tones of the men discussing colony business, and the quiet chittering of the women. It occurred to me the only difference was the absence of our Indian neighbors. All but Samuel, who after some initial awkwardness, had been accepted by the Cushman children and the Bradford brood.

I'd just called the children to come to the table when I heard Isaac ask Major Bradford, "What has happened to the remaining Wampanoags?" I stopped to hear the reply.

"King Philip's son and wife have been sent to Bermuda and the other members of his family were placed for safekeeping with some colonists in Rhode Island and eastern Connecticut. Many of the others have been sent to Barbados as slaves, although some survivors escaped to join western and northern tribes."

"Is there a chance these various tribes will reunite and rise up again?" my husband asked.

"It's very doubtful. Those who were not killed, or made servants or slaves, are now dispersed far from their original homes."

No matter the fear I had felt during the past years, my heart ached for the people of the gentle Squanto and of their intelligent leader, Massasoit. And for Samuel. What had happened to cause the war and its outcome I didn't fully understand, but I knew that in a terrible way we had all changed forever.

Chapter 43

An End to Witchcraft Trials

Mary Cushman, Rocky Nook, 1676 – 1680

After King Philip's war ended, the colony was occupied with rebuilding the many towns that had been destroyed—more than fifty. Thomas, who saw some of the destruction on his church rounds, told me one day, "Plymouth hasn't the trade and commerce of Boston and the Massachusetts Bay colony, and some of what we had before the war may never be replaced. I feel in my heart our colony is now considered just an adjunct of Massachusetts."

I knew this bothered him, since he'd always hoped our colony would become a busy place of trade and commerce. However, it did please me, as life here ran at a leisurely pace.

My daughter Mary left our home late in 1676, marrying Francis Hutchinson. Thomas and I missed her greatly, but since she and her new husband lived not far away, she visited often and was now with child. Our daughter-in-law Rebecca safely delivered a son, named Isaac after his father, and Elkanah married Elizabeth Cole in 1677. They soon informed us we would be blessed with yet another grandchild.

ꙮ ꙮ

On a cool breezy day early in the fall, I decided to visit my old friend, Priscilla Alden. I missed her company. Now in her seventies, she remained spry. Her oldest children had married and moved away, but Jonathan, Ruth and Rebecca lived in Duxbury. Priscilla kept occupied with her grandchildren, whom she claimed, with a smile and twinkle in her eyes, made her feel young.

We sat outside, warming ourselves in the sun, while I knitted stockings and mittens for Samuel, who had come with me. Priscilla had collected enough bayberries to render for wax, and she now oversaw her grandchildren in the making of candles for winter. We had molds for candles and could buy them ourselves but it was a fun chore for the children who dipped their tapers, hanging from a stick, into the pot containing the wax, then ran around in the garden until the wax had set enough for the next dipping. Samuel took part, but I worried whether he would keep to his task, since the boys tended to veer off to play as they ran around.

"Is it strange to have a Wampanoag child living with you?" Priscilla asked.

"It was difficult at first, adjusting to our life together, but more so for him. Especially the clothes. He took them off so many times during those first months, and I never knew where I would find them. But time has made him more and more a part of our family. It must be the hand of God that I see him no different from my own children. And he now keeps his clothes on."

Priscilla chuckled. "He seems a happy little boy, I must say. You're doing a good job raising him in the ways of the Lord."

Just then there was a loud scream from the far reaches of the garden. "Perhaps not," I said, knowing that voice.

Sometime later, when I had explained to Samuel that the sticks with the tapers were not to be used as spears, along with the promise of punishment when we returned home, we resumed our seats and our conversation.

"What have you heard of the recent witch trial, Mary?" asked Priscilla. "Witchcraft seems to have replaced the fears of war in the minds of many of us."

"I heard some—Thomas was a jury member for that trial."

"Did Governor Winslow preside?"

"Yes, and according to Thomas, Winslow had no taste for it." I frowned as I said that.

"What were the accusations? Isn't the woman from Scituate?"

"Yes, she is, and she was charged with bewitching a young neighbor, causing her to fall into fits with great pains in parts of her body. She claimed she nearly lost her senses. The girl said the accused did this with the help of the devil. The woman—her name is Mary Ingham—is elderly and widowed. I wonder if that was a part of the problem."

Priscilla's hand went to her chest. "Was she found guilty?"

"Mistress Ingham pleaded not guilty and said, according to Thomas, that she placed herself in the hands of God and the people of the county. The jury found her not guilty, although Thomas told me they had no clear reason for the verdict."

"That is good news, at least. But the poor woman. She must now be greatly afraid of attacks from those who disagreed with the verdict." Priscilla looked out over the garden, watching the children.

"Thomas told me she suffered much humiliation when her body was searched by authorities for evidence of her crime. You know they hanged a woman accused of witchcraft in Charlestown when they discovered she had an extra teat."

"Did they find anything like that on Mistress Ingham?"

"No, only that she was splay-footed. She had God's blessing that no one else spoke out against her at the trial."

Priscilla nodded in agreement. "If any woman could be found guilty of witchcraft because she has turned-out feet, many more would be brought to trial." She smiled and stuck out her feet, which were indeed somewhat turned out.

Thomas and I prayed that no further trials for witchcraft would occur in the colony, and in that God answered us, for Mary Ingham was the last ever accused.

ꙮ ꙮ

During this time, Samuel grew in God and we came to see him as an intelligent, curious and happy boy, who now followed our youngest son, Eleazar, everywhere. Eleazar, on his part, seemed to enjoy Samuel's company, patiently teaching him various chores and reading him stories from the Bible. In turn, Samuel improved Eleazar's skills in tracking wild animals. Some of the members of our church criticized us for making Samuel a member of the family, instead of treating him as a slave, in retribution for what his people did during King Philip's war. They never spoke directly to us because of Thomas' position within the church but whispered it behind their hands. Thomas finally became irritated enough to speak out at one of our Sunday meetings.

"Today I will read from Matthew 7. '"*Judge not, that you be not judged,*"' he began. '"*For with the judgment you pronounce you will be judged, and with the measure you use it will be measured to you.*' I'm sure you know to what I refer.

"And from Colossians 3: '*Put on then compassionate hearts, kindness, humility, meekness, and patience and if one has a complaint against another, forgiving each other; as the Lord has forgiven you, so you also must forgive. And above all these put on love, which binds everything together in perfect harmony.*' Let us pray you will find it in your hearts to accept one amongst us who is different. I hope these words are sufficient, as I will say no more."

Such was the standing of my husband, who had ministered to everyone in the church at one time or other, that the whisperings stopped. The children of some of the congregants now occasionally greeted Samuel with smiles of acceptance, and he charmed many adults by bowing and greeting them by name.

ஐ ஐ

Our son Thomas wed again in October of 1679. Abigail Fuller was a resident of Rehoboth. Mutual acquaintances had introduced Abigail, a widow with children, to my son, a widower with children in need of a mother. Her two children, ages one and three, joined Thomas' and Ruth's three, so their household immediately became, as my husband would say, 'overrun with little ones.'

I very much liked young Thomas' choice. Abigail seemed a good mother to Ruth's children, most not yet grown and in need of her oversight and kindness. Her energy and caring quickly overcame any resistance from the children, and I prayed she'd survive for this marriage to endure.

Our son came to visit us one late fall day, bringing Abigail and all the children. We left all but one of the children outside, while young Thomas, Eleazar and their father came inside to sit at the table and smoke their pipes, adding to the indoor aromas.

Feare, Lydia, Abigail, young Sarah and I saw to the midday meal, talking as we worked at the hearth with our various tasks, Abigail placing her youngest in our old walking stool. One or the other of us occasionally went outside to check on the clamor we could hear.

Lydia asked Abigail, "How do you manage with so many children at once? Have the older children shown any resentment at your marriage?"

Lydia!" I chided her. "How can you be so disrespectful? Pray pardon her words, Abigail. She needs to ask for God's forgiveness tonight for her thoughtlessness." Lydia, my last-born child, had grown up with a measure of freedom her brothers and sisters did not enjoy. *Had I been too old and tired to discipline her forthright tendencies? She occasionally reminds me of my younger self.*

Abigail smiled and said, "She just asked me an honest question. And the answer is yes, there have been some small problems. But we have prayed over them and the children have been strongly admonished by their father." Here she glanced over at my son Eleazar, who had brought Abigail's son John inside and now had him on his lap. "Thomas' Robert is old enough to spend most of his time with his father in the fields, and Desire has taken well to my apron strings, although she often talks of her mother. Little Thomas seems to be having a hard time finding his place—he remembers his mother's love well and resents the attention I pay my own children. I pray daily that in time he'll fully accept me."

I admired Abigail's strength and thought how lucky my son was to have found her. Her serenity and goodness matched that of Ruth, which may have been what drew him to her. I snuck a peak at her—round cheeks reddened from the heat of the fire, pale brown eyes, light hair tucked tidily into her coif, and a smile constantly hovering around her mouth. I only hoped there would be no strife in the marriage because of little Thomas, as I knew well how this could happen. Just then we heard a piercing scream from outside, and everyone ran to find its source. Nine-year-old Thomas was holding Samuel upside down over the well and saying unkind things about his heritage.

My husband grabbed Samuel and set him upright, while my son jerked his namesake away from the well. "Why do you do this shameful thing?" he asked the boy.

"He's just an Indian. Didn't you kill them during the war? Why should he be treated as one of us?"

I don't believe I'd ever seen my oldest son so angry, but he kept his temper under control. He'd become as much a man of God as my husband, and I knew he felt shame at his son's words.

My husband, finding Samuel unhurt, said to our son, "I'll talk with the boy. I know these words are not yours." With that he grasped his grandson's shoulder and walked out to the buttery. This was where our children were whipped for disobedience, and shortly, we heard some cries coming from within. Thereafter, there was a long silence. I knew if my husband were deeply affected by an event, he could preach for hours, and we did not see them again until the meal was on the table. Thus chastised, our grandson said not a word for the rest of his time with us but afterward was cautious around Samuel.

ꟷ ꟷ

The following year, the freemen re-elected Josiah Winslow governor. My husband told me Winslow filled this role nearly as well as his predecessors and sensed he would remain in this office until his death.

Although we considered the war over, there still occurred smaller problems with our native neighbors. Thomas knew about some of them from serving occasionally on the Plymouth Court. On a stifling hot day, when the heat from the hearth was nearly unbearable and the flies tried my patience, Thomas came home wet with sweat and red-faced. He came in the door and feeling the heat, beckoned me outside, where he slumped down on a bench.

"Let me fetch you something to drink, husband," I said.

Samuel, who stood nearby, said, "I'll do it," and taking a mug, went to the buttery.

Once Thomas had satisfied his thirst with a long draught of beer, he said, "This heat is nearly too much to bear. The sea shines like a mirror and was so calm that I had to row partway from Plymouth harbor and then up the river." Thomas had decided to sail rather than take our horse and wagon, and unfortunately, the wind had died that afternoon.

Next time I will send Samuel with him.

Thomas sent Samuel to gather wood for kindling before telling me about his day.

"Three Indians were tried in the court today," he said, as soon as Samuel had left. "They were convicted of stealing twenty-five pounds from the house of a Plymouth citizen. No one spoke for them, nor did the man recover his money."

"What was the verdict?"

"They will be sold into slavery."

"I would think even hanging might be preferable to a life of slavery," I said. "Slaves are often treated miserably. Did they steal the money to buy food for their families?"

"That might be the truth, although the Indians said nothing. They are proud, and the war has reduced them to penury."

Thomas would not want Samuel to hear of this. His kindness extended to everyone, and he despaired of the fate of the Wampanoags, especially Samuel.

ꕥ ꕥ

The next year, 1680, Thomas and Abigail had a son, Job. Abigail had survived the birth and recovered quickly, for which I'd prayed daily. I must confess I found it increasingly difficult to keep all my grandchildren's names straight in my mind. Thomas now had four children of his own and our daughter, Mary, two. After the deaths of their three daughters, our daughter Sarah and her husband Thomas Hawkes had three more children, two boys and a girl, and thus they were now blessed once more with six. Even Isaac had two, named Isaac and Rebecca. There had never been a time when we were altogether, for which I felt almost grateful, given this number. With Elkanah now married, I expected still more, and Feare, Eleazar and Lydia still lived at home.

In December of that year, Thomas lay sick and abed with fever, a deep cough, and congestion in his lungs. I worried God would take him from us, so sick had he become, and I awoke with dread each morning thinking he might die. I had sweated him early to try to break the fever and had given him seared sugar in aqua vitae for the cough, but he grew sicker. I then made him a pasty mass of powdered betony, caraway seeds, dried skirret, and hound's tooth mixed with honey, what Alice Bradford had called an electuary. I made him take it morning and evening.

I fussed over him so much that he finally said, "Mary, my good wife, leave me be. What you give me tastes so dreadful that I cannot possibly die, except from your fussing."

Nevertheless, the electuary, plus hot liquids, did soothe him and he finally began to eat again, sleeping soundly between meals.

While Thomas still lay in his bed, Eleazar came into the kitchen with a rush of icy air and went directly to sit by his father, who lay close to the hearth.

"What is so urgent," my husband asked in a raspy voice, "that you would disturb an Elder trying to rest?"

"I'm sorry to do that, Father, but I bring sad news. I just heard Governor Winslow has died."

Thomas pushed himself up from his pillow. "I had been expecting this—he's been unwell for some time now. He died at home?"

Eleazar nodded.

But Master Winslow is not old! He is two decades younger than Thomas!

After coughing violently, Thomas leaned back on his pillow, tired from the effort. "You know, he was our first governor born here," he told us. "I didn't like his intransigence and hostility when it came to dealing with the Wampanoags, and I deplored his wish to eliminate their last survivors after King Philip's War…but he dies in God's grace, a righteous man." He grew thoughtful. "I never ministered to him, knowing he would not want to hear words from an Elder who kept a Wampanoag child in his household. But he was never harsh or disrespectful to me."

I stood still, thinking of his words. *Ah, Samuel.*

"We must pray tonight for his soul, and for the well-being of his family." At that, Thomas closed his eyes and went to sleep, exhausted from this short conversation.

A few days later, when Thomas found his strength had returned and at last rose from his bed, Eleazar returned from a trip to Plymouth. I had sent him there to buy some metal buttons for a woolen coat I planned to make my husband, over which he could wear his cape on cold winter days. I had dyed the wool with woad, an herb we had imported from England and which I now grew in my garden. The resulting cloth, made by the weaver when he last stopped, was a lovely deep blue. I set the cloth on the table, placing the buttons Eleazar had bought against it, hoping he would see it and admire what I'd made.

Thomas, sitting at the table with a cup of hot mulled cider, paid scarce attention to the cloth, drawn only to the news Eleazar brought.

"They have elected a new governor, Father. Do you know Thomas Hinckley?"

"I do, and I'd expected to hear this. He's an excellent choice."

"Why do you say that?" Samuel asked.

Thomas glared at him. "It is not respectful for a child to interrupt an adult, Samuel," he said rather forcefully, unusual for his interactions with the boy.

His illness has made him short-tempered, I thought.

"If you promise to mind your tongue, I'll tell you."

Samuel hung his head and said quietly, "Yes, sir."

"Master Hinckley was born in England, unlike Josiah Winslow, and lived originally in Scituate. After he became a freeman, Hinckley moved to Barnstable…"

I could tell he was returning to health because he had slipped easily back into his teaching mode.

"…because he had differences with the preaching in the Scituate church. He has served our colony as a representative, a deputy, and a magistrate. There is even a law named after him—'Thomas Hinckley's Law,' created to limit the activities of the Quakers. That was when the Quakers were considered heretics, but since then Hinckley has moderated his view. I'm sure you'll recognize him when I point him out."

Samuel squinted his eyes, thinking. "Does he have a narrow face with a long nose? And a sandy-colored mustache, I believe." Then he slapped his hand over his mouth, realizing he'd interrupted again.

Thomas chuckled at that and replied, "Yes, that's Master Hinckley."

"But how was he made governor so quickly?" asked Eleazar.

"Actually not so quickly, son. We elected Hinckley to a new position of deputy governor when we re-elected Winslow. We all knew the governor ailed, and his senior assistant, John Alden, is of such a great age, that we feared the burden of the governorship would be too much for him. So we decided to provide for a deputy governor."

That night we gave thanks for the recovery of my husband, prayed for the soul of Josiah Winslow and called for God's blessing on the new governor in his endeavors. Little did we know at the time he would be the last of Plymouth's governors.

Chapter 44

More Shame for the Family

Mary Cushman, Rocky Nook, 1681-1687

With the passage of time, more and more of the Old Comers left our ken, their losses felt acutely by Thomas and me. Used to being at the center of the colony's business, Thomas found himself less and less involved in matters of government as he grew old, despite years of experience and his position as Ruling Elder of the church. The next generation now governed the colony.

He never considered himself limited by his age and ailments—the pain crippling his joints and back, the loss of his teeth, and the partial dimming of his vision. Or the fact I often had to yell to get his attention. Thankfully, Thomas did have one role remaining to occupy his time—tending to his growing flock in Plymouth, Rocky Nook, Duxborough and Plympton. Our son Isaac now followed in his father's footsteps and, because of Thomas' increasing frailty, frequently went with him on his visits to church members. Watching Isaac with his father, I wondered if his piety and devotion to the church would lead him to be a pastor of a church one day.

Thomas did still meet from time to time with our sons and neighbors for discussions of the larger world. One such a day occurred the year after Thomas Hinckley became governor, in the early spring when the sun was watered through puffy white clouds and the breeze carried the smell of new growth. Despite the chill, the men sat outside, wrapped in their cloaks and enjoying their pipes, near a crackling and hissing fire for warmth.

Isaac and young Thomas were there, along with John Alden and Alexander Standish. Master Standish still not remarried. I came outside to churn butter, an activity that needed the cooler air and it also gave me an opportunity to listen in.

"Thomas Hinckley has proved an active governor," commented Master Alden. John Alden was more than eighty years old, but he still had a lively mind and was spry enough to visit his neighbors from time to time.

"I have to agree with you," said Thomas, "based on what I've heard from our church members and whenever I catch our governor for a short discussion, I understand he feels we need a royal charter."

"But the colony has been without one these many years. Why would he think we need one?" asked Isaac.

"Because the crown never granted us the authority to establish our own government. He thinks without a charter, King Charles will take on the governance of our colony in the same way he now tries to control the Massachusetts colony," replied Alden. "He thinks to do this because the Massachusetts charter didn't give them the right to self-governance either."

Thomas took a pull from his pipe and blew out the smoke before saying, "I heard from Hinckley the king sent a number of royal commissioners to settle land disputes. Also to reform the Massachusetts government. It seems the leaders of the colony refused to co-operate. I wonder what the king will do next."

"But there hasn't been any punishment for their defiance—right, Father?" asked Isaac.

"True, but the king's anger must simmer like sop in a pot." Thomas chuckled at his characterization.

"So what exactly is Governor Hinckley doing?" asked Standish.

"He's determined to get a charter for Plymouth which includes the right to our own governance. He sent requests to the king each time a boat sails. The lack of an answer from the crown indicates the king isn't well disposed to Hinckley's proposal. There are some who say the governor hasn't been forceful enough. Others worry that his constant appeals make our colony more visible to the king and thus likely to invite his meddling."

"And if we do get a royal charter, wouldn't that give the crown an easier path to interfere with us?" asked young Thomas.

"I have thought that myself," replied my husband.

Governor Hinckley nevertheless continued to pursue this goal for the next several years, providing fodder for many such political discussions.

ꙮ ꙮ

My daughter Lydia wed William Harlow early in January of 1683. Her husband was the son of Sgt. William Harlow, the man who had built his house from the discarded lumber of our old fort meeting house. Neither Thomas, nor apparently Sgt. Harlow, had known of our children's contract to marry until the previous fall, when Lydia revealed she carried a child. Her choice of husband didn't displease us, for he was an industrious young man, much like his father. However, we knew there would be a reckoning with the church when their child, Elizabeth, was born scarcely a month after their marriage vows. Thomas bore all of this in silent anger, as this was the second of his children to flout God's laws. And as he had with young Thomas, he told me of his guilt and frustration that he'd failed to raise his children to be submissive to our church's tenets. In truth, this situation happened frequently in the colony, so while I understood Thomas' feelings and, like him, felt the shame of it, I could not judge my son and his wife as harshly.

In April, William and Lydia faced the church congregation for judgment. I sat quietly, wanting nothing more than to sink into the wood of the floor, as William and Lydia were asked to come to the front. Our pastor, John Cotton, read the charges. My husband, as Ruling Elder, stood at the head of the congregants, dressed in black and with a hardened expression. His shame burned in his eyes.

Reverend Cotton stood before the couple, saying in a loud voice, "You're charged with breaking the laws of our church, your child being born within six weeks after your marriage. And also with disobedience to your parents for engaging one to another without their knowledge and consent. Finally, you sinfully hid your guilt until it became evident. What do you say to these charges?"

Lydia sobbed and clung to her husband. William's head hung so low that his face was obscured and his voice muffled, as he replied, "We know we have transgressed God's rules and are very sorry for it." They both fell to their knees. "We sincerely repent of our actions and pray that God and his church forgive us. We will do whatever penance is levied and will freely accept the decision of the church in this matter."

To which, Lydia added, "I'm truly sorry for bringing such shame to the church and my family."

"Our members must now decide if they should be discharged from the church," Cotton announced.

Lydia and William left the room and the men gathered at the front of the church to discuss the situation. Thomas said little but voted against excommunication, along with the majority of the others. After more discussion, the men decided on Admonition.

Lydia and William were recalled, and the pastor passed judgment. "You both have sinned grievously, but we believe you're truly repentant. For that reason, you will not be expelled, but I give you an Admonition in censure of your conduct. You will be counseled, but be warned that henceforth, you must keep yourselves on God's path to righteousness."

I breathed a deep sigh of relief but could see the condemnation of Thomas and me in the faces of the congregants. The long years of selfless toil Thomas had given to the church wouldn't stem the firestorm of gossip that would burn through the colony, from town to town.

After the meeting, Thomas left without saying a word to his daughter and son-in-law, and I could only follow him, although I longed to comfort my daughter. The couple would be living with Sgt. Harlow and his family for the present, and I could only imagine the tension they brought to that household as a result of the Admonition. Thomas seemed intransigent in his feelings toward the couple, but he never disapproved when I went to visit Lydia and spend time with the baby.

"You know your father bears you great love and affection," I told her during one of these visits.

"I'm not so sure, Mother. He avoids speaking to us and when I catch him looking at me, I can see his shame."

"His love is stronger than his disapproval. Give him time. He will bend to God's will that he is, above all, your father and love is God's way."

As I predicted, Thomas' anger slowly abated and his feelings softened over the following year, so much so that he finally began speaking cordially with William and Lydia after our Sunday meetings. When they later moved some miles south of the town to a site with the Wampanoag name of Manomet, we both would occasionally travel to see them.

The same year of my daughter's great shame, the construction of our new Plymouth meeting house was completed. Its soaring Gothic roof, diamond-paned glass windows, and a small cupola with a bell to call worshipers made it quite grand. I sometimes missed the coziness of the old fort.

ꟷ ꟷ

My daughter Feare, the last child still at home, had never been particularly strong—doing some of our many daily chores exhausted her and she often napped. She seemed to resent the constraint her weakness placed on her life and perhaps this is what caused her to have a sharp tongue. She often criticized Sarah Standish and Samuel without apparent reason and daily slighted everyone around her, including her father and me. I prayed nightly for a change in her health and temperament, but God didn't hear me, even though I tried even harder to be more understanding and forgiving.

In October of 1684, long before winter crept over the land, Feare fell ill with congestion in her chest and shortness of breath. I used every receipt I knew to ease her distress but with little result. Her continued coughing took what little strength she had, until she couldn't even rise from her bed. She lacked any interest in food, drinking only a little beer or horehound tea, and Thomas and I watched in agony as she wasted away.

We prayed with her each night, and I believe she finally came to welcome the thought of being in the arms of her Maker.

"Mother," she said drowsily to me the night before she died, "I'm so tired. I beg you to forgive any harsh or unkind words I've said to you and Father, and I need to ask forgiveness from Samuel and Sarah as well. I've been so angry with God for giving me a weak body. I did so want to have a husband and family, and I blamed God for taking that from me. For some reason, I felt stronger when I was harsh with everyone. Now I can see this is His plan, and I accept it."

Tears welled in the corners of her eyes. She had become so small and withered from lack of sustenance, I wondered that she could even produce them. My own fell unchecked as I held her hand and stroked the hair from her forehead. Words of comfort escaped me, but I sang her some of her favorite psalms as she drifted to sleep.

The next day, at my husband's calling, various members of the family came to visit and say good-bye. Her eyes lit up seeing them, and she had a kind word and asked for forgiveness from each. That night, while a cold wind whistled in through the chinks in the house and we stoked the fire higher to keep her warm, she fell asleep for the last time. Her death cut my heart in two.

Losing children in childbirth or during their first years was common with the women of the colony, and because of their unending work to ensure their family's survival, they had no time to grieve. But Feare was grown and part of our lives, and the unfairness of her death before mine pained me greatly.

We buried Feare on a fall day with brilliant leaf color but a dull gray sky, which mirrored our grief that she'd had so little time to experience the fullness of life.

Reverend Cotton and my husband intoned the prayers, and my surrounding family and friends tried to comfort me. Returning home, I felt the house empty and hollow, and I wallowed in my sadness for weeks, until my children accused me of the sin of self-indulgence. For once, my husband didn't accept death with his usual stoicism, but instead voiced his grief in irritability and occasional anger. It took many nights of prayer for us both to accept her death.

ജ ഌ

That winter, I went as often as the storms and snow allowed to visit the woman who was my closest friend and the last Old Comer in my gossip, Priscilla Alden. Having more than eighty years, her life of late had slowed, and she spent much time knitting or by the fire, where she often fell asleep. Her husband John, a few years older but still active, passed much of each day at her side.

When I received word in February she had taken to her bed, Thomas decided to go with me to see her. In our prayers that morning, we thanked God there was little snow on the ground to make the trip difficult. Samuel hitched our horse to the wagon, and we traveled to the Aldens on the road that passed by their land. Even though this route spared us the wind and buffeting of the ocean, I was still chilled to the bone when we arrived, and after greeting the family, went directly to Priscilla's bedside. A small brazier next to her bed provided her with warmth, and after touching her shoulder to let her know I was there, I spread my hands above the fire.

"Why, Mary, how good to see you," she said, recognizing me. "How fare you? How grateful I am that you came to see me in this cold weather."

I looked at the finely wrinkled face of my dear friend, pale but serene. "I needed to see you for a good talk," I replied, smiling. Tears came unbidden to my eyes, as I realized this might be our last meeting.

Priscilla reached out and took one of my hands. "Don't grieve for me, dear Mary. We all must face our passing and I'm worn to the bone by this life. I hope heaven awaits me."

"I know it does." I held her hand with both of mine, now warmed. "We have had lives of adventure, have we not?"

"Indeed. And both of us blessed with good and living husbands." She looked anxiously at the door, clearly hoping to see John.

We talked for some time about our early days in Plymouth, where Priscilla, sweet of temper and blessed with great patience, had cared for the children, mended clothes, and with the other goodwives, did the cooking for us all. She laughed when I reminded her of Remember's attempt to plant a garden with her help. When she clearly tired from the conversation, I stood and said, "Let me get John. He'll be missing you."

Priscilla gave me a weak smile, and I bent down to kiss her forehead and called my husband in to give her his blessing and offer prayers. We then left the old couple alone together, holding hands.

She died in her sleep a few days later, and we attended her burial in the place where Myles Standish and other Old Comers had been buried in Duxborough and near the Aldens' daughter, Sarah. It was hard for me not to shed tears, and thereafter, when hearing some news or other, I would think, *I must tell Priscilla about this. She would be so amused.* Until I remembered she was no longer with us.

ഇ ഌ

Political talk was once more the focus of discussions at our home during the spring, and it seemed to enliven my husband. He could no longer travel as frequently to town and relied on our sons for news of the colony.

On a Sunday early in the spring of 1686, after our afternoon service, Thomas and Isaac and their families joined us for an evening meal. Isaac's wife Rebecca worked with me to prepare the meal, along with Abigail, young Thomas' second wife, and Sarah Standish. The oldest of my grandchildren split and carried in wood for the fire. Soon the kitchen filled with smells of garlic and onions in a stew of rabbit with vegetables, baking bread, and the usual smoke. The men remained near the hearth for warmth since the day was chilly, and we left the door open because of the many comings and goings of the children. Thomas lit his pipe and asked Isaac what he'd heard about the new Dominion of New England, since Isaac often attended the court in Plymouth and knew a great deal of the colony's politics.

"What is a dominion? Is Plymouth part of it?" asked Samuel with a voice that cracked as he spoke. Now fifteen, he had grown into an energetic and acquisitive youth whose responsibilities were that of a man.

"To answer your many questions," here Isaac smiled, "Yes, Plymouth is a part. The dominion is the gathering of all the different colonies under a single governor, something the king felt would streamline their administration. What he really wanted was to regulate our trade and make England richer, because we now make most of own goods. These goods compete with those manufactured in England."

"What do we make that competes with theirs?" Samuel asked.

"Textiles, leather goods, ironware, ceramics. England is losing a source of its wealth," replied young Thomas.

When Samuel was about to ask another question, my husband cut him off. "The king wants to make the cost of shipping our products to England expensive so their price would be less attractive to the English. If he also levied a tax on products made here, those imported from England would end up being less costly for us."

I signaled the men to move to the table, then brought the pot of stew for serving. Samuel returned from the buttery with a pitcher of beer. Conversation stopped as everyone helped themselves to food, but it resumed again with more questions from Samuel. "But I know there's a new king—King James. Does he see things the same way?"

"He's decided the dominion will be run by a provisional commission, headed by one Joseph Dudley." My husband took a slice of bread and dunked it in the stew.

"I know him," said my son Thomas. "He fought with us during the great swamp fight at the end of King Philip's War. I think he helped negotiate the boundary between Plymouth and Massachusetts."

"He did indeed," my husband said. "I think he'll govern wisely."

Young Thomas frowned. "Perhaps not. He's spent many years in England, and some say his loyalty to the crown won him this position and that he's now hostile toward the colonies."

Isaac looked to the men around the table. "I guess we'll have to wait and see how he governs."

In December of that year, news reached us that the king had had a change of mind and replaced Dudley with Edmund Andros, giving him the power of a governor. Little was known of him and his manner of governance, so we continued to wait and see.

ᘓ ᘒ

Our son Eleazar wed Elizabeth Coombs of Plymouth in January of 1687. The couple remained with us for the next year, and we were very thankful when a healthy daughter, Lydia, was born in mid-December. Eleazar planned to farm land my husband owned in Plympton, and they would move there the following spring.

In September, John Alden passed away quietly, and we buried him next to his beloved wife in Duxborough. At his burial, I felt a true emptiness and longed for the reassuring hands of Priscilla on my shoulders.

Thomas and I were now the last of the Old Comers.

Chapter 45

Troubles in Boston and the Death of Another Daughter

Mary Cushman, Rocky Nook, 1688-1690

Every time any of my sons came to our home, they spent an inordinate amount of time describing in highly colorful terms their irritation with the Dominion of New England.

One day in late winter of 1688, with the work of planting still a month or more away, my husband and three of our sons—Elkanah, Isaac and Thomas—were deep in discussion. They sat gathered to the hearth, wrapped in their cloaks to ward off the cold, sipping from mugs of mulled cider, puffing on their pipes and leaning toward the heat of the fire.

I had picked up my knitting and sat on our bench nearby. I also needed some warmth myself, but I knew my apparent disinterest wouldn't fool Thomas, so I pretended to instruct Sarah Standish, who had joined me on the bench.

"I hear Andros is a heavy-handed governor," said Isaac.

"Who told you that?" asked my husband.

Samuel sat on the floor between Elkanah and Isaac, and his head turned back and forth with the conversation.

"No less than Governor Hinckley," replied Isaac. "He represents our colony on the Dominion council, and many have criticized him for doing it—mainly those angry with Andros' rule. Hinckley's response is that as our representative, he is well-placed to counter Andros."

"Would that he could actually do that," said my son Thomas. "But I doubt anyone can really counter Andros. Did you know that shortly after he arrived, he asked each of the Puritan ministers in Boston if he might use their church for Anglican services?"

"Did any of them agree?" asked Elkanah.

"No, so Andros just demanded the keys to the Third Church of Boston. So now Reverend Robert Ratcliff preaches there—he's a close associate of King James, who's a Catholic. It wouldn't surprise me if Andros is fathering some popish plot."

"Do you know Reverend Ratcliff, Father?" asked Isaac, as Samuel rose to refill their mugs from a pot in the embers.

"No, this is the first I've heard of him. What is the Council doing? Isn't it supposedly advising Andros?"

"The Council of Representatives from each of the colonies will remain, but I also learned from Governor Hinckley that the king called for Andros to govern by himself. So what power can the Council have?"

Heads shook at this last question.

"What sorts of things has the Council legislated?" asked Elkanah.

"They're trying to make the laws of the individual colonies conform to English law. This is still occupying the Council's time, so for now we keep our own laws."

"Is Andros considering new taxes?" asked my husband.

Isaac gave a nasty chuckle. "Very perceptive of you, Father. You know Massachusetts has no tax laws."

"And I assume Andros intends to rectify that," Thomas said, in a voice dripping with sarcasm.

"Of course. Andros instructed the Council to create a scheme of taxation to apply to all the colonies. Now there will be higher taxes on my livestock, which I can ill afford. So the government will take more of what meager profit I make… from what we all make," said Isaac bitterly.

The men all nodded in agreement.

"Is there more?" asked my husband.

"I heard they're also attempting to assess town populations and estates," replied young Thomas.

Isaac rose and tapped the contents of his pipe into the embers on the hearth. "They've already met with resistance in some of the Massachusetts townships."

"What happened when they resisted?" asked Samuel.

"Arrests and fines," replied Isaac, "and the leaders are jailed until they agree to the assessment."

"Will there be a meeting of the Plymouth council to discuss this?" my husband asked.

"No," said Isaac. "Andros has cancelled town meetings, except when votes are needed for government positions."

As I took this in, I discovered I'd dropped some stitches. I angrily tore out everything I'd just knitted. We were all relatively poor because at times our land didn't produce enough to sustain us well from year to year. Higher taxes were just cruel, and it seemed more would be levied. *No town meetings? Andros is a dictator.*

ꕥ ꕥ

In February of 1689, another such meeting of my family occurred, this time in the yard where they stood warming their hands over the fire. Preparation of the evening meal kept me inside so I only heard snatches of their angry talk of rebellion, treason, and hanging offenses.

Samuel joined us at the hearth that night when I asked Thomas the cause of their anger.

"The heart of it is, as usual, Governor Andros and his rule. He has challenged the titles to our land. Furthermore, to be in accord with the taxation in England, Andros has introduced quit-rents to raise revenue from landowners."

"What is a quit-rent?" asked Samuel, before I could.

"It's a tax on owned or leased land," replied Thomas. "And anyone who doesn't have a legal title will lose their lands, unless they obtain a certificate of ownership from the government. And of course you must pay for that certificate. Andros has also issued writs of intrusion..."

"Oh dear," I said. "What do all these terms mean for us? Do we have a title to our land?"

"We do, but it's different for our neighbors to the north. All the lands in the Massachusetts colony were granted under its royal charter, so when the crown vacated this charter, it also voided all land grants. This is why the landowners must now recertify their ownership, and, of course, once they do this, they'll have to pay quit-rent taxes. Andros has created a spider's web. Perhaps it's God's blessing that Plymouth never had a formal royal charter."

"What will happen now?" asked Samuel, his dark eyes shining in the light of the fire.

"Well, many of the landowners are contesting these new rules in court, because if they don't obey, their lands will be seized. Now there's talk of rebellion."

"Rebellion? Really?" Samuel eyes were alight.

"Everyone is waiting for Reverend Mather of Boston to return from England, where the religious leaders decided to send him to press our case with the king. Andros had him arrested just before he left, but some Puritans freed him and got him on a ship bound for England just this month. We'll have to wait and see."

Wait and see again.

Thomas was apparently as concerned as I about our future, for both of us tossed and turned in our bed that night, unable to find peace enough to sleep. Finally, he asked me to join him in a prayer for our well-being in the face of such an uncertain future. Then we finally slept.

ꙮ ꙮ

In March, Thomas again had to attend the Plymouth Court. His son-in-law William Harlow was accused of having taken possession of a whale that had died on a shore within the boundaries of the town. The whale was by law the property of the town, and the jury found for the town and exacted a penalty of twenty-seven shillings and six pence, which they would return when the proper owner of said whale appeared.

I thought this was just foolishness. *Who owns a whale?*

Thomas had to assist William in the payment of that fine and bemoaned having to appear in court yet again on behalf of a family member.

ꕥ ꕥ

Eleazar, Isaac and both Thomases all owned horses and now travelled by our road system, still developing between the inland townships. In April, Eleazar made an unexpected visit, riding hastily into our yard on his horse.

Sarah and I were in the garden, weeding, as he leapt from his saddle, crying, "There's been a rebellion in Boston. Andros has been taken into custody!"

Samuel took the reins of the horse, as Thomas emerged from the house. "What did you say?"

"Andros has been arrested!"

"How do you know this, son?"

"I was there! I went with a small group from our militia."

"Come in and sit down. I want to hear all of it." Thomas directed Sarah to go to the buttery for beer, and we all followed him inside.

I must hear this! But who will I share it with? How I miss my friend Priscilla.

Eleazar sat at the table and thirstily drained half the beer Sarah had poured for him. Wiping his mouth on his sleeve, which earned a stare from me, he said, "We received word from Boston for our militia to gather a few days ago in Charlestown. So we sailed north and encamped there, across the Charles River from Boston. Boats took us early in the morning across the river, and after we'd met with other militias, we went about arresting Dominion and regimental leaders."

"Were they not warned by seeing your encampment?" asked Samuel.

"Yes, and some of them fled to Castle Island in the harbor."

"What happened then?" I forgot myself and asked, so enthralled was I by his story.

Eleazar just smiled at me. "A crowd followed us to Fort Mary, Mother, where Andros quartered with a large number of British troops. Outside the fort, I heard Boston Anglicans had also been rounded up, and sometime before noon, I saw an orange flag raised on Beacon Hill."

He finished his beer and Samuel poured him more. "The orange flag signaled to another thousand or more militia to enter the city. When Fort Mary failed to surrender, we left it guarded and went to the market square, where a declaration in support of the Prince of Orange—"

"Who is the Prince of Orange?" Another question just popped out of my mouth.

My husband answered with a sigh at my rudeness. "The Prince of Orange is William, son of the Netherlands king. He is married to Mary, the oldest daughter of King James. Parliament wants him to seize the crown from James. Please continue, my son."

"As I was saying," Eleazar said, glancing at me, "A declaration was read in support of the Prince of Orange, which called the citizenry to rise up because—as we had suspected—a popish plot had been discovered."

I could hear my husband's sharp intake of breath.

But Eleazar was anxious to continue his story. "At Fort Mary, former governor Bradstreet called on Andros to surrender, but Andros refused again. He made two attempts to escape, first by boat and then dressed in women's clothing."

"I would like to have seen that," said Samuel, smiling at the thought.

"In any event, both attempts were thwarted, and Fort Mary finally surrendered. Andros was transported to Castle Island for safe keeping. Then we returned home with our contribution, small as it was, at an end. It was quite an adventure, though, and rather exhilarating to all who participated."

"What will happen now?" asked my husband.

"I don't know," he replied, shaking his head. "I'm going next to see Master Hinckley and tell him what transpired, although he may already know."

"So if William and Mary become the king and queen, the Dominion and all of Andros' laws might go away?" I asked.

"Possibly," replied Eleazar. "I do think once all the colonies hear of the removal of Andros, the governments that were in place before the Dominion will be reestablished."

Later, thinking over what Eleazar had told us, I wondered whether the colonies might one day consider independence from English rule. I could hardly imagine it.

☙ ❧

That year, Alexander Standish at long last remarried. His new wife was Desire Doty, daughter of *Mayflower* passenger Edward Doty, who had died in 1655. The new Mistress Standish had lost two previous husbands, so I prayed for the health of her third. Sarah Standish, Alexander's daughter, was now twenty-three years old, but she chose to stay with us rather than return to her father's household. While I'm certain she did this out of love, I also believed she stayed to provide us assistance in our old age. She'd been living with us for so long that she'd become as much our daughter as any of those I'd borne.

Thomas and I lost another of our children that year—my daughter Mary. She had been living in New York with her husband, Francis Hutchinson, and we received a brief letter from him telling us of her death. It had been more than five years since we had seen her. As with all my children who had removed to a distance too far to lay my eyes on them, I longed to see their faces again.

It's a hard thing to have a child die before you, and we'd already lost Feare and our first Sarah, Sarah Alden Standish. Thomas and I managed to bear our pain only through prayer. With each passing of someone dear to me, I didn't know where I would find the strength to bear another.

ꕥ ꕥ

Isaac came with news in late March of the following year that there had been a revolution in England.

He sat at our table with Thomas, eating fresh bread and butter with some cheese, eager to share what he knew. "News has reached Boston that William of Orange finally made his move. He invaded England with a great fleet and by December, King James' rule collapsed without much opposition. James fled to France and now we have an avowed Protestant on the throne. The Dominion is certainly gone forever," Isaac said solemnly. "And we no longer have to worry about Catholicism becoming the religion of the land."

"And why is that?" asked my husband,

"Because William signed an Act of Toleration."

"Is that what the name implies?"

"It is, Father. The Act ensures religious freedom to non-conformists, such as ourselves."

"Then we must give thanks to God and pray that William has a long rule."

I believed the threat to our existence represented by the Dominion and its laws and taxes was now over, and I hoped life in the colony could return to normal.

ဢ ဢ

In the early summer of 1690, our sons who were then active in the militia—Eleazar and Elkanah—became caught up in yet another war, this one between the English and the French over territory in New England and Canada.

Both Eleazar and Elkanah came in early September to tell us the Plymouth militia would be sent to Canada. The weather belied my dread at the news—a day with warmth but no moisture in the air, bird sounds and the hum of bees coming from the garden, a gentle breeze ruffling the hair of my sons, and the soothing sounds of our animals foraging.

"Why is our militia being sent?" asked Thomas, with a touch of anger in his voice. We stood outside, sunlight gleaming off his nearly bald head and setting the many lines of his aged face into deep relief. He had become increasingly irritable in the past few months and complained frequently of minor things, much to my distress.

"Because with the restoration of the United Colonies of New England, our pact to provide militia for any conflict was also restored," Eleazar answered.

Why are we always caught up in England's wars?

"But what is the conflict? How is it that I know nothing of this?"

Eleazar sighed but answered respectfully. "It's very complicated, Father. We should sit while I tell you about it." My son had noticed that Thomas wavered as he stood.

Samuel pulled over the benches from the garden. Once we were seated, Eleazar told us, "I don't understand all that led to this situation, but it's common knowledge that the English have no love for the French nor the French for the English. Now the crown has appointed Sir William Phips as the major general in Massachusetts and has ordered him to command an expedition against the French in Acadia."

I must have looked puzzled because Elkanah explained, "That's what the French call their territory. It includes Quebec and parts of northern Maine, and areas along the Penobscot and Kennebec rivers."

Thomas frowned, his anger now apparent, but for a different reason. "We had trading posts there years ago, until the French drove us off, killing some of our settlers. Would this had been done forty years ago!"

"Last May," Elkanah continued, "Phips sailed with seven vessels and four hundred and fifty men to attack Port Royal—that's the capital of Acadia—and it surrendered without a fight. This emboldened Phips to try to take Quebec." Elkanah looked down at the ground, I thought to hide his frustration.

"By now they will have fortified Quebec, don't you think?" asked Samuel. "It's autumn and they've had time to plan for an English attack. Plus with winter coming, the French must think no attack can succeed."

"I know this," replied Eleazar, "and the militia knows this, but Phips is determined to win Quebec."

"Phaw!" said Thomas. "It's a fool's errand. It's always been like this between the English and the French."

"Must you go?" I asked.

"We're freemen and thus must fight with the militia, Mother," replied Eleazar.

My son Thomas was now too old to undertake active battle, and Isaac couldn't be spared, as he had become central to the work of our church as his father's strength decreased. *At least only two sons must go.*

We prayed with them before they left and extracted promises to have their families come to us whenever the need arose.

During the fall and into early winter, we heard nothing and expected the worst.

Chapter 46

The Passing of Thomas Cushman

Mary Cushman, Rocky Nook, 1690-1692

My sons returned with the militia in December, and I thought perhaps all the hours I had spent on my old and creaking knees praying to God for their safety may have had some effect.

I heard calls from the yard one afternoon, and when I opened the door, I saw the pretty pair of them, thin and ragged and leaning on each other in weariness as they walked toward the house. Elkanah trod slowly as if in pain, and Eleazar had one arm in a rough sling. Samuel ran immediately to help them, while I, not so spritely now, hurried after him, with Thomas not far behind.

"God's faith, it's good to see you home," I said, embracing each in turn. I was overcome with gratitude to God that they were home and cried with joy and relief.

"Mother, don't cry. We're home and doing well," said Elkanah, seeing my tears.

"Yes," I said, now laughing, as I looked them up and down. "I can see that."

Thomas thumped them on their backs in joy and took Elkanah's healthy elbow. We managed to get them into the house, where we sat them down gently. Without even asking, I undid Eleazar's sling and helped him remove what remained of his coat, waistcoat and shirt, so I could assess his injury.

"Don't worry, Mother, my wound is healing nicely, and the bone should soon be set firm."

"I don't trust the physicks traveling with the militia. They're crude barbers, good for nothing but cutting hair and bloodletting," I replied.

The injury had been halfway between his elbow and shoulder and was, as he explained to me, the result of a piece of lead fired from a flintlock at a range sufficient to break the bone but not shatter it. I ran my hand along his arm and felt nothing protruding beneath his skin. "Well, I would say you had the gift of God's grace that day." A long, twisted scar marked the site of the wound, and although raw and red, didn't look festered. "It seems the surgeon got out the lead but made a mess of the removal."

Elkanah smiled. "In truth, I didn't know what he did nor even when. I was quite drunk. I can thank my brother for getting me to him quickly, though."

I nodded and smiled at Eleazar. "And you're limping. What ails you?"

"Only my feet, Mother."

"Take off your shoes then and let me look."

The smell when he removed what remained of his shoes gagged me. I peeled off the remains of his stockings and gaped at his feet—black and red with blisters and open weeping sores and peeling skin. "Elkanah, take off your shoes and stockings as well." His feet weren't any better. "How did you manage to walk all this way in such condition? No, I don't expect an answer." Sarah stood at my shoulder, her face a mask of distress at the sight and smell of their feet. "Sarah, run and fill two buckets with warm water. Just dilute what is heating on the coals with water from the well. And bring in the lye soap."

I told them to set their feet in the warm water, then scrubbed one foot after the other with a cloth and lye soap. They moaned and jerked their feet from my hands, so Thomas leaned on their shoulders, while Sarah and Samuel held their legs. When all four feet had been thoroughly washed, I applied a balm made of pounded flax seed, which released linseed oil, and honey. I then wrapped each foot in a clean bandage. "Thomas, can you bring me some of your stockings?"

"There, you're ready to travel home now," I told my sons, after placing the dry and clean stockings on their feet. "I'm not sure if you'll want to keep those shoes, but you'll need something more than stockings on your feet. Samuel, can you take their shoes outside and clean them as best you can?"

I plied Elkanah and Eleazar with beer, bread, some salted pork, and cheese whilst biding my tongue not to ask them any questions. Nor did they offer anything about what they'd experienced but instead ate as if they had had no food in days—a reasonable probability.

While they ate, Thomas, wrapped in a coat and a warm cloak, scarf, hat and gloves, went out to retrieve the shoes and help Samuel to pull the wagon from the barn and hitch up our horse. He would take them both home. I embraced my sons again, before opening the door to the cold air. We were lucky to be without snow, but scanning the sky, I saw the thick, low clouds that typically preceded its arrival. The distance to Plympton was only six miles, and I hoped Thomas would get home before the snowfall.

When I later heard hoof beats in the yard, the first flakes drifted down.

ᔕ ᔓ

My sons were indeed reluctant to paint a picture of all they'd seen, except in private conversations with their father over the following week. After a fortnight had passed, they and their families gathered with us after Sunday services to celebrate their homecoming with a feast. I had to rely much on Sarah in the preparation, as I found myself less able to lift heavy pots and plates during cooking. We laid the table with roasted turkey—shot by Samuel the day before—roast pork, stewed turnips and parsnips, spiced pumpkin, bread, butter and cheese—enough food to hopefully relax my sons into to telling us a little of their time in Quebec. When it seemed our feast had nearly satisfied everyone's hunger, I said, "We're hoping to hear a little about your adventure."

"It was hardly an adventure, Mother," Elkanah replied, looking to his father for the decision to tell us. When Thomas nodded, he said, "We first attempted to take Montreal and thus pin the French forces south of Quebec, but we failed—mainly because we lacked supplies and suffered an outbreak of smallpox."

"Why didn't you turn back at that point?" asked Samuel.

Eleazar grimaced. "We wish our leaders had decided that, but, no, we were ordered on to Quebec, where the French forces from Montreal had joined those already there."

"How many ships did you have?" As usual, Samuel was completely engaged in the conversation and wasn't eating.

"We had about thirty ships, but only four were of a good size, and the wait for additional munitions from England delayed our travel up the St. Lawrence. We still lacked ammunition when General Phips finally decided to sail at the end of August. Then we had bad weather, contrary winds and pilots unfamiliar with the river. We only reached Quebec in mid-October." He stopped to take some cheese and bread, but Samuel was quick with another question.

"What happened when you got there? Did the French surrender?"

"Hardly," answered Eleazar, between bites. "As we'd suspected, the French had had time to build a palisade enclosing Quebec, along with many defensive emplacements for their cannons. And they had placed their gun batteries facing the St. Lawrence River so they could fire directly at our ships. Nevertheless, General Phips sent an envoy to deliver a summons for the French to surrender. He returned without a written response from Count Frontenac, and the messenger had been treated brutally." Seeing some puzzlement at the name, he added, "Frontenac was the leader of the French forces."

Elkanah paused in eating and leaned in. "I heard Count Frontenac said he had no reply to make, other than from the mouths of his cannons and muskets. At least this was the translation that spread through the troops. I came to believe it when we discovered the French forces were far superior to ours."

"Why didn't the general retreat then?" asked Samuel. I noticed he still hadn't eaten.

"Pride and ignorance, I would say," said my husband.

I deliberately dished more turnips and parsnips onto Samuel's plate and glared at him.

"The militia never got to engage in a real battle," said Eleazar. "At every place we tried to land, we were harassed by French forces and their field guns. In the meantime, the guns of our large ships began bombarding the city. The French shore batteries proved more than a match, and they pounded our ships from the top of the hill where the city sits. Our rigging and hulls were nearly destroyed."

"Were you in any of the skirmishes?" Samuel asked, finally taking a bite of meat.

"Yes, an attack on their earthworks which killed many of us, so we had to retreat. That is when I was hit. I'll say no more."

I knew from the stony look on Elkanah's face he meant it. We sat in silence for several moments, concentrating on the last of the food.

Finally, Eleazar said, "There isn't much more to tell. At the end of October, our general negotiated a prisoner exchange and we set sail for Boston. Seven of our vessels were barely seaworthy, and we burned three of them.

The men then asked for more beer and there followed a less exciting discussion of what might happen as a result of this failed expedition. Samuel, now disinterested, finished eating and went outside to chop wood. After refreshing their beer, Sarah brought a fruit fool to the table for a sweet, made with an egg custard and pureed apples. She set some aside for Samuel, who liked anything sweet. As Sarah and I cleared the remains of the meal and put the left-over food away, I was privy to a discussion of consequences of the loss.

"From what you've told me, Phips clearly lacked experience and had no book-learned military skills to offset this," said Thomas, sitting back and packing and lighting his ever-present pipe. Its smoke rose in a lazy eddy.

"I would have to agree, Father," said Eleazar. "I heard him claim only thirty of his men died in the fight, but I think the actual number is more like a thousand. I know many of those in our group who died came from Barnstable."

"That is a great cost to bear for a country so sparsely populated." Thomas' frown indicated a further unpleasant thought. "And the cost in money—I heard this expedition incurred a debt of some forty thousand pounds. I expect our taxes will be increased this year to offset that loss."

There followed some gloomy talk about the next year, and how the farmers might weather the increased taxation.

ꕤ ꕤ

Many things changed for both me and the colony in 1691. In early October, King William and Queen Mary issued a new charter, but not for the Plymouth colony. The charter combined Plymouth and Maine with the Massachusetts Bay colony. Plymouth colony existed no longer. I could scarcely believe it—all the many years of struggle and hardship, only to be part of Massachusetts. I wondered what William Bradford, Thomas Prence and Josiah Winslow would have thought.

In late summer, Thomas began to complain of a pain in his stomach, which grew worse with each passing week. I watched in fear as he ate smaller and smaller amounts, and I made all the foods he liked best, in the hopes of enticing him to eat more. His clothes began to hang on him as he steadily lost weight, and he lacked the strength to do the chores he usually did with ease. I woke each day with renewed anguish as he wasted away, becoming thin and gaunt. He had been such a large and vital man, the center and strength of our family, and my anchor for his entire life.

I found him at the table one morning in October, surrounded by our accounts, writing a document. "What are you writing, Thomas? A letter to someone?"

"No, it's my will, Mary. It's past time. I need you to send Samuel for Captain Standish and Reverend Cotton to witness it."

I knew then with clarity I would have him for only a short time more. The thought broke my heart.

I called all my sons and daughter together early November. I knew discussing Thomas' illness would be difficult, but I resolved to be open with them. I met them outside, and we spoke while Samuel took care of their horses and wagons. "My children, it pains me to say this, but your father is undoubtedly dying. I don't know the cause of his illness, but I think he will soon see the heaven he's told us about all these many years. Talk with him but not about his illness. He's in pain, and your stories and remembrances will distract him."

My sons stared at me, worry creasing their faces. "Surely there is something you can do, Mother. We can call a physick to see him," said young Thomas.

"Our new physick has already come and prescribed some medicines, which we tried to no effect. After his last visit, he told me in private he could do nothing more. Your father is very old and hasn't the strength to fight this last battle. Spend what time you have with him in good conversation and pray with him. He finds comfort in that." I left them and went inside, since they clearly wanted to talk amongst themselves first.

By the next week, all he could take was liquid—beer, mulled cider or wine, various teas made with such herbs as I thought might ease his pain. Sometime he vomited, even after a few drops, more and more with blood, and I agonized, feeling his suffering. Only laudanum, in increasing amounts, gave him relief. But his belief in God remained strong, so rather than find fault with God and cry out against this injustice, he found solace in prayer. I believed a lesser man would have given in to this affliction, but Thomas was strong and his will to live did not fade easily.

We prayed together many times during the day, and I ignored nearly everything but cooking to be with my husband. Samuel and Sarah offered their comfort and help, Samuel having completely taken over the heavier tasks and Sarah, the cleaning, mending and washing.

I was grateful that my children came often to visit.

ဢ ဢ

Nights were the worst, when Thomas groaned, his face contorted in pain, and prayed aloud, finally asking for me to give him laudanum. When he succumbed to the oblivion of that medicine, I would go outside, wrapped in my cape and blankets, and sit on the garden bench, thinking of all our years together, the warmth of his love, the hardships we had faced. I wept for both Thomas and me, who would be left alone without his comfort. I knew death to be one of God's gifts, to allow us to rest from our toil, and Thomas and I had had more years together than many husbands and wives. But *I* was the one angry at our Creator, that He would take him with so much suffering. There were times when I greeted the pink wisps of dawn, chilled to my core, and wondered if I would have another day with my husband.

Reverend Cotton came frequently, and I left him with Thomas to talk about church matters, which still captured my husband's interest. I heard their low voices from wherever I sat working, and they were a balm to my soul. My sons made frequent visits during that last month, and Lydia came to spend time with us.

Toward the end, he became so weak that he was unable to leave his bed. I sat beside him then, holding his hand and getting him to take at least a few drops of beer, which he liked, and wiping his face with a cooling cloth. We talked for hours of our lives, its humor and the challenges.

"Do you remember the time Isaac was gored by the lion?" I asked him one day.

He nodded, smiled, and said, "I also remember you asking me for a bigger knife for defense." We both chuckled at that.

His eyes still twinkled when he looked at me, reminding me of his youth. "Dearest wife, we've been blessed to have a long life together, have we not?" he said one afternoon. "By God's grace, we've enjoyed companionship and sharing for many years. I have loved you deeply all this time, even your forthrightness and stubbornness, although perhaps I didn't show you as much as I should have. Do you remember the night we sat in the Bradford's garden, eating apples for the first time?" His pale and haggard face stretched into a smile.

"And now we have our own trees, and as many apples as we want," I replied, patting his arm. "The children loved to put rotten apples on the end of sticks and fling them at each other!" Here we both laughed at the memory. "I remember when we first moved here, and you brought a skep for keeping bees. How many times the children and I were stung, trying to get the honey out—until you built us a better form for the hive...and built a good life for your family." I paused, tears coming unbidden.

Thomas reached out and clasped my hands. "Don't weep for me, Mary. I've had a good life, made all the better by your love and companionship. I'm so tired now, and I can hear God calling me. Remain at peace until your own time comes, then come to me for eternity. We are truly joined in our souls." Releasing my hand, he wiped away my tears, which fell freely.

How I love this man! I couldn't imagine life without him.

On the morning of December 10th, I awoke with my head on the bed beside Thomas, a blanket placed over my shoulders by Sarah or Samuel to ward of the chill of the house. I still held one of his hands, but it was cold and stiff. His struggle had finally ended as I slept. There were no more tears—I had cried them all out. I bathed and dressed Thomas' body and sent Samuel to tell Pastor Cotton and the members of our family.

ꕥ ꕥ

The following Sunday, the family—all of them—and so many friends, plus citizens of Plymouth I didn't even know, gathered on what we now called Burying Hill. It was a bitterly cold, gray, and windy day, and our cloaks whipped about us with the promise of snow's arrival. His grave was on the southerly brow of the hill at a beautiful wooded site Thomas would have loved, with a full view of Plymouth harbor, of the town, of the hills in the distance, and of the new church that stood on the site where he had prayed and worshipped for so many years.

We sang one of his favorite psalms, Psalm Four, after which Reverend Cotton spoke. "It has pleased God to take our good Elder, Thomas Cushman. He's been a rich blessing to this church for scores of years. He was grave, sober, holy and temperate, and always working for the peace and prosperity of the church and for the healing of all its breaches. Much of God's presence has gone away with the death of this blessed pillar of the church. He has truly served his generation according to the will of God."

Reverend Cotton called for a day of humiliation at the Plymouth church on December 16, a singular honor that comforted me in my grief.

ꕤ ꕤ

Thomas' will had been entered it into the town's probate records. In it, after first giving and bequeathing his soul to God and his body to dust in the hopes of a joyful resurrection, he had divided out all that he owned.

To me, whom he wrote of as his dear and loving wife, he left his home and all the buildings, uplands, and meadowlands in the township of Plymouth, for my use and support during the remainder of my life. In death, he had provided well for me, but I would have traded all of it for more time with him.

To his sons, he left various parcels of land in what was called the north precinct of Plymouth and in Middleborough. In his usual thoughtful way, he had provided for his daughters Sarah Hawkes and Lydia Harlow, as well as for the children of our deceased daughter, Mary Hutchinson.

He named me sole executrix of his will and designated our sons Thomas and Isaac and Elder Thomas Faunce of our church to help me. For the next months, seeing to details—debts, legacies and funeral charges—occupied much of my time, and I thanked Thomas in my prayers each night, first for his love and caring and then for his foresight in providing me assistance.

In early spring, all my sons visited me at home, where I had gathered my husband's personal effects to be given out, largely his books. Thomas had left me his best Bible, and I read from it each day, hearing his voice as I did so. The remaining books, except for two small ones for Lydia, were to be divided equally amongst his sons. I recognized the authors of many of them—Winslow, Bacon, Marcus Aurelius, Erasmus, Gough, Culpepper's Herbal—and had read from some of them myself, thanks to the teaching of my parents and Alice Bradford. There was even an old copy of *The Bay Psalm Book*, the first book printed in Boston.

I listened with amusement to the debate among the brothers about who would get which book. Young Thomas wanted Winslow's books, specifically asking for *New England's Salamander*, while the work of Marcus Aurelius interested Isaac. He picked up *The Bay Psalm Book* and said, "This book should go to Lydia. She likes to sing, although not always on key." We all laughed at that, and I thought how much Thomas would have enjoyed this discussion.

Eleazar picked up Gough's *Of Domestical Duties* and after looking through it quickly, handed it to me. "I think this is for you, Mother."

"If you look more closely, son, you will see it lays out practical rules for the family, based on the Bible. Since you're all now grown with families of your own, I have no need of it. I think my work is done." I smiled.

Isaac reached across the table, taking my hands in his, and said, "But your work isn't done, Mother. We'll need your advice and counsel for many years yet."

ઈ ૪

I scarcely remember the months that followed. When not dealing with Thomas' estate and arranging for tenant farmers to work the fields he'd bequeathed to me, I existed in a daze, doing my chores without thought, numb to life. I derived comfort from remaining in the home we had shared for so long, however, and working in my garden. This last had become more difficult as my body groaned its age and my eyesight worsened. Often Sarah would work there beside me, gently telling me which were weeds to be removed.

Samuel had remained with us, taking me to meetings on Sunday and doing the heavy chores that Thomas or my sons had done for so long. He chopped wood for the fire, did the occasional building and fence repair, worked in the fields, and helped Sarah make beer. The bounty of rabbit, venison, and fowl we enjoyed was evidence of his love of hunting. Watching him woodworking during the cold winter months reminded me of Thomas.

One day, after pulling weeds and pruning my flowers, I sat in the sun beside Sarah, who churned butter. She was my family now, but at twenty-six, she needed to have her own life. In many ways—her diligence at her chores, her smile and godly ways—reminded me of her grandmother, Priscilla Alden. Regarding her, I often thought of Priscilla with wistfulness from the love of her that remained in my heart.

I placed one hand on her arm. "Sarah, how good you are to care for me in my dotage! But it's past time for you to have a home of your own."

She paused and wiped the sweat from her forehead with the hem of her apron. "I remain because this is my home, dear Mary. You have become my mother, and I'm honored to care for you…and truth be told, I haven't met any man who measures up to your sons or my father."

I chuckled. "You're generous to say so, but perhaps you've set your standards too high? Has anyone caught your eye?"

She hesitated, then said, "Well…there is one man. I've met him at the Duxborough meeting several times."

"Do I know him?"

"Benjamin Soule. His parents are John and Rebecca."

I remembered the father, John Soule. He had been born in the colony when it was still young and struggling, and I recall his energetic young presence at our Sunday meetings at the fort. *Time has passed so quickly.*

"He is a yeoman farmer, as is his father, and has land in Plympton. But I don't know if my attraction to him is matched by his to me. We've only spoken a few times."

"Perhaps we might ask him to share a meal with us, on the pretext of something he could do for me?"

Joy lit Sarah's face and beautiful eyes.

ꟹ ꟹ

By early autumn, when the treetops were burnished in red and orange while their lower leaves remained heavy with the green, the harvest was in. Now I struggled with the assignment of our income until Isaac and Elder Faunce gave me help to complete the chore.

I missed the comings and goings of our sons on visits to their father, as these brought the news on which my mind and soul thrived. My sons were less likely to engage in these sorts of conversations with me, so my daughter Lydia became my ears to the outside world.

Lydia came as often as she could for a visit, bringing food—wheat bread, jellies and compotes, which I now had no energy to make. On one such visit, we sat at the table, mid-day, with Samuel now at the head and the women on each side, enjoying Lydia's gifts along with our meal.

"Sarah will soon be contracted to marry, Lydia." I smiled with love at Sarah, for indeed her attraction to Benjamin Soule had proven reciprocated.

"It's past time, Sarah," Lydia said with forthrightness—her inheritance from me, I feared. "Who is this man?"

After a discussion of the Soule family, while Samuel watched on quietly, I asked Lydia, "What do you hear about Plymouth?"

My daughter, as usual, was well informed. "I've heard that the counties joined with Massachusetts will now be governed from Boston. The last meeting of the Plymouth General Court occurred a month ago."

"But how will we be represented? By Puritan rule?" The thought of this vexed me.

"Well, there will be a governor's council, and our former governor, Thomas Hinckley, will be a member. He has stated that through him, the courts and the various departments of our former colony's government will be absorbed without difficulty into those of Massachusetts."

"I don't believe that." They could hear my sigh, and I felt some relief that Thomas had not lived to see all this. He would certainly have become embroiled in the transition.

The father of Lydia's husband, William, had died in March of that year, 1692, and his will had been probated and read. "William received good portion of land in Middleborough," she told me, "plus six acres of meadows on the west side of Plymouth. He now has much more land to manage."

I had long had reservations about my son-in-law, since he seemed to have little regard for the colony's laws or those of our church. But I thought perhaps having more land would settle him into a life of a yeoman farmer and set him on a righteous path. "The additional income must be welcome, Lydia, with four children to feed."

Lydia blushed. I had often noticed the threadbare condition of her children's clothing, and I regularly spent time spinning wool for material for their clothes. "We will pray for God's blessing on your husband tonight," I added with a smile.

And I would be present to see it, it seemed.

Chapter 47

Isaac Cushman Becomes a Minister

Mary Cushman, Rocky Nook, 1693-1699

My world continued to shrink while my extended family grew, as the years following Thomas' death rolled by. Eleazar and his wife had a third child in 1693, while the same year Elkanah's second wife, Martha, bore him his ninth and last child, a tiny daughter with dark eyes and hair, who took after her father in her energy and lungs. While I'd wished to attend both births, the trip to Plympton was too arduous for me now.

Sarah Standish married Benjamin Soule early in 1694. When their son Zachariah came into the world late in the year, the family moved to Plympton, where the Soules had land, and where it seemed most of my family now lived. That left me alone but for Samuel. My sons, seeing clearly my need for assistance in my old age, decided that Lydia and William would come to live with me, rather than moving me to one of my sons' homes. The comfort of this house, compared to that which Lydia and her five children occupied at the time, made it an easy decision for her and her husband. I wasn't asked for my preference, but I had hoped to stay in the house Thomas had built for us, and I was happy with their decision.

I was unused to having children about, the house having been occupied with only adults since Thomas' death, but Lydia's daughters, Elizabeth, now ten, and little Lydia, six, proved to be good assistants in the garden and with cooking, as long as I provided them with stories of the early colony on a regular basis. Wild animals, Indians, and life on the *Mayflower* were the subjects they liked most.

Lydia's son Thomas, at seven, worked in the fields with his father. Four-year-old William challenged our patience with his demands, while Robert, but two, toddled here and there, protected by the pudding around his head and his attachment by his shift strings to his mother's apron or mine. After a time, I came to enjoy what Lydia called 'mayhem,' with the number of blocks and poppets and spinning tops scattered about, on which we frequently stepped. Whilst there was discipline in the house, William was not the stern overseer of his children's behavior that my Thomas had been. Thrashing, except for extreme disobedience, was uncommon, William preferring to give them tasks he knew they didn't like, such as mucking the garden.

One fine summer day, Elizabeth and little Lydia watched me make bread and then took turns kneading it. Through the back door and the windows came a clean, refreshing breeze, driving out the smoke from the hearth and the other smells from so many people living in a small space.

"Grandmother, tell me again about the Indians," asked little Lydia. Great friends with Samuel, she often went for walks with him in the woods, where he taught her to recognize the tracks of small animals.

"There were many tribes," I began, "but our closest neighbors were the Wampanoags. Samuel is a Wampanoag."

"How did he come to be here?" Lydia reminded me of myself, always jumping from one question to another.

"He came to live with us after King Philip's war," I replied. "His parents were killed in that war."

"Oh. That's so sad. I'll ask him about his parents."

"I doubt he'll remember them very well. He was only five years old when we first met."

"What was King Philip's war?"

And so went our conversations. I wondered how much she retained, but I did hear her asking Samuel about his parents later that day.

ꙮ ꙮ

Samuel came to me not long after Lydia and her family moved in, sitting beside me in the sun just outside our door.

"Mother Cushman, now that I'm sure you will be cared for, I mean to find a life on my own."

Although I'd known this day would come, his words nonetheless pained me. I took his hands in mine and gazed at the face that had become so dear to me over the years. "You have been a good son, Samuel, and I want you to have your own place with a family and children. Where do you think to go?"

"When I was gone last week, I travelled to a praying town on Martha's Vineyard. It is a community of Wampanoags like me, all Christian, and is both tolerant and economically successful. I know I will be happy there, although I will miss you deeply."

I couldn't help it, tears started to fall. *What a problem with old age!*

"I will visit you so often, you will hardly know I'm gone."

There were still more tears on the day he left, and I often found myself looking for him, forgetting he had left. When he came back for his first visit, he told me that he now farmed and thought to marry a Pokanoket woman he had met there. Later, they both came to see me, often bringing gifts from Samuel's hunting.

Once, before he left, he told me with a glistening in his dark eyes that he'd come to think of Thomas and me as his parents. He would always be my son.

❧ ❧

My son Isaac came to visit me in the summer of 1694. We sat outside on a bench beneath a beech tree Thomas had planted many years before, which now gave shade to part of our enclosed yard. Thomas told me that he had a decision to make and needed my advice—he'd been nominated to become a Ruling Elder of the Plymouth Church, a position that had remained unfilled since the death of my husband. But while he was considering it, he'd received another offer.

"It seems the church in Middleborough has lost its pastor and teacher, Mother, and the town sent letters to the Plymouth church, hoping its leaders would consent to my filling that position."

"I'm not surprised, son. You're well known in the county for your preaching. Which offer seems the best?"

"I'm much honored by this latest request, but I feel I should accept the offer of our church to be an Elder there, since this nomination preceded the call from Middleborough."

I watched his face for a moment, unable to discern which path he would take. "Do you wish to enter the ministry?"

"I do. Father taught me well the tenets and precepts of our church, and I saw him as a great example as he walked in God's path for so many years. I wish to follow that path."

Isaac was now forty-six, and yet I saw him still as the inquisitive and rebellious young boy who filled our home with energy and questions. I knew our congregants regarded him as a man of strong intellect and devotion to God, much like his father, and he often led the prayers in the Plymouth church. But I knew in my heart it was time he led a church of his own.

"If you wish to enter the ministry, then you must become the pastor in Middleborough. I doubt our church would fault your decision."

ꝏ ꝏ

As pastor of the Middleborough church, Isaac improved his preaching and became well-known and respected for his gentle judgement and caring. After some time, he received a call to be the pastor of a new church in Plympton. While he loved the Middleborough church, I believed the fact his brothers lived in Plympton helped him decide to move there.

My oldest son Thomas came for a visit soon after Isaac had become Plympton's pastor, joining the family at our mid-day meal. As I grew ever more ancient, he came more frequently to see me.

After the meal, I heard Lydia's husband, William, ask Thomas, "How is your church doing under your brother's leadership?"

"Well indeed, William. He's well-suited to be our pastor. However, a difficulty has arisen."

I'd not heard of this and immediately felt a pang of anxiety for my second son. The men continued their discussion, unaware of my feelings.

"What problem is this?" asked William.

"It comes from Reverend Cotton of the Plymouth Church. He's asked whether, according to the rules of the church, a man can serve as pastor in one church who hasn't previously served as Ruling Elder in another and hasn't been formally ordained. Isaac and the majority of the church in Plympton argue, rather convincingly, that according to the long-settled principle of our religion, each church is entirely independent from all others and is self-governing."

"Didn't the Plymouth church give him permission to be pastor in Middleborough?" I had to ask and got a glare from Thomas worthy of my husband's. But he followed that with a smile.

"Yes, they did. I honestly don't know what will happen as a result of Reverend Cotton's objection, only that Isaac's preaching at the Plympton church continues, despite his lack of ordination. This has only served to add to the controversy."

With that, the talk about Isaac ended and the discussion turned to the usual topics of crops, weather, and children.

ꕥ ꕥ

Some three years later and after considerable ecclesiastical turmoil, Isaac was ordained, an event I was too old and feeble to attend. In the meantime, I learned that some members had withdrawn from the Plymouth church, irritated by the steadfast opinion of Reverend Cotton against my son. When it finally became apparent to Mr. Cotton that my son would continue to preach, and the people of Plympton would hear him, he asked for dismissal from the Plymouth church.

I felt saddened and slightly ashamed that the actions of my son would lead to this, since Reverend Cotton had served our church long and well for some twenty years.

Thomas, now sixty and the patriarch of the family, had come again on one of his regular visits. After greeting me and inquiring about my well-being, he and William lit their pipes and commiserated over a mug of beer at the table. I sat in a chair by the hearth, a wool blanket over my knees, closing my eyes in the appearance of sleep. My ears, however, were wide awake.

"I hear the Reverend Cotton is leaving Plymouth. Is it his continuing opposition to your brother that drove him to ask for dismissal?" asked William.

Thomas chuckled, sounding so like his father that a stab of longing spiked my heart. "No, something else."

He lowered his voice, but I could still hear him. "Charges were raised against him for an adulterous relationship with a married woman, Rebecca Morton."

"Wasn't he excommunicated by the First Church in Boston for the same thing?"

"He was, but the church there readmitted him after he made a public confession and an apology," replied Thomas. "We would not have accepted him to our church had he not worked diligently for several years on Martha's Vineyard, converting Indians there to Christianity. Apparently, this bleached the stains of scandal from his reputation in the eyes of our Elders. Because of that and the strength of his father's reputation in Boston, they accepted him as our pastor."

"I would think his many years of caring for our congregation restored much of his honor." William leaned back and drew from his pipe. "But it seems the devil was persistent. What was the judgment of the church?"

"The church Elders declined his request, voting instead to retain him—probably because Reverend Cotton convinced them the charges of adultery were false, created by political enemies."

"What enemies?"

"Those who resented his support of our colony becoming part of the Massachusetts colony. But I doubt his explanation." Thomas paused and drew on his pipe

"Why?"

"Because his wife has left him and now lives in Sandwich. Clearly, their marriage is strained by his sin."

"What will happen to him now?" asked William.

"He's leaving, without the vote of dismissal, which would have cleared his record of the charges of adultery. Many church members complained the church had turned a blind eye to his misbehavior, and with opinion so strong against him and his acceptance as pastor waning, he had no choice but to leave."

With that, my anxiety about the effect of my son's ministry on the Plymouth church was gone, but I despaired as I thought of the weakness of the body, even in those consecrated by holy vows. I wondered whether such men could lead us in God's ways.

Chapter 48

A Time for Good-byes

Mary Allerton Cushman, Plymouth, Massachusetts Colony, September 1699

Another year has passed and here I sit, on a bench in the garden outside my home, leaning forward on my cane. Autumn is upon us, and I enjoy the cool air and the rustle of the golden leaves over my head, basking in the sunlight filtering through them. My thoughts are almost always now of those who have gone before me and the history of my many years. I think of my father and sister, and of my brother, Bartholomew, who died many years ago without my ever seeing him again. And Governor Bradford, intelligent, far-seeing, and righteous, to whom Plymouth owed so much...and both my mothers, Mary Norris and Alice Bradford, each dear to me in their own way but dim to my vision with the passage of so much time... And of course my dear Thomas, the pain of his loss just as acute as the day he left me. I know in my bones I'll be reunited with him soon. I cannot help but wonder at what my grandchildren will see in their lives. Our roots are driven deep into the soil of this new country, but what of its future? I cannot imagine it.

Just now, I hear more than see the figure of my youngest granddaughter coming toward me. "Lydia?" I ask.

"Yes, Grandmother. Mother told me you were here in the garden. She seemed worried...are you well?"

"Yes, dear, I'm fine. I'm so enjoying this day. Here, sit beside me and enjoy it with me." I take her hand in one of mine as she sits.

"Grandmother?"

"Yes, dear?" I know what is coming from the tone of her young voice.

"Will you tell me a story?"

"Certainly. Which would you like to hear?"

"About your voyage on the *Mayflower*. It's a wonderful tale."

"Not so wonderful for those who lived it, I fear. Well," I begin, "we left England for the third time in September, when it was already cold, and the wind was blowing strong. We'd had to turn back twice because our sister ship, the *Speedwell*, had sprung so many leaks..."

Mary Allerton Cushman died on November 28, 1699 at 83 years of age. She was the oldest surviving passenger of the Mayflower and was buried beside her husband Thomas on the hill overlooking Plymouth harbor. The descendants of the Cushmans built a monument to the early family over the site of Thomas Cushman's grave. Mary lies there as well, surrounded by all the other Old Comers who established the Plymouth colony on New England soil.

It is estimated that there are 35 million descendants of the Pilgrims living in the United State today. Are you one of them?

ACKNOWLEDGEMENTS

The creation of this book was an intense learning experience, and I recognize the teachers who helped me fulfill my dream.

There are too many to name individually in the case of the written word, but three are foremost in my mind: William Bradford and his book, *Of Plymouth Plantation*, an invaluable if challenging read; Nathaniel Philbrick, whose book *The Mayflower* I read several times; and *The Midwives Book*, written by a seventeenth century English midwife, Jane Sharp, and edited by Elaine Hobby. I have books on colonial architecture, farming and farms, herbal remedies and seventeenth century medicine, the Pilgrim families, family life, and many on the history of the Plymouth colony, all weighing down the shelves of my bookcase. Downloads from hundreds of online sources sit in a staggering pile on my desk. Chief among them is the Plymouth Colony Archive Project at the University of Illinois, Plymouth Plantation, The Pilgrim Hall Museum, and the Plymouth Archeological Rediscovery Program.

I want to thank the input and encouragement I received from Donna Curtin, Executive Director of the Pilgrim Hall Museum, and the work of Craig S. Chartier, MA and principle archeologist of the Plymouth Archeological Rediscovery Program, which taught me much about how and where people lived in the Plymouth colony.

Numerous visits to Plymouth Plantation enhanced my visual sense of Plymouth and I am indebted to Anna Murfin, the artisan potter there, who introduced me to pottery and pipes, and to the reenactors at Plymouth Plantation and on the *Mayflower II*. I was lucky to be among the last to visit the ship before she was taken to dry dock for refurbishing for the 400th anniversary of Plymouth's founding. The visit reinforced the daunting conditions of living with one hundred and two passengers below deck.

The people to whom I owe a biggest thanks are the members of my critique group, who suffered through the many chapters of *The Last Pilgrim* over the last two years —Denis Dubay, Bob Byrd, Dawn Ronco and Elizabeth Calwell. Each offers a special contribution in addition to an overall critique: Denis for his astute feeling for the language of the book; Bob for his historical perspective and romantic input; Dawn for her encouraging "that's just lovely" comments and correction of my overuse of the passive voice; and Elizabeth for reminding me where I need to insert honest emotion. I couldn't have done this without them.

Kudos to my insightful editor Alison Williams, who managed to read the entire manuscript in a short time and offer astute and comprehensive suggestions. And I definitely must thank Mary Boutin, a good friend and my eagle-eyed copy editor, whose eyes have certainly crossed reading this book to find errors. She also found me an old but very useful book—*Major Bradford's Town; A History of Kingston.*

I am enormously grateful to the artists who 'got' my vision for the cover: Mary Louise Smith, a painter, and Michael Scott, President of MAS Graphic Arts. I have the original painting of the cover, framed and hanging above my desk. I also must recognize the enormous input from my publisher, Drew Becker, at Realization Press, who has the patience of a saint in dealing with authors.

I owe huge love and thanks to my husband, Gene, who despite back and shoulder surgeries during the creation of *The Last Pilgrim*, managed to take on household chores to leave me time to write. And to my parents, Jack and Audrey Parsons: My gratitude and my abiding love for giving me a wonderful childhood in Plymouth.

Lastly, my gratitude to Plymouth's Pilgrims for providing me with such rich material about which to write.

AUTHOR'S NOTE

The thin shoulders of the Pilgrim women bore much of the work to ensure the survival and growth of the early Plymouth colony. Despite the vital role these women played, historians and writers of historical fiction have largely ignored their contributions. *The Last Pilgrim* attempts to capture this.

Growing up in Plymouth, Massachusetts, I was steeped in Pilgrim history. Costumed in period clothing, I portrayed various girls and young women in the weekly reenactments of the Pilgrims' Progress up Leyden Street. Under the direction of the indomitable Rose Briggs, I learned the goodwife arts of cooking on a hearth, making candles, and the washing, carding, spinning and dying of wool at the Harlow House. Then, after a year of studying for the role, I became one of the first tour guides at the re-creation of the early Pilgrim village at Plimoth Plantation.

While working there, I became disappointed by how little we knew of the women who came on the *Mayflower* in 1620 and the *Anne* in 1623. I promised myself that one day I'd tell their story. That day has arrived, but it has taken most of my lifetime to get here.

I chose to focus on one woman, Mary Allerton Cushman, who was only four years old when she sailed from England. She held the honor of being the *Mayflower's* youngest passenger until the birth of Oceanus Hopkins. Mary lived through the entirety of the colony's history, first as Isaac Allerton's daughter and then as Thomas Cushman's wife. She lived to see her 83rd year (1699), as the oldest surviving passenger of the 1620 voyage. She was indeed the last Pilgrim.

I wrote *The Last Pilgrim* across the tapestry of Plymouth's history—its leaders, economy and growth, interactions with the native populations, wars, disease and continuous threats to its survival. I've made every effort to stay true to the real events and surroundings.

I took a writer's license in opening the book in Isaac Allerton's voice, since Mary was so young—in order to make the unlikely survival of the *Mayflower's* passengers and challenges of the colony's first years more immediate and real. As times passes and Mary grows, the story transitions to Mary's voice.

Mary's mother died during the first winter. Only five married women—goodwives —and a few older girls survived to support the forty-one survivors from the *Mayflower*, as well to care for the children and the baby Oceanus Hopkins. It occurred to me that as the youngest by two years of all the children, Mary might have been overlooked and frequently left to her own devices, without the instruction and care she needed. So I created Mary as a somewhat fractious child.

At that time, a common practice was to put children with other families, so they might grow in godly ways, without the 'over-love' of their parents. While boys were usually 'put out,' it seemed natural to me that Isaac Allerton, lacking a wife but with two other young children, might place Mary in the Bradford home to receive the instruction and discipline she lacked.

As for her marriage to Thomas Cushman, I decided to introduce an element of romance and love. So many of the Pilgrim marriages were based on immediate need and practicality, but Mary must have known Thomas for a long time before they married. I took the liberty of continuing her forthright nature in their relationship.

Another elaboration entails the acceptance into the Mary and Thomas Cushman's household of a young Wampanoag boy, following King Philip's War. This was not such a stretch since after the war, some of the orphaned native children were taken in as servants. I wondered how these children might have been treated. Knowing Thomas Cushman was a man of God, I decided that the child Samuel would grow up in a caring household.

The treatment of the native populations by the settlers in New England and New York was reprehensible to our way of thinking and sensitivities, and I found most of what I discovered about the Wampanoags and what happened to them ineffably sad and cruel.

Nevertheless, my objective was not to rewrite history through modern eyes, and I therefore tried to maintain a balance in telling of the Pilgrims' interaction with the tribes surrounding them. To any I might have offended, please understand this.

Disease and, above all, childbirth ranked as the major causes of death in 17th century New England. I feel fortunate to have found *The Midwives Book*, written by a 17th century midwife, Jane Sharpe. This allowed me to describe childbirth, and the role of the Plymouth midwife Bridget Fuller, in detail appropriate for the time. My husband, an obstetrician-gynecologist, was amazed at the correct procedures and detailed anatomy described by Mistress Sharp. With regard to herbal remedies and the treatment of injuries, I depended on many online resources and books. My introduction of laudanum to the Plymouth colony might have been a little premature. While its properties had been known for centuries, it wasn't until the 1660s that English physician Thomas Sydenham marketed it as a cure-all.

By the way, the Pilgrims were *not* Puritans but a more severe offshoot of the Puritan sect called Separatists. They were not called Pilgrims until William Bradford, the second governor of the colony, called the Plymouth colonists 'saints and pilgrimes' in his book, *Of Plimoth Plantation*. The manuscript for his book was lost for two centuries and was only published in 1856, when the name Pilgrim was finally given to these intrepid people.

I hope my readers enjoy learning about the lives of Isaac Allerton, Mary Allerton Cushman and her family, and especially the women of the Plymouth colony, as much as I did in writing about them.

Noelle A. Granger
Chapel Hill, January, 2020

CPSIA information can be obtained
at www.ICGtesting.com
Printed in the USA
LVHW062326041121
702427LV00014B/169